# SINFUL

## A DARK ASYLUM ROMANCE

## THE BOYS OF CHAPEL CREST

### BOOK FIVE

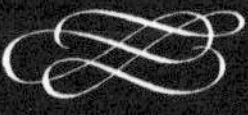

## K.G. REUSS

# THE CHAOS UNIVERSE

## DID YOU KNOW THE BOYS OF CHAPEL CREST IS PART OF AN ENTIRE DARK RH CROSSOVER WORLD?

**Black Falls High:**
In Ruins
In Silence
In Pieces
In Chaos
**Mayfair University:**
May We Rise
As We Fight
On the Edge
Into the Fire
When We Fall
**Kings of Bolten:**
Dirty Little Secrets
Pretty Little Sins
Deadly Little Promises
Perfect Little Revenge
Savage Little Queen
Dark Little Reign
**The Boys of Chapel Crest:**
Church

Bells
Ashes
Stitches
Sinful
Shadow
Asylum
**The Dare Duet:**
Double Dare You
Double Dare Me
**Standalone stories in the Chaos 'Verse:**
Snowballed
Hard Pass
Barely Breathing
Into the Rain
The Archangel

# FOREWORD

Dearest Readers

It's a rough ride, but seriously, that's what restraints are for. That is all.

-K

# ASYLUM

*I* bolted upright so fast I fell off my chair in Sirena's hospital room and grasped my head, gasping for air.

"What's wrong?" Sin demanded, lifting his head from her mattress where he lay while she continued to sleep soundly. His voice was scratchy, and his eyes were bloodshot. I hadn't bothered to question him earlier, but it was clear to me he'd cried several times just lying beside her for the last few hours.

"Fuck. FUCK!" It was the only thing I could get out as I stumbled to my feet and tugged open the door. "Watch her."

I rushed out of the facility and ran as fast as my damn legs could carry me to the woods, slipping on the ice the entire goddamn way.

*Run, run as fast as you can.*

*You can't stop Dante's knife.*

*He's a fucking madman!*

I can fucking stop it. Jesus fuck, could I not catch a damn break?

I stumbled forward, letting my sixth sense guide me.

*You have to hurry. Fucking faster. FASTER!*

*I don't have wings, motherfucker. . .*

I crashed into the dark woods, tripping over branches and logs, cursing the entire way.

The screams met my ears before I reached my destination. Surging forward, I launched myself over a fallen log and darted around several trees, my breath coming out in little white puffs.

Breath clouds.

Tired ones because tonight had been the ultimate shit show.

*Imposter Rabbit.*

*They just won't have it.*

*Play silly Rabbit games.*

*Get placed the ultimate blame.*

I tripped over a fallen branch and bounced off a tree, my shoulder shrieking in pain. Quickly, I righted myself and shot forward.

*Move faster! You're fucking too slow.*

*Too slow, turtle.*

"Fuck off," I snarled, shoving the second taunting voice out of my head.

I stumbled upon a gruesome scene, three watchers surrounding the screaming, bloodied body of fucking Bryce Andrews.

"Stop!" I threw myself forward and knocked Church aside. His bloody knife went flying into the white snow as I fell upon Bryce's trembling body.

"What the fuck are you doing?" Church demanded, snapping his knife up from the snow and coming back at me with a crazed look in his eye only lunatics wore. I knew it well since it was the same look that greeted me every morning when I looked in the mirror.

He rushed at me, knife at the ready.

*He's going to fucking gut you!*

*No fucking shit.*

Church swung the blade at me. Instinctively, I held my hand out, earning a nasty slash across my palm that had me cursing his name to hell and back.

He'd finally snapped and lost his fucking mind.

*It was only a matter of time.*

*Tricksy Dante Church can turn on a dime.*

Stitches jumped into the fray, trying to tug Church off me while we fought.

"I'll fucking go through you if I have to," Church snarled at me as I tried to hold his hand with the knife away from my pretty fucking face.

"Dante. Stop. Stop!" Ashes joined in to try to wrestle Church off me as I lay atop a poor, busted-up Bryce.

Church seemed to have developed superhero strength since the last time I'd seen him.

*He's out for revenge.*

*Clearly.*

I managed to get my leg between us and planted my foot in the center of his chest. I shoved hard, sending him flying backward. He landed with a grunt several feet away from me.

Quickly, I got to my feet, ready to continue to defend the dying rabbit at my feet.

"He hurt her," Church growled, getting to his feet. "He *raped* her. Move the fuck out of the way, Seth. He needs to die."

I ground my teeth together. "*Asylum.* My fucking name is Asylum. And he isn't the one." I frowned. "He can't be the one. It's not him."

"She said Rabbit," Church hissed out. "Guess who is out here bouncing around in the fucking clearing in a rabbit mask? How many fucking rabbits are on this campus?"

"Rabbits do tend to breed quickly," I muttered, the shit in my head a blurry mess.

Church let out an angry snarl and lurched forward.

I shoved him in the chest, leaving my bloody handprint on his shirt, but he came back at me. Twisting my fingers in his hoodie, I gave him a shake.

"Fucking *listen to me*, Dante. Fuck. What do you think killing him will do if he's the wrong guy, huh? If he's not the one, it'll fucking rip Sirena's heart in two. She'll hate you forever. I exist in her hatred. Wallow in it. Believe me. . . *Don't do this.*"

Church's chest heaved, his green eyes flashing through the moonlight.

"He's right," Stitches said, looking to a bloodied Bryce in the snow. "What if it's not him?"

"And if it is?" Church challenged, glaring in the direction of Bryce. "I've been out here when she didn't think I was. I saw her and him." His voice cracked. "I know she cares about him."

"Then we owe it to her to make sure," Ashes murmured. "We-we overreacted."

I released Church and stepped back. "We good on this? No skinning this rabbit? No more killing out of habit? He doesn't die tonight, and instead, we find out who else might?"

"Fucking rhymes," Ashes said, sighing. "Dante?"

Church continued to glare at a now silent Bryce on the ground behind me. I knew he was unconscious and needed help before he succumbed to whatever the hell Church and the guys had done to him.

"Fine." Church tucked his knife back into his boot and let out a deep breath. "But when we find out who did this, that motherfucker dies. Even if it's this little prick. Deal?"

"Without a doubt, and I can guarantee it'll be a lot more creative and fun than this," I said solemnly, an inkling of a shadow in my head. It was still too cloudy to make out, but it would eventually emerge. They always did in the end.

Church gave me a grunt and stiff nod, and I completely backed off and turned to stare down at the disaster that was Bryce Andrews.

"You fucking owe me," I muttered, dropping to my knees beside him and taking in the bloody mess that was once an imposter rabbit.

*And so do you.*

*We're in this together.*

*No more fuck-ups. This was huge.*

*I know. I couldn't get back in time. I'm sorry.*

*Enough. I have shit to do.*

*Just. . . tell her I'm sorry. Please.*

*Tell her yourself.*

I snapped off the voice and focused on the task at hand.

His face was beat to piss. Cuts littered it too. Church had spared no mercy on him. He'd practically gutted him.

I placed my hands over the deep wounds on his chest and abdomen.

"You're a mess. Don't die, you dumb fuck," I said, putting pressure on the biggest wound. "She'll be pissed at us all."

His lashes fluttered, but he remained unconscious.

"I need help carrying him. Be careful. Don't need his intestines on the forest floor. They can get slippery," I said.

We gathered around Bryce and got him lifted. It would be a long walk through those woods.

But it was worth it.

I smiled, the shadow taking form in my mind.

Yeah. Definitely worth it.

# SIN

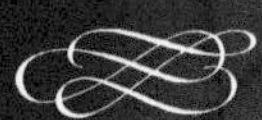

*I* was supposed to keep my distance.

No touching allowed, but I disregarded it, knowing it could get my ass killed, and clutched her cold hand in mine.

I stared at her bruised and swollen face as she lay in her hospital bed. My throat was tight. My chest hurt. I felt so fucking sick to my stomach.

*Raped.*

*She'd been raped.*

A soft cry left my lips at the thought of her being harmed. Again.

Fuck. Again.

She didn't deserve this.

I stared down at her hand and noted her nails were broken and jagged. She'd put up a hell of a fight.

It broke my heart further. This shouldn't have happened to her. I couldn't get it out of my head that it was somehow my fault. I'd created this entire fucking nightmare, and now everyone was paying the price for my terrible deeds.

"I'm so fucking sorry, Siren," I whispered, bringing her hand to my lips and pressing a shaky kiss to the top of it. "This is all my fault. I've

She didn't move. Her lashes didn't flutter. She simply continued to lie like a broken doll beneath her covers, her breathing shallow.

God, she was broken.

*She won't be able to come back from this.*

It was a thought I couldn't get out of my head. She retreated into the dark recesses of her mind. She'd be gone. Out of reach from even Asylum.

Nausea twisted in my guts like an angry serpent.

"You have to come back," I whispered. "I haven't gotten to tell you everything, Siren." A tear trickled down my cheek, and I hastily wiped at it. I wasn't a crier. Or hadn't been before all of this. A rustling outside her door had me removing my hand from hers, the cold from her touch making me ill. Hastily, I wiped at my eyes again.

Stitches entered the room, his attention focused solely on her.

"Angel," he murmured, his voice rough as he came to her. He reached out and brushed her hair away from her face and studied her for a long time before he looked to me. "Anything?" There was so much hope in his voice it broke my heart.

I shook my head, hating my answer. "Nothing."

His Adam's apple bobbed, and he nodded his head. "OK. Yeah. I-I guess I expected that."

He sat in the chair opposite me and took her hand in his. Neither of us said anything for a long time until he broke the silence.

"We found Bryce in the woods." He launched into telling me everything he knew about Sirena and the rabbit, ending it with Bryce being brought in.

"They think he's going to make it?" I asked, my mind filled with all sorts of shit regarding the rabbit.

*Fucking hell. Things needed to come out about that shit.*

"He'll be fine. He's busted up, but they're working on him. He lost a lot of blood, but you know how Church can get." He visibly swallowed. "How we can all get."

I looked away from him and stared out the small window. It was dark. Snow was falling again. I hated the snow. There was just so fucking much of it in Northern Michigan.

"Where's Asylum?" I asked finally.

"I don't know. He helped bring Bryce in and left. Said he'd be back. Didn't ask where he was going. Guess I didn't really care."

Sounded about right.

I glanced at Sirena. "What's the plan? She can't stay here. If Sully comes back—"

"She'll stay the night here." Church came into the room, Ashes behind him. Both crowded Sirena. I was forced to move away to make room for them. I backed against the wall, watching while they all doted on her.

"And tomorrow?" I asked after a long moment.

"She'll come home. Ashes is going to take Stitches and make preparations for her at home. I'll remain here with her." Church kissed her forehead while Ashes held her hand. All the guys were covered in blood. Based on what I knew, Bryce hadn't fared well out in those damn woods.

Stupid asshole.

"You can leave." Church straightened and looked at me, his voice hard. Despite knowing his level of anger, I remained against the wall.

"I don't want to," I said softly. "I'd like to stay—"

"Go, Sinclair," Church growled. "You're done here."

"Dante, man, come on," I pleaded, stepping forward. I hated being this pathetic sack of shit, but I'd learned some rather hard lessons as of late.

"Sin, just go home, OK?" Ashes said before Church could snap at me. "Get some rest. You've been with her for hours. Let Church take over. Go make sure Asylum isn't doing something stupid. You can come back later. Promise."

I swallowed hard before glancing to Church. A muscle popped along his jaw as he glared back at me, but he didn't say I couldn't. It was the best I was going to get, so I nodded and stepped forward. I paused at the side of her bed and stared at her for a moment, all the pain in the world constricting my chest.

I wanted to find who hurt her too and choke the life out of him.

And I would. Whatever it took.

†

"Where were you?" I asked, sitting up in bed. I'd tossed and turned all damn night, my dreams too fucked up and vivid to really get any meaningful rest. In them, I just kept seeing Sirena fighting off her attacker.

A fucking rabbit.

Asylum and I had a lot to talk about.

"Out," he muttered, flopping down in bed, his hand bandaged.

"Where?" I demanded. "You fucking know Mirage—"

"I know," he snapped, looking at me with tired blue eyes. "Bryce was a fuck-up. Shit is compromised now."

"Listen. I want to go home, and I can't do that if I'm keeping secrets—"

"For her, you will keep every fucking secret told. Don't run off and tell things so bold. If you want to go home, it's important to keep silent. If you open your mouth too quickly, things could get rather violent." He raised a dark brow at me. "Again."

I gave him a look of disgust. "So when?"

"In time. Until then, just play the game."

I shook my head and laid back down. Staring up at my ceiling, I let out a sigh. I was sick of games. It felt like I'd been playing them my entire life. More often than not, I also seemed to be the biggest fucking loser.

"Will Bryce be OK?"

"He will. Eventually. She is who I worry for." His bed creaked as he lay back in it.

"What do you know?"

"Not as much as I'd like," he answered, his voice soft. "I'm. . . in shock. I suppose that's the best way to say it. I'm hurting."

I swallowed thickly. "Me too."

"I was there, Sinclair. I was the one to push inside her body the first time. I felt her pain. Her terror. Her fear. The knowledge that we couldn't stop it. That if we tried, it would only get worse. *And it was me.*" He let out a soft snarl. "It was me doing that to her. I don't fucking rape women. I did my best that night with her to keep the monsters from seeing her. I tried so fucking hard to keep her dignity. Imagine it being someone else doing this to her. Then, for him to mutilate her? Beat her? Fuck." His voice cracked. "This will not go unpunished. We will find who did this, and he will pay for his sins in blood."

"He will suffer a long and slow death," I whispered.

"He is just the beginning," Asylum murmured. "No one fucking tries to tear the wings off of my firefly. *Fucking no one.*"

He didn't need to elaborate. I was there. I'd seen his reaction to it. I could hear it in his voice.

But he wouldn't be the only one bringing retribution.

I wouldn't stop until I found who did this to her.

Then. . .

Well, I'd probably end up committed for the rest of my life, but she was worth it. She was worth everything. I'd do whatever I had to if it meant saving her.

Now that I could see that, there would be no stopping me.

# CHURCH

*I* couldn't sleep.

Instead, I stayed awake at her side, trying to not lose my mind. All I could see, though, was red. My fury was beginning to take over. Shit would get bad if I let go.

I exhaled, my legs bouncing. Nausea twisting deep in my guts had me fisting my hair.

The thought that someone had forced my girl. . . robbed her. . . terrified her. . . hurt her.

My body trembled, the tears rolling down my cheeks.

I didn't fucking cry. That wasn't who I was, but the image in my head wouldn't stop playing on repeat. It brought with it an influx of ugly fucking memories from my childhood in the underground.

My specter didn't deserve this shit. She was all that was good in this fucked up world.

I was just about to tear my hair out and go on a killing spree, vowing to gut every motherfucker in this place until I found one who bled the truth for me, when a hand grasped mine.

I snapped my attention to Sirena, whose colorful eyes peered at me through dark lashes.

"Specter," I whispered, my voice laced with emotion. I grasped her hand back and brought it to my lips, where I pressed a fierce kiss to it. "Oh, god, Sirena. I-I—"

Tears trailed gently down her cheeks, further breaking my heart.

"Fuck, what can I do? I tried to find the rabbit, baby. I-it was Bryce, right?"

She let out a tiny whimper and shook her head.

"I saw you with the rabbit in the clearing. I followed you," I said thickly. "I knew. . . Fuck. I don't know what I knew, just that you met this fucker in the woods. And he hurt you. Bryce was behind the mask. We found him in the woods—"

More tears streamed down her face, and she shook her head slightly.

"No? It wasn't him?" My heart fell. "Then who did this? Who hurt you, Sirena?"

She trembled and squeezed her eyelids closed.

"Fuck, baby. You need to tell me. We can take care of him so he doesn't hurt you again."

"C-Cady. W-want C-Cady."

I stiffened. We hadn't told Cady what happened.

"She doesn't know," I said gently. "We didn't tell her. Your parents don't even know. We want to handle this."

She let out a soft cry, crushing the broken pieces of me further.

"S-Seth," she whispered. "P-please."

I studied her for a moment before nodding. If she wanted Asylum, I'd make it happen. In that moment, it was anything and everything for her.

"OK. I'll get Seth. Anything you want," I said.

"H-home," she choked out.

"OK, baby. We can go home. I'll have Doc come in and check you out, and then we'll go, OK?"

She closed her eyes and went silent, her body still trembling. Her lip had started to bleed again. Doc said it looked like she'd been bitten. The fury that radiated through my body at that was enough to drive me to the edge of my sanity alone.

The rest shoved me off the ledge of it and left me tumbling into the abyss of crazy.

I kissed her hand once more before getting to my feet and poking my head out.

"Get Doc O'Brien," I said to one of the wards.

He nodded and left. Doc O'Brien was the only one I trusted here. I had no idea if he was in my father's pocket, but based on his fairly newcomer status, I felt confident my old man hadn't sunk his claws into him too deeply. Yet.

I returned to my seat and held her hand again. Moments later, O'Brien came into the room.

He was young. Maybe early thirties. Dark hair. Dark eyes. A kind smile. Maybe that's what made me think he wasn't part of the shit my father had going on here.

"Mr. Church," he greeted me, going to Sirena's side and peering down at her. "Sirena. How are you today?"

She said nothing, as was her fashion. He didn't seem concerned with that.

"She wants to go home," I said as he checked her over.

"I think she should remain here for another night or two, just to be safe—"

"I don't want Sully or my father finding out," I said. "You know that."

He sighed, a frown on his face as he stared down at her. "I understand. It's just. . . they're probably going to find out. Maybe not today or tomorrow, but they will. People here talk. You know that."

"And when they do, she'll be home safely with me." I locked eyes with him. "She can't stay here. You know what happens here."

He cleared his throat. "I've heard rumors. I'm not privy to it all. I don't have that insider track, I suppose."

"Believe me when I say you don't want it."

He nodded and went quiet again for a moment. "Let's talk in the hall, OK?"

I glanced at Sirena, who stared at the wall with no emotion on her face.

*Fuck, baby. Don't retreat into your mind. Please. Stay.*

"I'll be right back," I murmured, leaning down and placing a kiss on her forehead. She didn't acknowledge me, which only raised the alarms in my head.

Quickly, I followed O'Brien out into the hall.

"You understand she's badly injured, right? She has substantial wounds, both physical and mental—"

"I know," I whispered. "I just want her home with me where she's safe. She's just not safe here. As long as she's stabilized—"

"It's been two days." He sighed. "Her wounds will need a lot of care. If I release her and something happens, an infection sets in or she regresses—"

"I will make sure she's cared for," I said fiercely.

He studied me. "Tell you what. I'll give her some time off from school. I'll call it a mental health break. You take care of her. If anything at all changes, you make sure you call me. I'll put my personal number on her discharge papers. I'll give her meds for her pain and some for her anxiety since once all this settles in, I'm sure it'll be hard on her. If you need anything, call me."

"Fuck. Thank you," I said, shaking his hand and meaning it.

"Of course. I'll have Brenda get her meds and paperwork together. Just don't hesitate to reach out. My first goal is getting people better."

"What's your second goal?"

He gave me a sad smile. "Making sure they stay that way. Go to her. I'll have someone I trust come in and help move her home."

"Thank you."

He nodded. "Be safe, Dante. Lots of monsters hiding in this place." And with that, he left me.

*Don't I fucking know it.*

I returned to her room and sat in the chair beside her bed. She continued to stare at the ceiling, her tears now dry on her face.

"We're getting you out of here," I said. "You'll stay home with me. Does that sound OK, baby?"

She said nothing, but I didn't really expect her to. Instead, she squeezed my hand lightly and hummed that damn song I'd heard her hum before.

It was better than nothing.

# SIRENA

My entire body hurt.

I kept retreating to my safe place, peeking out long enough to make sure things were still OK.

But OK still felt really awful.

I didn't even know the extent of my injuries, just that I had many, and it hurt to even breathe. The knife Adam had used had torn me up, and I was scared to even know just how much.

Which was why I stayed in the dark corner of my mind, humming my and Seth's song, hoping that this was all just a bad dream I'd wake from.

Something ugly lurked on the edges of my mind, beckoning me closer, though. I wasn't alone in my safe place. I knew this. It scared me, so I tucked myself deeper into the darkness, hoping I could make sense of everything soon. I'd felt this darkness before, but it had never been so pronounced. So. . . alive.

"She's been like this all day," Stitches murmured, his warm hand in mine as I stared up at the ceiling in Church's room. He'd brought me here after the doctor released me. I'd been here a long time it seemed.

Could have been a week or a month. I just didn't know, nor did I care. The only thing I wanted was the nightmare to go away.

"She's humming more than usual." Ashes commented. *My pyro.* "That's good, right?"

"She hummed when she was in the med ward last time," Church muttered. "Look how that went down."

"You said she asked for Claws. Maybe we should get her. We can't keep pushing her away. She's nuts and will fucking set the house on fire just to smoke us out," Stitches said. "Or Seth. Get Asylum. You always tell him no when he comes to check on her."

"Mirage," I whispered.

There was a scurry of activity as the guys gathered closer to me.

"What's that, baby? What did you say?" Ashes pleaded, cradling my face. "Come on, heaven. Just talk to us."

I said nothing, my heart hurting. I needed to see Mirage. And if I couldn't see him, I needed Asylum.

"Asylum," I murmured.

"OK. Fine." Church placed a warm kiss on my forehead with so much fierceness it made my heart jump. "Malachi, get Seth."

There was a scraping of a chair and then the sound of Stitches's heavy footsteps leaving the room.

"He brought her back before," Ashes commented, squeezing my hand.

"At what cost?" Church let out a sigh. "They grew closer after."

"Well, I mean, it's worth it, right?"

"Is it? What if he's right about all of this shit? That he gets her in the end?" Church asked, his voice soft.

*Get me in the end? I'm not leaving you. I'm not. God, why can't I just scream it for them to hear? Why was I so messed up?*

*I love you all so much.*

"She loves us. I know she does." Ashes kissed the top of my hand. "I'm not worried. Much."

Church snorted.

I closed my eyes, desperate for a little escape.

The curious tendrils of the monster lurking on the edges of my safe place raised its head and smiled.

Sleep couldn't come soon enough.

✝

THE ROOM FELT HEAVY. I opened my eyes and peered blearily through it, my body aching so much I wanted to scream. My gaze landed on him a moment later.

I let out a soft whimper.

He sat forward in his seat, his blue eyes fixed on me.

"Firefly," he whispered, cocking his head to the left.

I said nothing as I stared at him. Slowly, he rose from his seat and moved to tower over me. I sank a little deeper into the bed when he reached out and ran his thumb along my busted bottom lip. It was still swollen and stitched up. Eating and drinking were too much of a chore, so I hadn't been doing much of it.

"He hurt you," he murmured, his voice trembling. "He will pay, firefly. Do you want to help me make him pay? Do you want to be stronger and take him out? To slay? To kill? To maim? Your revenge to claim?"

I stared up at him, my heart in my throat, not understanding what he was saying to me and sad he wasn't Mirage.

He leaned down and ran his lips along my jaw. When he got to my ear, he stopped and whispered.

"I'm telling you, we will let you kill him. We will find him for you and let you kill him, firefly. All for you, my forever girl. A gift. Do you accept? You and the monster in your head?" He didn't move away from me.

I lay beneath his warmth, so many thoughts racing through my head until one stuck. That creeping darkness on the edge of my psyche became clearer, the intent much darker than I could have ever imagined. *My monster.* The heat from his body flowed into mine, opening my eyes to a world of potential. All the hurt. The fear. The pain. The unknown.

"You choose," Asylum whispered into my ear. "Tell me."

I let out a shaky breath, that decision going from a little flicker to a bright, burning flame of want as I embraced the monster inside me who wanted to come out to play.

"Yes," I rasped.

"Yes, what, my forever girl?"

"I-I w-want revenge."

"How do you want it?" His lips brushed against my ear, his warm breath sending goosebumps scattering across my skin, making me shiver. Not with fear. With desire.

So much desire.

"I want to kill him." I exhaled, sealing his fate.

Asylum shifted and brushed his lips gently against my busted ones, taking care to not put pressure against them in the most gentle kiss I'd ever gotten before.

When he pulled away, his blue eyes sparkled with all the wickedness in the world.

"So be it. It shall be done."

His words should have terrified me, but instead, they doused the flame burning inside me in gasoline, igniting some dark part of my soul I didn't know I had.

He let out a soft chuckle. "That dark part you feel in your soul, firefly? The one you've just illuminated? That's where *we* live. Welcome home, my little firefly. No more hiding. It's time to come out and play."

I liked the sound of that.

# ASHES

"He's been up there a long time." Church paced the living room, his fingers raking through his blond hair every few minutes while he cast quick looks to the clock.

"It's OK," I said, trying to cling to positivity.

Stitches sat forward on the couch and rested his elbows on his knees, his tatted fingers twined together. He looked exhausted. Hell, we all were. None of us had been getting much sleep since we'd brought Sirena home a week and a half ago. All had gone fine. Church stayed behind with her while we attended classes and therapy. Cady has been threatening our lives over not being able to see her. We'd told her she was sick, but after the first three days, it was becoming a hard sell.

When we'd gotten Asylum to come to her that day that she'd asked for him, she'd slept through it, and he hadn't been back since. Now, here he was.

"I'm worried, man. Whoever did this is still out there." Stitches glanced at me and then to Church.

I nodded. He was right. It wasn't Bryce. We hadn't seen him since we'd attacked him in the woods. We were beside ourselves, trying to figure out what the hell was going on with Sirena meeting whoever was in the woods. We were being patient, though. It's all we could do at this point with her.

"We'll keep her safe," I said.

"We said that last time. Look what happened." Church swore softly and stopped his pacing to stare up at the ceiling like he was contemplating it all.

We were all quiet for a moment before I said what I'd been thinking since this happened.

"Maybe you're right. Maybe we can't keep her safe. Maybe. . ."

"Don't fucking say it, Valentine. I'm not in the mood," Church said, glaring at me and going to his chair to sit. He slid back and scowled.

"What are we going to do about Cady? She threatened to feed me my own cock today on my walk back here after therapy." Stitches looked at each of us in turn. "She pulled out a fucking spork and told me it was what she'd use to mutilate my dick from my body before she toasted it over a fire and force-fed it to me."

I shook my head. Cady was wild.

"Claws will lose it if we tell her," Church said. "Sirena needs to be healed. She needs to decide if she wants Cady to know."

"It could be weeks. We can't hold her off that long. I'm not even sure we can last another day." I breathed out and rubbed my eyes. "Plus, it's the holidays, man."

I couldn't take this damn stress. I pulled my lighter out and went to flipping it opened and closed, counting softly as I did it while igniting the flame for a moment before starting all over.

"Fuck the holidays. We don't celebrate that shit anyway. We'll figure it out." Church turned his head as Asylum came downstairs.

"Watchers," Asylum said, inclining his head at us.

"How did it go?" Church demanded.

"It went. . . well." Asylum flashed a grin at us. "Little firefly has made a decision. We must help her carry it out with precision. To win the game. We stoke the flame. It's going to get bloody, boys. Buckle up."

I raised my brows at him. Asylum was nothing if not entertaining with his rhymes. He tended to confuse and frustrate me more than anything as of late, though.

"What happened?" Stitches asked.

I gestured for Asylum to sit. He did so at the end of the leather couch and surveyed us with his blue eyes.

"She has made a choice. We are going to guide her through it."

"She spoke?" Church was all ears while he stared Asylum down. She'd come a long way in the last few weeks and was communicating more. Then, this entire ordeal pretty much sealed her lips and made her regress. It was two steps forward and a million back.

Asylum nodded. "She has. It's unlocked the next step. It's a good thing because everything has just been a haze to me lately. Her choice tonight let me know where she is on things."

"Did she say who hurt her?" Stitches demanded before I could ask it.

Asylum's hands visibly shook. "She did not. I didn't push it either. She will tell us eventually. We just need to have patience."

"What if he hurts her again? Whoever it was?" I swallowed hard. "I swore I'd protect her, and I failed her."

"Me too," Stitches whispered.

"I think we all failed her. So many things could have been done differently." Church sighed, his voice shaking slightly. "I need to find this motherfucker and kill him. I need it more than anything else in the world right now."

We were all feeling it. It really sucked. It was definitely a contributing factor to my lack of sleep as of late.

I restarted my lighter ritual, hoping it brought me some comfort but knowing it was just igniting the agitation within me. I was a moth to the flame it seemed because I couldn't force myself to stop. It was my one vice, and I was going to use the hell out of it.

"Relax, Dante. All roads lead to our destiny. Even the rough ones. We must endure the pain so that we are made stronger in the end." Asylum's gaze traveled to the stairs. I couldn't help but wonder what he was thinking.

"Her," he answered softly. "Always her."

I glanced at Church, who wore a frown.

I swore this guy could get into our heads. It unnerved me.

"No worries, Asher. It doesn't work like that either." Asylum looked at me. "I'm not in your head. Your thoughts are safe."

I cast a quick look to Church and Stitches.

"Then how. . .?" I asked, not even knowing how to finish the sentence.

He shrugged and pointed to his head. "Voices. Messages from beyond. I just. . . know. I don't get to choose when it happens. It just does."

"So you're not in my head? Can't. . . hear my thoughts?"

He cocked his head left at me and narrowed his eyes. "We just. . . *feel you*. That's all."

"Like with Sirena?" Stitches called out.

Asylum nodded. "Yeah."

I'd have pressed the subject more if I thought his answer would change, but I knew Asylum. He never gave away secrets. At least not until he needed to. I worried about what all this meant. I didn't want to lose my heaven. The thought twisted my insides into a tight, painful ball.

"Why do you think you'll lose her?" Asylum murmured.

I looked at him, blinking rapidly and stopping the flipping of my lighter lid. If he wasn't in my damn head, it sure as hell felt like he was.

Stitches glanced at me while Church narrowed his eyes at Asylum.

The corners of Asylum's lips twitched before he spoke. "We could all be a big happy family someday if you relax a little."

We were quiet for a moment. I didn't even know what to say to that. It wasn't a shocker Asylum wanted in with us, but he'd never really come right out and said it. Everything had been a hint at it. But hell, maybe this was just another hint at what was inevitable. On the other hand, I knew she'd been scared of him, so I was confused about what the hell was actually going on.

"She chooses," Church murmured, a sad look in his eyes. Despite it, his voice was firm.

Asylum's blue eyes sparkled. "Indeed she does, Dante. I think you'll like where this is headed."

"But not Sin," Church continued, clearing his throat. "I'm open to the possibility of. . . you, but I will not entertain Sinclair Priest. Not after what he did to her and all the fucking shit it led to."

I glanced at Stitches, who frowned and sat forward. I'd never really considered anything past Sin locking her in the coffin with Asylum, but Church's words made me think. It really all snowballed from Sin's decision. Perhaps none of this would have happened had Sin not done that.

Asylum didn't move a muscle. He simply sat where he was, surveying Church.

When he finally spoke, his voice was soft and uncharacteristic of the psycho I knew.

"I am not without sin when it comes to my firefly. *My forever girl.* I think we are all guilty in some way in regard to her. Perhaps if we bonded in that darkness rather than repel one another, then maybe some good, some revenge, some beautiful retribution, could come from it. Let's not be too hasty. Let's allow her the time she needs to. . . blossom. To become our little monster."

I narrowed my eyes at him, his words sending a chill through me. "What are you planning, Seth?"

"Asylum," he corrected, looking to me. "That is my name. As for what I am planning. . . well, it's not really me. It's her. She wants revenge. I've promised it in any way I can make it happen for her. *We. We. WE.*" His legs bounced. He reached up and tugged at his black hair, and let out a snarl. "I fucking said we. Goddamn it."

I shot a quick look to Stitches and Church to see them watching him with the same confused looks on their faces.

Asylum let out a ragged breath before snapping his head up and letting out a groan.

"Fuck. Shut the fuck up. I can't get a fucking moment of silence. Just give me a fucking minute. I'll tell them. I'm going to fucking do it. Fuck. FUCK."

We watched as Asylum got to his feet abruptly, his chest heaving, his blue eyes flashing. He went to the wall and banged his head off it several times.

"What the fuck?" Stitches said, getting to his feet with Church and me.

"I said fucking shut up," Asylum whispered.

We stood watching Asylum as he continued to stare at the wall, his breathing deep.

Finally, he turned to us, a trickle of blood running from his forehead and down the bridge of his nose.

"She wants revenge," he murmured. "I've promised to let her have it. She wants to kill the person who hurt her. When she gives a name, we will secure whoever it was and let her have her way with him. There are no negotiations on this. *She chooses.* We've agreed."

I swallowed thickly at his words.

"Did she say she wants to. . . kill him?" I asked, nausea twisting in my guts. The thought of my sweet heaven murdering someone made me sick in all sorts of ways. Not all those ways were bad, though. Some of them were a joyful sickness. The kind I tried to not let out.

Because I wanted whoever hurt her to be dead too.

But I wanted him to suffer first.

"He will suffer." Asylum locked his eyes on mine. "We'll make sure of it. Are you in, Asher Valentine?"

I nodded without a word. I wanted this for her. I wanted her to have her revenge. To feel in control again. She needed it, and I'd never deny her what she wanted or needed.

Asylum nodded back at me and looked to Stitches. "Malachi?"

"If it's what she wants," he said softly. "Then so be it."

Asylum looked to Church, who stood emotionless in his spot, his green eyes dull.

"Dante?" Asylum asked. "Will you let this happen?"

Church was quiet for so long that I didn't think he'd answer.

When he did, his words were fierce.

"On two conditions," he said, stepping forward. "We play with him first if we get him."

"Absolutely. Playtime is my favorite time." Asylum's eyes glimmered with wickedness. He licked his lips. "And the second condition?"

"If her hand fails her, I get to be the one to kill him."

Asylum cocked his head to the left, the tiniest smile on his lips. "Are you certain that's what you want, Dante? You eat everything you kill."

"I am, and I do," Church said, the gleam back in his eyes.

"I'll let you use my favorite fork." Asylum grinned.

"No need. I have my own." A wicked smile spread across Church's face. Chills raced along my skin.

"Then let's get our little monster ready, shall we?" Asylum looked at us each in turn. "Let her blossom in her own unique way. We shouldn't force it, but we should encourage it."

We all gave him the confirmation he needed. His eyes sparkled, the blood still trickling down his face.

"I think this is the beginning of a beautiful friendship," he said, nodding.

I didn't say a word, but I had a feeling he was closer to being right than wrong.

We just had to figure out how we were going to get past the Sinclair Priest problem because I actually did miss him and wanted him back.

Church needed to realize he was worth it.

I sent out a silent prayer that Sin proved it in the very near future.

# STITCHES

$\mathscr{I}$ tossed and turned before I punched my pillow until I was breathless.

Whenever I tried to sleep, it failed me. All I could think about was the pain my angel had been in. The pain she was currently in.

Her silence always spoke volumes. I didn't want her to be silent. I wanted my girl back. The one who was coming out of her shell and really starting to live.

The fear I had of her retreating into herself made me sick with worry. I just couldn't let that happen again. It was an ugly place I had no desire to revisit.

I shuffled to my feet in nothing but my boxers and went upstairs to Church's room. The door was cracked open, so I peered inside, expecting to find Church in bed with her, but she was the only one in it.

Carefully, I stepped inside the room, grateful he'd left his bedside lamp on. I assumed he was out hunting. It was just his way of relieving stress, and I couldn't say shit about it. It was better than my way, which was beating on things or trying to kill myself to escape.

I slid into bed beside Sirena and stared at her while she slept.

Her pretty face was still slightly swollen and bruised. Beneath the new white nightgown Church had gotten her, I knew she had stitches and wounds littering her body. The motherfucker had cut her with his blade. If he'd have gone any deeper. . . I didn't like thinking about it.

I exhaled and placed my hand over hers on her stomach.

"I love you, angel," I whispered. "Don't go, OK? Don't leave us again. Stay, baby. Please. We need you here. *I need you, Sirena.*"

"I'm here," she whispered back in the sweetest voice. "I'm not leaving."

"Fuck, baby," I choked out, tears springing to my eyes as I drank her in. "It's so good to hear your voice."

Her lashes fluttered for a moment before her colorful eyes appeared. I sat up on my elbow and stared down at her.

"Do you need anything? Pain meds? Water? Anything," I said, both eager and desperate to please the pretty, broken angel in front of me.

"Help me," she said in her soft voice.

"Tell me what you need." I took her hand in mine and kissed her knuckles.

"Asylum. Mirage." She licked her cracked lips. *"S-Seth."*

I swallowed. "Do-do you want me to get Seth?"

Her eyelids drooped a little before she went silent.

"Angel?"

"Malachi," she answered in that sweet, soft voice that sent butter-flies flapping wildly through my guts and chest.

"I want you to feel better. What can I do?"

"Stay," she said, her lashes fluttering until they closed completely. "Forever."

"I'll always stay, angel." I scooted as close to her as I could get without disturbing her injured body. "I promise."

A little smile touched her swollen lips.

Her breathing grew deeper until her small body relaxed, letting me know she was completely asleep again.

I lay beside her in the bed, studying her beauty. Even hurt, she was breathtaking.

Knowing she wanted to kill the one who hurt her should have upset me. It should have made me want to protect her from it all and do it for her, but if she were serious about it, I'd hold that prick down and let her gut him until she felt her vindication and got her satisfaction.

She deserved that.

✝

I AWOKE in bed with just Church, our arms wrapped around each other like we'd been hugging in our sleep.

I blinked rapidly and looked at my watch. It was well into the afternoon. I tried to untangle myself from him, but he grunted and tugged me closer.

"Dante, man, stop," I said, trying and failing again. "Sirena. She's gone."

His green eyes snapped open, confusion in them for just a moment, before he shoved me roughly, sending me toppling over the edge of the bed.

I hit the floor with a thud, cursing his name.

"Motherfucker, my tailbone," I groaned, trying to right myself.

"Where's Sirena?" He jumped out of bed and rushed around the room and into his bathroom before coming out.

I managed to get to my feet and dash to the door before he could. With him on my heels, we rushed downstairs.

I skidded to a halt when I saw Sirena lying on the couch, her head on Ashes's lap, while cartoons played on the TV.

Ashes looked up at us and stopped raking his fingers through her hair for all of a moment.

"She came downstairs on her own," he said. "You two must be hard to sleep with."

Regret slammed into me. I'd fallen asleep beside her. Based on the way Church and I had woken, we were probably jostling her too much.

I took in her face. She was sleeping soundly.

Church moved past me and sat at her feet. He put them gently in his lap and covered them with a throw blanket.

Sighing, I shuffled into the kitchen and opened the fridge. My stomach gave a rumble, and I winced. I'd barely been eating again. Life had become far too stressful lately, but I was feeling it now.

"We're out of nearly everything," I said, closing the door. We didn't even have milk to make cereal. Hell, we didn't even have cereal.

"Snow is coming too," Ashes called out. "Just saw it on the news. It's supposed to hit late tomorrow. We're usually stocked up by now for the winter months. We're all going to be eating the things Church kills."

"I doubt you'd want to eat *all* the things," Church said.

I grunted. He was damn right about that.

"Well, we need to get some food brought in." I went back to the living room and settled on the couch, taking in Sirena's head on Ashes's lap. My stomach growled again, and I crinkled my nose. I had to eat. Quickly, I pulled out my phone and put in an order for a couple of pizzas and breadsticks.

"Pizza?" Church called out.

I got to my feet. "Yeah. I'll go meet them at the gates. By the time I get there, they should be near arrival."

"Want me to go?" Ashes asked, his voice strained. I knew he was trying to be kind by offering, but didn't really want to leave angel.

"Nah, man. I got it. I'll be back soon." I ran upstairs and dressed before coming back down and grabbing my jacket. I slid my feet into my boots, and headed out the front door.

The cold air bit at me as I put my head down and started the long walk to the gates. Snow was flurrying, and my breath came out in big white puffs.

I fucking hated the cold. I had no idea why I continued to live in it. I was of age. Leaving was an option after I finished my time at Chapel Crest. I'd spent my entire life thinking this was as good as it was ever going to get, but now that we had Sirena, I dreamed of more.

And more was someplace warmer than fucking Northern Michigan with the snow up to my fucking asshole.

When I reached the gates, I stood there, my hands stuffed in my jacket pockets, and my head ducked low. The wind was beginning to blow. The snow, which had already accumulated on the ground, was whipping across the main paved path as it wound its way through campus. Small drifts were forming.

The only good thing about this upcoming weather was that classes were typically canceled.

Didn't need any psychos getting frozen to death on their way to their classes. That would just be fewer bodies for Sully and Everett to play with.

On the other hand, knowing what I knew about Everett, he'd probably love it just as much.

I breathed out and closed my eyes, an ugly image in my head of me on my knees and crying softly for my mother as someone's warm body brushed against mine from behind. Warm lips. Tongue. The heat on my cock.

I swallowed hard, biting back the scream threatening to erupt from my mouth. More than anything, I wanted to smash these ugly memories into a million pieces so I couldn't discern what they even were anymore.

But I couldn't so far. I'd been trying. God help me. So much.

I didn't want to be weak. I didn't want to be some sick fuck's plaything.

It's what I'd been. It's what I was.

I wiped hastily at a tear that slipped down my cheek, not wanting it to freeze to my face.

I'd been trying so hard to move past it all. Being strong right now for my angel was what mattered.

"Hey," Sin called out, jolting me from my painful thoughts which had wandered back to my closet and the rope I'd put beneath my bed.

"Hey." I stared as he walked toward me with Asylum, who was too busy looking down at his phone to say anything to me. Seeing the pair together was still odd to me. They seemed inseparable these days, though. I was glad Sin had someone to talk to. If they talked. I assumed Asylum probably just drove him nuts like he did to us.

They stopped in front of me. Sin's hair was shorter. I'd noticed it before. It looked good on him. All shaggy. He was also thinner, with dark circles rimming his gray eyes.

A surge of sorrow swept through me. The pang of missing him hit me full force as we locked eyes. I shoved that feeling away too.

"How's Siren?" he asked, his voice low.

"I think better. She isn't locked inside her head like she was. . . before."

He visibly swallowed and looked away from me as he shuffled the snow at his feet.

"I'm glad," he finally said, looking back at me. "I-I worry."

"I know." I gave him a sad smile. It was good to know he was acknowledging those feelings. While Church was still pissed, I knew Sin might be able to redeem himself. Hopefully. I prayed he did because I missed his grouchy ass. Life just wasn't the same without him. It was hard putting the past where it belonged. It was a task I'd been trying to work on.

"Malachi. *Wolfy*." Asylum grinned at me. "Dinner?"

"Yeah, we're almost out of food."

"What? Why?" The concern in Sin's voice had me glancing over at him.

I shrugged. "I guess we've just been busy with everything lately."

Sin frowned at me. "You guys need to be stocked up. You can't rely on this shithole."

"Don't you?" I looked to Asylum, who winked at me.

"I always have a little something tucked away for when times get tough," he said.

I didn't inquire further because my delivery arrived. Apparently, they were getting food too. I took our order and turned away from the pair, ready to get back inside and see Sirena.

"Stitches," Sin called out to me.

"Yeah?" I stopped and turned to him.

He gave me a sad smile. "Can-will you tell the guys. . ."

"What?" I prompted, shivering.

"Nothing. Maybe I can tell them sometime."

"Yeah. Maybe." I gave him a smile which he returned, hope in his gray eyes.

"Always a pleasure, Malachi," Asylum said, opening their breadsticks and taking a bite.

I rolled my eyes at him. "See you guys."

I began my trek and looked over my shoulder to see they were headed into the woods with their food.

I frowned, wondering what the hell they were up to.

Making it a point to mention it to the guys, I picked up my pace and went home, eager to see my family.

What was left of it anyway.

# SIN

"Why are we out here?" I asked while we made our way through the thick, snowy forest. My concern over the guys not having themselves stocked for the winter was eating at me. And Stitches. Fuck, he looked so sad. When Stitches was sad, bad shit happened. The last thing I wanted was for him to take another nose-dive. The fact I wasn't there to stop him from it made me sick to my stomach. I could only hope Ashes and Church would be there for him. Knowing Sirena was a determining factor in all of this and was safely tucked away with the guys brought me a little hope that Stitches could hold his shit together. If not for himself, then for her.

"Why not? You love staring at the same four walls of that shithole we call home?" Asylum cast me a quick look.

"Beats being cold."

"You won't be cold. We have hot sandwiches to eat."

"Real fucking picnic," I muttered, clutching my bag of food tighter. I grunted as a bunch of snow went into my boot. Asylum and his weird-as-shit plans.

We walked in silence for what felt like forever before we took to a large hill. I watched as he practically slid down it in his long, black jacket, his hood filling with snow on the way down.

"Come on, Sinclair. The water's fine," he shouted up to me.

*For fuck's sake.*

I followed him down the hill, getting even more snow down my boots. I landed with a grumble at the bottom, dropping my baggie of food. Asylum was quick to scoop it up and hand it back to me.

"What the fuck are we doing, psycho?" I asked.

"This." He nodded for me to follow him along the hill. A large pile of brush and pine limbs stood in front of us and against the large mound. I watched as he continued forward before disappearing behind them.

Sighing, I followed him and was surprised to find the opening to a small cave. I ducked low and was able to still walk inside. The small hall opened up to a large chamber.

"What the hell is this?" I asked, spinning in a circle as he went around and lit several lanterns.

"I call it the bear den," he said, grinning at me before moving to a small propane heater and lighting it. "It's our home away from home."

I took in the furnishings he had in here. An old couch and a few old overstuffed chairs. A bed, complete with blankets. A small table. Random barrels of who knew what. Wood for a fire for when his fuel ran out.

"How long have you had this?" I asked, going to the chair he gestured for me to sit in. I flopped down on it, grateful for the heat the heater was putting off.

He shrugged. "Oh, since I arrived."

"I'm surprised Church doesn't know it's here."

"It doesn't run along his normal hunting trails. It's why I chose it." He bit into his sandwich and took a seat on the old couch. "It's pretty hidden. No one has been here. Ever. It's how I like it."

"No one?" I raised a brow at him.

"Well, except for *us*." He tapped his head before going back to his sandwich.

He didn't elaborate. Not that I needed him to. I knew the basic rundown of shit.

We ate in silence for a long time. When I finished, I tossed my wrapper into the small garbage bin by the door and sat down in the chair again. The place was warm now, so I removed my jacket and slipped my boots off before placing them in front of the heater to dry.

"I have a door," Asylum said, nodding to the old wooden door that he clearly wedged against the opening when he needed to be closed off. "There are some openings above us so that I can have fires in here too. I don't typically light them and opt for the propane route, but in a pinch, the fires work well."

I said nothing as I stared at the glowing red top of the heater.

"Come here. I'll show you my supply room." He got up, and I followed him, curious about what else he had hidden.

I'd completely missed a small room off to the side near the back of the cave. It wasn't much for its size, but inside there were all sorts of canned foods, water, pots, pans, dishes, blankets, pillows, and random other things, like a first aid kit and snacks.

"I don't completely depend on Chapel Crest," he said, leaning against the doorway and smirking at me. "I'm prepared."

"I'm surprised," I murmured, stepping out of the small room. He walked with me back to the seating area, where we sat again.

"Why are you showing this to me?"

"Well, there may come a time when we need a place to go. So now we have one. If I ever tell you bear den, then get here. Pretty simple. About half a mile north, I have a truck parked. There's a tree outside marked with a slash. Follow the slashes through the trees, and that's how you will become free." His blue eyes sparkled at his off-rhyme.

"Good to know," I muttered.

"Keys are under the floor mat. Full tank of gas and some supplies inside the cab."

I nodded, intrigued and a little impressed with the care he'd taken to having so many things in place. But it was Asylum. The weird prick probably had a vision he'd need this shit, so he'd put it all together.

"Now. Let's talk." He sat forward. "Firefly. My forever girl."

"What about her?" I swallowed thickly and looked back to the heater.

"She wants revenge. She wants to kill the one who hurt her."

I nodded. I wanted that too. Maybe not her killing him, but I wanted him dead.

"Did she tell you that?"

"Yes." He sat back. I could feel his piercing blue eyes on me. "I agreed. I spoke to the watchers. They're all for it. So now, we have to get her to come out of her shell a little more, and hopefully, we'll have answers. Then. . ." He pulled a fork out of his jacket. "We fuck him up."

I looked over at him.

"With a. . . fork?"

"This isn't just any fork, Sinclair. This fork has been forking amazing at removing eyeballs from motherfuckers' heads." He did an elaborate twirl of the fork over his fingers, a big grin on his face.

"What did you do with the eye you took from your stepdad?"

He continued to twirl his fork. "You know the answer to that. I made him eat it. He had a taste for human flesh anyway. I didn't really see the problem with giving him a taste of his own."

I figured as much.

"How many people have you actually killed?" I asked.

He was quiet for a moment before he stopped twirling his fork and let out a soft laugh, glancing to his left. I watched him interact with the fucking air for a moment before he focused back on me.

"Would you believe me if I told you?"

"Try me," I said.

He licked his lips. "Tell me how many you've killed first."

I scoffed at him and looked back to the heater. "Well, there's my old man."

"You didn't pull the trigger there," Asylum said, brushing me off.

"Yeah, but if I weren't part of the equation, he'd not have done any of the shit he'd done. He wouldn't have shot me. Hurt my mom. Any of it."

"He put the gun to his head and pulled the trigger. That was all him." He cocked his head to the left and hummed for a moment before a small smile turned his lips upward. "And he would have done it with or without you."

"How do you know that?"

He tapped his head. "I just do."

"You know that, but can't tell us who hurt Sirena?" I looked back at him.

He sat forward again, a muscle dancing along his jaw. "It's very fucking cloudy in regards to that. In fact, I only know what I know about your old man because I took a basic fucking psychology class. He was predisposed to violence. Depression. It was inevitable for him. With or without you, he'd have done it. Maybe even to a larger extent. End of story."

We stared one another down for a long time before he spoke.

"How many people have you killed, Sinclair?"

I swallowed hard. "Do I count the ones I've helped Dante with? Or just the ones I've personally killed?"

"Just your count, Sinclair. I already know the level of monster Dante Church is."

I closed my eyes, seeing Bells's face in my mind's eye. I heard her muffled cry. The way her body felt as she sagged against me, the life leaving her.

I shook the image away. "Three."

Asylum raised his brows.

"What?" I looked over at him.

"Not really all that impressive as far as numbers go." He shrugged and twirled his fork again.

"Sorry. I don't run around murdering people for entertainment."

"That's too bad." He winked at me. "It can be a hell of a stress reliever."

"You don't even like killing people. That's what you've said."

"I don't hate it. I should clarify that. I really don't. I just enjoy the torture more. Fuck, the screams." He let out a low groan as he stared up at the cave ceiling. "Gets my dick hard."

"Weird fuck," I muttered.

He smirked at me. "Forty-seven."

"What?"

"Forty-seven. That's my number."

"What the fuck?" I stared at him. "How?"

"Mostly with my fork—"

"No. I mean, how the fuck are you killing people like that?"

He shrugged. "I live an exciting life, Sinclair. I'm chaos. I relish it. It's my job to kill people. I was different growing up. My mom hated that I was. She tried to keep me contained, but when that failed, she let me go. Sold me."

"Sold you?" I blinked at him.

He nodded. "To the Underground. To Everett Church."

"What?" I frowned at his words.

"Oh yes. Daddy Everett. He's my daddy too." He winked again. "He gave me what I needed when I needed it. Allowed me to *work on myself*. All things are possible through death, Sinclair. Once you realize you control it, your life can change. I've witnessed a lot of things in my life. I know things. Some of those things may have made me a little. . . crazy." He let out a laugh. "But I would not change it."

"Was Sirena your first?"

"Sirena Lawrence is my first. My last. My always. My forever." His words were fierce. "I'm so glad she came back from the dead. They don't typically do that. Mostly because I have a thing about taking their eyes, but hers were just too pretty to steal. I love her eyes," he whispered, his hands trembling. "Or I take their hearts. I love hearts. Hands. Lips," he murmured, running his fork along his lips. "I take what appeals to me."

"What do you do with it?" I asked softly.

He chuckled. "Depends on my mood. Send it to their family. Give it to Everett as a gift to keep him happy and think I give a fuck about him. Stomp on it. Keep it in a box. Do you want to see my box of hearts?" He blinked at me.

"No. I'm good." I shook my head at him.

He laughed again. "That's probably more of a Church thing, huh?"

"Probably," I mumbled, thinking about Church's love of preserving the dead.

"But to further address my sweet little firefly, she is my first love. My first attempt at anything, really. She is my first survivor. That means she belongs to me forever. Those are the rules."

I said nothing and continued to stare into the heater, watching the heat lines dance off it.

"Dante doesn't know my secret, Sinclair. I'd like to keep it that way for now. My numbers. My...owner. I'm not really there because I want to be. Just like him, I want to be free."

"I won't tell," I said softly. "Your secret is safe with me."

"Good. I knew you were trustworthy, bestie."

I sighed but didn't say anything.

We were quiet again for a long time before I spoke.

"The box of hearts. That's not in here, right?"

He let out a laugh. "Of course not. I keep it under my bed in our room."

I rubbed my eyes. Of-fucking-course he did.

# SIRENA

"Come on, heaven," Ashes encouraged, his hands in mine, while he steered me to the bathroom. My body screamed at me to stop, but I needed to wash up.

When we got to the bathroom, the shower was already going. Church and Stitches had left an hour before to go into town to get supplies. They said it would be a few hours before they'd be back. I was OK with that. They needed a break from me. I could sense the stress I was putting on them, and I hated it.

"You can sit and wash," Ashes said, stopping at the walk-in shower that had a built-in seat.

I stared at it for a moment before looking to Ashes.

"I'll help you," he murmured.

He reached for my nightgown. I trembled, fear taking hold of me.

"What's wrong?" he asked, stopping.

I stared into his blue eyes, trying to figure out what was happening and why I was so scared. It was Ashes. My pyro.

"Heaven?"

I blinked at him, the answer coming to me.

I didn't want him to see me. The cuts. The fading bruises. The ugly

"Sirena? Hey. Talk to me," he urged, thumbing away a tear that had slipped down my cheek. "What's going on? What can I do to help?"

When I simply stared at him, my chest heaving with each gasping breath, he wrapped his arms carefully around me and held me.

"I won't look if that helps. I'll turn my back so you can wash, or I can wait outside the door. My only concerns are your safety and comfort, OK?"

I exhaled, the panic slowly ebbing away with his words.

"There. That's better," he murmured, pulling away and smiling down at me. "Do you want me to stay or go?"

I stared into his eyes for a moment before exhaling and stepping away. I wanted him to stay but not look at me. He studied me, clearly understanding, before he turned his back on me, allowing me some privacy.

Quickly, I undressed and stepped into the shower. Seconds later, I was carefully washing myself, noting Ashes hadn't tried to turn once. Instead, he seemed to be looking down at his phone and sending out a text. I assumed it was meant for Church or Stitches.

I forced myself to look at the damage and let out a shaky breath. I'd healed a lot. The cuts were beginning to scab over, and the bruises were fading to a dull purple and yellow. I would probably have some scars to remind me of the ordeal, both physical and mental. Even emotional. My body still hurt despite the fact that time had whizzed past since that night.

I ground my teeth as I struggled to get the flashes of that night out of my head. His laughter. The pain. The fear. The way his warm breath felt on my skin. His lips on mine. His teeth sinking into my lip.

Reaching out, I ran my fingers along my healing lip. The swelling had reduced a lot more, but it was still aching and bled when I moved my mouth too much.

Warmth rushed through my body as the images flashed even quicker through my head. One of them stopped and flared brightly in the forefront of my mind.

His soft moans as he fucked me. The sickness I felt. The defeat.

The defeat. The defeat. THE DEFEAT.

The warmth was replaced by cold slamming against my veins.

Rage. Rage. Rage.

Homicidal rage.

I didn't feel like myself.

I felt powerful. Out of control.

He was dead, and I was the one who was going to kill him.

"Heaven?" Ashes called out, his voice sounding so far away. "Sirena? Hey—"

I ignored him, only one thing on my mind.

"What the hell? Sirena?"

I was cold. So cold. So angry.

He didn't deserve to live. He needed to die. I had to kill him. Stab him like he'd stabbed me. Hurt him. Make him scream. Make him beg.

A cry left me as the cold intensified.

Warmth. Movement. I was being carried.

I blinked rapidly, the ugly thoughts and anger receding. The room came back into focus.

The living room. I was naked, and Ashes was cradling me in his arms on the couch.

"It's OK. It's OK," he repeated, his voice trembling while he rocked me on his lap. "I've got you. I won't let you go. It's OK."

I blinked rapidly before running my fingers through his soft hair. He pulled away and stared down at me, worry in his blue eyes.

"You scared me," he murmured.

I took his hand and traced letters gently onto his palm.

*Tired.*

He nodded, his Adam's apple bobbing.

"OK. Let's get you dressed, and then we can rest."

With ease, he lifted me into his arms and brought me to Church's room, where he placed me on the bed. Quickly, he grabbed a pair of panties for me and shimmied them up my legs before pulling one of Church's long shirts over my body and tucking me beneath the blankets.

Wordlessly, he rounded the bed and lay beside me after taking me into his hold.

"Sleep," he whispered. "You're not well. You need to rest."
The way he said the words made the fear swell within me again.
Because he was right.
I wasn't well. Something was happening to me.
Something really bad.
Something that could get someone killed.

Fuck the watchers.

I let out a groan and shuffled to my feet from my bed, my body feeling like I'd been run over on repeat, and then dragged for miles.

A creak at my door had me looking over to see who it was.

"Hello, bunny boy," Asylum said, cocking his head to the left at me, a tiny deranged smile on his lips that made me take a step back.

"Have a minute to. . . talk?" He raised his dark brows at me.

I swallowed hard. "All I have is time. You know that. This is my purgatory."

He pushed off my door jamb and came fully into my room, twirling a damn fork around his fingers.

"Put your weapon away," I muttered, not moving from my spot. I kept a close eye on the psycho as he slowly prowled my small dorm room. They'd let me out of the facility a few days ago, and I'd been here since. I'd left my door open to get some air in.

I was really great at making bad decisions.

"It's only a weapon if I use it to carve out your eyes. Or tongue. Ever had your tongue forked out, Andrews?" Asylum stopped his perusal of my room and turned to face me. Dressed in all black, he gave off the vibes of someone who would truly fork me to death before slipping away back into the shadows he dwelled in.

"Can't say I have," I answered tightly.

He studied me, still twirling his damn fork. "First time for everything, right?"

I exhaled.

"What do you want, Seth?"

"Asylum," he corrected me. "And I want to know how many times you've jerked off while thinking about my forever girl."

I winced at his words but remained silent. I was sure there wasn't a correct answer to any of it, and trying to give one would probably end with his fork jammed into my eye.

"You're right," he murmured, his blue eyes raking over me. I took note of the bandage wrapped around his hand. I remembered him protecting me in the woods and Church's knife catching him.

He cocked his head to the left again.

"You remember everything, don't you, bunny boy?"

"What do you mean?" My voice shook.

He moved to the corkboard in my room and studied the photos I had pinned to it. Me and my friends on campus. Photos of the cemetery and grounds. A picture of my dog back home. He reached out and ran his fingers lightly over a picture of me and Sirena. I stiffened, hating he was touching it.

"You're vanilla, Andrews," Asylum murmured, continuing to study the picture of me and Sirena. "A sweet vanilla cupcake. But you remember everything."

I remained quiet, my aching body stiff with anticipation.

"Tell me, *Vanilla,* when was the last time you held your cock and thought about my forever girl?" He didn't turn to face me. He simply continued to stare at the photograph.

When I didn't answer, he let out a soft laugh that sent chills down my spine.

"This morning, but you hurt too much." He turned to face me. "Yes?"

"Why are you here?" I demanded quietly, wishing I had some answer to how she was doing.

He let out another soft laugh. "She's fine, by the way. Little crazy, but aren't we all?"

I watched him walk to my bed and take a seat on the edge of it. He continued to twirl his fork.

"I'm here because you want what's mine."

I glanced to my open door, knowing he'd be on me before I'd made it halfway across the room.

He snickered. "You're right. *Run, run, as fast as you can. You can't escape the forking boogeyman.*"

"I care about her," I said, holding my chin up.

He nodded. "You can't possibly think you can compete with me and the watchers, right?"

"I'm not trying to." I shrugged helplessly. "I know where I stand."

"Good. Now that you know that, I have a job for you." He switched gears quickly, going from murderer with a fork to psycho with a fork. There wasn't much difference.

"I'm not interested—"

"I care not about your interest regarding the matter." He waved me off. "I need you to go to Miss Kitty and put your dick to good use. Think you can handle that?"

I crinkled my brows at him. "Who?"

He rolled his blue eyes. "Cady. She's poking around, trying to get to firefly. We can't have that. My girl must rest and not be reminded of such ugly things."

"What's going on?"

"Sirena was harmed." He gave me a measured look. "You fucked things up for us, Vanilla. Now I want your help fixing them."

I scoffed at him. "I can't help you. I can't even help myself. And in case you forgot, the watchers will probably finish gutting me if they catch me outside my room."

"Bunnies are fast, even wannabe ones. I'm sure you'll be able to escape. Get to Cady. Put your dick inside her. Distract her."

"No." I glared at him. "I'm not like. . . that."

He smirked. "Like what? Straight? Cut the shit. We know what you are."

"I've never said I wasn't straight—"

"Right. Your old man. I know. Get your dick wet, Vanilla. I *forking* need you to."

"No. I-I can't. I won't."

He stood and slowly stalked toward me. I backed away from him until I was against the wall. He didn't stop until we were nose-to-nose. His warm breath blew across my face.

I couldn't shake the feeling that he was staring straight into my soul and snagging all my secrets like a greedy monster.

He shifted, his nose brushing along my jaw as he inhaled deeply.

"Virgin," he murmured. "How. . . *Vanilla* of you, sweetheart. You want to lose it to someone equally sweet. *My firefly.*" He moved his face away from mine and closed his eyes for a moment before snapping them open. My heart jumped into my throat as he ran his fork along my cheek.

"She's not as sweet as you think she is. She's our little monster. She would destroy you, Vanilla. Rip you to pretty red ribbons. That is, if the watchers didn't get to you first."

I let out shaky breath after shaky breath.

"You're special. Like me," he continued, his fork at my temple before he skimmed it to my bottom lash line. "You remember everything. You know what you were doing April fifth, a Tuesday evening, at ten at night, don't you?"

I swallowed thickly.

"Answer me, Vanilla."

"No." I blinked rapidly as he teased the edge of my eye.

"You have really pretty eyes. I like them a lot. Hazel with little flecks of gold," he murmured. "I've learned one doesn't need to have both eyes to live a life where he remembers his fucking place."

I squeezed my eyelids closed as he continued to tease me with his fork.

"*They always close their eyes,*" he said in a soft, sing-song voice. "*They think it will save their lives. But I am a monster sent from hell to do the devil's chores. To fuck the world and its whores. To torment and terrorize the weeping. Now tell me, Vanilla, all the secrets you've been keeping."*

A gasp slipped past my lips as he slowly worked one of the tines from his fork beneath my eyelid. My pulse thundered through my veins while the fear bubbled within me.

"I saw my father making a deal with Everett Church," I choked out.

Asylum didn't stop his trek beneath my eyelid.

"And?" he prodded softly, his body pressed against mine.

"And he found out. He sent me here. He-he always knew I was different. My memory never fades. He-he was angry after finding my-my friend kissing me in my room. He let *him* touch me. . ." my words became choked.

"Everett likes sweet little vanilla cupcakes." The tine moved deeper.

A tear worked its way down my cheek at the ugly memory.

"Your father wanted to teach you a lesson," Asylum continued softly. "What a man's touch really felt like. When Everett was done, you were tossed aside. *A trust fall. A sacrifice because you disappointed him anyway.* Your father thought of you as a freak. You didn't fight hard enough. You disgust him. But Everett. . . you entice him. He's a collector of lost, special souls."

The tine was nearly as deep as it could go, the cold steel pressing against my eyeball beneath my lid. I was certain one wrong move from me would end in my losing an eye.

"Do you feed Everett information?"

"No," I choked out. "I don't. I'm just here until I'm released."

"You will never be released," he murmured. "None of us will until death finds the monster holding the keys."

I exhaled shakily.

"Now, if you're a good cupcake, I'll reward you with those keys. Do you want your freedom, Vanilla?"

"Yes," I rasped.

"Then do what you're told. Go to Cady. Distract her however you can. Tell her you've seen Sirena and she's fine. That the watchers are just protective assholes. That she has the goddamn flu. Whatever your pretty, little, extraordinary mind comes up with."

"And then?"

"And then, maybe if you do a good enough job, I'll be closer to handing you the fucking keys. Trust me when I say God has nothing on my kingdom of paradise." His breath feathered along my lips. "My keys open all doors. Even the doors where cupcakes wear masks and want pretty mute girls beneath a full moon. Think about it."

And just like that, he pulled the fork free from beneath my eyelid and stepped away.

"Sirena?" I whispered.

A crooked smirk cut his lips upward.

"Paradise, Vanilla. Now get to fucking work."

# CHURCH

*I* stared into the flames dancing in the fireplace in our living room. We didn't often light this thing up, but Ashes had it roaring when Stitches and I had come back from getting winter supplies. We'd hauled it all into the house, having spent several thousand dollars on it all. Winters here could be brutal. It was probably one of the reasons why Chapel Crest was situated where it was. Students weren't able to escape more than half the year. Made life easier for the people in charge.

Because of the dancing flames, I knew Ashes was struggling with something. He kept pacing the room, flipping his lighter open and closed. Clearly, he was trying to gather his thoughts. I watched the flames, worry unfurling in my guts. Stitches simply sat on the other end of the leather wrap-around, looking to the ceiling. Ashes said Sirena had been sleeping for hours now.

That was good. She needed the rest.

But seeing Ashes pace the way he was made me think we had a new issue to tackle.

*Like we needed any fucking more issues.*

"Shit got weird today," Ashes finally said, stopping and letting out a shaky breath.

"How so?" I looked over at him, taking in the way his Adam's apple bobbed when he swallowed and the way his blue eyes wavered.

"*Sirena.* I took her to shower. She didn't want me to look at her. I get it. I do. That wasn't the problem. I turned my back on her and let her get inside the shower. Everything was going fine. Then she got out and walked past me completely naked and soaking wet. She didn't respond to me calling for her. I didn't know what the fuck was happening." He breathed out.

"She doesn't talk or respond much anyway, if at all," Stitches said, frowning. "So what was weird about any of it?"

"She walked out like she was in a trance. She went straight to the front door and pulled it open. I managed to get to her the moment she made to step outside." His blue eyes widened. "*Her eyes.* She wasn't there. It wasn't until I got her back to the couch that she started to come out of it."

I rubbed my eyes, my frustration coming through. "I'll call Doc. See what he says. She was sleeping peacefully when I was up there."

"Maybe it's her meds," Stitches added, a note of hope in his voice. I knew what he was thinking, though. He was praying she wasn't losing her damn mind.

"Trauma does fucked-up shit to people," I continued. "Maybe that's all this is. We'll watch her. If it happens again, we'll figure it out. We always figure it out."

Ashes let out a sigh. "It was just weird, man. She was fine afterward. Pretty much just went to sleep."

"We'll watch her," I repeated.

We fell silent for a long time. The knock at the front door had us on our feet. It was rare that anyone came to our house without an invitation, and I knew damn well I hadn't invited anyone.

"Maybe it's Cady?" Stitches wrinkled his nose and awkwardly adjusted his dick in his pants. He'd mentioned she threatened to feed him his own cock if she didn't get to see Sirena. Obviously, the threat meant something to him as he made a move to protect himself.

I went to the door and pulled it open to find Sin holding two paper sacks of groceries.

"What's this?" I asked, frowning at him.

"I, uh, I saw Stitches at the gates. He said you guys didn't have much food. I thought I'd bring you some. It's not a lot—"

"We don't want it," I snapped, glaring at him. "Keep it."

"Church, I-I don't want Sirena to be without if something happens. Storms are coming—"

"I know how to take care of my girl," I snarled at him. "Don't come to my fucking door and insult me, Sinclair."

"What's going on?" Stitches came up behind me and stared Sin down. "Hey."

"I brought supplies," Sin muttered.

"Shove them up your ass." I slammed the door closed on him, anger coursing through me.

"Man, he's trying," Stitches said, sighing.

"Doesn't fucking matter. He fucked up. He can't unfuck what he did. Our girl up there losing her fucking mind and hurting is a reminder of that fuck-up."

"He's our friend. Our brother. At least he was. Let's just—"

"No. I'll fucking kill him if he steps foot into this house, Malachi. You know I will. Then I'll eat all fucking winter." I stormed upstairs and went straight to my room to find Ashes sitting on the edge of my bed, watching Sirena sleep.

"Who was at the door?" he asked, glancing at me.

It was hard for me to keep my anger in check whenever I was around Sin. He'd been one of my best friends. We'd bonded in our traumas, but that fucking asshole went a step too far.

"Sin."

He raised his brows at me. "What did he want?"

"He had supplies he wanted to give us."

"Oh. That's nice of him." He flipped his lighter open and closed, his attention back on Sirena.

"Fuck him," I said, my irritation continuing to build.

The flame from Ashes's lighter danced for a moment before he closed the lid and returned to his ritual opening and closing five times. A pause. A flame. Back to opening and closing.

"Maybe we should talk to him and hear him out," Ashes started.

"No. I already told Stitches that Sin can fuck off. He's not welcome in this house. He helped for a minute when Specter was hurt. I appreciate that, but it doesn't erase his sins. What he did fucked everything up."

"Dante, we agreed to let Asylum in here. To help. To. . . I don't know. I think maybe we should hear Sin out."

I ground my teeth together. "Asher, man. Enough. I'm already on edge with everything. It takes every ounce of control I have to not just gut him whenever he's close. The fact you and Stitches are so careless with your forgiveness baffles me."

Ashes sighed and looked back to Sirena. "You know Sinclair has issues. We all do. Would you cut me out for mine? For setting the house on fire? What about Stitches for fighting? For his anger? I mean. . . fuck, man. We all deserve a little grace."

"He meant for her to die, Asher. *Dead.* He hoped Asylum's crazy ass would take her out."

"And yet you're letting Asylum in." He looked back to me. "Do you get my point?"

I let out a huff of frustration. This conversation was going in circles and pissing me off.

"Let's put a pin in it," Ashes said, clearly catching on. He closed his lighter and clenched it tightly in his hand. I noted the slight tremble. "We can revisit this conversation later. However, you need to understand that Asylum and Sin have obviously become friends. If you're letting Asylum near, know that Sin will be too. You can't be pissed about that."

I said nothing, knowing he was right. Knowing that it wouldn't matter. Knowing at some point, I'd lose it on Sin again because he'd had a hand in the pain my specter was in. Knowing that he was responsible for. . .

Fuck.

For the way I felt. The pain and betrayal he'd inflicted on me.

I hated to admit it, but the grumpy fucker had broken my heart. After all the shit we'd been through together with Bells.

Bonded together in blood, death, and dark secrets.

And he'd fucking betrayed me.

I let out a sigh and sat on Sirena's other side, then stared down at her.

"I love you, specter," I murmured before placing a kiss on her forehead.

She let out a little hum in her sleep, and I looked to Ashes.

"Even in sleep, she hums that damn song," he said softly. "I wonder where she heard it and why it's so important to her."

"Me too," I said before twining my fingers with hers and clinging to her small hand.

In the end, it didn't matter. As long as she was happy and still here, it was what I'd focus on.

And fucking keeping her that way.

# MIRAGE

*I* rubbed my eyes, exhausted and worried off my ass, while I paced the length of the cave. My head was killing me. The snowflakes from the season's first major winter storm were just starting to fall.

I was sick to death of living this way.

*Him.*

*Me.*

*Where the fuck did I end, and he begin?*

I paced again, the voice in my head.

*Right here. You know that. In time.*

*Fucking damnit. Stop. Silence for one fucking day. Please.*

*You know we can't do that.*

*Be real fucking nice if we did.*

*It's not so bad. Could be worse, yes?*

I let out a grumble.

*Could try the meds again. They made us feel really fucked up, though,* the familiar voice continued.

*Not happening. We will suffer in silence.*

*I wouldn't say silence. I'd like to think we get along well, locked in our mind. Together. Forever. The same. Different. Us. Us. US.*

*Fucking damnit. Enough. Don't fuck with me unless it's important.*

*It's always important. For example, I'm only here to tell you to expect company soon.*

*That it?*

*No.*

A soft laugh in my head before the voice spoke again.

*I also wanted to tell you that I love you, my crazy fucking personality.*

I sighed.

*I love you too, my insane fucking warden.*

*I'd let you out to play more if you didn't get carried away. You know that.*

*And I told you that I was breaking free soon.*

*Yes, well, I saw what happened when you decided to do things on your own. You almost got poor Bryce killed.*

*He almost got himself killed. No one told him to play pretend.*

*Yes, well, he loves her too. She's easy to love.*

*And hard to stay away from.*

*Indeed. Look to the door. He comes.*

The voice faded, and I was left with silence in my head. I exhaled, relishing the quiet I so rarely got.

I looked to the door of the cave. A moment later, Sin stepped inside, covered in snowflakes. He closed the makeshift door behind him and looked to me.

"Welcome," I said, not bothering to go to him.

"It's fucking cold out there," he mumbled, stomping forward and putting the bag he was carrying onto the floor near the old couch. "I brought you some clothes like you asked for."

I raised my brows at him. "I didn't ask for clothes. We haven't spoken in a long time, Sinclair."

He rolled his gray eyes at me through the dim light of my heater.

"I don't fucking know when you're him and he's you. Excuse me to hell. . . *Mirage*. It is Mirage, right?"

It was my turn to roll my eyes.

"Yeah, it's Mirage."

"Good. You two are hard to keep track of."

"So we've been told," I muttered, looking to my right and scowling.

"If it helps, Asylum is fucking weird." Sin sat on the couch and stared at me.

"It doesn't."

He shrugged. "Didn't figure it would." He looked around the cave. "So. This is where you'll be hanging?"

"Yeah." I sat in the chair near the heater and rubbed my hands. It wasn't freezing in here, but it wasn't a sun-soaked beach either.

"Might need another heater," Sin commented.

I nodded without a word.

"I'll make sure to get one. I'll get more propane, too, so you can use that little stove over there. Beats eating beans out of a tin can."

"So what? I can eat it out of a pan?"

He shrugged at me. "Beggars can't be choosers."

I scoffed at him, irritated at the current situation.

"Listen, it won't be long. Asylum will let you out more."

"And you know this how?" I looked over at him.

He stared into the heater. "Because he said he would."

"Right. Healing takes time." I held my bandaged hand out.

"You know why he said you couldn't come out, right? Even with that bandage on your hand?"

"I'm aware. He's punishing me for fucking up. Bandage or not, I must pay my penance."

Sin nodded. "I know a thing or two about that."

I studied him for a long moment. His blond hair had been cut. It was shaggier than normal. He lost weight from his sadness but was still a big guy. His muscles still strained against his clothes ever so slightly. Enough to still be intimidating.

"Are you still hurting yourself?" I asked in a low voice as if these stone walls could hear my words.

He continued to stare into the heater. "Sometimes."

"You need to stop."

"Do I?" His gray eyes met mine. "What good would stopping do?"

"There are far worse things to be punished for, Sinclair. I would know."

"Then you also know that none of the shit that happened was your fault. You didn't hurt Sirena. That wasn't you."

"Wasn't it?" I raised my brows at him. "It may not have been me, but it was my fault. Asylum escaping and getting close to her. . ." I sighed and looked to the ceiling of the cave as if divine intervention would save my treacherous soul.

"I don't believe you or Asylum are sick," he said softly. "We're all fucked in the head in one way or another, but I don't think you're *sick*. Not like *them*. They need to die, and we need redemption."

"Ah, the villains' redemption arc." I let out a sour laugh. "Whatever could two monsters do to make our atrocities right, Sinclair?"

"She loves you," he said fiercely, his gray eyes boring into mine. "You know she does. Through all the shit, she loves you, Seth. Even Asylum. She loves him despite his crimes against her. I-I worry for her." He went quiet again.

I cocked my head to the right as I watched him.

"If she could forgive you and Asylum, maybe there's room in her heart to forgive me too," he finally whispered.

I studied him, hurting for his pain as if it were my own. Hell, in a way, it was.

"I believe you can have that. That we all can have that. Asylum is the way." I chuckled softly.

*Best believe I am. Follow me. I know the way.*

I focused on the silence and edged him out of my head. It was quiet once more.

"I don't even know how to go about proving myself." Sin scratched his head and shifted in his seat. "I beat myself. Cut myself. I-I pray to a god who probably only wants my suffering. I'm at a loss."

"I don't know other than to just keep going." I sat back. "With Asylum's plan, I think he'll get you close enough to her. It's you who needs to reach out and take what you want."

"And you'd be OK with that? Me taking her?" He crinkled his brows, his focus on me.

I shrugged. "Look, I understand she's capable of loving more than one person. I'd be honored to be included in it. If she wants me and wants you and the watchers. Asylum. I'd not hesitate. I'd fall to my knees for my goddess and worship her."

His Adam's apple bobbed. "What if I can't fix this?"

I sat forward. "We tried to kill her. She still kissed me willingly. She still sought me. I think there's hope for you, Sinclair. Just reach out."

He scoffed at me and shook his head. "I'm not good at this shit. Even this conversation feels uncomfortable."

I waved him off. "Don't worry about it. I rarely get to speak to people being so. . . locked up. Even the uncomfortable conversations are better than no conversations."

"Well, you have Asylum in your head."

I snorted. "Sometimes. At least you're near enough to punch him when he starts his shit. All I can do is wish I could pull him out of my head and lay him on his ass."

Sin gave me an actual smile. "You'd not do it."

I laughed at that. "Probably not. While he pisses me off, for better or worse, he's the voice in my head."

Sin let out a soft laugh. "He's the voice in mine too."

"The devil on your shoulder," I mused. "The wind at your back, pushing you forward."

Sin smirked at me. "That's you too, Seth. You're the same. I'd have killed myself already. Probably. One of my cuts would have eventually been deep enough."

I cocked my head to the right again and stared at him, my eyes narrowed. "No, I don't believe you would have. You wanted an outlet, not to be dead. Sometimes, hurting ourselves is the only way to bleed our emotional pain out and focus on something different for a moment. A different pain that can divert our attention. That can give our hearts a moment of peace. Give our minds some ease. I would know."

He glanced to my wrists, which were covered by the sleeves of my dark hoodie.

I swallowed hard. "I also have punished myself."

"Do you still do it?"

I chewed my bottom lip for a moment before answering. "Yes. On occasion. Asylum gets angry with me, but what are demons good for if not to get pissed off when you try to cut them out of you."

"He's not really in you, though," Sin said gently. "I mean, he is, but still. He's in me too sometimes."

"He's the parasite I can't live without." I let out a mirthless chuckle. "But I do love him despite it all. I suppose that says more about me than it does about him."

"I feel that way about the watchers. They wanted me dead, but I still love the hell out of them. Church still wishes for my death, I'm sure. In fact, he's made it clear I can fuck off and die."

I waved him off. "Dante will come around eventually. Besides." I shifted in my seat and gave him a sinister smile. "It's not actually him you need to impress to make your way back into their group."

Sin raised his brows at me.

"It's her," I finished. "Dante and the guys will give her whatever she wants. You know this. I know this. Asylum fucking knows it. Why do you think he's playing the angle he's playing? He knows if he just goes to the watchers and asks to fuck her, too, they'll tell him to go to hell. It's why he's working on *her*. He makes himself important in her recovery. He's worked his way beneath her skin as I have. Then she needs him. Needs me. Can't live without us. When she finally gives in, the watchers will witness it. They'll welcome us in with open arms *for her*. If you want to go home, Sinclair, she's your fucking compass, my friend."

He sat straighter. "I-I can't fuck up again."

I shook my head. "No. You can't."

"I don't know how to do this shit. I've always been a fuck-up with women. Fuck, I don't want to hurt anymore. What if it doesn't work? What if—"

"Stop." I held my hand up. "You think too much. If you need to think on it, consider this. What if it *does* work? Huh? I'm not a believer in manifesting destiny or anything like that, but I do believe that if you change your way of thinking, your journey will be more enjoyable. Don't you want an enjoyable journey?"

"I do," he murmured.

"Then positive thinking. Let the darkness belong *to us* and the night. For now, focus on being better and not doubting shit about yourself. You're a survivor, so fucking live, Sinclair. Don't do it for the watchers. For Sirena. Do it for you because you deserve it just as much as the next crazy fuck. Got it?"

"Yeah," he answered thickly, getting to his feet. "Yeah. I mean, fuck. I'll try."

"It's all we can do. I need a nap. My head hurts."

"Will you be OK here?"

"I've been here a long time. A little longer won't kill me."

"Where do you go when you're... gone?"

"Always working." I sighed. "Building a better life. Making points of contact. Taking down the man."

He stared me down for a moment before nodding, obviously deciding to not pursue questioning me. "I'll bring the propane and another heater. They're calling for at least a foot of snow. I'll try to get it back to you before it starts coming down hard."

I waved him off. "Don't kill yourself over it. Worse comes to worse, I'll blanket off one of those smaller rooms and take the heater in there. I'll be fine. I've spent a fair number of winters here."

He nodded and walked to the door.

"Hey, Sinclair?"

"Yeah?" He looked at me from over his shoulder.

"Tell Asylum he owes me fifty bucks."

"Can't you just dial him up in your head and tell him?"

I smiled at him. "I'd rather you get to see his face when you tell him."

He chuckled and shrugged before leaving me alone in the cave with nothing but silence in my head.

I couldn't ask for a more perfect evening.

Well, unless it included my Rinny.

But I'd get there. Eventually.
I smiled at that.
*One. Two. I'm coming for you. Three. Four. You'll scream some more.*
In fact, many would by the time we were done.
What a sweet nightmare that would be.

# SIRENA

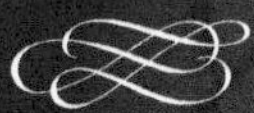

*I* exhaled. Inhaled. Exhaled. Inhaled.

A wave of dizziness came over me before slowly dissipating.

I was OK, and I wanted to live my life.

It had been far too long. The days kept weaving onward, and yet nothing was getting better. All I knew was that to get better, I had to be better.

Staying in that damn bed and staring at the ceiling wasn't fixing my problems. Being weak wasn't fixing them.

Something dark and angry was coming over me, and I was tired of pushing it off the last few weeks. Maybe I needed to get mad. Maybe it would fix things and put me in charge for once in my life.

But deep down, I was terrified. I would always be that little girl who struggled to get out of the locked box.

I swallowed hard at that memory before pushing my blankets off and getting shakily to my feet. As carefully as possible, I made it to the bathroom and turned on the shower. Church wasn't in bed. He usually wasn't in the mornings. He was typically downstairs or taking turns with Ashes and Stitches on attending classes, so someone was always with me. He'd leave in the middle of the night too. I assumed he was hunting.

I wanted things to get back to normal.

I took a shower, avoiding looking at my body the entire time, before I got out and dressed myself. I fell sideways, a wave of dizziness coming over me again, but I managed to catch myself on the edge of the sink before I could tumble to the floor.

Steadying myself, I finished getting ready, feeling almost human for the first time in weeks.

Slowly, I made my way downstairs to see Church was there, typing something into his phone while he sat in his chair. The smell of his weed hung thick in the air.

I approached him, finally catching his attention as I closed in.

"Specter," he said, getting to his feet, his green eyes drinking me in. "You look beautiful."

I felt my face heat at his words and looked down at the pretty sundress I was in. I was a bit cold wearing it, but it made me feel good and reminded me of Cady. By wearing it, I felt better.

He took my hand, pulled me onto his lap, and nuzzled against my neck.

"I love the way you smell," he said softly, his warm breath sending goosebumps flying over my skin. I closed my eyes as he inhaled deeply, his hand high on my thigh beneath my skirt. "I like that you came downstairs to me. Are you feeling well, baby?"

To answer, I turned to him and placed a gentle kiss on his lips.

He took control immediately, deepening it until I was breathless.

When he broke away, he placed a sweet kiss on my bare shoulder.

"I'm sorry. I've just missed seeing you this way."

I rested my hand over his on my thigh and gave it a gentle squeeze.

"Are you hungry? I can make you something." He stared into my eyes.

I gave him an eager look, which made him chuckle softly.

"OK. I'll get you something to eat." He lifted me easily from his lap and placed me on the soft cushion before getting to his feet and going into the kitchen. I watched as he worked quickly at the stove. Before long, the smell of oatmeal hung in the air.

My stomach gave a growl which made me wince.

Quickly, he put my oatmeal into a bowl, grabbed a glass of orange juice, and came back to me. I watched as he placed the items on the table next to his seat before he brought me to my feet and took his place on the cushion again.

He pulled me back onto his lap and grabbed the bowl of oatmeal.

"Open," he commanded softly.

He was going to feed me.

I parted my lips and allowed him to slip the food against my tongue.

"Eat, baby," he murmured.

I did as instructed, chewing the oatmeal quickly. It was really good. He had even put blueberries into it. The little berries popped with flavor, making my tastebuds dance with joy.

He continued to feed me until my stomach was fit to burst. I turned my head away from him. I thought he'd fight me on it and make me finish it all, but he downed it himself before grabbing the orange juice and offering it to me. I sipped it and pulled away. He was quick to polish that off, too, and then placed the empty glass back on the side table.

With care, he pulled me against his body and held me. I rested my head in the crook of his neck, enjoying the comfort he brought me. The way he smelled. Like cold, wintery forest. Cedar. Wood. Something distinctly *Dante*.

"Is there anything you want to do today?"

I remained silent, locked in my prison. More than anything, I wanted to speak, but the words weren't there. I hated it, but this was me. I wanted to be someone else. Wishing the words would come when I wanted them to didn't always work. Sometimes I was able to voice them, which was a huge accomplishment for me. Most times, though, I was stuck in silence.

"Do you think you're ready to return to classes? As much as I enjoy knowing you're here and safe, it's getting hard to keep Sully off my ass. Eventually, he's going to send word to my father. We don't want that," he said thickly.

He was right. We didn't.

I fingered one of the buttons on his dark button-down.

"Sirena?" he called out. "I wish you'd speak to me. I love the way your voice sounds. It's so. . . pretty and sweet. I dream of it."

I shifted closer to him.

He gave me a gentle squeeze as my fingers trailed to his wrists and played with all the leather bands he wore. One had a small rabbit on it. I traced the shape, feeling the soft leather.

I was sure it was made from a poor bunny.

I moved to the next bracelet and ran my fingers along the strange leather. It was sewn together in pieces, the leather different colors.

I stared up at him curiously.

"Do you like that one?" he asked in a rough voice.

I bit my bottom lip. I wouldn't say I liked it. It simply made me curious.

"Would you like to know the story behind it?"

I ran my finger along the leather again, noting that one piece had an intricate design embedded deep within it.

"When I lived at home, my father made me do things for him. Things pretty little girls like you should never have to witness."

I swallowed, my heart rate picking up.

"This one." He pointed to the first bit of leather. "This is from a man who owed my father money. He sold flesh for him. He would keep a chunk of cash with each transaction. Father didn't like that, so he sent me in. It seemed only fitting that I take his flesh as a souvenir."

I shivered at his words, the nausea at what he meant twisting through my guts like an angry serpent. I jerked my hand away from the bracelet, but he captured my fingers and pressed them back against it.

"The second piece is from a man who ate. . . things he shouldn't," he said in that rough voice. He slid my fingers to the next piece.

"This is from a man who tried to touch me."

Another piece.

"This is from a woman who fucked my father while he was married to my mother. I do not tolerate betrayal. I was able to get to her. My father's time will come someday as well."

Another piece.

"This is from someone who tried to buy my mother from my father. My father watched me do this one. He laughed the entire time I hacked the man to bits."

He continued on, telling me the story of each piece of leather until we reached the last piece. It was a band connected to the others but was solid and wasn't Frankensteined together like the rest were.

"And this," he said softly, his voice wobbling. "This is my mother."

My breath came in a shaky gasp at his words.

"*Calista,*" he continued in a whisper. "The queen of the Underground."

He paused. "I've never told you the story of my mother, have I? Of my story and how I came to be this way. I know you're aware of Ashes, Stitches, and Sin's stories, but mine has alluded you."

I trembled on his lap. He ran his knuckles along my jaw and turned my face so I was staring into his moss-green eyes.

"I am no saint, Sirena. I'm a very bad man." He thumbed my bottom lip. "If you leave me, I'll find you and weave you into my mother's bracelet."

I shook at his words.

"Whether you like it or not, you belong to me. I never let go of things that are mine. And nothing that ever hurts what belongs to me gets to live for long."

I turned my face from him, fear washing over me.

"Look at me," he commanded, turning my face back to his with a firm hold.

I stared into his eyes, my breath held.

"I will find the person who caused you harm, specter. When I do, I will deliver him to you. I will watch you carve him to pieces if that is your wish, but I swear on my life, you will have your revenge if it is what you seek. For you, I'd give the world. I'd give you your own heaven."

The darkness I'd been trying to keep at bay peeked out from the shadows, eager to get to work. The fear washed away, replaced by excitement.

I licked my lips, the numbness of this new part of my soul coming out to look around.

"What if I want hell, Dante? Should you deliver it?"

His eyes darted to my lips, where I had the bottom one pulled between my teeth.

"I would deliver hell and all its fucking demons anywhere you'd like, my love. For you, I'd do anything. Kill anyone. All you need to do is give the command, and it will be yours."

"Promise?" I leaned in.

He exhaled and closed his eyes briefly. I studied his peaceful face. So beautiful. So flawless. Such a beautiful, perfect monster.

His lashes fluttered for a moment before he opened his eyes.

"I vow it. Yours. All of it. Anything. You are my reason for everything now. Both my sanity and insanity. You drive them. Steer them well, my specter, because once I let go, I really will unleash a hell you couldn't even fathom in that pretty little head of yours. So call my name. I will come to you and go to my knees, then await your command. I am yours, Sirena. Forever."

I let my eyelids close, relishing his words. This darkness within me adored them. The light feared them.

Who I was, I didn't know, and that scared me.

But not as much as Dante Church did.

"Tell me your story, Dante," I demanded softly, now reeling in the darkness. Maybe if I let the darkness out, it would keep me safe. It would protect me.

I wanted to be safe inside my body.

He cradled my cheek when I opened my eyes.

"You may never look at me the same way again," he murmured.

I pressed my lips to his. He immediately kissed me back, dragging the breath from my body.

"I am not myself," I whispered against his lips between kisses.

"I know," he answered in a trembling voice. "We all snap in here. You are no exception."

I nipped his bottom lip, earning a soft groan from him.

"Tell me your story," I commanded again.

His lips trailed down my neck. I loved the way it felt. So firm and in charge. So. . . Dante.

His lips left my skin and was replaced by his hand in a firm hold around my neck. He gave it a squeeze, making me gasp out.

"If you try to leave me after hearing it—"

I reached out and wrapped my hand around his neck before squeezing like he did to me.

"Then we will both die," I whispered.

"Don't tempt me with a good time." He crushed his lips to mine in a fierce kiss. All senses left my head as he took control of my body.

"Tell me who owns you."

"You do," I choked out.

He sucked against the sensitive skin of my neck, releasing his hold on me. I moaned softly as he cradled my breast.

"You're not my specter," he whispered into my ear after trailing kisses and bites along my jaw.

"I am. I'm just a different version."

"I want *her* right now. She needs to hear my words. Bring her back. I want my sweetheart, not her monster."

"No."

"Bring her back to me," he commanded, pulling away and glaring down at me. "Now."

I blinked rapidly, heat sweeping through me. Dizziness. Nausea. Confusion.

I stared up at him, wondering how we'd gotten into the position we were in. Why I'd snapped the way I had. It was the darkness inside me. I was sure of it. I was her. She was me. A demon sent from my own personal hell. One meant to protect me from the bad men in our world.

The lines were blurred. We were all bad here it seemed.

"There you are," he murmured, cradling my cheek. "*Specter.*"

A tear worked its way down my cheek. Fear blanketed me. Something was wrong. Really wrong.

But it felt so right. So safe.

"It's OK. We're all a little crazy here, baby." He kissed me sweetly before pulling away. "You were asking about my story. Do you still want to hear it, or would you like to save it for our next walk through the cemetery at midnight?"

With a shaky hand, I reached out and squeezed his hand.

"Now," he confirmed. "So be it. Just don't run. There's nowhere you could ever go that I wouldn't find you. Understand?"

I stared back at him, knowing exactly what it meant. He was scared he'd lose me by telling his story.

He wouldn't, though. I'd stay.

"Your eyes are so expressive," he said in a gentle voice. "If I stared long enough into them, I could know the secrets to the universe."

He brushed his lips against mine. "Let's begin, shall we?"

I exhaled and gave a slight nod of my head.

That seemed good enough for him because he began speaking.

"My mother's name was Calista, and she was beautiful."

# CHURCH

*I* licked my lips, my ugly story tainting my tongue. I never spoke of my mother. It wasn't a memory I liked, but the guys knew it, so my girl should also know it. I shoved all the shit out of my head that had transpired with Sirena moments ago. It was a subject I'd broach another time. Right now, I needed to focus on this moment.

"My father forced my mother into marriage," I said in a soft voice. "They attended Mayfair together. She was beautiful. A singer. A scholar. A model. Hair like spun gold. Eyes green like emeralds. When I was a young boy, I'd stare at her beauty, mesmerized by it. I'd never seen a woman so beautiful in all my life." I thumbed Sirena's bottom lip. "Until I met you, that is."

Her soft, warm breath blew across my thumb.

Fuck, I wanted to devour her.

And maybe that monster she'd let out earlier. I'd love them both to fucking death without a second thought.

I pushed those ideas from my mind, deciding I needed to speak to the guys about what I'd witnessed with her. Ashes hadn't been overreacting the other day when she'd tried to go naked out the front door.

She really had snapped.

I tabled those thoughts once again and focused.

I cleared my throat.

"My mother never willingly loved my father. He demanded it, but she was strong-willed. A fighter," I continued. "I was born out of hatred and rape."

Sirena's colorful eyes filled with sadness and pity.

"Do not pity my origins, specter," I warned. "I do not."

She bit her bottom lip and remained silent.

"My father wanted an heir. Needed one. He wanted a son, of course. Men are stronger than women in his world. I came into the world born of hatred, yet my mother loved me despite it. I grew with her guiding me. When I was five, my father bought me a rabbit for my birthday. I loved that rabbit. I was young, but I knew what love was. My mother had taught it to me despite the dark world we lived in."

I let out a soft breath, hating this next part.

"For my sixth birthday, my father gave me my first hunting knife. He commanded me to kill my friend. When I refused, he beat my mother in front of me. She told me to stand my ground. To defy. I did, my body shaking with fear. He would kill my mother, though. He knew how much we loved one another. Perhaps he was jealous of the small family we'd made without him. Unable to handle watching my mother being beaten, I knew I had to make a choice. My mother or my pet." I paused, inhaling, the ugly memory stirring my hatred. "We ate my kill for my birthday dinner. I threw up the entire night, my broken mother consoling me in her bed."

I paused, focusing my mind to continue.

"After my sixth birthday, my father began my training. Weapons. Fighting. Killing. I killed my first person when I was six and a half," I murmured. "A man. I didn't know him. My father's men held him down in a white room. My father stood over my shoulder and whispered into my ear, '*Pathetic. Disappointment. Weak. Dante, you're fucking weak. No one will ever love you. Your mother will grow to hate your weakness.*' His words hurt me. Angered me." I clenched my teeth so hard my jaw ached. "I was young, Sirena. I didn't know how to control myself. I didn't know how to ignore the pain he inflicted on me. So I took my knife and pushed it through the man's throat. It wasn't easy. He screamed so fucking loud until it gave way to gurgling. His blood stained my hands. My clothes. The white room. For once, I felt a freedom I'd never felt before. A way to express my anger. *An outlet.*" I breathed out. "My father made me pick the part I liked the most on the man. I chose his arm. He had a tattoo of a skull on it. My father made me carve off that part of the man. I did so, then. . ." I sighed. "He taught me to eat everything I killed. It started with the rabbit."

Sirena's soft fingers brushed along my cheek. I took her hand in mine and kissed each delicate finger, my throat tight.

"I did not mourn that man's death nor the end of my innocence. I didn't know how to. I was a child. I knew it was wrong, but it made my father proud, so I took refuge in that, hoping he would be kinder to me and my mother. I embraced that freedom and let myself go. It upset my mother. She fought with my father. He hit her. Hurt her. My hopes were crushed. When I was nine, she defied him by trying to escape with me in the dead of night." I let out a sad laugh.

"We didn't make it to the front door before he was on us. He dragged us back to my mother's bedroom, where I was forced to watch her punishment. Beaten. Stripped naked. *Fucked.*"

"'*Do you love your mother, Dante?*' my father screamed at me. '*Do you love her?*'"

I stared at Sirena, noting the sadness swimming in her colorful eyes. Telling my story wasn't something I ever longed to do, least of all to her because I knew she was someone who felt too much, and god help me, I didn't want her to hurt. I didn't want her to pity me or feel sorry for me. I didn't deserve that from her.

"He screamed that at me on repeat until I answered and said I did. He made me move closer. He said it was a lesson in love."

My throat tightened more. The words were hard to say, the memory still raw and bleeding even after all these years.

"H-he said he'd kill her if I-I didn't. . ." my voice trailed off. "I couldn't lose my mother. I loved her. She was my whole world. My protector. She lay in that bed, her eyes barely open, her face swollen and bruised." I released a shaky breath. "She was so cold. She didn't fight the punishment. She let it happen, but I remember the tears that mixed with her blood as I did it. As I-I. . ." Fuck, saying the crime was painful.

Sirena's brows were knit so tightly.

I could do this.

My mother would tell me that speaking my feelings would heal me. It had been many years since I spoke of my feelings in such a way. I figured my soul was an ugly scab that would never heal, truths or not.

"I beat her," I whispered. "He told me to pick my weapon. The only thing I had was my belt from my pants." I cleared my throat. "Her blood. Her tears. Her-her body. He forced me to hurt her. He guided my hand. He said it was a glimpse of my beginnings. He said it would make me stronger. I still remember the way she sounded as I cried from my position. The pitiful, soft cries. The way she reached for my hand when it was over to hold me. To comfort me." I shook my head, hating the fucking memory.

"When father was satisfied with my job, he pulled me away from her and finished her punishment. She didn't make the same noises for him that she'd made for me. For me, she'd given me muffled cries of pain. For him, she screamed." I paused. "I didn't want to hurt my mother that day, specter. Don't run away thinking that. I simply had the sampler my father wanted me to have so I could be damaged further by his sickness. So I could see my future. So I could have a taste of power. The next day, he gifted me Stitches, my broken and torn brother. It made life easier. I had someone besides my mother because looking at her made me sick to my stomach. What I'd done was wrong, but I was a selfish boy wanting to keep my mother with me. Wanting to save her and always have someone who would love me no matter what."

I rubbed my eyes, the familiar nausea twisting through my insides.

"I continued killing for my father. I've killed so many people, specter. I became bored with it. Hundreds of the dead haunt me. I was growing up and had friends, though. Troubled ones. Stitches. Ashes. Sin. We became broken brothers bonded in our collective darknesses.

I took solace in having them in my life. They broke up the ugly I lived in."

"Mother wasn't happy yet. She would kiss me goodnight each night and make me promise I'd get out. When I screwed up, my father would use her to punish me. I watched my father hurt her. I stood by, unable to do anything because it would end in her death. Death would have been a far kinder fate, but again, I was selfish and wanted my mother with me always. Love can make us do ugly things. Keeping my mother alive was one of them."

I took a moment to brush a stray piece of Sirena's dark hair away from her face.

"My mother took to staring into my eyes while she was beaten. Tears would streak down her cheeks. I'd cry with her. As I got older, her punishments, and mine, were worse. Men. So many men wanted her. She was so beautiful," I whispered. "Even beaten and broken, she was still so breathtaking. My father sold her to high bidders. The men would have their way with her and then spit on her after. I'd watch her curl into a ball and cry softly. I'd go to my knees and hold her hand through her tears, just like she'd do for me."

"'*Dante, please,*' she'd whispered to me after one brutal night where four men had their way with her. They'd hurt her beyond words. She screamed. Threw up. They'd run their cocks through her sick and fucked her with it. And I was forced to fucking listen to it. Sick. Sick. So fucking sick." My voice shook. "The night that happened, I realized I was hurting my mother more than saving her. There wasn't a way out for either of us, and she didn't deserve to suffer as she had been. So I went to her room later that night and lay in bed with her. I was fourteen."

I drew in a breath in a pathetic way to calm myself for the next part.

"I whispered to her that I loved her. I kissed her. Held her. Told her how much she meant to me. I wanted to show her the love she deserved." My hands shook.

Sirena widened her colorful eyes at me, her lips parted.

"She whispered against my ear, her voice barely there from all her screaming. Her words were, *'Please, moy sladkiy d'yavol. Please.'"* I cleared my throat. "I would never deny my mother the things she wanted. I moved so I was over her, her body beneath mine. *'Let me go. Please. Let me go.'* I can't tell you how many times she'd tried to end her life over the years. Slash her wrists. Try to hang herself. Each time, she'd be found and brought back into our dark world. But I could give her this. I could do this for her."

I reached into my boot and pulled my hunting knife out. I ran the blade along Sirena's jaw, along her soft lips, down her throat, and over the tops of her breasts. Her breathing picked up.

"I kissed her forehead again. Her cheek. Held her. And pushed my blade deep inside her body. She let out a soft moan against my skin. She gripped my arms tightly as I continued to cling to her as she clung to me. As I continued to kill her she whispered, *'Kak ad menya blagoslovil'.* It means, *how hell has blessed me."* I took a moment to collect myself before continuing with the next part.

"She stilled beneath me, a tear working its way from her eye and dripping onto her white pillowcase. Her blood was everywhere, even in my mouth. Beneath my nails. On my face. I swallowed it, hurting so much I didn't think I'd ever heal. But it was the smile on her face which let me know she was at peace. That I'd finally saved her. I'd done it. I'd given her the freedom she'd been desperate for."

"With that in mind," I continued softly. "I took my knife and chose my favorite part of her. That was the rule. We take our favorite parts and make them part of us by feasting. I took my mother's heart. She was pure in heart. My father came in and caught me holding it in my hands, her body having grown cold. I'd taken great care of her during my operation."

*"'It took you long enough.'"* I stopped moving my knife along Sirena's breasts. "That's what my father said to me. He walked past me and looked down at my mother's mutilated body before he crawled onto her and fucked her one last time. I watched, satisfied she wasn't there to hurt anymore." I let my knife fall away from Sirena's soft skin.

"He took her tongue, and we ate together that night. I went back later and took some of her skin and made my bracelet with it. Her heart is part of me now. I joke and tell the guys she's my soft spot. And the bracelet. . ." I shrugged. "I always liked the way her skin was so soft. I like knowing she's still with me, no matter how small a piece of her."

Sirena's bottom lip trembled. I moved my knife back to her breast and stopped it over her heart.

"If you ever run from me, I will find you and cut your heart from your chest and devour it," I husked out. "Then I will fuck your dead body before I preserve you for eternity. Because my love is forever, specter. When I vow it, I mean it. I fucking love you, and you will always be mine."

A tear leaked down her cheek before she was crying silently.

"Don't cry," I whispered. "And don't run. I told you it was a bad story." I licked her tears away, relishing the way she tasted.

I thought she'd pull away from me. I thought she really would run. Instead, her lips met mine in a deep, soul-shattering kiss. My knife fell from my hand, clattering to the hardwood floor at my feet. The monster inside took over, and I pushed my way into her tiny body, her scream of protest against my lips.

"Mine," I growled as I forced my way inside. "Your body belongs to me. Not him. Get him out of your fucking head." I shoved upward into her, making her tears flow harder. "This pussy is mine. Not fucking his. I will fuck you until you forget that night. Now fucking scream for me, Sirena."

And she did.

Music to my fucking ears.

# SIN

*I* caught a glimpse of Siren for all of a moment before Cady swooped in on her. She'd barely made it across the courtyard. Weeks had passed. My heart clenched in my chest at that small glimpse. A pink hat atop her head. Her long black hair a wild tangle around her ankle-length pink puffy coat. Her mittens. Not gloves, because a girl as sweet as Siren wore mittens. The guys flanking her.

My spot empty.

I ground my teeth at the thought, hating I was having it and hating I was hating it. I wanted more than anything to go home and prove myself, but I also had self-loathing which didn't seem to want to fuck off. I had a belief I didn't deserve her, and it would ruin everything.

"Everything is already ruined," Asylum said, smacking the back of his hand against my chest and taking a bite from a muffin he had. "Why not fix shit now so you can ruin it later?"

"Shut up," I muttered, glancing at him. "And stop chewing so fucking loud."

He took another bite from his muffin and ignored me. "Go talk to her."

"No, Church will kill me."

"Pussy." He let out a laugh and stepped away from me. I caught the rest of the muffin he tossed my way and watched him saunter toward the group.

In disbelief, I shook my head. He wasn't afraid of shit. I was once that way, but I'd been humbled a bit in the last few weeks. I'd also made that vow to Church after everything happened to her in the woods. I'd keep my distance. I was to be seen and not heard. That was my place. In the background.

I watched Asylum join the group and shove Cady aside. She was quick to shove him back, but Stitches reached out and tugged her away as Asylum completely took center stage. He produced a black rose from the inside of his jacket and handed it to her.

For a moment, she hesitated before taking it from him.

I thought Church might attack, but he simply brushed a snowflake from her nose before giving Asylum a curt nod and moving Sirena forward, the guys falling in step, Cady joining them.

Asylum watched them go, a tiny smirk on his lips.

Mirage had a point, it seemed. If Sirena wanted it, Church gave it. So I just had to get her to want me so I could go home.

Not that it would be the only reason I'd do it. I cared for her deeply. I'd admitted it as much as it sucked to do. That sort of shit wasn't my style, but it was what it was.

Asylum came back to me and brushed his shaggy black hair away from his eyes.

"It's easy, Sinclair. Simply walk up and say hi."

"Untrue," I muttered, eyeing the watchers and Sirena enter the main hall, Cady bouncing along behind them. The doors closed, leaving my heart empty.

"Suit yourself. You'll eventually cave. I know I'm an exciting guy, but you aren't having as much fun as you could have. You're a grouch. An angry potato."

"What?" I scoffed at him. "Fuck you. I'm not a potato."

"You are. You just sit around all the time, hurting yourself. Moping. Rotting away. Like a fucking potato. You'll start smelling soon if I don't kick you out of the room."

"Fuck, you drive me nuts," I snapped at him.

"Do I?" He brightened at my words. "I do like to make people crazy. Makes my cold, dead heart twitch a little. Fucking love that for myself. Thanks." He clapped me on the back before doing a little skip away from me like the absolute fucking lunatic he was.

✝

I DIDN'T HAVE the balls to speak to Sirena in classes. I sat in the back watching her like I always had, though. For an entire fucking week, I did it, breaking a little more each day.

It was a Friday when I sat up straighter while Sister Esther focused her attention on Sirena. I'd threatened this woman before about picking on her. Knowing she was an absolute bitch made it easy for my anger to flare whenever the old sack of shit opened her mouth.

"Answer the question, Miss Lawrence. Headmaster Sully has stated you've spoken since arriving here. We've been over this before. We do not fake disability in my classroom."

Sirena remained quiet, her body hunched forward, her dark hair covering her face. I noted the visible tremor in her as she tried to calm herself.

"Speak, you ungrateful mutt!" Sister Esther brought her ruler down and smacked it repeatedly on Sirena's desk. "Useless excuse for a girl! Useless! A waste. God has long forgotten you, you insolent brat. SPEAK!"

I stood at the same time Sirena grabbed the ruler and jerked it from Sister Esther's hands. In a flash, Sirena was on her feet. I watched, horror-struck and fascinated, as Sirena brought the ruler back before swinging it forward. It connected with Sister Esther's face, making her cry out as the blood burst from her busted nose and lip.

The older woman stumbled back, clearly shocked at what had transpired.

"Do you want to go to hell?" Sirena snarled at her, stalking forward with the ruler raised. "Because I will send you there, you old bitch."

I dashed forward and grabbed Sirena roughly, tugging her from the room amid the gasps from the students. Sister Esther shouted for someone to call Sully for her and to get a nurse with a ward. The sound of scurrying faded away as I hauled Sirena down the hall.

I didn't stop until we got to her locker. I tugged her jacket out and forced her into its warm confines before leading her out of the school. She came without a fight or a word. I didn't know what to do with her, so I brought her to the forest and the only place I could think of.

The bear cave.

# SIRENA

$\mathscr{I}$ let Sin lead me away. I didn't know what was happening or why, but I accepted that this might be my end.

*Good.*

*I was tired.*

He brought me deep into the woods. I struggled at times through the snow, but he pushed us onward until we'd reached a small cave. Quickly, he brought me inside and closed a door behind him.

I sucked in a sharp breath at the darkness we were in. He moved past me, and within moments, the cave was illuminated by a light from a lantern he'd lit. I watched him start a heater before he looked at me.

"Sit," he commanded with a grunt.

Nervously, I stepped forward and went to the old couch he sat on, then settled beside him. The heater immediately thawed me while we remained in silence.

I was scared. My brain was having these angry moments that terrified me. All I knew was that I'd get too emotional and just. . . hell, I didn't know. Leave my body? Go on autopilot? I'd always been that way, though. Zoning out. But this felt different. It felt like I was stepping back so that someone else could step forward. Over the years, I'd ignored it. Checked out. Assumed it was a mini vacation for my troubled mind. Now, it was becoming more pronounced and terrifying. I'd always had control of it. Now I felt like it had control of me.

"What happened back there?" Sin finally asked, his voice barely above a whisper.

I said nothing. I had no answer. Saying I didn't know didn't seem helpful, so I just stared into the heater, my hands twisted on my lap.

"You clearly speak, Siren. So speak. Talk to me." He sounded almost desperate. He reached for me, but I jerked away from him.

"I'm not going to hurt you," he said. "I want to help you."

I glared at him, remembering the coffin and the pill. I shouldn't be angry with him, but I couldn't help myself. I cared about him just like the watchers did. I didn't want harm to come to him, but in that moment, I didn't want him touching me. I was still leery despite everything I knew. Despite what he'd done for me recently.

His Adam's apple bobbed as he stared back at me. "I'm an asshole for what I did, OK? We both know that. I'd-I'd like to move on from it. So talk to me. Tell me what's going on."

I turned away from him, still silent.

He sighed but didn't push the subject. Instead, he got up and went to a small carved-out room before returning with a bag of potato chips and two bottles of water. He opened the chips and offered me some.

I hesitated before dipping my hand into the bag and bringing out a handful. He seemed satisfied with that because he took his own handful out and munched along with me.

His phone buzzed several long moments into our silence, and he pulled it out and stared at the screen before sending a message and sighing.

"I'm sure you're aware you're in trouble," he started.

I swallowed hard and tightly wrapped my arms around myself like they would protect me.

"That was Asylum. He's coming."

I shivered at his words. Asylum was coming. He'd know what to do. Hopefully, that didn't include shoving me back into a coffin and throwing away the key. Even though I was getting better about all that had transpired between us. I was still a mess at times. The emotions were so conflicting.

"I'm sorry, it's Asylum and not Church or the guys."

I looked to him at that comment.

He raised his brows at me. "What? Do you want to see Asylum?"

I said nothing. All I knew was I didn't want to see Sully or anyone related to their sick madness.

He narrowed his gray eyes this time. "Or is it someone else?"

I bit my bottom lip and glanced away from him. I knew he was talking about Mirage. I hadn't seen him in what felt like forever. I tried to not think about it, but being successful in those endeavors clearly wasn't my strong point. I felt guilt over the entire situation. The fact Church hadn't tried to kill me over it had surprised me.

But I knew that didn't mean shit in the long run. Just because Church loved me didn't mean he wouldn't put me to rest in a grave somewhere. He'd told me as much already.

And if Church knew about Bryce and his feelings. . .

Or mine.

I was a mess. An absolute disaster.

"Whatever. Not my business," he muttered. Before he could elaborate further, the door slid open, and a snow-swept Asylum came in. Quickly, he shut the door and strode toward us. I got to my feet, my heart in my throat as he approached, his blue eyes focused on me.

"Firefly," he murmured when he reached me. "Are you well?"

I twisted my fingers in front of me, my heart banging hard. I needed to get back to campus. This was wrong. It was dangerous. Church would lose it. Or Asylum would. Neither was something I wanted to be around for.

"You're freezing," he continued, reaching out and taking my hands in his. His touch was gentle and sweet, not anything like his personality.

He led me back to the couch and sat with me on it.

"Sinclair, get our guest a blanket," Asylum said without looking away from me.

Sin retrieved a blanket from the chair and handed it to Asylum before going to the chair and sitting, his gray eyes on Asylum as he unfolded the blanket and draped it around my shoulders.

"This isn't the most civilized place to be, but it's the best we have," Asylum said. "I can work on making it more accommodating for you."

I wasn't quite sure how he could accomplish that without adding real heat and electricity, but I wasn't about to comment on it.

He let out a soft chuckle. "Trust me, my forever girl, I can make it better."

I cast a look to Sin, who looked away from me quickly and focused on the heater.

"It is rather chilly in here. We do have another heater. Sinclair, get that going. She's cold."

I thought Sin might object to being told what to do, but he wordlessly rose to his feet and set to work starting another heater.

Asylum ran his hand up and down my back in an attempt to warm me a bit more.

"You've created quite the stir, firefly. Word of your wrongdoing spread like wildfire. I told Church and the guys I was going to find you. I need to message them and let them know you're safe."

He removed his hand from my back and pulled his phone out. He sent a message to Church before a laugh left him, his phone buzzing with a call, Church's name on the screen.

"She is safe. I have her," he answered. He listened for a moment, nodding his head. I could hear Church's voice but couldn't make out what he was saying. Relief flooded through me. Knowing Church and the guys were aware of who had me put me at ease. While I knew Asylum had done many good things for me, and he made me feel. . . things, I was still apprehensive around him sometimes. I chalked it up to our past. The fear that one day he may snap again terrified me.

His gaze swiveled to me, and he crinkled his dark brows.

"Never," he said, his voice a deep rumble. "Firefly."

I blinked at him, and he disconnected the call. He reached for my face and cradled my cheeks, his blue eyes locked on mine.

"*Fucking never*. Do you understand me? *Never, Sirena.*"

The way he said my name made goosebumps rush along my skin.

"I swear it to you. I do not make promises I'm unable to keep. You are my entire fucking universe. Losing you would cause my stars to weep. Understand?"

His words made my heart pump harder.

In a flash, he hauled me onto his lap to straddle him, his hands firmly on my hips before they slowly moved up. He tangled his fingers in my hair and brought me nearer to him, his lips at my ear.

"You belong to me, my forever girl. I would die for you. What's worse is I would live for you, even while hating everything about the life I'm in. You are that bright spot I focus on. And now. . ." He moved a hand slowly back to my waist and gripped hard. "You are the darkness I want to fucking get lost in. I'm going to prove to you how worthy *we* are. Do you want it?" He tightened his fingers in my hair, making it hurt.

I let out a soft gasp.

"Answer me." He brushed his lips along my jaw until he was at my neck.

I gripped his shoulders tightly. He shifted ever so slightly beneath me, showing me how hard he was as his length pressed against my center.

A whimper slid past my lips.

"Take it," he murmured. "It's yours."

I ground my teeth, forcing the lewd thoughts from my mind of how much I just wanted to try on my terms.

"You're curious." His lips swept to my ear. "Try me, firefly. First ride is free, baby. I don't tell secrets." He bit the tender flesh of my neck, making me bite back a soft groan.

Before I could answer him, though, Sin's deep voice called out.

"Knock it off." The sound of Sin's heavy boots coming closer sounded out around us. One moment, I was on Asylum's lap. The next, I was being torn off, with Sin's firm, powerful grip around my biceps. I crashed against him as I tried to stay on my feet from his rough tug.

"She's the watchers' girl, not yours," Sin snapped. "You know that.

Church would fucking skin you alive and wear your ass like a hat if he saw you touching her like that."

"I'd become an ass hat?" Asylum's lips quirked up in a teasing smirk. "I bet I'd be stylish."

Sin let out a disgruntled snarl before shoving me onto the chair away from Asylum. I went down quickly, the air whooshing from my lungs.

He was right.

I hated he was.

I was wrong. So damn wrong, but I couldn't help the feelings I was developing.

I chanced a look to Asylum, who winked at me.

"I'll let Sinclair have this one. We're meeting with the watchers at seven. May as well get comfortable, my dear, as hard as that may be."

I smoothed my skirt and paid attention to my hands on my lap.

Sin and Asylum spoke to one another, but I didn't take in anything they were saying. Instead, I cast a brief peek at Asylum before letting my focus trail to Sin. He must have sensed me looking because he glanced at me for a moment, making my heart jump.

There was something in his gray eyes that made my breath catch.

I didn't explore it, however. Sin had taught me a lesson.

Be careful who you developed feelings for because sometimes they could change your life. I was beginning to have a problem, though. I could feel the trouble brewing as that bit of darkness skirted the edges of my mind.

Asylum cocked his head to the left, a tiny smile on his full lips.

"Admitting you have a problem is the first step in recovery. And sometimes recovery is simply taking what you want," Asylum murmured.

Sin didn't move. He simply stared back at me.

"Do you have a problem, firefly?"

I swallowed hard and slid my gaze from Sin back to Asylum, that darkness I was desperately trying to keep contained seeping out.

"I believe I might," I said, licking my lips, a warm buzzing making my head feel funny.

Asylum grinned at me.

"Then come sit on my lap. Maybe we can fix a few of them."

I blinked rapidly at him, the odd feeling and confusion replacing the void.

"Ah, too bad. Maybe next time," Asylum said, still grinning at me.

And just like that, the buzzing in my head was gone, and I was myself once more.

I glanced back to Sin and couldn't miss the look of concern on his face.

Quickly, I averted my eyes and went back to staring at my hands.

Truth be told, I was concerned too.

And grateful. Grateful he'd brought me here and away from the harm Chapel Crest held. I knew I would be punished for what had happened even though I was certain it hadn't been me, at least conscious me, hurting that nun.

I clenched my teeth.

*Fuck her. She deserved it.*

I exhaled and caught Asylum's eye again.

"She did, firefly. She did," he murmured before looking back to Sin and speaking to him about a new door for their cave.

Whether she deserved it or not didn't make it right, but then again, everything in my head was a mess.

Maybe this entire world needed to burn.

And, maybe Ashes would help me.

That thought brought me solace, so I focused on my watchers, eager to see them tonight while praying they had a solution to keep me out of the facility.

Because I wasn't going to go back. Sully could bank on that.

Both me and the darkness inside my head knew that.

# ASHES

She'd struck a nun and had drawn blood. Sin was in her class and had the sense to get her out of there before the wards and Sully intervened.

I exhaled and glanced to Church, who had been pacing in our living room for the last twenty minutes. I was going to break my damn lighter with how fast I was flipping it open and closed. Or worse, use it to set something ablaze.

"I'd have hit the bitch too," Stitches said, eyeing Church as he continued to wear a path into the hardwood floor. Church grunted, but he didn't say anything. He'd been quiet. Way too quiet. He was clearly upset. As soon as he'd heard what had happened, he'd rushed away and met Sully before he made it halfway down the hall to us.

I had no idea what deal he'd worked out, but I was sure we'd be hearing about it soon.

"Me too," I muttered, knowing damn well Sister Esther was a bitch to begin with. It was no secret she liked to create problems just so she could punish students.

I was stress cooking. I'd made a lasagna, salad, and homemade bread. I'd put together a cheesecake earlier, and now I was waiting for Asylum to bring Sirena home.

It had been a trying day.

Stitches had to assure Cady earlier that we'd get it sorted. I thought she was going to bust our living room window out when we didn't answer the door. It was why Stitches went to it and spoke to her.

He promised we'd reach out to her the moment we had news. She'd been blowing up my phone for the last hour. I made her promise not to come here until after everything was done.

She'd seemed agreeable, and I'd had the last fifteen minutes without my phone screaming at me with messages from her.

The doorbell rang, and we snapped our attention to it quickly. Church was faster than I was and made it there before I was able to step foot out of the kitchen.

He tugged the door open, hauled Sirena into his arms, and hugged her tightly before pulling her deeper into the room. Sin and Asylum followed after closing the door behind them.

When Church got to the living room, I was there with Stitches, waiting to hold Sirena.

Church let out a grunt and released her, and I was quick to take her into my arms.

"Heaven," I murmured before kissing her gently. "Are you OK?"

Her answer was to give me a tender kiss in return before going to Stitches. He didn't say anything. He simply held her tightly before Church snagged her away from him and dragged her onto his lap.

"Sit," he commanded to Asylum and Sin.

Both wordlessly picked their spots on the couch. I sat with Stitches on the L part of the wraparound while Church sat in his chair with Sirena.

"You made me dinner?" Asylum asked.

"I guess," I muttered, taking my lighter out to open and close it five times. Flame. Close. Repeat.

He smirked at me. "Surprised you didn't burn it."

I rolled my eyes at him. "Funny."

He gave me a wink. "It's all in good fun, *Torch*."

"What's going on with Sully and your old man?" Sin demanded, ending my conversation, if it could be called that, with Asylum.

"I will be leaving soon," Church said, his voice a low rumble.

I tensed in my seat at the news, flipping my lighter open and closed faster. Sirena was quick to snap her focus to him, the worry evident on her face.

"It's OK, specter. You'll be safe. The guys will be here with you, and I'll be in touch as much as possible."

"What does he want you to do?" Stitches demanded, his leg bouncing while he stared Church down.

I glanced from Stitches to Church, knowing damn well Stitches was on the verge of freaking out. He'd practically grown up in the Underground with Church. He knew the atrocities better than Sin and I did. We'd heard the horror stories and had caught glimpses ourselves, but that was different than living in it. Hell, I wouldn't even call it living. I'd call it surviving.

"Dante, man," I started, but he held his hand up to stop me.

"It's done. I'm going. It was part of the deal I made so Sirena wouldn't be punished. Instead, I take the punishment."

Sirena buried her face in his neck and held onto him. He turned his attention from us to her, whispering things we couldn't hear.

"This is fucking stupid," Stitches snarled, looking to me. "We should just kill all of them and be done with it."

"We will," Asylum said.

Stitches and I both turned to look at him.

"In time," Asylum continued. "Now is not the time."

"I say you're wrong," Stitches snapped, pounding his chest with his fist. "Now is the perfect fucking time. I'll go there myself and hang Sully's ass right now. I don't need a fucking schedule to do it."

"If you want to take down all of them, we wait. We aren't in any position to do any of this shit," Asylum snapped back.

I'd never seen him look so fierce.

"What have you seen, Seth?" I asked gently.

He looked to me. "My name is Asylum."

"Asylum," I corrected. "You always know things. Tell us what you know. We need a really good reason to not just end it now."

"We simply aren't ready. Firefly wants revenge. We won't get it if we start mindlessly killing the players. The monster will run. Hide. He will not come out to die. This game has always been a long game. Taking shortcuts would fuck everything. Once we grab the little fucking snake who touched my forever girl, then we can move forward. Until then, we wait."

"Who the fuck made you boss of any of this?" Stitches shouted, getting to his feet.

I followed and put my hands on his chest in a sad attempt to calm him.

"Malachi," Church's voice boomed out. "Sit."

Stitches glared at Church. "You fucking know what the Underground is like, Dante. We grew up there. It's not rainbows and Christmas gifts. It's a nightmare born from the underside of the devil's dick. If you're punished—"

"The punishment is to kill. How many have I ended, brother? Huh? How many?" Church said in a deadly calm voice. "This is *nothing* to me. *Nothing.*"

"Sit down," I murmured to Stitches.

He let out a disgusted grunt but sat. He buried his head in his hands, his elbows on his knees while his legs bounced. I knew him well enough to know he was on the verge of completely losing it.

"It'll be OK. Let's just trust in Asylum. Just for a little longer. We need to get the guy who hurt our girl, man. Can you do that? Just wait a little?" I rested my hand on the middle of Stitches's back.

He said nothing, continuing to shake with his anger.

I hadn't noticed Sirena get up, but she had because she moved to stand in front of Stitches for a moment before she went to her knees for him and cradled his face. We all watched as she lifted his head and stared at him.

"I don't like this," he whispered, staring at her. "The longer they live, the more dangerous they become. Not just to you, angel, but to all of us."

She pressed her lips to his, quieting him.

We sat in silence, watching as she deepened their kiss until he was tugging her onto his lap, his hands all over her.

I cleared my throat and looked to Asylum and Sin.

Asylum's eyes were narrowed while he watched the exchange. He was clearly not happy about seeing it, but not appearing like he was going to do anything about it.

Then there was Sin.

He'd balled his hands into tight fists, his gray eyes focused on the pair.

"Malachi, take her to your room," Church called out. "Our guests don't need to see a show."

Stitches didn't even break his mouth away from hers. He simply stood, her cradled in his arms, and walked with her to his room, the door slamming closed behind him.

"Sorry about that," I said, forcing a smile onto my face. "She has a way with him."

"She has a way with us all," Asylum murmured, his blue eyes focused on the hall where Stitches had disappeared with Sirena. "I want in."

"Uh." I flipped my lighter open and closed five times and looked to Church, hoping I wasn't going to have to hold off a death match in our living room. Asylum had already made his desires clear before, but tensions were high at the moment. Seemed like a bad idea to bring it up.

"I know you do," Church said, his voice low.

"She chooses," Asylum added, raising his brows as he stared Church down.

A muscle thrummed along Church's jaw before he answered.

"She does," he said.

"So if she chooses all of us. . .?" I cast a quick glance to Sin, who was staring at his feet, his body tense.

"It's a discussion for another time," Church said. "And don't worry, Sinclair, you're not part of the equation."

*Fucking hell.*

"Dante," I started. "Can we just not—"

"I made my promise. My vow. I'm only here to protect her," Sin murmured, his voice thick. He looked from Church to me. "I won't touch her unless it's to save her. She would never choose me. She has enough monsters to deal with."

Church scoffed and pulled a joint out before I went to him and offered him a light. He took a deep inhale of the drug before offering it to me. Taking it from him, I toked on it for a minute before going to Asylum and offering it.

He waved me off. "My head gets too calm when I'm high. Feels like I should be on high alert right now."

Fair enough.

I turned to Sin. "You want some?"

Sin looked at the joint for a moment before he reached out and took it, taking a deep hit before handing it back to me. I brought what was left to Church, who sat staring at Sin. I could only imagine the thoughts rolling through his mind.

I didn't think any one of them were pleasant. If I knew anything about Church, it was that once he was pissed at you, he stayed that way. Many people had lost their lives to his wrath before. Sin knew it too.

The bleakness of that situation haunted us.

I hated to admit it, but Sin might not ever get to come back to us. Yeah, he'd screwed up, but I still gave a damn about him, and it was clear he was willing to try again.

"So you're just going to leave? Do you know for how long?" I asked, sitting back in my spot.

"I'll leave tomorrow morning. I don't know for how long. Until he's satisfied. If I do a good enough job, I expect it won't take long."

I sighed. "Man, I don't like this."

"Nor I, but it's either me or her, and I would easily die in her place," he answered simply.

"Then come back to haunt nightmares." Asylum smiled. "I would be happy to assist you with your father. I can come with you."

"No," Church said quickly. He closed his eyes for a moment. "No. Stay here. More hands here are better."

"I knew you'd say that." Asylum settled back in his seat. "But I'll still help."

"Of course you did," I mumbled.

"I'd prefer Sin didn't have to work too hard," Church continued. "Ashes and Stitches will already be here. Asylum as well. I don't see why Sin's service would be required."

"Every single one of you was here when this shit went down," Sin said, his voice laced with his anger. "And it was me who fucking got her out of there. I'm useful. I-I can be useful."

"Easy, slice and dice," Asylum said, resting his hand on Sin's shoulder.

I winced at the nickname. I knew it had to do with all the cuts Sin had given himself over the past few weeks.

"You are useful," I said. "You are. It's just. . ."

"I'm not going to hurt her," he whispered. "I'm not. I swear I won't. I just. . . I only want to help. I said I'd not touch her. It wasn't a lie. I won't unless it's necessary. If you all make this happen, and I'm the odd man out, I'll deal with it." He let out a shaky breath. "I made my hell, and so I'll burn in it. I accept this."

"Sin." I sighed, ready to say to hell with it and welcome him home. So much pain was laced in his words. I hated he was hurting, but damnit. He'd really fucked up.

He had helped today, though. He'd kept her safe. Acting fast, he managed to get her away. The fact she hadn't tried to get away from him had to mean that perhaps she was more accepting of him than we were. Or at least Church was.

"Cry me a fucking river," Church said before taking another hit from his joint and blowing out the smoke. "You're lucky we let you live. Be happy with our fucking compassion, and stop trying to weasel your way back in. You're not wanted. No amount of heartfelt words will change my mind."

"You're right." Sin let out a bitter laugh. He got to his feet and went to the door. Without another word, he pulled it open and left.

"Damnit, Dante," I muttered, getting to my feet. "We do fucking need him. All hands on deck right now. *For her.*" I didn't wait for his rebuttal. I swept from the living room and went to find Sin.

I didn't know what I was going to say, but hell, maybe it would help.

At this point, it sure couldn't hurt.

# SIN

"Sin! Hey! Wait up!" Ashes jogged through the falling snow toward me, his breath coming out in white puffs.

I paused, turning to wait for him to catch up to me.

"What?" I muttered when he was at my side.

"Hey, man. You know how Church is—"

"It doesn't matter. It's fine," I cut him off, my words soft. "I get it. I'm not such an idiot that I fail to remember how badly I fucked up. I know what I did. I know why I did it. I regret it, but regrets don't fix problems, do they?"

"Maybe they could. You're obviously trying."

I scoffed. "Asher, it's fine. Don't worry about it." I started walking again, but he grabbed my arm and pulled me to a stop.

"It's not fine," he said, his gaze raking over me, sadness in his eyes. "I'm not against you coming home."

My throat tightened at his words.

"I appreciate the sentiment, but that doesn't fix anything."

"Church just needs time," he continued. "I think in time he'll come around."

"What about you? Huh? What do you need? Because I know you

Asher. You're not ready for me to come back, either. You can say you are all you want as a way to try to soothe the wounds I've been licking but cut the shit. Be honest with me."

He sighed and was quiet for a few moments before speaking. "I'm scared. OK? You can be unpredictable. Given what happened, yeah, it's hard to trust you. I mean, the *what-ifs* are there, man. They're there. I won't lie about them. Stitches tried to kill himself, and then that shit in the facility happened to him. I barely kept my shit together. Church was a mess. He fucking heeled for them, Sinclair. It had to be bad to get him to heel. You know that. Then her. All she went through just because you couldn't just let love in. So yeah. I'm fucking terrified you'll get pissed off and lose it again and make shit decisions. I don't want to have these feelings, but fuck, man. I do. OK? I fucking do."

I nodded, absorbing his words like a punch to the gut.

"I understand," I whispered. "It's why I vowed to stay away from her. I want to keep her safe. Call it my penance. I meant what I said about that. The only way I can prove it is to simply do it. I'll do it over and over again if that's what it takes. If I never get to come home, so be it, but at least I can say I tried."

We stared at one another for a moment.

"I'm going to go home. I'm tired," I finally said. "You have my number if you need me. I'll come if you call."

"Come back to the house. I made some food—"

"I appreciate it, but I'd rather be alone."

"Sinclair, come on."

"I'm not trying to get your pity. I really do want to be alone right now. You have enough to deal with having Asylum there. Worry about your plans and getting Church home. I'll be around." I didn't wait for him to ask me again because I knew he would. Instead, I continued down the trail, letting the snow fall around me.

I LEANED against the shower tiles, my eyes closed and the knife firmly in my hand. I didn't press the blade in as hard as I could. I ran small, shallow cuts along my abdomen, relishing the burning ache it brought. The ache that dulled the other one in my heart.

I hated feeling so fucking pitiful, but that's what I was.

Pitiful.

Watching Sirena with the guys tonight only made me realize how alone I was now. How sad I was. How pathetic.

The knife slipped from my hand, clattering at my feet. I was done. I was too tired to keep hurting myself, at least for the night. Tomorrow was a new day.

I finished my shower and got out. After dressing, I went and lay in bed and thumbed through the photos on my phone. All of us guys. There were random, stupid photos, like Stitches catching a fish. Then him chasing Ashes with it. Ashes setting a garbage can on fire in the men's room. Church giving the camera the finger, a joint hanging from his lips.

I paused over a picture I'd taken when Sirena first arrived here.

It was a picture of the guys just standing around and talking. It was a casual photo I'd taken. At the time, I hadn't noticed Sirena in the background, but there she was.

I zoomed in and screen-capped the photo.

She looked so innocent and pure. So scared.

I swallowed hard while staring at the image before I traced my fingers lightly over her face. While blurry, it was the only photo of her I had.

Closing my eyes, I envisioned the way her lips parted when she was on the verge of communicating. How big and colorful her eyes were. The way her long black hair whipped around her in the breeze. The way she chewed her bottom lip when she was thinking or nervous.

The way she smelled like something I could devour.

I stroked my cock beneath my blankets, yearning to hold her. Kiss her. Get her to forgive me.

What a homecoming it would be.

But one I knew I could never have.

It didn't matter what anyone said. Church was always the one who finalized decisions. As much as I wanted her to tell me to come home, I knew he'd never allow it. I'd never be going back.

I forced the ugly thought out of my head and focused on the way she looked in my mind's eye. In my mind, she reached for me. Caressed my face.

Her lips met mine.

I groaned as I continued to jerk it to the image of her in my head.

In my imagination, I pushed her gently onto her back before kissing my way down her body to her pussy where I licked and sucked, making her squirm beneath me.

"Fuck," I hissed out as the image faded, and I came all over my abdomen. The jewelry from my Prince Albert piercing made me feel like the orgasm was even stronger. I hadn't been laid in what felt like forever. This was as best as it got as of late, though.

Fucked up dirty thoughts of a girl I couldn't have.

I disgusted myself.

Sighing, I got up and cleaned up the mess I made before getting back into bed. The room was dark, with the exception of the moonlight streaming in through the window. I lay in bed for what felt like hours before sleep finally took me.

I wasn't asleep for long when the door opened, and Asylum entered the room.

Groaning, I cracked my eyelids open and peered blearily at him as he stripped out of his clothes, down to his boxers, before he grabbed his pajama bottoms from his dresser.

"You were gone a long time," I commented gruffly.

He slid into his bed and turned to face me, the moonlight on his face. He looked exhausted.

"Those watchers are a lot of work. I wanted to stay back to see my forever girl, but Stitches must have kept her beneath him for the better part of two hours before they finally came back out," his words were sour. "I had to listen to Church rant about you and pray Ashes didn't burn the damn place down. That guy is a mess. He tries to hold it together for all of them. Poor bastard."

"Yeah, Ashes is a good guy. He tries," I muttered.

"He's on your side. Mostly. I think maybe even Stitches is, although he didn't come out and say it." Asylum rolled onto his back and stared up at the ceiling. He was quiet for a long time before he spoke. "She came and sat next to me when Ashes was warming the food and the guys set the table."

I watched him in the moonlight, taking in the way his Adam's apple bobbed and the look of vulnerability on his face. I'd never seen it before, so it was surprising to me.

"She let me touch her," he whispered, his voice trembling. "It was for only a moment, but she brushed her fingers along my palm. I felt her before she pulled her emotions away from me."

"What did you feel?" I whispered back, my heart in my throat.

"She's so full of love and light, but that darkness within her beckons me. I was already obsessed with her, but she's changing. The darkness and the light will meet in a crash of violence. I can't wait for it to happen so she can truly become whom she's meant to be."

I exhaled. "A monster like us?"

He looked over to me. "No. Not like us. She's more than we could ever hope to be. She will always be kind, but she will be just. She will not tolerate being hurt. She will seek her revenge and be a force to be reckoned with. That is if I can teach her. Or. . ."

"Or what?"

He was quiet again before he cleared his throat. "Mirage can."

I sat up on my elbow and gave him my full attention. "You hardly let Mirage out. Are you going to?"

He licked his lips and closed his eyes.

"Asylum? Are you letting him out?"

"He's dangerous," Asylum murmured. "More so than I."

"You're both dangerous," I corrected.

"I think things through. Mirage is insane when it comes to her. I suppose I am too, only in a different way." He was quiet for a moment before letting out a soft laugh. *"Don't fuck this up. I can't have you fuck this up."*

I knew he was communicating with Mirage, so I said nothing, simply watching him.

"Tomorrow," he said softly. "No. Train her. Fix this mess that's been made. See to it, revenge is paid."

Asylum's eyes opened, and he looked at me again. "Sinclair, make sure everything runs smoothly. I will be leaving and giving Mirage the chance to make things better. It's best I duck away into the shadows so he can come out. He's a sweet boy, but he can be unpredictable when upset. So don't let him get upset. He's been doing a good job lately of managing his anger. He can be the hurricane to her sunshine." He laughed softly. "I suppose we both are, in a sense."

I said nothing. I knew Mirage to be kind most of the time, but I also knew he was part of Asylum, and there the crazy flourished .

"You need a friend, Sinclair," Asylum mused. "While I'm away. Mirage will be too obsessed working on finding who hurt her."

"I'll be fine," I said, rolling onto my back to stare at the ceiling. "I'm always fine."

"We're best friends, Sinclair."

I looked over at him. "Are we?"

He chuckled. "Of course we are. Who else do you have?"

I grunted a response. I had no one but him. Lucky fucking me.

"So I promise to get you a friend as a thank you. Someone you have for when I'm away so you don't miss me as much."

"You're delusional."

"And you love me for it," he commented, the smile in his voice. "You'll have Mirage, but we aren't the same, him and I. We are as different as we are the same."

"You're both confusing fucks."

"We are, aren't we? I suppose that's why we work so well together."

We were both quiet for a moment.

"How long will you be gone?" I asked.

"However long Church is gone," he said. "I will return when he does. With him gone, it'll give Mirage room to. . . wiggle."

"How. . . convenient." I grew quiet for a moment. "Asylum?"

"Yeah, bestie?"

"You're not only fucking with us all, right? Like, you're still not wanting to kill Sirena to keep her safe? Because that shit you did was fucked up—"

"I'm here to stay, regardless of any feelings anyone has on the subject. I'm a fucking terminal disease and won't leave this world without her."

"That doesn't bring me much comfort," I muttered.

"I want her, Sinclair. I will have her. Hurting her isn't what I want. I didn't even want it then. I simply wanted her safety, and death could render a soul untouchable, so it was the best option I had." He paused. "I was young and stupid. I hadn't learned to harness my gifts yet. I have my shit together now. We both do." He tapped his head for emphasis. "She will always be safe with me. And with Mirage. He loves her like I do. His love is tender but fierce, like mine. Perhaps older than mine, but that doesn't mean shit to me. All I know is that I'd bleed this world dry if it meant she smiled for me." He sighed. "So she will always be safe with me."

"And Mirage?"

"You know Mirage well enough to know he wants the best for her. She will be safe with him, provided he doesn't let his rage out. Not that he would harm her with it. But others could be harmed. He's fine until he loses it. Then, well, carnage. But you'll be here, making sure he's OK. If we play our cards right, Ashes and Stitches might let you come over and hang out with them. Or let you take Sirena. Never know."

I scoffed at that despite the pounding of my heart at the prospect.

"Don't be so sad. Take what you want. Life won't be so bad. Kiss her. Touch her. Spread her legs wide and fuck her. You won't know until you try. And until then, you'll continue to cry."

"You're absurd," I said, shaking my head.

"She chooses, Sinclair. Don't forget it. Just make her see *you are the way. The light she needs.* You can do that, right?"

I said nothing, not knowing if I could do that. The way I currently felt, my answer was no, but there was a little part of me that was so desperate to prove myself to her that it was driving me insane.

"So, become insane," Asylum said with a yawn. "Nothing wrong with being a little crazy, bestie. After all, that's why we're here."

He had a point.

# STITCHES

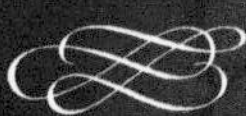

*I* watched Church fuck Sirena doggy style on the bed while she sucked Ashes's cock. We'd put her through her paces tonight. I'd taken a step back since I'd buried myself inside her twice in my bedroom while Asylum and Sin were over. I'd been gentle with her even though all I wanted to do was drive my cock home inside her tight, hot pussy. I'd held back though because I knew she might need me to be gentle and slow for her.

Since I'd had so much time with her earlier, I figured I'd let Church get his fill since he was going to be leaving. It only seemed right.

"Get over here, brother," Church rasped as he slowed his movements.

"I don't mind watching—"

"I want you to fuck her with me," he said, slowing to a stop. She continued sucking Ashes off without hesitation. He looked like he was having the time of his life because he'd let his head fall back and had his fingers tangled in her hair, guiding her along his shaft.

"I want your cock in her pussy with mine," Church said.

I nodded, wanting that too. I moved and lay on my back next to Sirena.

Ashes hadn't been so far gone that he hadn't heard us because he pulled his cock free of her throat and helped her straddle me.

"Hey, angel," I murmured, cradling her face. Her response was to kiss me deeply. I fell into it without protest, my cock painfully hard and desperate to burrow inside her.

Church's warm hand wrapped around my dick, and he guided it into her heat. I let out a soft moan against her lips as I buried myself inside her again.

*Fuck, she felt so good.*

I thrust upward into her, making her gasp against my lips.

Church let me have the moment for a long beat before I slowed to a stop so he could join.

"This is going to hurt," Church called out thickly while he nudged his cock along mine in an attempt to join me inside her.

Her breathing picked up, her nails digging into my chest.

"Breathe," Ashes instructed softly.

"Easy, baby," I murmured, my hands on her hips. "Let Church in. Relax. It's going to hurt, but then it's going to feel so fucking good. We want to fuck away all your ugly memories."

I could tell she was trying to relax, but her body was fighting her on it.

A soft cry left her lips when Church's thick cock spread her enough to break his head in.

She buried her face in my neck, her nails deep into my flesh, her body heaving with her heavy breathing.

"I fucking love her this way," Church husked out. "God, it's so fucking good."

She whimpered, her nails digging deeper. Little droplets of my blood blossomed out, but I ground my teeth and let it happen because it brought her comfort. Fuck my comfort.

"Fuck, she's got a tight pussy," Church continued, finally sliding his cock deep against mine inside her. "Damn, Asher. You're missing out."

Ashes grunted and stroked his cock. "Stitches and I can try together when you're gone."

She cried out as Church withdrew and slammed back into her.

Her body writhed and squirmed, but I held her tightly against me.

"Easy, baby. Easy," I whispered. "It's us, OK? Just us. We love you."

She relaxed slightly as I slowly began to pump in and out of her, matching Church, who had the sense to slow it down. Judging by the way he shook, it was a big feat for him to do. She'd recently gotten out of one of the worst experiences of her life. We needed to be careful with her.

Her breathing slowed, and she withdrew her nails from my flesh.

"There you go. Take it, angel. Take our cocks like a good girl," I cooed in her ear as we slowly fucked into her body.

Church rested his body gently over hers and kissed her shoulder.

"Let us erase all the fear, specter. All of it. Give it to us to take. I love you," he whispered breathlessly. "And I'll take care of you always. We all will."

She relaxed further, so we took that as a good sign and picked up our pace.

Her writhing became pushing as she tried to gain more from us.

"There you go, baby. Your pussy wants more cock," Church said.

"Fuck," Ashes murmured, a soft whimper coming from him. "I want in."

I chuckled, imagining how rough he had it watching us fuck her.

"Help Ashes, baby," Church called out breathlessly. "Suck his dick."

Slowly, she moved her head and parted her lips for him. He wasted no time pushing his cock into her mouth, a soft moan leaving him as she sucked.

It was hot as fuck. We'd never done this with another girl before. I felt so connected to her and the guys.

*Sin would have loved this.*

I pushed him out of my head. Shit hadn't gone great tonight, and Church had been bitching about him since I'd come back into the room.

It didn't matter. Right now was what mattered.

"I'm going to fucking come," I groaned out, the heat building. "Fuck."

Church moved faster against my cock, making the entire rhythm we had fly off the handle. I gave up and came hard, shooting my load deep inside my angel, my body trembling from the intense pleasure.

Ashes followed, his body tensing as he filled her mouth.

"Swallow me, heaven. Fuck yeah. That's it. Good girl. Fuck, you're good," he rasped.

She did what he wanted while Church continued to pound into her. Her mouth slid off Ashes's cock and found my lips. I kissed her, the taste of Ashes's release on my tongue.

"Oh fuck." Church groaned out.

His cock twitched against mine as she tensed in my hold, her soft, sexy little moans filling my mouth as she came. Her release flooded us, soaking the sheets.

Fuck, I loved when she came like that.

She shuddered in my hold before going still, our kisses coming to a standstill.

Church slapped her ass, making her whimper, before he leaned down and tugged her mouth from mine and kissed her. He pulled out a moment later, leaving just me and her.

He left the room and came back a few minutes later, and I withdrew from her body and laid her on her back in bed. Ashes was quick to curl up next to her.

I looked to Church to see the fond look on his face.

"Let's clean up," Church said softly.

Ashes sighed but untangled himself from Sirena, who offered us a bashful smile before I took her hand and helped her off the bed.

"Get her cleaned up. I'll take care of this," Church said.

He didn't need to tell me twice. I rushed her to the bathroom and started the shower, barely able to stay away from her. The moment the water was warm enough, I hauled her beneath the spray and impaled my cock inside her again.

We were both coming again within minutes. It was probably a record for me, but I didn't give a shit. I wasn't a minute-man, but fuck, she had an incredible pussy. My dick and balls ached from how much sex I'd had, but to hell with it. It was worth it.

"I'll never get enough of you," I said between soft kisses while the shower rained down on us.

She held me tighter, her breasts pressed against my chest.

"I'd take you again right now if I thought my dick could handle it," I said.

She smiled against my lips before pulling away and washing her body. I looked to my dick.

Fuck. Tomorrow. We'd do it again tomorrow.

I wanted Church to be able to spend some time with her tonight anyway since he was leaving.

So I helped her wash, and she helped me wash.

When we were done, we got out, and I toweled her off before myself. Then, we returned to Church's room, where he and Ashes were already on the bed, murmuring to one another about his impending trip.

I forced myself to not contemplate it and shoved my concern away.

Tonight, we'd have a good night because, honestly, I didn't know how many good nights we may have together.

Sirena crawled between Church and Ashes, and I slid in next to Church.

"Let's watch a movie," Church said as Sirena cuddled him, Ashes at her back.

I knew what he was doing.

He wanted it to be just another normal night.

But we all knew it wasn't normal, and tomorrow he'd be gone.

"It'll be OK," Church murmured into the silence as Ashes pushed play on a comedy.

I nodded and gave my brother's hand a squeeze before focusing on the TV.

It would be OK. I'd make sure it was. It was the only thing I could do right now.

# SIRENA

*C*hurch was gone when I woke.

A tear rolled down my cheek. Knowing he was doing this for me hurt my heart. I didn't want anyone to suffer on my behalf. He'd told me he had no problem doing it because he loved me.

*It should be me.*

The thought had been going through my head since last night when he announced he was going to help his father. All of this was because I lost it. Because I'd let the darkness out of me. Being constantly poked and prodded by people made me so frustrated, though. Even the normal side of me felt it. I dealt with it better with the lighter part of me. I was more logical and was a critical thinker. The other part of me, the part I assumed was just fed up and had been lurking deep inside my mind for a long time now, was the opposite of everything I was outwardly.

It terrified me, but at the same time, it brought me a sense of relief. It was like I could separate from that part of myself.

I wasn't sure exactly what was happening to me, but I assumed that's what it was. Two parts to the same soul. The sweet part and the fed-up part.

"Don't cry," Ashes whispered, thumbing my tears away. I hadn't realized he'd woken, but clearly, he had because now he was wiping away my tears, his voice strained with concern and sadness.

I took his hand in mine and shakily wrote on his palm

*This is my fault.*

"Oh, Sirena." He sighed. "It's not your fault. Yeah, you let go a little bit, but we all do. That bitch had no business pushing you around like that. I've wanted to knock her ass out for years, but you beat me to it. If it wouldn't have been you, it would have been us. So don't be sad it happened. It was meant to. She brought it on herself with her shitty attitude. She's twisted and foul, like the rest of them here."

I traced more words onto his palm.

*I'm worried about what's happening to me. I'm worried about Church.*

"Baby, you are my perfect girl. You will always be," he said gently. "Everyone gets fed-up sometimes. This was just your breaking point. You've been through so much. You're so strong. You're OK. I promise. And Church will be too. He grew up in the Underground. He learned to fight there. He learned to survive. He's going to be fine," his voice trembled with his words.

I scrawled more words onto his palm.

*Why don't I believe you?*

"Trust me. It's scary. I get it. It's even more scary when you've survived the shit the monsters are capable of, but Sirena." He paused and traced his thumb along my bottom lip. "I hate to say it, but Church is a monster too. So are me and Stitches. Sin. Asylum. We're monsters. It's why we're here."

I wrote quickly.

*I'm a monster too.*

"You are too pretty to be a monster." He lightly kissed my lips. "If anything, you're a righteous angel sent to save us all."

I smiled a little at his sweet words.

He took my hand in his and kissed my knuckles. "Let's get Stitches up. We'll eat. We'll build a snowman. Do some online shopping and hope it can get delivered despite all the snow. Watch movies. Make cookies?"

I kissed him again, really liking his ideas.

"Then it's settled," he murmured. "A day of fun. Maybe you can paint for us later. I love watching you paint."

I nodded, liking that idea too.

"Good." He kissed the tip of my nose before he got out of bed. "Stitches. Hey. Stitches!"

Stitches grumbled in his sleep and rolled over but didn't open his eyes. Instead, he let out a soft little snore.

Ashes shook his head.

I rolled over and rested my head on Stitches's chest. His arm immediately wound around me and hugged me to his hard body. Gently, I ran my fingers along the plane of taut muscles on his abdomen before moving to the tattoos he had covering his torso. He mumbled in his sleep as I traced a cross near his belly button.

"Malachi," Ashes said, moving to stand on Stitches's side of the bed. "You hungry?"

Stitches's eyes snapped open. "I could eat."

I smiled at that, knowing he needed more food in his body. He'd lost weight like I had while locked away in the facility.

I kissed his cheek before straddling him to take Ashes's hand. Stitches was quick to put his hands on my waist and hold me over his impressive, hard length.

"Good morning, angel," he said, smiling at me.

My face heated beneath his stare.

"Let's make breakfast and get her fed before we do any of that," Ashes interjected. "Church is gone."

Stitches released my waist, and Ashes helped me to stand.

"I know. I was awake when he left." Stitches sat up and rubbed his eyes. "It was around five this morning. He hauled ass out of here quickly. Said he didn't want a prolonged goodbye because those hurt more." A look of despair washed over Stitches's face. "He drove to the airport and left his car there."

"I assume he took his father's private jet out?" Ashes asked, kissing my temple.

"I guess. Sounds like that's how he sent for him." Stitches stood and adjusted himself in his boxers. He winked at me when he caught me looking, making my face heat again.

Quickly, he put his fingers beneath my chin and tilted my head up so we were staring into each other's eyes.

"Don't be embarrassed about wanting what you want, angel. I have no issue with it. It's yours to take."

I gave him a bashful smile, which he ate up before he pressed his lips against mine. It was easy to fall into the guys' kisses, and I wasted no time doing it with him. His hard length pressed against my belly, letting me know exactly what he thought about it.

"Come on," Ashes urged. "I'm hungry."

"We can spread her legs and eat her pussy on the table," Stitches murmured against my lips. His words sent a thrill through my body. "She's the perfect meal."

"I'm not opposed to that." Ashes dragged me away from Stitches, and they both helped me to dress before they led me downstairs.

"I want you to sit and relax," Ashes said, handing me the remote. "I'm going to make breakfast. Stitches is going to —"

"Start eating now," Stitches said, his dark eyes roving over me.

I squirmed beneath his gaze.

The doorbell rang, making him scowl.

"Stitches is going to answer the door while I make breakfast." Ashes let out a laugh and went to the kitchen.

"Hold that thought, angel. Let me deal with this," Stitches said, getting to his feet and going to the door. I watched him open it and groan.

"Fucking hell, Cady. Really?"

"Out of the way, stranglehold. I'm here with stolen waffles and to see my sister."

"And you brought Bryce?" Stitches let out a sigh. "You're lucky Church isn't here. This wouldn't go over well."

"Long hair, don't care." Cady pushed past Stitches and came straight for me, a bag in her hands I assumed housed stolen waffles.

"I heard Church left," she said, hugging me.

"How did you hear that?" Ashes asked from the kitchen.

"He texted me." She looked at me, her eyes rounded. "He said I'm supposed to let you assrods handle things, but he said I could come to stay the night if I wanted to. So here I am."

"What about you?" Stitches asked as Bryce stepped into the house. Stitches closed the door behind him. "Why are you here? I'm surprised you're even able to walk."

I frowned at his words, unsure about what they meant. I hadn't seen Bryce on campus. Rumor had it he was sick. He definitely looked pale and in pain. My plan was to go see him this week. I just hadn't known how to address it with the guys. We had so much we needed to air out.

I got to my feet to go to him, but Stitches moved forward and captured me in his arms before I could get to my destination.

"What are you doing, angel?" he cooed in my ear.

I looked up at him to see a muscle thrumming along his jaw. I reached out and brushed my fingers against it. His expression softened, and I untangled myself from him and went to Bryce.

"Hey," Bryce greeted me softly, his voice holding a slight tremble to it. The last time we'd spoken, he'd told me his feelings. How much he cared for me. I'd been trying to process them along with everything else.

I reached out and took his hand, then gave it a squeeze.

"Sirena," he whispered, his eyes glassy.

My heart broke looking at him.

He wasn't OK. Something was wrong, and there was no way I could just ask him. I tried to get the words to come out, but they were stuck, making me frustrated.

He must have taken notice because he squeezed my hand back. "We'll talk about it later, OK?" His voice was so low I had to lean in to hear him.

"Sirena," Stitches called out, the tension evident in his voice.

I tugged Bryce forward, and he came along easily. His movements were slow, though, and I took note of the wincing he was doing when he sat on the couch.

Stitches quickly dragged me to his lap on the L part of the wraparound and nuzzled into my neck, his words a warm brush along my skin.

"We're mad at him, Sirena. We can talk about it later, OK?"

I crinkled my brows at him in confusion, but I gave him a nod anyway because I wanted to know what had happened. Judging by the uneasy looks Bryce was casting Stitches, I wasn't going to like it.

The smell of Ashes's cooking met my nose, and my stomach gave an audible grumble. My face heated when Stitches chuckled.

"Rina, do you want to do some online shopping today? I found a website that has loads of discounted clothes." Cady looked to me with excitement in her eyes.

I smiled at her, letting her know I'd like to do that.

"Hell yeah," she said, giving Stitches the finger when he shook his head at her. Bryce remained quiet on the couch, focusing on his hands in his lap. Even more concern washed over me.

The doorbell rang once more.

"What now?" Stitches grumbled, sliding me onto the cushion and getting to his feet. He stomped to the door and pulled it open.

"Morning," a familiar voice rang out. I knew that voice.

Immediately, I got to my feet, my heart in my throat as I watched *him* come through the door.

I wasted no time in rushing to him. I was so fast that Stitches couldn't catch me. Mirage opened his arms for me, and I fell easily into them, noting Sin stood awkwardly behind him.

"Rinny," he murmured in my ear as he hugged me against his hard body. I took note of his rabbit mask in place.

"What the hell, Asylum?" Stitches snagged me back, and I scowled at him. "Why are you wearing that damn mask?" Tension radiated from him. "What the fuck is going on?"

Mirage offered him a quick smile that didn't quite reach his blue eyes. "I'm Mirage. I'm wearing the mask because I'm a rabbit. Sirena loves rabbits."

"A rabbit hurt her." Stitches frowned at him. "You didn't..."

"I would *never*," Mirage said fiercely. "I'm not who you seek. I'm who *she* seeks. That is all."

"So you were the one meeting her in the woods?" Ashes called out.

"To help her. She needed a way to relieve some stress. Nothing more. Nothing less. I was just a friendly rabbit who was able to help."

"I get it," Stitches murmured. "You were meeting up with her as a… rabbit. The one who hurt her knew that. That's a clue. Something to go on then. Right?" Stitches looked to Ashes then to Mirage. "It's something, right?"

"It is," Mirage said with a nod. "It's just not much. We'll get there though."

"Well, you don't need to wear that damn mask here," Stitches continued. "It's fucking weird, dude."

"It doesn't come off."

"Asylum." Stitches sighed.

"Mirage. I'm Mirage. A rabbit."

Stitches rolled his eyes. "You're crazier than I thought."

"No, you thought right." Mirage grinned at him. "I'm living up to the thought."

"Right, well, what's going on? Why are you guys here? Also, Church may lose it when he learns you were the damn rabbit the whole time," Stitches continued, narrowing his eyes at him.

Mirage waved him off. "He won't. And if he does, he'll get over it and see it for what it is. A friend helping a friend. Again."

Stitches grunted as I watched the exchange, grateful Mirage came out and said who he was. I didn't like keeping the secret.

"To answer your other question though, we stopped in today to see how things were going. Figured it might be nice to get a jump on everything."

Sin had been silent the entire time.

"Everything?" Ashes called out from the kitchen. "What's everything?"

Mirage shrugged. "Church is gone. I think strength in numbers is a good thing." His blue eyes moved to Cady and Bryce. "It's good to see you, Bryce."

Bryce grunted a reply.

"I don't really think you're needed," Cady said, her eyes narrowed.

"We're here. We have it covered. Go back to your padded room, you nutsack."

I shot her a look, wanting her to be quiet. She caught my eye and sighed before looking away, clearly annoyed at Mirage's presence.

"It's fine," Ashes said, coming closer with his spatula in hand and a yellow apron on. "I like the idea of strength in numbers. Sirena seems happy to see him and Bryce, so I say, let's roll with it. Weird mask and all. Mirage." He gave him a nod. Mirage inclined his head back, seemingly good with it all.

Stitches rolled his eyes and steered me back to the couch.

"Sin, it's nice to see you," Ashes said.

I knew he felt awkward. Sin gave him a quick nod before finally toeing his boots off and hanging his jacket next to Mirage's in the closet.

"So, Asylum, you look weird today," Stitches said when Asylum sat on the couch next to Sin.

"Do I?" Mirage smirked at Stitches. "How so?"

"I don't know." Stitches studied him, his hand on my thigh. "Almost like you had a good night's sleep and combed your hair. Plus, that stupid mask."

Mirage chuckled at that. "I'm the same, yet different. It's who I am."

*Tell him who you are. Who you really are.*

Mirage winked at me and pressed his finger to his lips like he was keeping a secret. I frowned at that. I didn't know why it mattered, but it wasn't my place to tell. Maybe he would.

"You even sound weird." Stitches frowned at him. "You OK?"

"I'm fine. I assure you. Excited to be here. I'm just...Mirage."

Stitches rolled his eyes at him. "Whatever. No need to be sarcastic about it."

"I do like being here. You know that, Malachi." Mirage's gaze was fixed on me.

"Well, we were planning something a little more exciting than entertaining guests," Stitches continued.

I placed my hand on his thigh and gave it a little squeeze.

Cady laughed. "Ah, I see. You guys were going to get dirty before breakfast."

"During, actually," Stitches said. "But then you showed up with Bryce and ruined it."

"Glad to hear I wasn't the cause of ruination," Mirage piped up.

"You already know you are. You're the icing on top of the bad company cake these fucks made." Stitches pointed to Cady and Bryce.

"No fighting. We have enough problems. We're going to eat and have a good day. It's Saturday. We can hang out. Watch some TV. Play some games. Let's just chill," Ashes said, placing a steaming pile of pancakes on the table next to the stolen waffles.

"I'm glad you aren't kicking me and Sinclair out," Mirage said. "Or Bryce, for that matter, considering everything."

"Not now," Stitches snapped.

Mirage held his hands up in a surrender motion.

"I agree," Mirage said. "I was merely pointing it out. But soon, Malachi. It's only right we divulge that little tidbit of truth."

I glanced from Mirage to Stitches to Bryce, confused about what they were talking about.

"It's not a big deal. I'm over it," Bryce said. "Sirena, the guys thought I was getting too close, so they came and talked to me. That's all. You don't need to worry about anything. I've learned my place."

"Have you?" Sin asked, snorting.

"Yes. For now." Bryce openly glared at Sin, a move which surprised me. He was usually pretty withdrawn around the watchers. And Sin. And even Asylum. So, to hear him stand up for himself made me happy.

"For now." Sin shook his head. "You're as bad as I am, aren't you?"

"Let's eat," Ashes called out. "Forget all this shit. Good food. Good times."

I got up, agreeing with Ashes, and went to my spot at the table. Ashes had added a leaf, and Stitches went and got more chairs from the basement. We all settled around the table awkwardly. It was the first time we'd all been together.

I missed Church being with us, though. He completed the little family I'd gotten since arriving here.

Quickly, I cast a look to Sin sitting across from me. He was staring right back at me with those penetrating gray eyes.

I wasn't quite sure what to call Sin, but I knew it probably wasn't my enemy.

At least, I really hoped not.

# CHURCH

The last place on this planet I wanted to be was in the fucking Underground.

"Dante," a guard murmured, inclining his head at me as I passed by.

I said nothing, continuing to walk with my head held high. I was a king in this hell on earth. I made sure everyone here knew it too. Being gone as long as I had, I assumed maybe they'd gone lax without me. The fucks in this place sure scrambled to welcome me though.

Last summer, I'd spent my time traveling. I'd returned home long enough to grab a few things before heading out. I hadn't even stepped foot into this hellhole in nearly two years.

But here I was now, walking the halls and having these fucks bow to me.

They weren't bowed far enough. That's all I knew. They should have been on their fucking knees with my knife to their throats.

"Welcome home," another said when I walked past.

I remained wordless, irritated that I was even here in the first place. But it wasn't because of my specter. I'd do this happily in her place. Here, she'd become twisted and broken. I didn't want that for my girl. I was pissed because it shouldn't have to be this way. My entire life, all I wanted was a normal family. A father who loved me, my mother, and Stitches. Maybe a little fluffy dog. I'd have played football or hockey. Went to a regular high school. Wouldn't have a mental health history as long as my fucking leg.

Alas, I didn't like dwelling on that shit.

But sometimes, it crept through my mind, so I'd give it a few moments in the spotlight before kicking it out as I did to everything else in my life that bothered me.

I pushed open the door to the punishment center and strode forward, dressed in all black like the demon I was.

"Dante, my son," my father greeted me with a smile and his warm hand in the center of my back. "Right on time. It's one of the finer aspects of your personality."

"What needs to be done?" I asked, ignoring his bullshit and speaking in the monotone I'd adopted just for him and these circumstances.

I'd only been here a few hours and already I was growing bored.

My father chuckled as the man with the blindfold on whimpered between the two hulking assholes who held him.

"A lot of the same old nonsense. He owes me money. Tried to touch what didn't belong to him. Punish him as you see fit." He clapped me on the back and took a step back.

I stared at the man for a moment, falling into my old routine. It was like riding a bike. It wasn't something easily forgotten.

"Get me a table," I snapped to no one in particular. This place was dark magic, though, and seconds later, someone was scurrying inside with a table for me. They placed it in front of the man, who let out a soft cry through the gag in his mouth.

I stepped toward him and stopped on the other side of the table.

"Kneel," I commanded.

The man shook violently and pissed himself.

I let out a soft snarl when he remained on his feet.

The guys holding him knew me well enough. They knew I wanted complete submission from the people being punished, which was why they hadn't put him on his knees for me.

"Remove his gag and mask," I said.

The deed was done, and I was met with the dark eyes and snotty nose of some fuck I recognized from long ago.

He'd been a regular in the Underground. I caught him staring at my mother more than once. I was certain he'd even tried to purchase time with her, but my father hadn't approved the transaction because Jack didn't have the kind of money it took to fuck the queen of the Underground.

"Jack, Jack, Jack," I murmured. "We meet again."

"D-Dante," he whimpered. "Please."

"Knees. Now," I barked at him.

He sobbed softly and went to his knees for me. I paced in front of him, my monster free from the cell I kept it in.

"What did you do?" I demanded after a moment.

"I-nothing. I-"

"Do not fucking lie to me." I turned abruptly and fisted his hair. "Speak only the truth to me."

"I'm s-sorry. I can get the money I owe. I swear I can. I only need a few more days—"

"Who did you touch?"

"I-I—"

I pulled my knife out and twirled it between my fingers. A newer knife. I'd left my old one with Sin, but it made no matter. I'd killed with it before.

Jack cried out, snot dripping from his nose.

"Consider your next words carefully," I said softly. "And make sure they're truthful. I do not like liars."

"I-I've watched you grow up, Dante. With your mother. Calista—"

I let my fist fly. It connected with a crack against Jack's face, busting his nose and lip, the blood flowing freely.

"Never say her name," I hissed at him.

"I-I'm sorry. P-please," he blubbered.

"Who did you touch?"

"I-I, her name was Misty. I didn't have the cash, but I can get it now—"

"Put your hands on the table," I instructed.

"No," he wailed, shaking, the smell of his piss wafting off him.

"Jack, don't make this harder than it already is. Hands on the table. Now."

With a soft sob, he put his hands on the table, each digit trembling with his fear.

I didn't hesitate. I brought my knife down hard and fast and removed several fingers while he screamed, his blood gushing out. The men held him in place.

I took my time carving off the last digit. A pinky.

He vomited into the bloody mess before he passed out.

The men woke him for me, but he was barely conscious from the abrupt blood loss.

I was growing bored. Plus, he was filth, so I slit his throat in a lightning-fast movement. He slumped over in the mess we'd made together, his body limp.

"Not as clean as I prefer," Father's voice met my ears.

"Not as exciting as I prefer," I answered back. I turned to leave, but my father's voice had me stopping, my back to him.

"I have more work for you. Meet me in my office."

I cast a look over my shoulder at him before leaving the room.

Fucking figured it couldn't be a one-and-done thing.

✝

I settled in the leather chair across from my father's desk, watching as he poured us both a drink. He slid it over to me and settled in his seat.

I took the drink and sipped it, grateful he at least had a better taste in drink than he did in food.

"You always perform," he commented before taking a drink. "I can always depend on you."

"It is my job to serve," I muttered, slamming back my drink and sliding my glass back across the table. "Especially when you're using my girl and my friends against me. It helps we cut a deal."

He let out a soft chuckle. "You'd have come to me anyway. You always have. We're family. Your roots run deep beneath this blood empire."

"You know I don't like small talk, father. What is it that you require of me?"

He rapped his knuckles on his desk before refilling our glasses. I took my glass and sipped at it again, watching him closely.

After a moment, he opened his desk drawer and pulled out a manilla folder. He then passed me a picture of a pretty young woman.

"What's this?" I asked, picking the photo up and studying the girl. She was about my age. Dark hair. Dark eyes. Slim.

"That's your sister," he said, his hands folded on the desk in front of him.

I frowned and placed the photo back on the desk. "I don't have a sister."

"Well, half-sister. Her name was Macy."

I ground my teeth and stared at him from over the photo of her. "*Was?*"

He nodded. "She's dead. I suspect Matteo De Santis killed her. She was working for me, infiltrating the horsemen. She was a gem. Incredibly intelligent. She was better than I hoped because she got tight with the Sugar Daddy. The creator of sugar. She was supposed to get the recipe to me, but she was taken before she could. Originally, I just sent her in to get close to them to learn of their inner workings. Luck would have it the Sugar Daddy came into existence during her time there, which would have proved useful had she not died. I've heard she had a hand in its creation. Of course, she refused to tell me everything. It's caused some issues for me."

"Why didn't I know I had a sister?" I demanded, forgoing the other information. "Why was that kept from me?"

He refilled our glasses even though I didn't need another.

"*Siblings.* You have two."

I ground my teeth. "Where is the second one?"

"I suspect *comfortable*."

*Great. A fucking riddle.*

"I want to know what you know. No more lies," I snapped at him, frustrated out of my mind. If I had family, I wanted to know about them.

"I expect nothing less. Before you were born, I helped couples have babies," he explained. "Sometimes, I paired them with the men or women who could bring their dreams to reality. It was a lucrative business model but one I found rather boring. It's why I discontinued it after I'd created one of my own. The fact that Macy came out female was a disappointment. I was fortunate your mother was woman enough to grant me my boy. A *legitimate* heir." He stared fondly at me. "With you, I didn't need to continue fucking worthless women in the hopes of obtaining my son. I could simply fuck to fuck."

I held nothing but contempt in my heart for him, though, and didn't give a rat's ass how he felt. The man was a sick, perverted monster who probably never should have sired offspring. Given Macy seemed to be so easily swayed to do his bidding, and then the fact I was a fucking monster didn't give me high hopes for my remaining sibling.

"You have adopted children. Stitches. Isabella. They aren't actually my blood, are they?" I would love for Malachi to be my blood brother, but I wanted nothing to do with Bells. Fuck that dead bitch.

"I have sired three children. A female. A male. And you. There is no one else. This kingdom is yours. It's safe. Only my eldest, legitimate son shall have it."

I didn't give two fucks about this kingdom of sin and sorrow. It could burn to the ground, and I wouldn't piss on it to put it out. Yet, I couldn't stop my next question.

"Then how is it you created another child? For what purpose if you already have me to take over?"

He smirked at me. "Sometimes I do things because I grow bored. That is all this is. Business during a dull time. Fucking to fuck. He means nothing. Just a little eager helper. I need more of them. Willing. Excited. Desperate for my approval." He chuckled and drank again.

I sighed, not even wanting to know who my other sibling was. In this world, it was unlikely he'd last long anyway. Besides, he was created not through a marriage like I was. He had no real place in this world, therefore I rendered him a waste of time and space.

"How do you know Matteo killed Macy?" I asked, moving the conversation forward.

"I just have my suspicions. He thinks I killed his daughter, so he killed mine. An eye for an eye thing. You know how they can be."

I shook my head, disgusted by all of it. This world was sick. Innocence was always lost. Not that I knew if anyone involved was innocent, but I couldn't help but think of my specter and how sweet and innocent she was, and how she didn't deserve any of the shit she'd been forced into.

"What do you need from me, Father?"

"I want you to be a good brother and watch over your remaining family when the time comes. Bring him home. I want you to be a mentor. Teach as I have taught you."

"Home? Here?" I snorted at that. "Why? What would be the purpose of any of that?"

"Because he is blood, and blood is meant to be home."

"Then why let him go in the first place? Why create another kid who isn't a legitimate heir to the Underground then ask to have them mentored and brought here?"

"It was part of the deal I made."

"While I enjoy games, Father, I assure you your guessing games aren't one of them. Give me the information I need so that I can see to the task."

"It is simply someone who came to me, desperate for his wife to have a child. I wanted another son. We had an agreement that we would give his wife a child and that I would come to collect someday. My terms were clear. I fuck his wife and put a baby inside her. He keeps the child safe."

"And has he failed? Did you not vet properly, Father?"

He glared at me. "Watch yourself, boy."

"I'm sorry, Father, but you're asking me to mentor some lost brother of mine. All so he can come live in this hell? So he can be as crazy as we are? Help me see the logic in this."

"Blood belongs at home," he said, a muscle popping along his jaw. "You will do as you're told, or you will pay with the blood of those you've grown attached to."

"Did you force her? The mother?" I needed to know this. It was gnawing at me.

He inhaled deeply, his gaze fixed on me.

"She wanted it despite her screams. Her husband watched from the darkness of the alley as I took what I wanted. He was paid for his sacrifice."

I said nothing, disgusted by the man in front of me.

"It is another task, for another time. I was only making you aware of it."

"Of course, Father. Give me the information I need and a time in which I need to do it."

"Perfect." He offered me a wicked smile which did nothing but encourage me to want to kill him faster. It was sad, though, that he'd sunk his claws into another family's lives. He had a way of tearing apart anything that might be able to thrive.

"Fine. Send word when you're ready. I am at your service."

"Excellent. Now. We need to discuss the next point of business."

"And that is?" I raised my eyebrows at him, tiring of his company.

"The horsemen. You've heard of them?"

I nodded. Of course, I'd heard of them. They were up and coming. They were headed by Lorenzo De Luca, son of Anthony De Luca. They were taking over the city, piece by piece. Block by block. Rivals to the Kings and the De Santis syndicate. Rivals to the Ivanovs. It was quickly becoming a battleground.

And here we were. The Underground. Smack dab in the fucking center.

"Which side are you on, Father?"

He smiled at me, knowing exactly what I meant, and sat back in his seat. "Mine, of course. Let them feud. In their violence, we shall rise.

Let them kill one another off. Let us plant the seeds. We take over and claim this city as ours."

I scrubbed my hand down my face. "And what of Sirena?"

"What of her? If you want her, you'll do what you're told. I will let you keep her. I'll let you keep all of them. Malachi, Asher. Sinclair. Anything you want will be yours. Just do my bidding and do it well."

"For how long?" I whispered.

"Forever, of course." He surveyed me for a moment when I didn't answer. "I want their sugar recipe. With Macy's passing, I have no in. So I need one. They have a girl." He handed me a photograph of a gorgeous redhead with vibrant green eyes and then several more photos of who I assumed were the horsemen.

"Lorenzo De Luca is training to be head of the syndicate. His father, Anthony, has gone into hiding, leaving his only child to handle business. He's ruthless, but young. He will no doubt make a few mistakes."

I stared at the photo of the dark-haired man in the picture. He looked every bit the future head of a mob syndicate.

Father went through and showed me a blond named Cole, Lorenzo's right-hand man, and then a photo of someone I recognized from watching football. The quarterback for Mayfair, Fox Evans.

Surprising, but then again, this world was twisted, so why the hell not?

"And this is him. The Sugar Daddy." Father pushed a photo of a guy with dark hair and green eyes at me. The guy looked sad as hell. I studied the photo, taking in the exhaustion in his features. The haunted look in his eyes. This was a man who battled demons.

None of the people in the photos were much older than me. In fact, I knew Fox Evans was nearing his twentieth birthday because I'd heard it on some spot they did on him for TV. He was only months older than me.

"His name is Ethan Masters," Father continued, smiling. "Luck would have it, I have a photo of him as a boy, as well." He showed me another picture of the guy, but this time, he couldn't have been more than nine years old. Same haunted expression graced his face. The bruises on his arms were visible, but that wasn't what drew me to look closer.

"This was taken here," I said, looking up from the photo and to my father.

He gave me a sinister smile. "He was one of my very favorites."

My stomach twisted at his words.

"A sweet boy. Trusting. Loved fire trucks. Wanted to be a fire-fighter someday. Do you remember what you wanted to be when you were young, Dante?"

I averted my gaze from him and stared down at the picture of the sad boy in front of me again.

"I wanted to be free," I whispered.

"And to be free, you'll get me the Sugar Daddy. To have the family you seem so desperate for, you'll do what it takes to ensure I get what I want. The girl is the way in. I want Rosalie Bishop."

I glanced to her photo again. She was so vibrant. There wasn't a doubt in my mind that this was the type of woman who brought sunlight into a room with her. That she filled the tormented soul of Ethan Masters with the motivation to keep fucking going.

He and the horsemen would do anything to get her back. Even give up the recipe that was the key to their new kingdom.

"So what say you, Dante? Will you be everything I need you to be? Will you conquer worlds with me?"

I closed my eyes for a moment, gathering myself. Could I do all this shit for the rest of my life? I didn't mind taking life. I felt nothing when I did it. But was it what I wanted? To rule this hell someday?

The bigger question was, how far was I willing to go to protect the ones I loved?

A vision of my mother flashed in my mind. Her long blonde hair. Her sweet smile. The way her green eyes sparkled when she was happy. The way it felt to be hugged by her. To be loved by her.

"You know the rules." He pulled a knife from his drawer and slid it toward me before taking out a piece of paper, the terms of the arrangement clearly spelled out for me.

I read over it, everything in order that stated I'd get Sirena for good and my guys would be safe as long as I fulfilled my duties. It was something to buy us some time until I came back and was able to kill his ass.

Reaching out, I picked up the knife and twirled it between my fingers before pushing the blade against my other palm and making an X on it. The blood ran red, and I pressed my hand to the sheet of paper, sealing a deal with the fucking devil.

Everything came down to what I wanted. What I needed.

I missed being loved.

Now I had that with Sirena.

I wasn't about to let it go.

It didn't matter how many empires I had to conquer. Kings. Horsemen.

I'd do it. Without question, to keep the ones I loved safe, I'd do it.

"Perfect." He rose to his feet. "Let's go for a ride, shall we?"

*A*shes dropped a kiss on the top of my head and went outside to Sin and Stitches, who were smoking on the back patio while the snow fell around them. Cady was fast asleep on the end of the couch.

Bryce had barely spoken to me today. In fact, he maybe said ten whole words total to anyone.

I was torn between him and Mirage. I wanted to go to both. Instead, I sat with cushions between us all on the couch.

"Rinny," Mirage called out. "Sweetheart."

Bryce snapped his attention to Mirage, a sour look on his face.

"What's wrong, *Vanilla?*" Mirage cocked his head to the right. "Mad because I'm brave enough to reach out to her?"

I didn't like him provoking Bryce. Bryce was sweet and kind. Seeing the sadness morph across his face didn't sit well with me.

Quickly, I slid over to Mirage and pressed my finger to his lips.

He went silent, his blue eyes drinking me in.

My breath caught in my chest when he leaned in and whispered in my ear.

"Go to him. I already know you want me, my sweet dream." His lips brushed against the shell of my ear. "They won't be back in for many minutes. I promise it's OK."

I pulled away and stared into his eyes.

How was it OK? It was wrong because my feelings were confusing. And it wasn't confusing in a way where I didn't know what I wanted. The longer I was around Bryce, the more I was realizing these feelings were growing. The guys would never allow it, though. But damn, I missed him. Wanted him.

I shoved that last thought away.

We were friends. It would be weird. . .

"It won't be weird," Mirage said gently. "Is it weird for us?"

I frowned.

Of course, it was weird. There wasn't even an us. There were just these weird thoughts in my head I was trying to shuffle through. Even with Bryce, it was that way. What I was supposed to do about it, I had no clue. I knew the guys were more likely to be OK with Asylum/Mirage joining than Bryce. Maybe.

I cast a look to the outside to see Ashes and Stitches standing on either side of Sin, their backs to us. They were clearly getting along and chatting like they once did. I smiled, the thought that maybe they could get over everything making me happy.

My gaze slid to Bryce, who was staring down at his hands on his lap.

To hell with it. I cared about him.

I slid over to him and placed my hand over his.

He looked up from his hands and into my eyes.

"Hey," he said, his voice low.

I struggled to get my words out. When they failed me, I let out a frustrated grunt. Hatred for the person I'd become spread through my body, making me shiver. We sat in silence for so long it became awkward because all I wanted to do was talk to him. I glanced to the guys to see that they were still out there, but for how much longer, I had no clue. Not long, I'd assume. It was cold outside.

I closed my eyes, letting the darkness peek out.

The darkness had an easier time speaking, but it frightened me. I'd always kept it locked up. I'd ignored it all these years, pushing it to the back of my personality. My mind. Forcing it away because I had no idea how to really control it.

I had to try, though. As terrifying as it was, I had to try.

Inhaling, I focused on controlling it as much as I could.

It slipped out further. My body felt fuzzy.

"Are you OK?" I asked Bryce, my words low.

He blinked rapidly at me. "Sirena?"

"Are you OK?" I repeated louder.

"I-I'm OK. I'm hurting," he answered, his Adam's apple bobbing in his throat. "I meant to meet you in the woods. I-I got hurt."

"Did he hurt you?" I demanded, my anger slowly rising to the surface.

"I, who?" he asked.

Mirage slid closer.

"You know who. The one who hurt me."

"I-I, no. No. Church found me out there. He got angry with me. We-we fought." He winced. "I fought with the watchers. I'm OK, though. At least now. I saw you meeting with the rabbit. With Mirage. It was the only way I could get you to speak to me again after. . . after I told you how I felt." He licked his lips. "I'm sorry about that. I am. I understand we can't happen, but I don't want to not be in your life. I care about you and want to be with you however I can be. Even if it's only as your friend."

"You want me?"

"I-I do, but I already know—"

"Did you see him? In the woods?"

"Sirena, I only saw the guys. I didn't see anyone else. I know you were hurt," his voice cracked. "I blame myself. I-I should have gotten there sooner. Then you wouldn't have been hurt. Hell—"

"He'd have hurt you too," I said. "He's a monster. A fucking monster!" The words came out in a scream. I saw red. Images of that night flashed through my mind.

"I'll kill him. I'm going to kill him!" I tugged at my hair, snarling and screaming. My body went fuzzy again, and I couldn't stop the loud sob that tore from my lungs as those ugly images kept flooding my mind.

I couldn't take it. I couldn't.

God, help me.

I was hot. So hot.

I couldn't escape. I can't escape. He's going to hurt me. He's out there. Waiting.

I tore my top off, and Bryce got to his feet.

"Do something," he shouted at Mirage, who was on his feet, trying to hold me while I screamed.

I heard the patio door bang open. Footsteps thundered toward me. The sound of Cady calling out to me in a frantic confusion.

Ashes. Stitches. Mirage. Bryce. Cady. Even Sin.

"Sirena. Sirena. Hey. Hey, stop. Stop." Stitches pulled me away from Mirage and wrapped his arms around me as I continued my meltdown.

"What the fuck happened?" Ashes demanded.

I didn't hear what Bryce and Mirage recounted.

*I couldn't breathe. I couldn't breathe.*

"Sirena. Angel, baby. Look at me." Stitches forced my face upward. "You can do this. Focus. Focus."

I couldn't do this.

In my mind, Adam cackled and teased me. Hurt me. Forced his way inside me.

"Fuck," Stitches snarled. "Asher, meds. Now. Top shelf in my bathroom cabinet. There's a syringe and vial there. Bring them."

I had no idea if Ashes left. All I knew was that I couldn't breathe. My fingers and lips were numb. I was going to pass out.

"She's hyperventilating," Mirage said. "Give her to me."

"Fuck off," Stitches snapped. He pulled me between his legs and lay against the arm of the couch, his hand on my chest.

"Remember this, angel? Remember?" He whispered frantically in my ear. "I'll keep you safe. Breathe, baby. Keep breathing. I got you. I got you. Breathe with me. Please, Sirena. I need you to focus."

Ashes came back and went to his knees next to us. I was going insane. More flashes in my head. Jerry hurting me. Sully. Everett Church's Cheshire smile. The people behind the mirror. Adam. Adam. ADAM.

I was going to kill them. I'd kill them all. I struggled to get up so I could go to them. So I could slay the monsters so they couldn't hurt anyone else.

Stitches forced me back down.

"Fucking hurry, Asher." Sin let out a frustrated hiss. "She's fucking losing it, man."

"I'm going as fast as I can."

There was a tight band around my bicep. I heard Cady crying in the distance. Then, a pinprick in the crook of my arm.

My body relaxed. My breathing slowed. The room came back into focus for a moment before it grew fuzzy.

"I'll kill him," I whispered.

Or at least I thought I did.

I had no real idea because I drifted off, the concerned faces of Ashes, Bryce, Cady, Sin, and Mirage's rabbit mask fading away, Stitches's soft words in my ear.

"Sleep, angel. Please. Just sleep."

So I did.

# SIN

*I* stared down at the text on my phone a week after Sirena's meltdown in the living room. She'd missed classes earlier in the week, but I knew she was back because Ashes had just sent me a text to grab her from classes and walk her back to the house. He had his therapy session, and Stitches was being forced to do group therapy at the same time. Cady had detention, the guys seemed leery about having Bryce help, and Mirage was off doing god knew what. I hadn't seen him all day.

He'd been acting strangely after the shit with Sirena happened. I was used to Asylum being in the room at night. Mirage rarely slept there. If he did, he came in during the four in the morning hour wearing his rabbit mask, then only slept for a few hours before going to classes. If he even bothered going at all.

Mirage was a world apart from Asylum in how he behaved. The fact he was able to pull himself together around people and blend in spoke volumes of his talents.

I shook my head, not wanting to get caught up in the mess that was Asylum/Mirage. Instead, I sent a reply message to Ashes to let him know I'd get Sirena, then take her to their house and sit with her

After waiting a few more minutes, I made my way to Sirena's class. It was another Bible study class. The Sister who ran it was quiet and not nearly as bad as the other assholes at this place. I leaned against the brick wall and stared at the lockers in front of me.

The bell rang a few seconds later, signaling the end of classes.

The moment Sirena came out with her head down, I sidled next to her. She cast me a quick look, her colorful eyes wide.

It was always uncomfortable being around her. I never knew what to say or what the hell to do with my hands. Stuffing them into my pants pockets, I walked beside her to her locker.

"Everyone was busy with after-school stuff," I finally said when the crowd had thinned. "I'm supposed to take you back to the house and stay with you."

She glanced at me again but didn't say anything. Ashes told me she'd been having a lot of sleeping issues since her meltdown. He'd texted me some updates here and there, for which I was grateful. While Ashes had come around a lot, Stitches was still a little withdrawn. I didn't blame him, though. He talked to me, but it wasn't like it used to be with us. He'd gone through hell because of me. We all had. I hated myself for it. I tried to not focus on that shit, but it haunted me like an old ghost.

She opened her locker and grabbed her coat. I waited while she put it on and filled her book bag with what she needed before she put her head down and walked toward the exit. I followed her, pulling my jacket tighter around me.

Several minutes into our trek, she slipped on some ice. I caught her by the arm before she went down completely and brought her back to her feet. I couldn't tell if her cheeks were red from the cold or from embarrassment. I hoped it wasn't embarrassment.

Once she was firmly back on her feet, I released her arm, grateful she hadn't tried to tug away from me. We continued in silence to the house. When we arrived, I inserted the key I still had and opened the door. She stepped inside, me behind her, and I closed us in.

Quickly, she dropped her bag to the floor and removed her jacket before going to the couch where she sat and stared straight ahead.

I didn't really know what to do, so I went and sat on the L section of the couch.

"Are you hungry?" I finally asked.

She bit her bottom lip but remained quiet.

Fuck it. She had to be hungry.

I got up and went to the kitchen. I'd lived here for a good portion of my life, so it wasn't hard to find shit. Not knowing what she liked to eat, I stared down at a box of plain macaroni noodles before checking the fridge to find a various assortment of cheeses and milk. Coming to a decision, I pulled a pot out of the cupboard, filled it with water, and put it on the stove.

From my view in the open kitchen, I could see she'd pulled her books out of her bag and was working on her homework.

Such a good girl.

I pushed that thought out of my head. Homework and I didn't mix. Fuck that shit. I wasn't going to go out into the world and be a scholar. Making it through was based on my intimidation factor and my role as a watcher. Of course, that may not work so well for me now in that department. It didn't matter. The only way out of Chapel Crest was to pass. Classes. Therapy. Bible studies. All of it. Or death. Judging by how shit had gone down for me throughout my life, I was certain Death had long forgotten me.

I stayed in the kitchen, leaving Sirena to her work. When the water boiled, I put the noodles in, and when it was ready, I made the homemade macaroni and cheese for her. I never cooked around the guys. Ashes typically was the cook. He was a decent cook. Sometimes, he burned things just to see how many flames he could create. One time, when I'd asked Church why we let him near the stove, he'd smirked and said it was good tolerance building for Ashes.

Honestly, I was surprised Ashes hadn't burned the house down long ago. I knew he struggled with his pyromania daily. In any other facility, they'd have taken his lighter away from him. But here? I think they wanted the excuse to corner him.

After I pulled the food from the oven, I made Sirena and myself each a plate and brought them both out to the living room. I placed the food in front of her on the coffee table.

She looked up at me in surprise, those colorful eyes of hers sending a jolt right through my heart.

"I made you something to eat," I muttered. "I figured you might be hungry."

Surprisingly, she closed her book and picked up the plate. A tiny part of me thought she might shun my attempt and go without, but I was happy when she lifted the fork to her lips, all the cheesy goodness on display.

With my breath held, I waited for her verdict. I hadn't cooked in ages. When I was a kid, I'd cook with my mom. That shit went to hell, though, after my old man shot me.

Another sour memory I pushed away.

The tiniest moan slipped past her lips as she chewed and then swallowed.

"Do you like it?" I sounded far too eager for her approval. Desperate, even. I hated that, but fuck it. There it was.

While she never really said shit to me or communicated, it was when her gaze met mine, and that tiny smile graced her pretty face that I knew that was it. I was done for. If I had anything holding me back before about pleasing her, it was gone in that moment.

That smile. The little bit of sparkle in her sad, pretty eyes. All I wanted to do was make her smile for the rest of her days.

I couldn't, though.

I wasn't that sort of guy. The only thing I was good at was fucking everything up.

All the potential happiness whooshed out of my body at the thought that I'd never be good enough for her. That I didn't deserve her or any bit of happiness. My name was Sin, for fuck's sake. That didn't exactly inspire good things.

I looked down at my plate still on the coffee table, lost in my miserable thoughts.

It was when the weight of someone next to me made me realize she'd moved to sit beside me.

I looked over at her, my heart in my throat.

So much innocence greeted me. Sweetness. Gentleness.

I swallowed hard as she leaned forward, picked up my plate, and handed it to me. Gingerly, I took it from her, my fingers brushing along hers for but a moment. A moment that made my heart leap higher and the flames slowly building in my soul spark brighter.

Reaching out, she gently brushed her fingers along my lips. I closed my eyes at how wonderful it was to feel the touch of someone else.

"Sinful," she whispered softly.

I opened my eyes and stared at her, my throat tight.

"I am," I answered back just as quietly, my voice shaking.

*Fuck, get it together, pussy.*

Her gaze darted over my face before her fingers fell away, making me exhale slowly.

"Eat," she murmured, her focus still on me.

I forced out a slight smile, suddenly realizing why the guys were completely obsessed with her. She was everything we weren't. Everything all of us had been missing in our lives. Everything we'd always wanted.

And I'd gone and fucked it up by locking her in a goddamn box with Asylum.

He'd paid his penance and won her back. He'd protected her in the facility. What had I done aside from running through the woods with her? Anyone with half a heart would have done that for someone.

All the shady shit I'd done couldn't ever be made up. I'd accepted that. Hated it, but accepted it.

But the way she looked at me made me think maybe I could be wrong.

*It always hurts. Love always hurts.*

I didn't want to hurt anymore. God help me, I didn't.

Fuck, what I wouldn't give to be normal.

She scooped noodles and cheese onto her fork and offered it to me despite me having my own.

*Fuck, Siren, you're making it so much worse.*

*Please, don't give me hope.*

*I don't deserve it.*

I didn't want to take her food since I had my own, but I didn't want to push her away, either. Fear gripped me as I parted my lips for her.

Carefully, she put the food into my mouth. The guys always fed her. I'd even seen them doing it at lunch. Maybe she associated this with caring.

*Fuck, I can't get wrapped up in the tiny details. She probably just wants me to eat to prove I didn't poison it. Quit overthinking.*

She blinked at me, waiting for me to chew and swallow. I did so before offering her a small, wobbly smile.

I felt like a complete idiot sitting here. If she were any other girl, I'd have buried my cock inside her body already and have walked away. I'd learned my lesson with getting too attached.

But damnit, why did I want it so much?

Maybe because I couldn't have it.

Damnit.

Seemingly satisfied, she went back to eating, not bothering to move away from me. I forced myself to not overthink it. I simply ate beside her, telling myself she was only being nice. Despite my sins, she was still the sweet girl she'd always been.

Except I'd seen her darkness only nights ago as she'd faded away and let whatever monster that lived inside her mind out into the world with her proclamation she was going to kill him.

*Him.*

I wanted to find out what his name was and kill him too.

But if she wanted the honors, then I'd bring him to her and put him on his knees so she could have the pleasure of slitting his fucking throat.

I think we all had that desire.

We ate in silence, and when she was done, I took our plates and returned them to the kitchen before coming back and taking my seat again.

She still hadn't moved away from me.

We sat in more silence for several long minutes before I finally spoke, not even knowing how to talk to her.

"Um, I, uh, don't know what to say."

*Real fucking smooth, Sinclair. Way to state the obvious.*

She fidgeted for a moment before she got up and went to her bag. Defeat coursed through me at her distance.

Hope sprung back to life, though, when she returned, a notebook and her pen in her hand, and sat next to me again.

I watched while she slowly scrawled words onto the lined pages. Her writing was beautiful. All loopy, like what I imagined a love letter would have looked like ages ago. And she had a message for me.

**Are you OK?**

I stared down at her words to me, my mouth dry.

She wanted to know if I was OK.

I couldn't say the words, so I took the pen from her and wrote back.

**I will be.**

It began an exchanging of the pen and words. She wanted to speak to me. It was our first real conversation, and I didn't want to screw anything up.

**Do you promise?**

I stared down at her words, hating the feelings burning my chest.

*I'm trying to, siren.*

I paused before writing more for her, hating that my writing looked more like chicken scratch than anything else.

**Are you OK?**

She took the pen from me and stared at the paper momentarily before finally writing back.

**I don't know. Sometimes. I'm scared.**

I read her words, my heart aching for her.

**What are you afraid of?**

She took the pen.

**Everything.**

Her hand shook as she handed the pen back to me.

**When I was younger, I was afraid. After my father shot me. I'm**

**still afraid, but I've found that sometimes I can use that fear to be stronger.**

I paused, feeling like a damn hypocrite. I was anything but strong.

**I'm not the greatest at advice. I'm sorry.**

She stared at the words for a moment before writing back to me.

**What are you afraid of?**

Fuck. Same answer, siren.

**I'm afraid I'll never be good enough for anyone.**

I exhaled and decided to give her a little story about my past.

**When I was younger, I had this necklace. Well, it was a rosary. I'd pray with it. It brought me peace during my parents' divorce. The divorce was ugly, and I was raised on God. So I'd pray with this rosary every night. I'd say my novena. Begging God to save my family. To make my dad a better man for my mom.**

My hand shook.

**Church found me with it once. Asked me what it was for. I told him. He asked his mom for one, and she got it for him. Then Asher got one. Then Stitches. It seemed we all needed a little extra help in our lives. I lost mine, though. When my dad took me, I'd prayed with it that day. I begged God, the saints, and anyone who could hear my terrified prayers to save me. Maybe they did hear me because I'm still around. But the rosary is gone. I wish I had it because sometimes I think I could use the prayers. So I could have hope. Maybe God would hear me if I had it.**

She read my words and didn't move for a long time before she got to her feet and went upstairs, leaving me alone in the living room.

I felt like an idiot telling her that shit. I wasn't the type to open up like that. My stomach twisted with the embarrassment of it.

Thinking she wasn't going to come back, I sat there, wallowing in my self-pity. It was when she came back downstairs and sat beside me again that I perked up.

She took my hand and turned it palm up before placing her hand over it. Something cool dropped against my skin. Her eyes met mine for a moment, making my heart skip before she pulled her hand away.

I stared down at what she'd given me, my throat tight.

A rosary.

Blue and silver. A cross.

She took the pen and paper and quickly wrote another message.

**For you. So you can have hope again.**

The words became blurry as my eyes filled with tears. My inner thoughts pleaded with me.

*Don't fucking cry. Please, don't fucking do it, Sinclair. Hold it in. She doesn't need to see that shit. God, why did she have to be so perfect?*

I rolled the beads between my fingers, trying to keep the tears at bay. It had been a long time since anyone had ever given me a gift, and this gift hit home for me.

Her warm fingers brushed along my jaw before she gently lifted my head to look at her. As hard as I tried to contain it, a tear worked its way down my cheek.

She cocked her head, her pretty plump lips parted, and leaned into me.

I held my breath as she placed a kiss on my cheek, taking the tear with her. I exhaled a shaky breath when she pulled away, everything within me telling me to just take the moment and kiss her lips. Tell her how sorry I was. Tell her I wasn't worthy.

Fuck. I'm not worthy.

I can't. I want it, but I can't.

"Sinful," she whispered. "Pray."

I nodded, my throat tight, wanting to say so many things to her. Instead, the front door opened. Ashes and Stitches came into the room, ending our conversation. Quickly, I wiped at my eyes before tucking the rosary into my pocket. I glanced at our note before grabbing that, too, and stuffing it down beside the rosary. No sense in leaving it behind.

It was proof she gave a shit about me.

And that was worth saving.

# ASHES

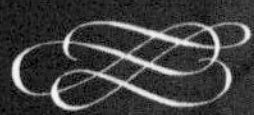

"You cooked?" Stitches looked from the macaroni and cheese to Sin.

Sin nodded. "Yeah. Sorry. I didn't know if she'd eaten—"

"It's homemade?" Stitches narrowed his eyes at Sin.

I looked at the food. It definitely looked homemade. It smelled otherworldly. My stomach gave a loud growl.

"Yeah." Sin shifted awkwardly as he stood with us in the kitchen and rubbed the back of his neck before he looked to where Sirena was sitting on the couch watching some documentary Stitches had put on about Bigfoot being in Michigan.

I didn't think it was a good idea for her to be watching that on TV since a lot of the stories from eyewitness accounts came from the area we were in. She didn't need the stress of more bullshit. I hated the thought that crept into my head, however.

*Maybe it'll keep her out of the woods.*

I wanted her to be safe. Peaceful sleeping had eluded me since everything happened. My fear of her sneaking out again kept me from completely going to bed. Even the slightest of noises jolted me up these days.

I'd told Sin and Stitches this very thing a few days ago when we'd smoked on the patio the night Sirena had to be sedated.

"I didn't know you could cook." Stitches grabbed a bowl and piled the food onto it before he took a big bite. "Fuck. That's good. What the fuck, man? Why didn't you ever tell us? We've been tempting fate with Asher making dinner every damn night. I think I've eaten more burned meals than properly cooked ones."

"Man, shut up," I said to Stitches, rolling my eyes at him. "I'm not that bad."

Stitches shrugged and took another bite. "Yeah, it's not that bad. It's not Sin's macaroni good, though."

I had to find out what he was raving about, so I got some and ate it, swearing softly after my third bite.

"See? It's good, right?" Stitches asked around a mouthful of noodles and cheese.

"It is," I agreed. "I like this."

Sin gave us a small smile that didn't quite reach his eyes before he looked back to Sirena on the couch.

"Should she be watching that?" he finally asked.

"I'm hoping it scares her enough to keep her out of the woods," Stitches said unapologetically, voicing my exact thoughts. I was torn on it. He didn't seem to be, in any case.

"Yeah, but it might trigger her too." I looked in her direction to see if she was showing signs of another freakout. She appeared to be watching it without issue.

"Thanks for watching her tonight," I said, focusing back on Sin, whose attention was still on her.

Stitches glanced at me with raised brows. I gave him a quick smile. Sin had it bad but didn't realize it yet. Or maybe he did and knew he was backed into a tough corner that Church didn't seem to have any desire to let him out of.

Me?

I could see the change in Sin. Seeing him broken and sad was hard, but I also saw his strength. I wanted him to come home. Having our lives return to normal would be a godsend. Knowing Stitches was more on my side than Church's helped too.

"Sin?" I called out when he didn't answer me.

"Huh?" He turned and looked at me.

"I said thanks for watching her tonight. How was everything?"

"It was fine."

Stitches and I exchanged another look.

"Fine?" I pressed. "What did you guys do?"

"Nothing. I made some food," he muttered. "We sat on the couch. She did some homework. That's, uh, pretty much it."

"Is it?" Stitches asked. "You two were close when we came in."

Sin shook his head. "Just... I don't know. Nothing. Just sitting there."

He looked back to her again, ending the conversation. It took him a beat before he walked forward. Paused. He shook his head and muttered something we couldn't hear.

I looked at Stitches again, knowing something was definitely up.

He gave me a knowing nod and studied Sin.

"You leaving?" Stitches asked.

"Uh, yeah. Yeah, I should probably go. I told Asy-Mirage I'd watch a movie with him tonight."

"What kinds of movies does he like?" I asked, curious what sort of stuff Asylum was into. Or Mirage. Whoever the hell he was today.

Sin scoffed. "Weird, obscure horror. Shit sucks."

"Figures." Stitches rolled his eyes. "He's so fucking weird."

"He is," Sin agreed, letting out a sigh. "I'll see you guys."

"See you," I said wistfully as he pulled his jacket on. He paused at the door when Sirena got up and went to him.

We watched the exchange wordlessly.

Sin took a cautious step toward her. She simply stared at him.

"See you, siren," he said softly before backing away. She remained silent, watching him open the door and leave. The cool breeze from the Michigan night fanned across her face, feathering her dark hair.

"Something's going on," Stitches said when Sirena returned to the couch and sat back on it.

I nodded. "Seems to be."

"What do we do?"

I mulled it over before answering. "I think we let it happen, whatever it is. Maybe Sin will come home."

"What if he fucks up again?"

I pulled my attention from Sirena as I scooped another forkful of noodles and cheese into my mouth and chewed.

I swallowed, hating the words coming from my mouth but knowing they were true.

"You know the rules. None of us will go unpunished if we hurt her. He had his warning. Next time, I'll burn him until his screams fade into the night," I whispered.

"Just wanted to make sure we're on the same page."

"We are," I said, finishing my food before putting the bowl into the sink.

"And Church?"

"I think if Sirena wants Sin, Church will allow it. I know I will."

Stitches considered my words before scraping his bowl with his fork. "I will too. I might punch him in the face so he remembers, but I think I'd welcome the grouchy fuck with open arms." He ate quietly for a moment before speaking. "And Asylum?"

I sighed and rubbed my eyes. "I think it'll be the same deal. Even Bryce. We're not blind."

Stitches scowled. "He's too fucking nice. We'd break him."

"Might be fun."

He grinned. "Promise?"

I pulled my lighter out, then opened it and closed it five times. The flame flicked on the fifth time, and I looked at Stitches from over it.

"I do."

I snapped my lighter closed and started my ritual all over again, my eyes fixed on my girl on the couch.

If Bryce wanted in, he'd have to be initiated.

I was sure the complete hell we put him through would be worth it in the end.

And if it wasn't, it gave us something to kill.

I reeled my ugly side back in and went back to flipping my lighter open and closed, my eyes on my girl.

# STITCHES

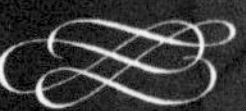

*W*e sat and watched TV with Sirena that night before taking her upstairs to her bedroom. We'd been making it a habit to sleep with her every night that Church had been gone. She seemed calm. Like she was better.

But I was the poster child for faking my outward appearance for others. After watching Sin tonight, I felt like maybe something happened between her and him. Something that had him in a choke-hold over her.

Hell, we all were, if truth be told.

I wasn't opposed to her wanting Sin. It was the original plan. He pissed me off like no one else, but I was slowly getting over it. Dwelling on it was making me miserable. I had enough shit wrong in my head and didn't need to add something like one of my best friends fucking up to it and then holding that grudge.

It was hard. Fuck, was it hard. Everything Sirena had endured was because of the snowball effect he started.

I drew in a calming breath, trying to keep my mind off that shit. If Sirena was able to forgive him, then I knew I could too. Maybe. Someday.

"Can I braid your hair?" Ashes asked her when she pulled her pajamas out of her dresser.

"What?" I looked at Ashes. "Did I hear you right?"

"Yeah." He shrugged. "I want to try something."

I shook my head. He was always doing weird shit I didn't understand. She offered him a smile, which I took as a yes, before turning her back and undressing.

We both watched in silence.

I loved the way her hips had that sexy as fuck flare. The way her long black hair hung down her back and brushed the top of her hips. The cleft of her ass teased me from beneath her panties. I adjusted my hardening dick in my pants, noting Ashes was flipping the lid to his lighter open and closed as was his ritual.

She came back to us with her brush and settled on the floor between Ashes's legs. He smirked triumphantly at me and took the brush from her before he began plaiting her hair in a thick braid.

"Where'd you learn to braid?" I asked, mesmerized as he continued to gather her hair.

"Abby," he said, his voice low.

I didn't push the subject. He so rarely spoke of his dead twin sister. It was a painful subject for him.

I watched him tie off the braid with a black band. Sirena turned and stared up at him from her knees.

*Yeah, that's fucking gorgeous.*

"Hey, heaven." He ran his knuckles along her jaw. "Did you and Sin have a good time?"

We hadn't asked her about it yet. I knew we sure as hell would, though. If Ashes hadn't done it, I knew I would.

She took his hand and kissed his palm before scrawling words onto it.

He smiled at her. "I'm glad. What did you two do?"

Sin told us nothing much, but I knew Ashes was curious about Sin's behavior tonight like I was.

She wrote more on his hand while he nodded, and his brows crinkled while he deciphered her words.

"Really?"

She nodded.

"What did she say?" I asked.

"She said what he told us they did."

I breathed out, grateful Sin hadn't lied to us.

"Come here," Ashes instructed in a seductive voice. She rose for him, and he pulled her onto his lap so she was straddling him. His lips met hers, kissing her deeply.

I watched, mesmerized by them, my dick begging me to let it out and join in.

My phone buzzed, making me let out a soft hiss. I pulled it out of my pocket and caught Church's name on the screen.

"Hello?" I answered it.

"Stitches. How is everything?"

I looked to Ashes, who had his hands beneath Sirena's nightgown and was clearly cupping her perfect ass in his palms.

"It's good."

"You sound distracted. What are you doing?"

"I'll show you." I snapped a picture of Ashes and Sirena making out and sent it to Church. He was quiet for a moment before he let out a groan.

"What are you doing?" I asked, continuing to watch Ashes as he removed her nightgown and kissed along her collarbone.

"Wishing I was there so I could fuck her with you two."

"I wish you were here too, brother. How is our dear old man?"

Church snorted. "Way to kill the mood."

"My pleasure," I murmured, watching Ashes remove Sirena's bra and suck her nipple into his mouth. Her head fell back as she ground against him.

"Well, I'm just updating you on what's going on. Father wants me to check out this girl. Apparently, she's connected to these horsemen who are making sugar. He wants the recipe and thinks getting their girl will make them hand it over. I'm to learn their habits. Their routines. All that shit."

"Ah, the great hunter," I said, forcing my attention away from Ashes and Sirena. He'd lost his clothes already.

"I suppose."

"How long do you think you'll be gone?"

"I'm hopeful this girl and the horsemen are boring as fuck and are creatures of habit. I don't expect to be gone for too long."

"Is that all he has you doing?" I knew Everett. He wasn't only making Dante scout out his next victims. He made use of him whenever Dante was around.

"You know how it is here," Church said with a sigh. "I killed someone today."

I swallowed at his words. Everett had taken me to kill people before too. Not nearly as many as Church had, but I'd seen Church unhinged in the punishment rooms. He was a murderous robot, void of all feelings. I'd thrown up the first time I'd killed someone.

I was ten.

Church had comforted me after.

*"It's OK, Malachi. Close your eyes and think of your favorite place in the world. It's where I go when I do it."*

*I closed my eyes and envisioned myself at home, watching my mom cook before everything went to shit. I thought of my dog Farley at my side, licking my hand. The way the house smelled from dinner. My favorite program playing in the background. The sound of birds singing outside. The setting sun shining through the windows, casting pretty colors along the old wooden floor.*

*"Are you there, Malachi?"*

*I nodded. "Yeah."*

*"Then stay there. Whenever you go to the punishment room, go to your favorite place in the world. You can't be hurt there."*

*"Do you promise, Dante?"*

*"I never lie," he answered, hugging me tightly.*

"What did he do?" I asked, falling out of the old memory.

"Fucked around and found out," he answered. "Owed money. Touched something he hadn't paid for. Same shit as always. I don't know why they're always so fucking stupid. Like they don't know they'll be caught and have to pay."

I grunted at that. The people who frequented the Underground were all dicks and no brains. Or tits and no brains because women went there too. Maybe not as much, but there were some sick bitches in this world.

Nausea twisted my insides as the ugly memory of the facility filled my head. Men and women. Both monsters.

"Malachi?"

His words pulled me out of an incoming panic attack.

"Yeah. Hey. Sorry. Got distracted." I cleared my throat. "I, uh, needed to tell you something. Asylum. Or Mirage. Whatever personality he is or was, is who was meeting Sirena in the woods. He was here and told us. Mirage, I mean. Wearing a fucking rabbit mask."

Church was silent.

"He said they're friends and he was simply being her friend by offering her a shoulder to lean on, basically. This personality is just weird though. The rabbit thing? Weird."

"So someone knew he wore that to meet her and impersonated him," Church said dully.

"Seems so."

"Fuck, he's nuts. I want to beat the shit out of him more than anything else." Church sighed. "Sirena was fine with him? In the mask? No weird outburst?"

"She ran right to him and hugged him. She seems to like this Mirage personality a lot more than Asylum, but we all know she likes Asylum." I'd gotten up and moved out of earshot of Sirena and Ashes and had lowered my voice. "Are you mad?"

Church sighed. "I'm pissed she lied about it. But I get it. I can be… difficult. We all can be."

I nodded. He was right about that.

"How is our girl?" Church asked, seeming to be willing to let it all go. Or maybe he'd stew on it overnight before raging.

I looked over to Ashes and Sirena, who were still doing some heavy making out. Of course, Ashes was taking his time.

"She looks like she's having a good time," I said with a soft laugh.

"I want to watch."

I hesitated for a moment before I invited him to video call. His face came onto the screen, his green eyes tired, and his blond hair a wild mess. He was smoking weed and drinking a fifth of scotch.

Typical Church behavior when he was forced to spend time with Everett.

He propped the phone up so I could see him fully sitting in a chair in his bedroom. He was dressed all in black, and I watched him undo his tie and unbutton his shirt.

"I love you, brother, I do, but I'm going to jerk off, and it's not you I want to do it to."

"Sorry." I genuinely laughed that time and turned my phone so it was aimed on Ashes and Sirena.

"Asher," Church called out.

"Yeah?" He pulled away from Sirena to look over at Church on my phone screen.

"Fuck her for me."

Ashes let out a laugh before returning his attention to Sirena and tugging her down on top of him as he lay back on the bed. Church and I watched Ashes continue lavishing her tits in his face, her ass in the air.

"Give me a close-up," Church demanded.

I did as requested and moved the phone close to her pussy. She glistened with want as she rubbed against Ashes's cock.

"Lick her pussy for me, Malachi."

I did the best I could with the phone situation, hoping he could see, and licked Sirena's pussy for him before moving to her ass. A gasp left her as I ate her asshole.

"Finger her pussy," Church instructed.

Gladly.

I pushed a digit into her heat, earning another whimper from her before I went back to eating her ass.

Keeping the camera propped was a job I wasn't so sure I was cut out for. It was hard to keep my focus on what I was supposed to be doing.

"Just fuck her," Church's voice sounded out. "Put the camera on you guys so I can watch."

I did what he wanted and placed the phone on her bedside table before I removed my clothes and crawled onto the bed with her and Ashes. Gently, I pulled her face away from Ashes and kissed her soft lips, my cock brushing against her damp pussy.

"We're going to fuck you so Church can watch," I whispered against her lips. "Is that OK?"

She nodded, and I released her, going to her ass since Ashes was quick to claim her pussy. Not that I expected him to fuck her elsewhere. I wanted her ass anyway. It was time I got to claim it.

I gathered all her dampness and smeared it around her hole and along my cock. I spit on her as an extra precaution and slowly worked my finger into her tight rosette. She squirmed beneath the pressure for a moment before relaxing. I worked her for a moment before adding another finger, wanting to get her a little looser for me so she wasn't hurt. Having my long, thick cock up in her ass might cause her a great deal of discomfort, but I knew she'd taken Church before, so she could handle it. He was rougher than I was. At least in the beginning. Once she acclimated, I'd rail her until she howled my name.

Ashes slowed for me when I withdrew my fingers and pressed my cock to her asshole. She stiffened, and he whispered quickly into her ear. Words I couldn't hear. I was too far gone now. I had to have her like this.

I pushed forward, breaching the tight ring of muscle. She let out a hiss, her body still tense. Ashes growled because she was clearly clawing the fuck out of his flesh with her nails.

I drilled slowly inside her, listening as her breathing changed.

"You OK, angel?" I called out in a shaky voice when I bottomed out in her ass.

I received an answering whimper, which sounded a hell of a lot like yes. So I pulled out and slowly pushed back in a few times, Ashes patiently waiting for me.

"You good, baby?" Ashes asked.

Another soft whimper from her.

"Oh, sweet girl, we're going to make walking hard tomorrow." Ashes kissed her, speaking all sorts of dirty words to her as I worked in and out of her, him slowly beginning to move with me while buried in her pussy.

I stopped and spit on her hole again before really moving.

Her breathing picked up, her small body jostling between us.

"Fuck her harder," Church barked out, breathless. "I want her to come for both of you."

"Gladly," Ashes grunted out, picking up his pace. I matched my pace with his, both of us plunging in and out of her body, nothing but the wet sounds, moans, and heavy breathing sounding out in the room.

I glanced to my phone on the bedside table and saw Church was jerking his cock in time to our movements.

"Come on, Asher," I encouraged. "We can go faster."

He picked up his pace until we were fighting for control of her body, her cries music to my ears.

"Fuck yeah," Church husked out. "God, that's fucking good."

Sirena's body tensed before she trembled violently, her pussy soaking both me and Ashes. I couldn't take it. I came hard, filling her ass and cursing loudly as I shuddered against her body. Ashes followed, a low, feral groan leaving him.

We slowed to a stop, leaving her quaking between us.

I leaned forward and kissed her bare shoulder.

"Love you, angel," I murmured.

Her lashes fluttered as she lay in a boneless heap on Ashes's chest. I chuckled softly at her sated, blissed-out state and pulled free from her body. Ashes stayed embedded in her, and I went to my phone to find Church cleaning the mess he'd made on his bare abdomen.

"You like it?" I asked.

"You fucking know I did. I love watching you guys fuck her."

"Well, come back home so you can join us."

"You can count on that." His phone shifted, and his entire face came into view. "Let me talk to her."

I walked the phone to her and held it in front of her face.

"Specter," Church murmured. "You're such a good girl. You know that?"

She smiled tiredly at the screen, making his lips curl upward.

"You let Ashes and Stitches take care of you, OK? And. . . take care of them too. For me. Promise?"

She nodded for him. He exhaled, a sad look on his face.

"I'm sorry I left without saying goodbye. It would have made leaving harder."

She reached out and brushed her fingers along the screen.

He let out a soft laugh. "I can't wait to see you again." He lowered his voice. "I love you, Sirena. I'll see you soon, OK?"

She shifted and moved forward to kiss the camera lens, Ashes shifting with her so he could stay inside her pussy.

"Oh, specter," Church said. "Sleep well."

He cleared his throat. "I'll talk to you guys later. Be safe."

"Of course," Ashes said. "You too."

I moved away from Ashes and Sirena.

"You sure you're OK?" I asked.

"I'm fine. I was raised to survive and conquer. So were you," he said, giving me a pointed look. "I'll see you soon, brother."

"You better." I went to the small bathroom off of Sirena's room and closed myself in.

He hesitated for a moment. "Has Sin been around?"

"Sin took care of her today when we had therapy. It went well. She seemed like she was happy. No issues with either Sin or Asylum, er, Mirage."

"I see."

"Sin is getting better."

"Fuck him," his words were bitter. "He pisses me off."

"I think he wants her. Seriously. His attention was all on her today. He was barely able to hold a conversation with us."

"He can want what he wants. Doesn't mean he'll get it."

I sighed. I didn't want to argue the fact. Time would sort it all out. I still had a bit of it to get over, and Church clearly did.

"And Asylum?" Church pressed. "Or Mirage. Whatever the fuck name he's using now."

"I don't know. He wasn't around today."

Church grunted. "Just watch her. I think he means well, but he is fucking weird."

I laughed at that. "I know."

"OK. It's late. I have to get up and kill people tomorrow. I'll talk to you later."

"Night," I said.

"Go take care of our girl." He disconnected the call, leaving me in silence.

I smiled down at the black screen, deciding to fuck with him.

I took a picture of my dick and sent it to him.

A moment later, he sent me a middle finger emoji with a laughing face.

I grinned at that, hoping it helped him relax, and cleaned up before returning to Ashes and Sirena.

They'd both fallen asleep, him still inside her, his dick beginning to finally soften. I chuckled softly at him and his cock warming before covering them with the blanket and sliding in beside them.

"Night, Malachi," Ashes mumbled sleepily.

I twined my fingers with Sirena's.

"Night, Asher."

# MIRAGE

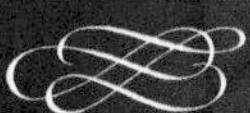

The night air was cold on my skin as I raced through the dark forest, my breath coming out in heavy white puffs. I ran and ran as if I could escape my demons. I was no fool. I was a demon.

I skidded to a halt at the edge of the woods and stared out at the dark, snow-covered cemetery before I made my way to the mausoleum and stared up at it, my white rabbit mask in place.

This was where Asylum took her. Where he made us players in a game where there were no real winners.

*We always win.*

I scoffed at the familiar voice in my head. Closing my eyes, I let my head fall back, feeling the darkness creeping around inside me.

*Inside us.*

*Please, not now.*

*Why not?*

*Because I only want to be. . . me.*

*But we are we.*

*Let me, please. Just for. . . now. I-I want to have this. On my own. I never get to. . .*

All went quiet in my head for a moment before that familiar voice came back.

*Fine. Win her over. We need her.*

*I'm trying. It's hard to get her alone.*

*Church is gone. Go to her. You know she will come to you. And for you.*

*I'm not doing that.*

*I have.*

*Not the way she'd have wanted.*

More silence

*Make a damn move, or I'm taking over.*

*I will. Give me time. Please.*

*Tick tock, little rabbit.*

My head went quiet, and I opened my eyes and stared back at the moon.

I'd make a move tomorrow. Tonight was meant for the forest.

✝

"YOU'RE QUIET," Sin commented as we sat in the cafeteria the following day. I'd barely slept, but that was how life for me was. I'd been this way since I'd lost Sirena. Asylum bitched at me about it because it would give me dark circles around my eyes. He hated it.

Whatever. He hated a lot of things about me. The scars. The turmoil. The way I could get too violent when pushed too far. At least the depression had gotten better since Sirena came back to us.

*You know I fucking love you.*

I sighed, ignoring the voice, and looked across the cafeteria. I hated winters here. We were stuck inside with snow up to our backbones. The summers were short, but at least we could be outside. Seasonal depression was a real thing. I didn't care what any of these bitch nuns argued.

Just read the Bible. It'll cure everything.

That's what they shoved down our throats.

I'd read the Bible. I was still sick.

"I'm tired," I answered, wondering where the hell Sirena was. I hadn't seen her today. I hadn't seen the guys either, and that was unusual. I mentioned as much.

"I saw them this morning," Sin said, picking at his French fries.

That offered me some semblance of relief. I shifted awkwardly, wishing there was a better way to carry carrots on me instead of my back pocket since sitting on them made my back hurt.

"Good." I turned back to my food and frowned. "I don't even think these fries are made out of potatoes. We kept one in a fish tank for two months, and it never spoiled."

"How do you know it didn't spoil?" Sin held a fry and looked to me. "Didn't it get furry or some shit?"

I shrugged. "No. We ate it. Still tasted the same."

"Fucking gross." He shook his head. "And why was it in a fish tank?"

"Asylum. He named it Kevin."

"You had a French fry named Kevin?"

"*Asylum* had a French fry named Kevin. I had a science project."

"Fucking weirdos," he said, going back to his plastic sticks. Er, French fries.

He wasn't wrong.

"This sucks. Want to go do some listening?" I dropped my gross fry onto my tray.

"Listening? I don't know if you got the memo, but I'm not psychic or whatever you are."

I rolled my eyes at him. "I meant to see if we could hear anything about what happened to Sirena that night. Someone is bound to talk."

Sin stiffened. He said nothing for a moment before he dropped his fry onto his tray and got to his feet. "Let's go."

I was quick to join him. We left the cafeteria and walked the hall in silence for several long moments. We passed a few of the wards who paid us no mind.

"What are you thinking?" he finally asked me.

"That we should talk to Danny Linley. He had a thing for her. It's why he got his ass kicked."

"You mean carved?" Sin raised his brows at me.

"Same thing."

"Definitely not. Ask Andrews about that."

"You mean Vanilla?" I chuckled at that name.

"He might be one of those quiet freaks." He shrugged. "You know how that goes. I think of him as more of a shadow. Always around. Slinking. I'm sure he knows all sorts of Chapel Crest secrets."

"Shadow," I mused. "He could be a spicy little pepper. I know he wants Sirena."

Sin let out a snort. "He had her. Clearly, that shit didn't pan out."

"He didn't have her like the watchers had her. Like I had her."

"You didn't have her. Asylum did."

"She was mine before anyone else's," I said fiercely. "Everyone who gets to hold her should be grateful I'm willing to share. Not many would be so willing to share their corpse bride."

"Corpse bride? That's morbid." Sin glanced at me. "You do realize she's alive, right?"

"She was dead to me, Sinclair. I-I thought I'd lost her forever," I said, my heart aching with all those ugly memories I had from that time in my life. "Hearing she was alive has changed everything. And now I get to be here."

We stopped, and he turned to face me.

"For how long?" he asked.

"Forever if I can help it."

"And Asylum?"

I let out a soft chuckle and cocked my head to the right. "I can't seem to shake him, but he loves her, and I do love him, so I guess that's OK."

Sin stared me down and looked like he was going to say something, but he narrowed his eyes and moved past me.

I turned to see what he was looking at and saw Danny Linley round the corner.

"Perfect." I stalked forward, Sin at my side.

Danny caught sight of us and stopped in his tracks, his eyes wide as saucers.

"Hello, Danny," I said, circling him in the opposite direction of Sin. "Just the guy we were looking for."

"A-Asylum. I-I swear. I've stayed away from her. I-I jerked off to a picture of her last night, but I swear, I've not gone near her—"

"My name is Mirage," I snarled in his ear. "Say it."

"M-Mirage," he choked out, squeezing his eyelids together.

"Now forget it," I instructed. "Because I am he, and he is me, and we are we."

Danny snotted and blubbered, nodding his head, his body shaking. "O-OK."

"Prove to me you're not the piece of shit who touched my girl in the woods," Sin snarled out, nose to nose with Danny.

"I-I'm not. I swea-swear I'm not. I didn't. I didn't, Sin. Fuck, man. I didn't."

Sin raised his knee and connected it with Danny's stomach, making him double over and fall to his knees.

I cocked my head to the right, watching Sin work. He was really something.

"Tell me what you know," Sin demanded.

"I-I don't know anything. I didn't even know Sirena went to the woods without Ch-Church."

Sin tangled his fingers in Danny's greasy hair and tugged his head back.

"You swear you don't know anything?"

Danny's Adam's apple bobbed, and he nodded.

"Then find out who hurt her in the woods for me. I want that fucking information."

"W-why do you think I can get it?" Danny whimpered.

"Because you're Danny-fucking-Linley. Your life is spent at the bottom of the fucking barrel, trying to scrape by. It's where the monster is who touched my girl. Who hurt my siren. I want a fucking name."

"O-OK. I-I need an incentive m-maybe. . ."

"How about this?" I asked, bending so I was eye to eye with him. "If you get us a name, the right name, I'll not turn your trachea into my new wind instrument. How does that sound?"

"I-you're going to kill me if I don't get it?"

"Oh, I won't kill you," I said, smiling at him as I pulled the carrot out of my back pocket and bit into it before chewing slowly.

Danny's gaze darted around, clearly terrified.

"Look at me," I instructed.

His gaze snapped to mine, and he opened his mouth to speak, but I jammed my carrot deep into his maw, making him sputter and choke as I held it there.

"If you don't fucking get us what we want, I'll let Asylum out to play. You remember how fun he is, right?"

Danny let out a choked, garbling noise before I drove the carrot deeper. His face turned bright red, tears dripping down his cheeks.

I cocked my head to the right at him again and smiled.

"Do we have a deal? Blink once for yes. Twice if you're ready to die."

Danny blinked once and stared fiercely at me.

"Perfect." I pulled my carrot free from his mouth. He let out a shuddering breath, coughing and wheezing roughly as I tossed the carrot to the ground. Sin released his hair, and Danny fell forward to his hands and knees, trying to suck in mouthfuls of air.

"Keep that. A token to remember this moment by." I backed away from him, Sin coming with me. Movement caught my eye, and I swiveled my head swiftly to see a shadow dart away. With narrowed eyes, I watched the spot where I'd seen someone before I smiled.

*A shadow indeed...*

I'd give our shadow a freebie this time.

"A name, Danny," Sin called out. "Sooner rather than later."

Danny said nothing, but his soft cries let me know he was on the same page as us.

"Why the fuck do you carry carrots in your back pocket?" Sin asked as we walked down the hall, Danny's whimpers fading away.

"For times such as these, Sinclair." I gave him a megawatt smile.

He shook his head at me. "You might be crazier than Asylum."
I smiled at that.
It wasn't the first time I'd heard that. I doubted it would be the last.

# CHURCH

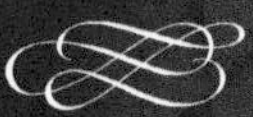

*I* watched from a dark corner as she sang.

She was breathtaking. Beautiful. Long, red waves. Bright green eyes. The voice of an angel. Her energy was palpable. And she was untouchable.

Her men were everything to her. And the spare.

I studied the pair with narrowed eyes as the Archangel kept close to her side. Everyone in the Underground knew who the Archangel was. A monster created from the sins of the very man who took him in.

He just didn't know he'd spent most of his life doing the bidding of the very same man who put him in the position he was in now.

Well, mostly.

Being neutral in our world only went so far, and money talked.

When the Ivanovs sent a messenger to my father to meet with them, he'd done so, dragging me along for the adventure.

Kill Delilah Beyers, the former mistress of Matteo De Santis. Kill her children. Kill the heir.

I was a child, still learning the ropes, but I'd seen the dark sparkle in my father's eye that night. He saw their mistake in requesting his help, so he jumped on it.

*"You want the family dead?" Father asked, surveying Sergio Ivanov and his men on the docks, the moon hanging over our heads.*

*"Yes. Take out the heirs. My son will handle his remaining heir at Bolten." Sergio eyed my father.*

*Father looked to one of Ivanov's men situated behind and next to him and smiled before dragging his attention back to Ivanov. I noted he focused on two in particular in the background.*

*"What of payment?"*

*"Two million dollars. Half now. Half when the job is done."*

*Father nodded and was quiet for a moment. "Have you met my heir? Dante?"*

*Ivanov focused on me, a muscle along his jaw thrumming.*

*"I've only heard. . . things."*

*"All good, I'm sure," Father said with a soft, wicked laugh.*

*"Of course. He is. . . remarkable."*

*"Indeed. I thought tonight would be a good night to demonstrate his skills."*

*Ivanov shifted uncomfortably, his men taking steadier stances.*

*"How so?" he asked.*

*"I'm not happy with the payment. I'd like to negotiate."*

*"Oh?" Ivanov cast a glance at me. I hadn't moved an inch. I wanted to go home and hang out with Stitches. He was alone. He didn't like to be alone.*

*"More money?" Ivanov gave a wobbly smile.*

*"No. Money isn't an issue. What I require is. . . dinner."*

*"Dinner?" Ivanov blanched, clearly understanding where the conversation was leading. "Surely, we can arrange a nice restaurant—"*

*"I prefer to have my chefs do my cooking."*

*"I see." Ivanov visibly swallowed. "What is it that you'd like?"*

*"Well, it seems as if you need this Beyers woman dealt with in order to move pieces on your board so you can come into power after assassinating Matteo De Santis. With his older brother. . . gone. . . and Carmine out of the game, you stand to win it all. I'd say two million isn't really up to snuff for me." Father smiled. "And if you go elsewhere now that I know your plan, you risk me telling De Santis. We both know you'll be unlikely to kill me tonight, and it would be impossible once I walk away. So. Dinner. I require sacrifice."*

*Ivanov studied my father for a long, tense moment.*

*"Who?" Ivanov finally asked.*

*A tiny smirk cut my father's lips upward before he nodded his head to the quiet man standing behind Ivanov and the one next to him who looked scared.*

*"I want that one and the one beside him."*

*Ivanov looked over his shoulder to the tall man, his face visibly paling.*

*"I cannot give you him—"*

*"Then we don't have a deal." Father inclined his head at Ivanov. "Come, Dante, perhaps some ice cream would hit the spot—"*

*"Wait." Ivanov squeezed his eyelids closed as we turned back around to face him. "I-I'm sorry, Nathaniel," he whispered, stepping aside.*

*The quiet man's eyes widened, and he took a step back. That was nothing because our men were quick to descend on him. It was the nervous man who darted off into the night.*

*"Dante." Father stared directly into Ivanov's eyes as Nathaniel tried to fight off our men. "See to it that you catch our dinner. I do so love fast food."*

*I didn't hesitate.*

*I loved the hunt, and he knew it.*

*I caught sight of the man dart into the woods. What I loved more than the hunt was the woods. Smiling, I swept forward into the night, my knife clutched tightly in my hand.*

"Hey, handsome. Can I get you something?" A pretty brunette asked, breaking me out of my memory.

I stared idly at her through the pulsing club lights.

"Unlikely."

She offered me a coy smile and reached out to touch me, but I was quick to wrap my fingers around her wrist.

She let out a cry, her eyes filled with fear as I leaned in and narrowed my eyes at her.

"Why do you think you can touch me?" I demanded in a low growl.

"I-I just thought you'd like some company—"

"If I didn't request it, then how could you arrive at that conclusion?"

"Please, you're hurting me—"

"Go." I released her. She stumbled backward but didn't waste any time putting space between us as she scrambled through the crowded club.

Ready to get out of there, I moved along the back of the club toward the exit. I saw him before he saw me.

Deciding I'd fuck with fate, I didn't move aside when he passed by me.

*Lorenzo De Luca.*

His shoulder knocked into mine. He didn't even bother to turn to look at me. He simply kept going.

It was all I needed to know.

He thought of himself as being at the top of the world. No one was worthy of a second look. Or even a first.

I smiled at that.

That's the sort of thing that could get a guy into trouble.

He'd find that out soon enough.

# SIRENA

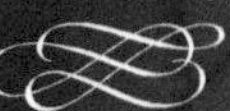

*I miss Church.*

I scrawled the words across Ashes's palm three weeks after Church had left us. He hardly ever called. From what I understood, Ashes had asked him about that. His answer was that it was easier not to. That he trusted everything was going well here for us.

I supposed that translated into no news was good news, but that didn't make me miss him any less.

"I know, baby." Ashes kissed the top of my head. We'd just finished eating dinner and were relaxing on the couch.

The urge to go to my room and take a photo of myself, then send it to Church was overwhelming me. The little dark part of my soul was definitely encouraging it.

"Want to smoke?" Stitches asked, pulling a joint out and looking to Ashes.

"Fuck, why not." Ashes got up, but not before kissing my head again. Stitches tilted my chin up and dropped a sweet kiss on my lips before he went out to the back patio with Ashes. Ashes's lighter's red glow illuminated them for a moment as they lit the joint.

Deciding it was now or never, I went upstairs to Church's room, my phone in hand, and lay in his bed in my white nightgown.

Carefully, I took a photo of myself sprawled in his bed, hoping I looked seductive and not like a nervous wreck. I'd never sent anything racy to anyone in my life. My goal was to get him to video home. He hadn't done that yet with me. It was always to the guys. Even all his calls were made to Ashes or Stitches. None to me. I didn't expect him to call, though. It wasn't like I could blame him. Who would want to call and listen to someone breathe on the other end?

Instead, he'd call one of the guys, and they'd relay his messages to me. He missed me. He'd be home soon.

But soon wasn't coming fast enough, and I was growing frustrated.

Drawing in a deep breath, I sent him the photo and waited nervously for his reply.

It felt like forever that I stared at his ceiling before my phone buzzed. Excitedly, I looked to see that he was requesting a video call with me.

Using a shaky finger, I accepted the request.

His handsome face came onto the screen.

"Specter," he greeted me in his deep voice. "My naughty girl."

My heart banged hard as he leaned forward, his shirt off.

"What are you doing all alone in my bed? Where are Ashes and Stitches?"

I bit my lip and moved the camera so he could see the window. Hopefully, he got my meaning.

He smirked at me. "I understand. So you thought you'd tease me?"

I stared at him, noting how tired he looked. All I wanted to do was reach through the screen and hug him. Thinking about the awful things he was doing at home made my stomach twist with a sickness I didn't know I could have.

"Well." He sat back and raised his brows at me. "Take off your clothes so I can see you, baby."

I stayed sitting for a moment before I got up, propped my phone on his dresser, and backed away. Slowly, I removed my nightgown, panties, and bra, my arms moving to cover the scars I now had.

"I want to see all of you," he husked out while sitting in his chair, smoking something.

I let my arms fall away so he could see me.

"Fuck, you're beautiful," he said, his voice thick with want. "You don't know how much I've missed you, specter. You're in every fucking thought I have."

My heart lifted at his words.

"Give me something else to think about, OK? Can you do that for me, baby?"

I gave him a small nod that seemed to please him because he smiled.

"I want you to lay on the bed with your legs spread. Can you do that?"

I hesitated for a moment before moving back to the bed and doing as he requested, my nerves taking over, making my legs tremble.

"Relax, baby. This is the fun part. I promise. Spread your legs for me so I can see that pretty pink pussy."

I felt the heat sweep over my body, but I spread my legs wider for him.

"There you go. I like that."

I watched as he pulled his dick out and stroked it slowly, his green eyes filled with want.

"Do you have any idea what I want to do to you right now?"

I shook my head, not sure what I would even say if I could say anything.

He chuckled as he continued to stroke himself.

"Touch yourself for me." His words sent a shiver up my spine. Nervously, I let my fingers wander between my legs and gingerly slid my fingers through the folds, noting the wetness.

"Fuck, you're a real sweet girl, aren't you?" His deep voice sent goosebumps popping along my skin. "Taste yourself for me."

I blinked, nervous about doing such a thing.

"What's wrong? Scared?" He let out a soft laugh. "Don't be scared. I promise that pussy tastes like magic, baby. Do it. It'll make me so fucking turned on to see you do that for me."

I drew in a calming breath and put my damp fingers to my lips, and sucked on them. The groan that slipped from his lips made me ache with want inside.

"Fuck, what are you doing to me, specter?" he called out, stroking himself faster. "I want you to come with me, baby. Fuck your tight pussy with your fingers."

I'd never done anything like this before.

Nearly deciding this was too much for me, I paused, the little bit of darkness peeking out to survey what I was doing.

Maybe it wasn't darkness. Maybe it was bravery. Bravery that was angry and fed up with being who I was. I wanted to be more. I wanted people to know I couldn't be messed with. I couldn't be pushed around.

I'd spent my life being a ghost.

That needed to end.

But fear... fear was who I was right now.

"Specter?" Church's deep voice interrupted my confusing thoughts.

I squeezed my eyelids closed and ran my fingers through my damp folds, the sparks of electricity soaring through me.

With my breathing ragged, I touched myself for Church, earning his groan of approval.

"Push a finger into your pussy for me. There you go. That's my girl," he rasped.

Opening my eyes again, I slid my finger in and out for him, doing everything he demanded of me.

"Fuck yourself for me, baby. Two fingers. Perfect. There you go. God, you look so fucking perfect right now." His movements had become faster, his breathing heavier. "Rub your clit now. Yeah, just like that. Go faster for me. Can you go faster?"

I did as he instructed, the heat slowly taking hold of me.

"Squeeze your tit, specter. Yes, perfect. Like that. You enjoy touching yourself for me?"

I nodded, feeling breathless from the impending pleasure stirring between my legs.

"Fuck, you look good like that. When I get home, I'm going to fuck you so hard you'll scream for me. I love it when you scream."

I worked my finger quicker, continuing to squeeze my breast, before I rolled my nipple between my fingers.

"Look at me. Eyes on me, specter," he grunted, his hand moving like a blur along his cock. "When you come, I want me to be the one you see. Understand?"

I let out a soft whimper of confirmation that made him groan.

It hit me like a ton of bricks. The heat. The pleasure. It rolled through my body.

I came hard, my eyes on him, my release gushing free from me in a wet mess, soaking his sheets. His feral groan followed, letting me know he'd gotten off with me.

We both sat panting for several long moments before Church let out a soft laugh.

"Oh, specter. You are so full of surprises."

I sat and pulled his sheet over my body. He'd moved the phone so it was focused on his handsome face, his green eyes illuminated in the light from the screen. I brought the phone closer to my face and stared at him, missing him so much my heart hurt.

"I'm coming home soon," he said gently. "I'm sorry I don't call as much as I should. Honestly, specter, it pains me to see you and know I'm not there. Seeing you makes me want you even more, and that's dangerous when I'm here, but fuck, baby, I miss you." He exhaled. "I love you more than life itself, Sirena. I'm always watching over you. I'll be home soon, OK?"

I nodded, my eyes burning with unshed tears.

"Thank you for tonight. Soon, I will hold you in my arms again and make love to you in our cemetery. Be my sweet, strong girl. Keep the guys happy, but give them hell when you need to. I like knowing they're scrambling." He smiled at me as I wiped at my eyes. "I would slay the entire world for you, Sirena. Sweet dreams, my little ghost."

The feed cut off, leaving me in silence and sadness.

The call should have made me feel better, but it made me feel worse. All I wanted was to hold him. Love him. Be with him. All of us together, but as long as his father and the monsters were calling the shots, it would be this way.

What I needed to do was find Adam and just start the fight here and now.

The darkness ebbed through me, making me inhale deeply.

I focused on it, feeling it taint the edges of my light.

Someday, I'd have to be brave enough to embrace it. Today wasn't that day, though.

Today, I curled around Church's pillow and closed my eyes, wishing I could change things and knowing that without strength, I'd never get to. Wishing I could love the men I loved, all of them, even the ones I dare not whisper their names.

Maybe tomorrow would change it all.

It was the best I could hope for.

# SIN

"Sin! Hey, wait up," Ashes called out, trotting down the hallway toward me. I stopped and waited for him, taking in how he seemed exhausted with the dark circles around his blue eyes and the way his smile wasn't quite as bright as I was used to seeing.

It felt like too long since I'd been alone with Sirena. When they didn't need me, I kept my distance as promised, but it was eating me up inside to be a silent bystander.

"Hey," I greeted him. "Uh, what's up?" I winced at the gnawing ache on my side. I'd whipped myself earlier that morning, and the wounds were tender on my broken skin.

"I was wondering if you could hang out with Sirena tonight. I need to burn, and I don't want to take her out into the cold. Plus, I don't want her to freak out since we'll be in the woods." He sighed. "I think her being home in the warmth would be best."

"So just you and Stitches would be going out?"

"And me." Mirage joined us, his rabbit mask in place.

Ashes raised his brows at Mirage. "You want to come with us?"

"Yes. I already know that I will, so there is no sense fighting it." He winked at Ashes, who didn't even look interested in fighting it.

Instead, we stopped our walk and made a small circle to converse.

"You look different today," Ashes said, narrowing his eyes at Mirage.

Mirage grinned. "Do I? How so? Same mask. Same...smile."

"I don't know. Did you cut your hair or something?"

"No. I brushed it, though."

Ashes chuckled. "Do you not brush your hair?"

"Some of us aren't responsible like that, Asher. I'm lucky if I can find my carrot in the morning."

"He means the vegetable," I cut in. "Not his dick. He always has that in his hand."

"Fuck you." Mirage chortled. "Asshole. You're one to talk."

I caught the small smile on Ashes's face at our bantering and fixed one on my face that, for once, didn't feel so forced.

"I lived with Sin. I know too much about his carrot issues," Ashes said, bumping his shoulder with mine.

It almost felt like the old days when I was still a watcher. The smile faltered on my lips at the thought that now I was just the odd man out, looking in.

"So, Sirena?" Ashes looked to me.

"Uh, yeah. I, um, I can do that."

"Awesome. Thanks, man. I set Stitches's homework on fire in the sink this morning."

I winced at that. It wasn't often Stitches even bothered with homework, so for Ashes to have burned it on him. . .

"Hey." Stitches rounded the corner with Sirena and joined us, his arm around her waist.

Her colorful eyes met mine for the briefest moment, making my heart lurch with want. I inhaled deeply to calm myself before watching her gaze move to Mirage. I studied them, noting Ashes and Stitches weren't paying attention as they talked.

Mirage's blue eyes sparkled, a tiny smirk on his lips as he stared back at her. Her cheeks darkened a pretty pink color, and her bottom lip pulled between her teeth.

I wondered if he was doing some head shit with her. He told me he couldn't read minds, but that didn't make me believe anything because he still always knew things.

It wasn't a secret to me that Mirage and Asylum wanted her and wouldn't stop until she was theirs. Sometimes I wished I had their stamina for getting their lives fucked up by Church and the guys. And their hearts because I wasn't so sure any of this was going to work out for anyone.

Especially once Church figured out she had room in her heart for the psycho.

"Faith, Sinclair." Mirage's voice pulled me out of my thoughts.

"What?" I blinked at him, stopping Stitches and Ashes's conversation.

"Faith. It's what you lack. Have some, OK?" Mirage's voice was gentle, but he was the gentler one if I had to label him. He was also more unpredictable than Asylum was. Sometimes, though, it was hard to tell where one ended and the other began.

I pushed my hand into my pocket and felt the rosary Sirena had given me. I'd prayed with it every night since I'd gotten it. I'd even gone to the lake and sat in the cold, looking out at the frozen water, making wishes and saying prayers I hoped were heard.

I offered Mirage a brittle smile and looked to my feet.

"OK, well, that was weird, but what did I expect?" Stitches called out. "Asylum, man, you're nuts. Anyone ever tell you that?"

"I'm Mirage," Mirage said instantly. "Not Asylum."

Stitches rolled his eyes. "You're nuts."

"I don't disagree." Mirage shrugged, still smiling. "So. Heard your homework got torched."

Stitches let out a sigh. "Ashes set it on fire this morning in the kitchen."

"It wasn't like you did it," Ashes shot back.

"Dude, I did, like, three questions on there."

"Malachi, you literally wrote, *Fuck this. Fuck that. Fuck you.* That doesn't qualify as doing your homework."

"*Asher,* I was going to finish it."

I looked to see what Sirena's take on the entire thing was. She was watching, the tiniest smile teasing her plump lips.

I licked mine, remembering what it was like to kiss her. She'd been so out of it when I'd last kissed her. Drugged. Hadn't even kissed me back.

How I wondered what it would be like for her to kiss me the way she kissed the guys.

But I knew it wasn't going to happen. Church made it abundantly clear there was no way in hell, but the Mirage/Asylum ordeal told me to get in there and play anyway. That she chose.

I tightened my hand around the rosary in my pocket, my thoughts getting progressively more morose, until I felt Sirena shift beside me, the guys continuing their bantering.

It took me a moment to realize she'd slid a note into my pocket.

My heartbeat thundered in my ears at the prospect of what she'd written to me.

I cast a quick glance to her only to see her watching the guys with a hint of amusement on her pretty face.

"Hey, asslicks." Cady came into the fray. "And Rina."

"Cadence, never a pleasure," Stitches said, no venom in his words.

"Haha, douche nozzle." Cady rolled her eyes at him before looking to Ashes. "It's Friday. That means burning?"

Ashes smiled and nodded at her. "You want in?"

"Does Seth Cain creep you out? Hell yeah, I want in," she proclaimed, jerking her thumb in Mirage's direction.

"Easy, Cady Cat," Mirage said easily. "You're not exactly giving off wholesome vibes with all the trash you've been dragging back to your room."

Cady stiffened and turned on Mirage.

"I know everything," he simply said with a shrug.

"What are you doing? Stalking me?" Cady countered, a curious look on her face.

"Well, I know you brought a certain someone to your room last night. Someone you don't want Sirena to know about."

Sirena's eyes widened before she looked to Cadence, whose face had gone red.

"We were just talking. He was apologizing for being a dick that night."

"Why hasn't he been in classes? Seen on campus?" Mirage countered.

I frowned, watching the exchange. Apparently, Stitches and Ashes were just as confused about what was going on because they watched with narrowed eyes and crinkled brows.

"Adam has a note. He's taking a mental health break," Cady said, her voice shaking.

I didn't give a shit about that, though. It was Sirena I cared about because her hand brushed the side of my leg before she turned tail and ran.

"What the fuck?" Stitches said, looking confused for a moment before he hauled ass after her. She was fast. I'd give her that.

"Uh, sorry. I gotta go," Ashes muttered before he loped off behind Stitches to get to Sirena, who had disappeared around a corner already.

I stood looking between Cady and Mirage, wanting some context.

"Adam was a dick one night," Cady explained, frowning. "He said some nasty shit about Sirena. Like extremely nasty. The guys kicked his ass and left him on the side of the road. He's been in and out of it since. It wasn't him," she continued, her blue eyes bright, her words making me think she was begging us to believe her. "He has different personalities. The one that night was one he hates. He wanted to apologize for what was said. He's been in the med facility and his dorm, trying to get his mental health back on track."

I'd heard Adam Larson was a real prick. We all had mental health shit going on here, so it was hard to discern when people were truly being pricks or when it was something going on with them mentally. I supposed there was an argument for both sides of that coin, one I didn't have the desire to debate.

All I knew was if he got his ass kicked by the watchers, he must have fucked up badly. Church didn't typically beat you to near death unless you really pissed him off. He was levelheaded like that.

And Ashes certainly didn't. He was the calm, collected one. If he was angry enough to beat a motherfucker, chances are, it was deserved.

"Why are you trying to convince me?" Mirage asked.

"I'm not. I'm just saying we talked. He told me what happened—"

"Cadence, I say this to you as someone who cares about Sirena," Mirage cut in. "But fuck that guy. He's not worth it."

"You don't even know him, Seth—"

"I know her," he interjected. "And if it makes her uncomfortable, why would you want him around? Clearly, the shit he did bothered her. It bothered the guys enough to beat his ass. Did it bother you?"

She stared up at him for a moment. "Yes."

"Then why entertain his excuses? Mental health or not, it upset her. He could snap and do it again. Why risk it?"

She chewed her bottom lip nervously, a look of defeat on her face.

"Cadence," Mirage called out, moving into her space and resting his hands on her biceps. "Look at me."

She forced her gaze to his.

"He's not worth it. She's come a long way. She's been through a lot."

"I-I know," she whispered. "I just, I'm always living my life around hers. I love her so much, but I-I—"

"Are being selfish," I said.

Both she and Mirage looked at me, her eyes wide.

"It's OK to be selfish," I explained, my voice soft. "As long as it doesn't hurt anyone. When it starts to hurt those we love, we need to examine the reasons we're doing it. If those reasons don't align with who we are deep in our hearts, then it's time to back away from them."

"Sinclair, I didn't think you had it in you," Mirage said, a smile working its way onto his lips. "You know what you've experienced?"

I crinkled my brows in confusion at him. "What?"

"Personal growth," he said. "Nice."

I blinked at his words, rolling over what I'd said. It had been like some forgotten part of my soul had spoken those words.

"Cadence." Mirage focused on her again. "Sin is right. You can forgive the guy for his mistake, but that doesn't mean you need to let him occupy your time. OK?"

She nodded. "OK."

"Now smile for me."

"Go to hell."

"I already live there," he murmured, chucking her in the jaw before backing away. "Go on now. Git."

"I'm not a dog," she said, scowling at him.

He unearthed a carrot from his back pocket and bit into it, chewing as he considered her.

"No, you're more like a cat, aren't you, kitten?"

"You're so weird."

"Like a mangy kitten."

She gave him the finger and turned to leave.

"Cadence?"

"What, psycho?" She stopped and turned to look at him.

Mirage bit into his carrot again. "There are better men out there than Adam."

"Like you?" She smirked at him. "You want my sister. Are you doing it because you love her, or are you selfish?"

"Both," he answered simply.

Her lips parted as she stared at him, apparently surprised at his honest, direct answer.

"You're not good enough for my sister."

"No, but sometimes the bad guy wins." He offered her a smile that didn't quite reach his eyes.

She shook her head at him and left us.

We didn't say a word until she'd rounded the corner and disappeared.

"I wonder what little old Adam said to upset Church and the watchers. I wonder what he did to scare Rinny." Mirage stared at the space where Cady had disappeared.

"We could always just ask the guys," I said, knowing Ashes would be the one to go to. He'd answer without dancing around it.

The edge of Mirage's lips curled up. "We could, or. . ."

"Or what?"

"We could pay a visit to Adam. I get a much better feeling from people when I'm near them."

"Yeah? Or do you mean when you're choking them?"

He chuckled. "Same thing, right?"

I shook my head. "In your world, I suppose it is."

✝

WE DIDN'T FIND ADAM. He wasn't on campus or in his room. His name wasn't registered as the day's patients in the med facility, so we simply returned to classes. I was bored out of my head in some Bible course when I remembered Sirena's note.

Eagerly, I pulled it from my pocket and stared at the perfect square in my hand before glancing around to make sure no one was watching me. Satisfied no one was, I carefully unfolded the paper, my heart bumping a hard rhythm in my chest.

Her words were scrawled perfectly across the page.

*Sinful,*

*I had a good time with you the other day. I know it's been quite some time since then, but I needed to tell you how I felt. I'm trying to be a stronger person. A better person. It's not only for myself but for everyone who has to be around me. I don't like being me sometimes, and I get the feeling you don't like being you sometimes, either.*

*Stitches told me they were going to ask you to stay with me tonight. I hope I'm not out of line when I say I'm looking forward to seeing you. I want to get over the trauma of our past and move forward. I hope you want the same. I feel like we've both changed a lot since then and are better for it.*

*Hopefully, I'll see you later. Maybe we could watch another movie? Or we could talk like this. I really enjoyed it.*

*Yours,*

*Sirena*
*PS- You make the best macaroni and cheese.*


I SWALLOWED hard and reread her note before scrawling a reply back to her on it.


*SIREN,*

*I would love to watch a movie with you, and if you're feeling up to it, I could teach you how to make that macaroni and cheese.*

*I want to move forward too. It's just. . . a lot. I struggle. It's easier writing that rather than saying it. It doesn't hurt so much that way.*

*Anyway, I look forward to seeing you tonight.*

*I'll bring a notebook with me so we can talk if you'd like.*

*Yours,*

*Sinful*


I STARED down at my note to her, my heart in my throat. I knew it was only a note, but I'd never even remotely opened up like that to anyone before. I hope it didn't come back to bite me in the ass. The bell rang then, signaling the end of class, and I got up. When I reached the door, I spotted Bryce in the hall.

Quickly, I pushed my way through to him and tapped him on the shoulder.

He turned, a copper-colored curl bouncing on his forehead, his hazel eyes wide. Maybe he expected to get punched or something. I had no idea. In fact, I didn't even know why he was here. He seemed rather normal and boring.

"Hey, I need you to do something for me," I said, clutching the note tightly in my hand.

"What?" He visibly tensed.

"You're in Sirena's class next, right?"

"Yeah. Why?"

I held out the note to him. "Make sure she gets this. Don't fucking open it, or I'll break your pretty face. Got it?"

"Yeah. Yeah, I got it." He took the note from me and put it into his pocket. "That it?"

"Yes. Just. . . make sure she gets it."

He nodded, and I stepped aside from him to pass through. I watched him go, really hoping I wouldn't have to kick his ass.

# BRYCE

*I* clutched the note Sin had given me and went to class to find Sirena already seated. Carefully, I moved past the throng of standing students all chatting and went to the seat next to her.

"Hey," I greeted her.

She turned and offered me a smile, which made me relax. After the events at the watchers' house with her freaking out, I hadn't been able to talk to her. She'd avoided me, or I'd been out of class, doing mundane office things. My grades were the highest at Chapel Crest, so it was nothing for me to randomly be pulled out to do office work for the lazy women who should have been doing it.

I licked my lips. "Sirena? Uh, Sin gave me a note for you." I pulled it out of my pocket and handed it to her. Not wanting to get Sin's fist implanted in my face, I hadn't read it.

She took the note, her face brightening.

My heart fell. She was going to give him the time of day after he'd screwed up with her and that damn mausoleum shit.

But I didn't know why I thought differently. Sirena was a sweet girl, plain and simple. Of course, she had forgiveness within her

I cleared my throat, watching as she read the note, her lips curling up higher.

My curiosity was getting the best of me now. She never spoke to anyone, so seeing her writing notes to a guy who tried to hurt her made me frown. And if I were being truthful, it made me have a little self-loathing because she certainly wasn't giving me the time of day.

She'd really gotten beneath my skin and had gone straight to my damn heart since she'd arrived here. I cared about her more than I ever cared for anyone before in my life. I didn't know how to get her to see that. To even give me a damn chance.

I knew my competition.

There was simply no way in hell I was going to make the cut.

Instead, I'd just be here for whatever she needed. I'd rather have her as my friend than nothing at all, even if it hurts.

She finished her letter and turned to me with hopeful eyes.

Like I could say no to her.

Sighing, I held out my hand, and she was quick to place the note back into it. After stuffing it in my pocket, Sister Hazel began her droning, so I sat still in my seat, tuning her out.

The damn note was burning a hole in my pocket, though. I wanted to know what was going on. If nothing else, as a way to protect her. I knew Church was gone. It made sense Sin would try to wiggle his way back in.

By the end of class, I was beside myself. My decision had been made. I was going to see what was going on. If it was bad, I'd reach out to Church and let him know. Because I'd seen Ashes and Stitches chumming around with both Asylum—or Mirage as was the current name—and Sin on campus recently, I knew they were both slowly working their way in.

I was tired of being the odd man out. My whole life was spent on the outside, looking in.

Damnit, I wanted in this time.

Even if I didn't fit in with any of them except her. It was all that mattered. Her.

We got up when the bell rang, and I walked next to her out of the room like we used to do.

"So, um, do you want to talk?" I asked, feeling dumb as shit.

She pulled me to a stop and stared up at me, making my heart tumble awkwardly.

"Sirena?" My throat was tight.

She gave me a sweet smile and squeezed my hand, moves that all but broke me before leaving me alone in the hall and disappearing into another class.

Sighing, I stared at where she'd gone before my phone buzzed in my pocket. Figuring it was one of my friends, I pulled it out and saw her name on my screen. I blinked in surprise at it before fumbling to check the message from her.

> I do want to talk. Soon, OK? I'm trying to work through some stuff. It's a lot for me.

I stared at her message for a moment before quickly thumbing out my reply to her.

> OK. I'm here if you need me. . . cupcake.

I didn't want to push her on it, so I tried to play it cool and add a little nickname for her like the guys had. It was a feeble attempt at connecting with her on a different level.

After I hit send, however, I felt like an idiot.

I let out a groan at calling her cupcake. We'd eaten cupcakes a few times in her room since her arrival. She always seemed to really like them. It felt right to call her that, but now that it was out there in the wild, I wanted to kick myself.

*Chocolate. Cherry icing. Pink cupcake wrapper.*

The memory of our first cupcake together flashed through my mind, every detail recalled in perfect recollection, right down to the soft sound she'd made when she took her first bite and the damn fly that walked along her windowsill that had driven me nuts. I'd ignored it, not wanting to ruin our evening, but man, I hated flies.

I didn't expect a reply from her, but one came just moments later.

> I still think about that chocolate cupcake with the cherry frosting.

It wasn't her words that got me. It was the little heart emoji after them that swept me off. It probably didn't mean anything, but it came from her, so it meant something to me.

Smiling, I tucked my phone back into my pocket, vowing to get her another cupcake, before I headed out to where I figured I could find Sin.

✝

I DIDN'T OPEN the note.

As much as I'd wanted to, I was still high on Sirena's little heart emoji. Instead, when I reached him sitting in one of the quiet rooms I'd seen him go into a lot lately, I walked right up to him. I took a seat beside him in one of the overstuffed chairs and took out the note.

"Here." I handed it back to him. "She replied."

He took it wordlessly and opened it, a smile blooming on his lips.

I shifted in my seat, my guts tight.

"Must be good," I said softly. "If it has made you smile."

Sin folded the note and placed it into his leather jacket pocket before going back to staring at the wall.

He didn't say anything to me, but I couldn't let it go.

"She's a good person. Don't hurt her again."

He dragged his gaze to me, his face expressionless.

"I won't."

I nodded, not knowing what else to say. Instead of sticking around feeling like an idiot, I got up to leave.

"Bryce."

I turned to look at him.

"In another life, she could have used someone like you."

I let out a soft, sad laugh. "Yeah, but here we are. In hell."

"Here we are," he repeated sadly.

"And now she has you," I added.

He scoffed. "Does she? What she has is a dreamer. I'm not with her. Probably won't get the chance to be, but I do dream of it. It's all I have at this point."

I adjusted my backpack on my shoulder, getting what he was saying. "I'm a dreamer too, I guess."

He chuckled softly. "Welcome to hell, friend. You can sit next to me." He looked pointedly to the chair beside him.

To hell with it.

May as well join another demon in this hellhole.

Wasn't like I had anywhere else to be.

# SIRENA

"Sin is going to hang out with you tonight while we're gone," Ashes said, coming into the room wearing all black. He matched Stitches, whose arms were wound tightly around me on the couch.

"You're going to be good, right?" Stitches murmured in my ear.

I nodded for him, earning a kiss.

Truth be told, I was excited to see Sin tonight. I felt like we'd had a major breakthrough the last time we'd been together. I wasn't so scared to be around him now. I wasn't sure when that had happened. Perhaps it was when I realized I was afraid of nearly everything and needed to prioritize what I needed to truly be fearful of.

He didn't make my list.

Maybe it was because I knew my watchers would take care of him again if he toed out of line. Or maybe it was because I saw more than the sinner before me. I saw someone who was struggling and hurting like I was.

I saw someone broken and scared.

Sin was all of us. He just screamed it louder than we did.

And for that, I wanted to hold him close and let him know every-thing could be OK if he'd let it.

Like I was one to talk.

I was terrified of Adam. Everett. Sully. All the monsters hiding in the dark here.

I'd been waking up nearly every night with a nightmare of it all. Ashes was always so sweet over it, but it was Stitches who was the one to offer me the comfort. Not that Ashes didn't. It was simply that Stitches had lived through many of the horrors with me, and I knew he still struggled with them. We were sort of bonded in that darkness.

With Asylum.

I sighed, thinking of him. It was weird for him to not be around. But Mirage. I smiled at that. Mirage was. . . everything. They all were though.

Even Bryce.

I didn't really know when the transformation happened in my heart, but it was there. I felt for him. For Asylum. For Mirage. For Sin. For the watchers. It was a lot, and it made me feel overwhelmed. I didn't like to think about it, so I focused on one thing at a time.

Right now, it was getting Sin sorted so he could come home. Even if Church was angry, I knew Ashes was already past it, and Stitches was working on it. I just needed to get them all to see that even if Sin decided he wasn't interested in me, he was still a part of our family. Or his family since they were his way before they were mine.

I knew what love did to Sin.

It made him feel. It made him crazy. It made him kill.

I breathed out, untangled myself from Stitches, and went to Ashes, who hugged me against his body.

"I'll miss you, heaven."

I kissed his soft lips before pulling away and taking his hand in mine.

*I'll miss you too.*

He smiled at my words as the doorbell rang. Stitches answered it, and Sin stepped into the room a moment later, snowflakes in his blond hair and a notebook in his hand.

His gaze swept over me briefly, with no emotion on his face, before he focused on the guys.

"We won't be gone long," Ashes said, breaking away from me to go all business.

"Take your time. Get it out of your system, or you'll end up needing to go mid-week," Sin said knowingly.

Stitches nodded. "He's right. You do it every damn time you cut a burning short. Or you set something on fire in here."

Ashes grumbled out something before sighing. "You're right. Fine. Call if you need anything. We worry."

"She's in good hands. I have Cady's number. The psycho I live with. Bryce. Church. I don't have a shortage of people to call if I need something."

"Speaking of that psycho you live with," Stitches started. "How's that going? Is he that weird all the time?"

"He's. . . weird in different ways. Always. It's tiring." Sin looked to me. I knew what he meant. The switch probably made his head hurt. Always the same, yet always different. Unless you knew, you didn't know shit. Then again, I'd always known something was up. It took nearly dying and seeing my monster again to put the pieces together to get the full picture.

I didn't hate Asylum, though. I didn't even fear him anymore.

Not really. I mean, he was terrifying, but so was Mirage. And Sin. And all the guys.

But I'd decided I didn't want to hate any of them, so I didn't. There were far more important people out there who deserved my wrath than a couple of guys trying to get their heads in the right space.

"Does he watch you sleep at night? He reminds me of some creep who would watch you sleep," Stitches continued.

"Like Church?" Sin smirked at Stitches.

"You've got a point there. And to be fair, Church only watches Sirena at night." Stitches winked at me. "But something tells me baby girl likes that about him."

I winked back at him, making his grin bigger.

"He actually called me today," Ashes said after putting his boots on. "Church. He's been busy dealing with Everett's bullshit." Ashes moved his gaze to me quickly. I had no idea what he'd been doing. I tried to not dwell on it because I was scared of what Church was capable of in the hands of his father.

"Is everything OK?" Sin asked.

Stitches shrugged. "Is it ever?"

"Good point." Sin let out a sigh.

"Everett has him following around some people, learning about them. I think at some point Everett's going to call on him to do some real damage, aside from what he's already doing in the Underground."

Sin nodded and rubbed the back of his neck. "I see. Well, I'll be here to watch over Siren if that happens. Just text me."

Ashes and Stitches exchanged looks. It was Ashes who spoke, though.

"Maybe Church and you could talk when he gets back—"

"It's fine, Asher. I'm good. Really. I'm not going to bother him with my shit. I know what I did was fucked up. I'm making peace with the consequences. Even if they fucking hurt." He glanced at me, his Adam's apple bobbing.

He'd changed so much. He was still grouchy, but that exterior had become cracked and worn, and I was able to see the man beneath it. The one who wanted to love and be loved. The one I could even. . .

Damn.

I smiled at him, making the sadness in his gray eyes recede.

Stitches cleared his throat.

"Uh, we should get going. It's getting late. Angel, baby, don't do anything. . . well, don't do anything I wouldn't do. Keep Sin in line, OK?" He kissed me, lowering his voice. "I'm serious. I worry about you. Alone."

I squeezed his hand, letting him know I would be safe with Sin. It seemed Stitches still had his reservations despite the niceties happening between the three of them.

Stitches released me, and Ashes took his spot, kissing me slowly.

"I love you," he whispered against my lips. "We'll be back soon."

I nodded at him before going up on my toes for another kiss. He gave it freely before pulling his lighter out and flipping it open and closed five times, the flame burning bright for a moment before he snapped it closed and did it all over again.

"Sin, take care of our girl," Stitches called out once he got to the door.

"I will," Sin answered, inclining his head at them before they opened the door and left, leaving just me and Sin alone.

We stood staring at one another for a moment before Sin cleared his throat and gave me a nervous smile.

"I, uh, brought a notebook." He held up the black notebook for me to see. "And a pen."

I said nothing as I went to the couch to sit and looked over the back at him. He shuffled from foot to foot for a moment before he came over.

"Can, I mean, do you want me to sit next to you?" He seemed so bashful about it all, and it made me smile. I'd have never thought Sinclair Priest could be this nervous guy. He was always so cold, withdrawn, and rough.

I patted the cushion next to me. He moved forward and sat before he opened the notebook. I watched while he wrote quickly in it.

I wasn't sure why he didn't want to just speak to me, but I didn't hate that he wrote the notes. In fact, I rather liked the effort he put in.

**What do you want to do?**

I took the notebook from him and answered.

**Talk? I like doing this.**

He smiled at me, and I wrote another note.

**How are classes?**

He frowned and took the pen.

**Lame. I'm not a fan of school. I can't wait until I'm done.**

I studied his answer, wondering what he planned next in his life. The possible answer made me nervous because, ultimately, I hoped it had to do with me and the guys.

**What will you do after you graduate from the program?**

He took the pen back from me and poised it over the paper for a long time before he finally wrote.

**I honestly don't know. I guess I never thought past Chapel**

Crest. I like building things, so maybe I'll work in construction or something. What about you?

I bit my bottom lip for a moment before writing my plans. Hopes. Dreams.

I want to paint. Mayfair has an excellent art program. When I was younger, I dreamed of attending there to learn to sing better. Now, I'd be happy to go so that I can paint with some of the best.

He stared at the page for a moment.

Do you sing?

I hesitated before writing my response.

I used to sing and dance. I did ballet for many years. I even tried after I was hurt. I just couldn't anymore. My body didn't want to move like it used to. I loved ballet. I always wondered if maybe I could grow up to be a famous ballet dancer/singer. Silly, huh?

He took the pen back from me.

It's not silly, Siren. It's a wonderful dream. When I was a kid, I wanted to be a professional hockey player. My dad loved hockey. Maybe I thought if I played, it would make him proud of me and create some semblance of happiness in his life since he seemed so angry about everything. I played for a few years and did good, but then shit happened to me too. So here I am.

His words saddened me. I hadn't known he played hockey and had loved it.

Do you think you'd play again? For you this time?

He quietly contemplated my words before snagging the pen from me and writing his answer.

Maybe. I don't really have a reason to do it anymore, even if I do still love it.

That made me sad. I even said as much.

What about doing it for you and not worrying about anyone else?

He let out a soft chuckle.

In case you didn't know, one of my toxic traits is that I'm always doing things for myself. I'm trying to do things for others as a means to an end to the noise in my head. I'm trying to be better for those around me.

I paused before writing my answer because I wanted to get it just right for him.

**You're better than you think, Sinclair. I wish you could see what I see.**

His bottom lip quivered for a moment as he held the pen. I wasn't even sure he was going to write back before he finally put the pen to the page.

**I'm so fucking sorry I hurt you, Siren. I will punish myself every day for my sins against you and the guys. Until my dying breath. I pray every night it's my last night in this perpetual hell. And each day, I awaken, forced to bear the pain another day. I only hope someday you can forgive me. If you can never do that, then I accept it.**

I watched him finish writing. He wiped quickly at his eyes before handing the notebook and pen to me. Quickly, he got to get to his feet and walk away. My chest clenched at his words, and my heart filled with pain.

I didn't want him to punish himself. He was sick like the rest of us, and it wasn't a good enough reason to be punished. It wasn't our fault. It was the monsters before us.

Everything fell into place in that moment. I was seeing him. The real Sinclair Priest. The lost boy who was struggling to find his way out of despair.

Carefully, I got to my feet and went to him in the kitchen, where he was banging around, pulling pots and pans out to cook the macaroni and cheese.

I went straight to him and took his hand in mine.

He paused what he was doing and looked at me, his blond hair hanging in that shaggy way I liked around his face. It was the look in his eyes that sealed the deal.

He was a man with very little hope or happiness in the world.

He wasn't a danger to me. Not really. Maybe he'd stomp on my heart someday, but I didn't see that day being today.

"Siren," he started, a pained look on his face.

"I forgive you, Sinful."

A breath whooshed out of him, and he stared me down, so much turmoil on his face.

"You shouldn't have to. I fucked up. I shouldn't have done what I did. If I'd have just given you a chance. . . or given myself the chance." He let out a breath and stared up at the ceiling before looking back at me. "Bells fucked me up. I loved her. Or believed I did. It was the only kind of love I knew, I guess. The love from my mother seemed to have come to an end after my dad tried to kill us. I was violent and unpredictable. Angry. I pushed her away, and I guess it probably worked because she walked away from me one day, and now I'm here."

I watched him, wishing there was something I could do to make him feel better.

He sighed. "What I felt for Bells wasn't what I thought it was." He visibly swallowed, his Adam's apple bobbing with the motion. "I-I thought that was love. She was my entire world. We were going to have a kid." He rubbed his eyes. "I still deal with that. Knowing my kid was killed by her out of her anger and sickness. She betrayed me and worked for Church's old man. She never even loved me, even though she told me she did. Led me on. Made me feel like I had a chance at happiness only to rip it away from me and leave me like this." He looked away from me, his hands trembling.

I stepped forward and reached for him, taking his face gently in my hands and steering his attention back to me.

"I'm a fuck up, Siren. I'm afraid it's all I'll ever be. I-I even ruined my family. I want to come home. I'm not the same person I was then. I swear I'm not. Church doesn't believe me, but it's not like I blame him after the shit I did."

"You're just lost," I murmured.

"Who would even care to look?" His gray eyes flashed with his pain, making me hurt even more for him.

I went for it. I wrapped my arms around him, earning a soft cry from him, his body jerking.

Quickly, I pulled away, feeling like I'd done something wrong.

The twisted look of agony on his face made my heart jump.

"S-sorry," he managed. "I-I punish myself. I'm just a little sore."

His words sickened me. I'd heard he was doing that, but I didn't realize it was to the extent that he couldn't even be hugged.

I reached for him again, but he jerked away.

My words failed me, so I tried again, backing him into the corner of the kitchen counter. My words didn't work, but my body sure as hell did.

I reached out and began unbuttoning his top. He stopped fighting me on it, his breathing shaky.

I'd never had the chance to take Sin's shirt off, but when it finally fell open, it was to see beautiful planes of corded, thick muscles and bruises. So many painful bruises in different levels of healing. And the cuts.

They were deep and weeping with little trickles of blood. He hadn't even bothered to bandage them.

My nostrils flared as I took him in.

My name was etched deep into his chest. Scarred forever in my name.

"I'm sorry," he choked out.

I said nothing. Instead, I took him by the hand, led him back to the couch, and had him sit. Quickly, I scribbled a note to him.

**Don't move. I'll be right back.**

I left him before I went into the downstairs bathroom and rummaged around until I found all the first aid supplies the guys had. I brought it all back out and went to my knees before Sin. He stared down at me, his lips parted.

Wordlessly, I pushed his shirt off and began doctoring him up, taking care to clean the wounds on his body.

When I'd gotten all of them taken care of, I stared at my name carved into his chest. The scarring looked like it had been a painful ordeal. The redness was still surrounding it, and the skin was raised slightly with each letter.

Gently, I traced my fingers along the letters.

S-I-R-E-N

"Why?" I whispered, staring into his eyes.

He captured my hand in his, wrapping it around my small one.

"So you'd be near my heart," he answered in a soft voice. "Always."

I closed my eyes at his words. As if I couldn't hurt anymore for him, then he goes and tells me these things.

His words hurt my soul.

There had to be something I could do. Something we could do.

Maybe he was still scared to fall. To let go.

But I knew I was too afraid to say my feelings or make a move to show him how I felt about him.

So I did the next best thing.

I leaned in and placed a tender kiss over his heart.

His eyes were closed, his breathing deep, when I pulled away from him. I watched him, intrigued by this beautiful man who was terrified to feel anything.

Once he finally gave in, though, it would be a hurricane.

I wouldn't mind being the girl caught in the eye of it, but I didn't know how to say it, so I took the notebook and wrote him a message instead.

**Macaroni and cheese?**

He looked at my words for a moment before he smiled and cradled my face.

"Yeah, Siren. Let's make macaroni and cheese."

I gave him a smile, hoping he could see how much I cared. He thumbed my bottom lip for a moment.

"I would give anything to make you macaroni and cheese forever if it's what you wished."

Leaning in, I hugged him gently, making sure to wind my arms around his neck instead of his torso. He exhaled and hugged me back, his face buried in my neck. We stayed that way for a long time before he broke away.

"Come on. I'll tell you my secret recipe."

I grinned as I took the hand he offered and let him lead me away.

# SIN

*I* stared down at the note in front of me. Keeping the smile off my face was impossible at this point, so I didn't fight it. In fact, I was embracing it. Being able to smile made me feel not so worthless. It made me feel like maybe there was more in the world that was possible for me.

Sirena and I had been passing notes back and forth to one another all week. Each day, I'd wake up and actually be happy to be alive because I knew I'd get a message from her. We'd discussed my love of random facts in our previous note-passing. Sometimes, we talked about the weather. The nuns. Our favorite foods. Books. Sometimes, though, the conversations got deeper, like her telling me she wanted to dance and sing again or me telling her I could play guitar and was taught by my dad and wished I could pick one up and play again without remembering him.

Today was a random fact day, however.

**Sinful,**

**Did you know snakes can predict earthquakes? You said you liked weird facts. I thought maybe you'd like that one.**

**Yours,**

**Siren**

. . .

TAKING MY PENCIL, I wrote back.

SIREN,

Did you know the Mona Lisa doesn't have eyebrows? A lot of people overlook it and never even notice it. It's because it's been cleaned so much that the eyebrows have faded.

I didn't know that about snakes. Thank you for the information. I'll be sure to run if I see snakes slithering out of Michigan.

In other news, Ashes messaged and said he's going burning tonight. He asked me to come over just a few minutes ago and hang out with you. I said yes.

I'm really looking forward to it. You make me forget how to be sad.

Yours,

Sinful

I FOLDED the note and held it in my hand. The moment the bell signaled the end of class, I was out of my chair and headed to the cafeteria, knowing I'd find her there.

Rounding the corner, I saw her already sitting with Stitches.

I slowed my rush, knowing I couldn't just walk up and hand it to her in front of him. Our notes were our secret. Being unsure if the guys even knew she was communicating to me like this, I didn't want to be the one to put it all out there. Sure, I'd hand Bryce notes to pass for me, but that was a one-time thing. It didn't count.

"There's a package for you," Mirage's voice was in my ear.

I glanced over to see him at my side, his blue eyes fixed on Sirena at the table with Stitches. He kept trying to feed her, but she brushed him off, a smile on her face, before taking his fork and attempting to eat on her own. We watched as he quickly turned her attempt into a playful fork fight, their forks clanging against one another as she tried to eat on her own. She finally succeeded, making a grin spill over Stitches's face.

I smiled at the scene, wishing I was part of it.

"In a way, you are," Mirage murmured as Cady joined Sirena and Stitches at the table, Ashes soon adding to their group. "Part of it. You get to see the happiness from afar."

"It's not the same."

"It's good in a different way. Embrace that." He clapped me on the back. "Anyway. The box is on your bed. It's pretty big. You should probably go and open it. It was moving."

"Moving?" I looked sharply at him.

He nodded, not bothering to look at me. "Yep." He pulled a carrot out and bit into it, not paying me any attention. His blue eyes moved from Sirena and Stitches as he took in the rest of the students slowly, like a hunter, surveying which small defenseless animal he'd attack next.

He was doing whatever weird thing his brain compelled him to do, so I backed away with a sigh, really hoping there wasn't something alive in a box on my bed.

✝

I STARED down at the note on the moving box. Asylum's scrawl met my eyes.

*SINCLAIR,*
*I promised you a friend. I think he's perfect for you. You're welcome.*
*Your Neighborhood Forking Madman,*
*Asylum*

"FUCK." I sighed, hoping whatever it was wasn't venomous.

Carefully, I opened the box and peered inside. It took me a moment to realize what it was.

A smile touched my lips as I reached inside and lifted out a fairly large reticulated python from the box. He curled around my arm and hand as I turned to see his face. His tongue darted out, checking the air.

"Hey, there," I murmured gruffly beneath his weight.

He stared back at me for a moment before twisting around to check out the rest of the room.

One night after the events where the watchers nearly killed me, I'd told Asylum I'd love to have a snake again. Growing up, I had one my mother hated. When she married Rudy, he'd made me get rid of it and reprimanded me for only caring about myself and not my mother's feelings about the snake. I think a lot had to do with the fact that it had been a gift from my father years before, and it reminded her of all the shit we'd gone through.

But I loved that snake. I guess I loved my mom a little bit more, however, so I let my snake, named Log, go. I'd cried over it, but I never let anyone see that.

Somehow, though, Asylum saw all. So did Mirage, but he just didn't talk about it often. I liked that about him.

"What will I name you?" I studied the snake, trying to come up with the perfect name for him. When nothing settled, I took him over to the other larger box on the floor and opened it. Inside was a complete setup for him. Smiling, I placed my snake back into the box he came in and closed it before going about setting up his new habitat.

Asylum went all out on it. I appreciated that he'd done this for me. I had no way to repay him, but I'd at least tell him thank you.

Once I had it all put together, I took the snake out and held him for a while before kissing the top of his head and placing him in the large habitat. Once the lid was closed, I looked at my watch to see nearly two hours had passed. It was almost time to get Sirena. If I made it back in time I might be able to see her before her last class. I checked the snake's habitat once more, making sure everything was secure, before heading back to classes.

I'd made it right before the bell rang. Sirena came out of her class with Cady. Breathing out a sigh of relief, I waited eagerly for her.

Her eyes found me immediately, and a tiny smile teased the corner of her pouty lips.

Her smile did something whenever she turned it on for me. My heart beat faster. My palms grew sweaty. I felt like I was flying.

It scared me.

"Hey, weirdo," Cady greeted me as I fell in step with them. "Getting brave lately, huh?"

I ignored her and pressed the note I'd written earlier into Sirena's hand without Cady seeing. She took it with ease from me.

"Sinclair, you missed therapy this afternoon," the droning voice of my therapist called out.

Fucking hell.

I watched as Cady and Sirena rounded a corner, Sirena looking over her shoulder at me before disappearing into the crowd.

I sighed and turned back to the asshole who was annoying me.

"I wouldn't say I missed it," I muttered.

She raised her eyebrows at me. "We can do a make-up now. I have a free hour."

"Whatever." I followed the bitch to her therapy room, not wanting her to know I felt anything other than annoyance.

But in my heart, I was elated.

At my snake. At Siren.

At the prospects for the night. To speak with her again.

It was my secret, and I wasn't telling anyone.

SIRENA

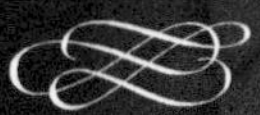

**You make me forget how to be sad.**

Sin's messy scrawl made my breath catch.

I hated that he was sad. It was burning a hole through my soul.

He'd be here soon, though, and I was hopeful I'd be able to make him smile. He was quickly growing on me.

"What are you making?" Stitches came into the kitchen after I'd tucked the note back into my dress pocket and wrapped his arms around my waist before planting a kiss on my cheek.

I lifted my pasta fork out of the steaming pot and showed him a nearly limp noodle.

"Mm, spaghetti." He continued to hold me while I stirred the pot, enjoying his warmth on my skin. "You're cooking for Sin?"

I felt him tense slightly.

Carefully, I put the pasta fork onto the counter and turned in his arms.

He stared down at me, his dark eyes filled with an emotion I couldn't place. Maybe fear? Sadness? Worry? Or a mixture of all the things.

"Malachi," I whispered, finding the words inside me. I had the

253

desperate need to let him know I wasn't going anywhere despite the growing feelings blooming within me for all the current men in my life. The watchers were where I wanted to be. Sin coming home was important. Asylum and Mirage joining. And Bryce...

My face heated at the thoughts, not knowing what I was going to do to make it even happen. Maybe it was a pipe dream. If Cady were here and I'd have said that, she'd laugh and wiggle her brows at me, making it dirtier than what I intended. Pipes and dicks. She had a way about her like that.

He blinked quickly in surprise. "Angel?"

"I love you," I finished, going up on my tiptoes and pressing my lips against his.

"Fuck, baby," he groaned against my lips before deepening it. "I love you too."

A gasp of surprise left me as he lifted me quickly and sat me on the kitchen table, his fingers in my hair, his tongue tangling with mine.

He broke the kiss off abruptly, a dark look in his eyes before he put his hand on my chest and pushed me flat on my back.

With ease, he lifted my legs and placed my feet on the table.

I made to lift my head, but he tutted at me.

"Here's what's going to happen. I'm going to eat your pussy before I fuck you. If Ashes comes in before I'm done, I'm going to let him have some fun too."

Quickly, I looked to the pasta cooking on the stove. Catching my meaning, he swept to it and turned off the burner before pulling the pot off the stove and draining the water from it.

He returned to me immediately.

"I've never cooked and fucked before," he said, smiling at me. "I'm going to need you to hold on, angel. It's going to be rough and fast."

With those words, he shoved my dress up and tugged my panties off before diving between my legs.

He wasn't kidding.

I gripped the edge of the table as his tongue flicked expertly over my clit, sending bolts of electricity through my body.

I squirmed beneath his mouth as he ate me before bucking my hips up to meet his tongue.

His hands gripped my hips tightly, and he tugged me roughly against his mouth, deepening his feasting.

The heat built within me as he ate, and soon, I was coming hard, dampening the table and his shirt with my release.

He didn't stop. Instead, he pushed a digit inside me as he continued his onslaught. My body trembled with the movement, and I gasped when he pushed a second finger into my heat.

He was going for another one, and he was damn well going to get it.

I came for him again, earning that soft groan of approval from him that drove me wild. He slowed his work on my pussy before coming to a stop and pressing against my damp mound.

He straightened and stared down at me, his face moist from my orgasm, his shirt spotted with the wetness I'd gushed out.

My cheeks heated at knowing I'd done that.

"I like it," he said softly, his dark eyes sparkling. "When you come on my face and cock. You're my favorite meal, baby. If I were dying, you'd be my last meal request."

My face heated further, earning a sexy-as-hell smirk from him while he undid his jeans.

With his cock in hand, he rubbed it against my damp pussy, teasing me for a moment, before he pushed his way in amid a soft moan.

I noted the slight tremble through his body. He was trying to be gentle with me. I appreciated that.

"Look at me," he whispered, pulling out and thrusting back into me. "It's me and you."

I knew he was worried I was having some weird flashbacks. And honestly, I was. I'd been having them whenever I had sex, but I wanted to do this with him. With all my guys. I liked the way it made me feel. They tried to make me feel safe, and I wanted that safety. I craved it.

I focused on him.

"Breathe with me, baby," he instructed in a gentle but rough voice as he pushed into me again. Out. In. Out. In. Slowly. Gently.

I inhaled deeply, my eyes focused on him.

"There you go. Good girl," he husked out. "I'm going to go faster. Is that OK?"

I nodded, knowing how fast and deep Stitches could get. Then again, Church and Ashes could too.

He pulled out and slammed back into me, making me arch my back off the table and let out a hiss of pleasure.

With his hands firmly on my hips, he fucked into my body, clearly having something to prove to me.

He didn't need to prove anything to me, though. He was my Stitches. My watcher.

Mine.

All mine.

Just like the rest of them.

I sat up, slowing him down, and crushed my lips against his. He groaned again as I shifted to grind on his dick, eager to explode for him.

Easily, he lifted me, my ass cupped in his hands, and fucked me that way.

I wound my arms around his neck and tried to match pace with him, but lost out moments later because I came hard, my chest heaving, my orgasm soaking everything.

"Fuck. Good girl. Do it again for me," he said breathlessly as he lifted me up and down on his long, thick cock.

I came again seconds later, my body trembling, and my breath lost to him.

He followed, slamming deep inside me and holding me in place as he filled me, my name on his lips.

He bounced me on his cock a few more times before kissing me gently.

"You're incredible," he whispered against my lips. "You're going to stay, right?"

The fear I figured was there came out in his words.

My answer was to kiss him again.

"Why didn't you guys tell me to come down?" Ashes called out.

I pulled away from Stitches and cast a guilty look from Stitches to Ashes, who was taking in the scene with a frown on his face.

"Looks like a good time was had," he continued, staring at the mess we'd made. "Damnit, Malachi."

"Sorry," Stitches said, grinning at him. "She was cooking. I love a woman who can cook."

"Food?" Ashes widened his eyes at me.

I gave him a bashful nod. Quickly, he pulled me off Stitches, who was still impaled deep inside me, and kissed me. I stumbled against him, but he caught me easily.

"Malachi, clean this up," he said between kisses. "Sin is about fifteen minutes out. I need to take care of some business before he gets here."

And with those words, he swept me to his room and buried himself deep inside me.

"What a beautiful fucking mess he made," he commented as he kissed me, moving in and out of me at an even, delicious pace.

I clung to him as he made love to me. Not fast. Not slow. Just. . . Ashes.

"I want to take more time, heaven, but Sin really is on the way. I need you cleaned up before he gets here. Do you mind if I go faster?"

I silenced him with a kiss, letting him know he could use me however he saw fit.

He let out a groan and moved quicker, his cock moving in and out of me so fast the heat made me squirm.

Within moments, I was clinging to him, my nails deep in his back as I came for him. He followed, my pussy milking every last drop from him before he collapsed over me, balancing himself on his arms, his lips on mine.

"Fuck, I bet you're sore. I'm sorry. I just. . . you're beautiful to me, baby. I couldn't resist."

I kissed him gently, earning a contented sigh from him.

"Come on. Let's get you cleaned up." He pulled free from my body before bringing me to my feet and taking me into the bathroom, where he was quick to help me wash. Soon enough, I was clean, and he was running a brush through my hair.

"I love your hair," he mused, smiling. "It's so thick and silky. Soft."

I smiled at that. I liked that he liked it.

There was a knock on the door, which caused him to sigh. I turned and faced him, taking in the tired look in his eyes.

I took his hand and traced letters on his palm.

*Are you OK?*

"I'm fine," he answered. "Just. . . wish things were different, you know? And not so cold."

I nodded, understanding him.

"I want us all to get along. I know it'll be a long road, but I'm here for the ride if it's what you want," he continued thickly. "I've seen the way you look at Sinclair. You've always looked at him that way. Like you do to us. But I've also seen you look at Bryce and Asylum like that too."

My heartbeat pounded in my ears, and I made to back away from him, shame washing over me.

"No," he said, pulling me back and tilting my chin up so I was staring into his blue eyes. "I want your happiness at any cost. I just want you to know this might not work with everyone, so. . . be prepared, OK?"

I nodded, my throat tight.

He let out a soft sigh and pressed a kiss to my forehead.

"We'll pray for the best, OK? I'm on your side, baby. I want Sin home too. Asylum and Bryce? I don't know. It's something maybe we can visit soon."

I traced more letters onto his hand, which made him smile at me.

"Don't be sorry for having a good heart and wanting to love every-one. We're all jealous pricks, so know that going into this. For now, let's only focus on one thing at a time. Sound good?"

I nodded, feeling a little better.

Ashes was so easy to talk to. It was one of the many things I loved about him.

"I may slip along the way and complain a little, but ultimately, it's all you, heaven." He kissed the tip of my nose. "Just be good while we're gone, OK?"

I went up on my tiptoes and kissed him, letting him know I was agreeing to his terms. He returned the kiss before breaking away.

"Come on. You need your panties back," he said with a soft laugh, which made me smile back.

And with that, he led me back to the living room, my hand in his.

One watcher down, two more to go.

Hopefully.

# SIN

It didn't take a genius to know the guys had fucked her before I got there. Not only were her cheeks flushed, but I knew the guys. When they got laid, they were more cheerful and relaxed. Stitches even cracked a joke with me, while Ashes was more talkative than usual.

Plus, I'd seen Stitches try to discretely give Sirena her panties back when he thought I wasn't looking. She'd left the room after, letting me know she'd been out here with her long legs on display and nothing on beneath the pretty blue dress she wore.

*Chairs. Grass. Rocks. Boats. Snails. Dirt. Sister Esther.*

I ran the most boring or gross things through my mind to alleviate my desires and the fact that I was close to pitching a tent in the kitchen.

"Same as last week," Ashes said. "Cady is staying behind, so if you need her, text her. You know how she is. If it's really serious, just call us, and we'll come back."

"She'll be fine," I said firmly, knowing in my heart I'd make sure of it.

Ashes clapped me on the shoulder. "I know you'll take care of her."

Stitches cast me a narrowed-eyed look but didn't refute Ashes's words, which brought me some relief.

After they kissed her goodbye, Stitches making a decent show of it, they left us alone.

I pulled my notebook out of my jacket and went to the couch while she darted off to the kitchen. Moments later, the smell of something delicious filled the air. Curious, I got up and went in to see what she was doing. I was surprised to find her doling out noodles and sauce onto a plate.

She blinked at me so innocently I nearly melted, but I took the plate she offered and watched her take a basket of garlic bread and a salad to the table with two bowls and some dressing.

She got her own plate and settled down in Church's seat as I took my old spot.

I watched her get up and grab the notebook. She brought it back before she placed our other note into its pocket for safe keeping.

Quickly, she scribbled out a message to me.

I looked at it and smiled.

**I haven't cooked in a long time, but I wanted to try. I hope it tastes OK.**

I took the pen and wrote my message back.

**It smells and looks amazing.**

I paused and scooped some salad into my mouth after putting dressing on it and chewed quickly.

Whatever the hell dressing she'd used was incredible.

Next, I ate some spaghetti and bread before nodding and grabbing the pen again.

**It's official. It's probably the best meal I've ever had. Thank you.**

Her cheeks flushed pink before she went back to eating.

In silence, we ate, both of us finishing off our food. When we were done, I helped her clean up before we went back to the living room and settled on the couch next to one another.

I scribbled a note out to her again.

**I got a pet.**

She widened her eyes at me, so I continued.

**Actually, Asylum got me a pet. It's a snake. Reticulated python, or a retic as many call them. I haven't named it yet. I thought maybe you could help me give it a name?**

She smiled at that and wiggled in her seat, the pen in her hand.

**Snakes scare me.**

I wrote back, pulling another pen out of my pocket so we wouldn't have to keep exchanging. She grinned at my brilliance. At least, that's what I told myself.

**Maybe we can work on that.**

She smiled again.

**I'd like that,** she wrote back.

I contemplated my next question before posing it back to her.

**So. . .? Want to help me name him?**

She bit her bottom lip for a moment before writing.

**I can't name him without seeing him. Can you show me?**

I hesitated for a moment before nodding and offering her my hand. Eagerly, she slid her palm against mine, and I pulled her to her feet and grabbed my jacket before tucking the notebook into the inside pocket.

Quickly, she put on her snow boots and her fluffy pink jacket, which went past her knees. I grabbed her hat and pulled it over her head, delighting in the smile she gave me, my heart so full I wasn't sure how I hadn't floated away yet.

*Bring it in. Don't get too close so soon. This isn't going to last. You know that.*

I swallowed thickly at my thoughts, the smile sliding off my face. She took notice and parted her lips. Before she could question me in whatever manner she was going to, I led her outside into the cool night air.

Again, we went silent, walking to my dorm. When we got there, I brought her into my room. She stepped in and looked around. Mirage was gone for the night, most likely out running through the forest like a maniac in his rabbit mask. I wasn't sure what that was about. Past the woods and eating carrots, he wasn't very rabbit-like.

I'd have asked him, but I honestly didn't want to know the shit that went through his head. Same with Asylum.

I went to my snake's habitat and pulled him out gently. Sirena backed away, her eyes wide.

"It's OK," I murmured, going to the bed and sitting on the edge. "I promise."

Nervously, she took a careful step toward me, then another and another until she was near enough that I could touch her if I reached for her.

"Sit," I instructed softly. "We can go slow."

She did as she was told and sat next to me. Not nearly as close as I knew she would have had I not been holding the snake, but near enough to satisfy me. Mostly.

"He's a little bigger than my last one," I started, watching him curl around my arm and stick his tongue out. The care card that came with him said he'd eaten a rat just a few days ago, so I knew he wasn't hungry.

She watched, visibly swallowing, as the snake darted out its tongue.

"Touch his head," I said. "He won't hurt you. I have him."

Carefully and with a shaky hand, she reached forward and slowly rubbed the top of his head before jerking her hand away and shivering. I smiled at her innocence. Knowing the snake was unnerving her, I got up and put him back into his habitat before coming back to her.

She visibly relaxed, and I pulled out the notebook. She took it from me and wrote me a note.

**That was scary.**

I smiled at her words.

**You were safe. And brave. I'm proud of you for petting him.**

It was her turn to smile.

**I was still scared.**

I chuckled and wrote back.

**You did great. I didn't doubt you for a moment.**

She wiggled in her seat before taking her boots, hat, and jacket off, then getting cozy in my bed and lying back against my pillow.

I swallowed hard and stared at her for a minute, watching as she patted the spot next to her.

I'd already taken my jacket off, so I pushed off my boots and scooted in beside her. The bed wasn't the biggest, so we were body to body on it. I bent my knees, and she mimicked the movement, her dress not covering nearly enough leg. She didn't seem to be doing it on purpose, though, but my dick wasn't listening.

I cleared my throat and placed the notebook on our thighs between us.

**What name do you think now that you've met him?** I asked with my pen.

She tapped her lips with her pen for a moment before answering.

**Hisstopher?**

I chuckled at that.

**Not bad. What do you think about Danger Noodle?**

A soft laugh left her, sending my heart soaring for what had to be the millionth time that night. We spiraled into listing ridiculous names after that. We probably had a hundred names by the end of it, both of us laughing. I'd never heard her laugh that way before. It was music to my fucking ears. I wondered if the guys had ever heard her before.

**William Snakespeare.**

I snorted at the new name she wrote.

**I like that. It's settled. His name is now William Snakespeare.**

She looked over at me, a beautiful smile on her face, her eyes sparkling. They were so vibrant and full of the life I longed for.

I'd never seen eyes like hers.

I realized in that moment that I loved looking into them, and it was really going to fucking hurt when I no longer could. I knew our days with one another were numbered.

It fucking sucked because I wasn't ready to go anywhere.

I hadn't even realized I'd leaned into her until her soft, warm breath scattered across my lips.

I was a breath away from fucking everything up, but I didn't move away. Neither did she.

Instead, she reached out and cradled my face. I closed my eyes, absorbing the way it felt to be touched by her.

This was definitely different from anything I'd ever had before.

And this different was terrifying because I knew I'd do terrible things in her name. There would be no limit to just how far I was willing to go. She wouldn't ever need to ask. It would be done without hesitation.

"Sinful," she whispered, her warm breath blowing across my lips.

"Siren," I answered back, opening my eyes to stare into hers.

*Fuck it. I was going to do it. It was worth dying for.*

I always made shit decisions. I knew this and did them anyway. A way of self-destruction or self-sabotage. Whatever fancy word people wanted to use for it.

The moment the thought went through my head, the door to my room banged open, and Mirage stomped in, looking like a wild man, with his black hair disheveled and snow clinging to him.

Sirena and I jerked away from one another as Mirage slammed the door behind him and peeled his coat off .

"We have company," I muttered, watching him toss his shirt onto his bed.

Mirage turned and looked to us, a small smile on his lips.

"Hey," he said, his body relaxing.

Sirena was quick to sit up before she straddled my waist to get over me and to him. She didn't do it slowly, but she did falter. I caught her before she tumbled off me and hit the floor, the movement brushing her against my aching dick.

I swallowed down the groan at her over me like that. Again, I knew she wasn't thinking it through and was just eager to greet the half-naked guy who interrupted probably one of the biggest mistakes of my life.

Mirage helped her off me, tugged her against his body, and held her tightly. I watched, having never seen him like this with anyone. Not that he was around a lot for me to witness, but this was different. I was catching a glimpse into something from their past.

Something I really had no business watching. I sat up, still unable to tear my eyes away from them though.

They were different together.

It was almost like watching two missing pieces find one another. Or magnets.

He cradled her cheek when she pulled away and stared down at her in wonder. There was so much focus and adoration on his face that it made my chest clench.

Dante and the guys were going to have their work cut out for them. I would, too, if I ever became part of that equation again.

Mirage leaned in, and Sirena placed her hands on his bare chest. Asylum/Mirage was fucking ripped. Asylum and I would often work out together in the evenings when we were bored. I supposed Mirage worked out in the forest doing whatever he did in the darkness, which only added to it.

I watched as Mirage whispered in her ear before he pulled away and stared down at her. He cocked his head to the right, a tiny smile touching his lips again.

She went back in for another hug, both of them holding one another tightly.

So that was what true love looked like. Like the kind of love that started young and progressed. That had gone through heaven and hell and still found its way back.

I finally looked away, knowing I wasn't the guy who could have that.

"The self-loathing is a bit early," Mirage called out.

I snapped my attention back to him to see Sirena had separated from him and had gone to stand at the window. She was staring out into the falling snow, her lips parted.

"Fuck off," I muttered.

I glanced to Sirena again to see she wasn't paying us any attention.

"And put a fucking shirt on," I snarled at Mirage.

He chuckled. "Why don't you take yours off?"

I looked up at him standing by his bed and scoffed. "Why?"

"Because you're worried she likes the way I look more than she likes you," he said softly, so I knew she couldn't hear him.

I ground my teeth at his words. "Untrue, fuckhead."

He laughed again. Then, he grabbed a clean hoodie from his drawer and pulled it over his head before flopping back onto his bed and watching Sirena stare out the window.

The room suddenly felt too small.

"Siren?" I called out, grabbing our notebook and jacket. "We should probably get back. I don't want the guys to get home and you're gone."

She looked over her shoulder at me before moving away from the window. I grabbed her jacket and helped her into it when she reached me. She allowed me to help and even let me pull her pink hat over her head.

"Your mittens," I said, clearing my throat and holding them out for her to put on. She did so without a word, silent as always.

I caught Mirage's eye, and he winked at me before going back to the book he'd picked up. He read a lot. He was currently reading a lot of books on physics and the metaphysical world, but I'd seen him a week ago going through sci-fi novels. He was all over the place. I could have sworn I even saw him reading a math textbook one day.

"I'll, uh, be back in a bit when the guys get back," I said.

Mirage tossed his book aside and got up.

Sirena turned to face him again, and he dropped a kiss on the top of her head and then gave her another hug.

"Soon," he said gently, almost a whisper to her. "Believe me?"

She nodded, and he sighed and released her before backing away, a sad look on his face. I gave him a nod, and he went back to the bed and his book as we left the room.

It was a quiet walk, but I didn't expect anything else. With my hands stuffed into my jacket pockets, we trudged through the accumulating snow. When we reached the house, I opened the door for her, and she went inside and took off her jacket and gear.

Needing a moment to myself, I stayed outside and grabbed a

shovel. I cleared off the patio and the walkway before going back inside to find her sitting on the couch with our notebook on her lap and writing.

A sad smile touched my lips, and I removed my jacket and boots and went to sit beside her.

She slid the notebook onto my lap and got up. I took it and read what she'd written.

**I'm sorry if I made you feel uncomfortable tonight with Mirage. I didn't mean to. I had so much fun with you. I don't want the night to end or end weirdly, so I was thinking we could talk more? I like doing this with you. I almost feel normal when we do it. I also feel awkward because I don't want you to feel like you're being forced into this. If you don't want to talk, we could just watch a movie, or I can go upstairs and give you some space.**

She came back to the couch holding two mugs of hot chocolate, complete with marshmallows, and offered me a nervous smile.

"Sit," I murmured, taking the mug from her that was intended for me.

A look of relief swept over her face, and she took the spot next to me, her mug in hand. We sipped our drinks, and I nodded.

It was some good shit.

Sirena clearly knew her way around a kitchen. Or at least spaghetti and hot chocolate.

I had a feeling the sauce and dressing she'd made tonight were homemade too.

Placing my mug on the coffee table, I pulled out my pen and wrote a note back to her.

**I want to still talk. I'm just not used to seeing Mirage that way. That's a me problem, not you. Any of my feelings are my issue. I don't intend on making them yours. I know I've been dumping a lot of it on you lately with our notes, and for that, I'm sorry. I'll work on that.**

She stared at my message, a frown on her lips.

**I like you telling me things. I don't want that to stop.**

I sighed, deciding I didn't want to have this conversation and I'd go ahead and change the subject. I took the notebook back from her and wrote more.

**Tell me about dancing.**

She nibbled her bottom lip for a moment before answering me.

**I know what you're doing.**

**Unlikely,** I wrote back. **I want to learn about ballet. Tell me about it.**

She looked at me, a suppressed smile on her face, before she put her pen to paper and wrote to me.

*It's like flying but on your feet. It's freedom in song. In movement. I loved it.*

I watched her face morph from content to sad in a matter of seconds with her words.

**Show me?**

I had no idea if she even would.

She scoffed at my words and paused her pen over the paper.

**I can't. It's been too long. Things change.**

She wiped at her eyes quickly.

I took the notebook from her and offered her my hand. She stared up at me, her face damp.

"Siren, dance with me?"

She blinked and wiped her tears again before taking my hand. I brought her to her feet and led her to the large space between the back of the couch and the kitchen.

"I can't dance," I admitted. "But we can stumble together."

She smiled at that and moved closer to me.

"I definitely don't know ballet," I continued, putting my other hand on her waist and ensuring I kept holding the hand I already had. "But I do know the chicken dance if that helps."

She let out a little laugh that warmed my heart.

"Shall we?" I asked, raising a brow at her.

She nodded at me eagerly, and I shuffled awkwardly with her until we were both laughing at how clumsy I was. It was when I spun her and pulled her against my body, rocking us together, that I realized it didn't matter what I did.

She was it.
She was the one.
No amount of fighting it was going to work.
I'd die with her, for her, or because of her.
There was no other ending to our story.

# ASHES

"I can't believe you let Sirena hang out at Cady's," Stitches stewed, pacing the living room a few days after we'd returned from my night of burning. It had gone well, and we'd returned home to find Sirena sleeping on the couch, her head on Sin's shoulder while he sat beside her, watching TV. Something told me he hadn't really been paying attention to the TV, however. Seeing her sleeping and so peaceful against him solidified what I already knew.

She cared a hell of a lot for the grouchy asshole, and that might cause some problems later on. Her feelings were growing exponentially, and so were his. I meant what I'd told her, though. I could be on board with it all. I only wanted her happiness.

I was going to try to fix things because if she wanted Sin, I was more than willing to let it happen. It just had to be something that happened with everyone on the same page.

I'd have my work cut out for me.

"She wanted to go. Cady looked like she was going to eat my soul if I said no. I can't say no to Sirena, and I definitely wasn't going to with Cady staring me down," I said.

"She goes to you because she knows you're a pushover," Stitches muttered.

"I'm not," I argued. "I want her to be happy. She needs a little freedom."

Stitches grumbled but didn't push the subject. His phone rang, and he quickly pulled it out.

"Hey," he answered.

I went over to him and saw that Church was video calling.

"How is she?" Church demanded without fanfare.

"She's good. Perfect as always." Stitches glanced at me, his face saying everything he wanted to say with the look.

*We should have kept Sirena home because now Church was going to be pissed.*

"Good. Where is she?" Church pressed.

"Uh, she's with Cady right now," I said. "They wanted to do their nails."

Church's expression hardened, and he reached for a napkin and quickly wiped at the dots I'd noticed on his skin. It took me a moment to realize he was wiping blood off his face. Even his knuckles were stained with it.

That could only mean he was already in a shitty mood.

I took out my lighter and began my ritual.

"Why the fuck aren't one of you with her?"

"She needs time to grow, man. We can't be with her all the time. She hates feeling suffocated," I explained. "She's in Cady's room. The door is locked. It's only for a couple of hours."

"Why couldn't she be at the house doing her nails?" Church threw the bloody rag aside and gave us his stern glare.

"Because she's here all the time," I said. "Classes or here. She needed a change of scenery."

"Unacceptable—"

"Dante, man. Seriously. I don't want to argue," Stitches broke in. "What's going on? We haven't heard from you in forever."

"I'm probably coming home soon. I'm waiting to meet with my father this evening. I've done everything he's asked of me. He seems pleased."

"How many did you kill today?" I asked thickly, the bloody rag still hanging out on the edge of the screen.

"Only three," Church answered stiffly.

"Do you want to talk about it?" I started, but he cut me off.

"What I want is for you to get your ass over to Cady's and get our girl home."

I sighed. "She hates being controlled like that—"

"I understand," Church said through clenched teeth. "But she needs to understand some prick is probably still running around out there. We don't know who he is or what else he's capable of. Don't you think you should be watching her? Our home is the safest place. You know this. You promised her safety. Just get her home."

"Fine." I gave in. He was right. We did have the safest place. Even though I knew Cady would protect Sirena with her life, it wasn't right to leave her alone the way we had. Or rather, I had.

"Good." Church unbuttoned his shirt and sat with it open. The blood spots weren't visible on the black, but I knew they were there. He lifted a glass of alcohol to his lips and sipped before lighting up a joint and taking a deep hit. "How has everything else been?"

"It's been fine," Stitches said. "No noise here. Haven't even seen Sully."

"It's because he's been in and out here," Church grumbled. "Saw his prick ass yesterday. Father let him watch me disembowel someone. I wanted to wrap the entrails around his fucking throat like a necklace."

I winced at his description.

"I assume it was a way to remind him to stay in line, but you know Sully. The twisted fuck has dick for brains."

I couldn't argue that. The guy was trash.

"Vice Headmaster Atkins hasn't been around either. I think Emerson and the nuns are holding it down," I said.

"He's not here. He's never been here, that I know of, so whatever the piss he's doing doesn't concern us, at least outwardly." Church took another hit.

"To be fair, you didn't know Adam or Asylum were involved with your old man," I pointed out.

Church blew out the smoke. "You're right. So who the fuck knows. I'm only saying they aren't here, to my knowledge."

We were quiet for a beat before Church spoke again.

"What's up with Sinclair?"

Stitches and I looked at each other.

"What do you mean?" Stitches asked.

"You know what I mean. Has he been spending time with Sirena?"

"He has a few times. Asylum. Him. It's not been substantial. He's been helpful taking over when we have therapy and all that bullshit," I said, feeling on edge at Church's terse tone.

"Shit better not happen there. We're already dealing with this third rabbit shit. We don't have a name. She was meeting Asylum, Mirage, whatever fucking name he's using now, in the woods, then was hurt by another who wasn't Mirage or Bryce. So some shit is going on. What have you found out about it?"

"Nothing," I mumbled, hating that we hadn't. If it was someone on campus, they were remaining tight-lipped on it. It was frustrating, but we weren't exactly actively looking. Our concern was simply keeping Sirena safe and happy.

"I see." Church's face was emotionless. "Get your asses out there and get some kind of information. Sinclair is a last-ditch fill-in. He's not coming back. I won't allow it. He fucked everything up with his shit. I'll let Asylum and his twisted white prick rabbit alter ego in before I fucking allow Sinclair back."

"Right," I said tightly, hating the way he was behaving, but I knew arguing wasn't the way to win this, so I let it go.

"It'll be handled," Stitches broke in. "We'll do more digging. Everything so far has been radio silence."

Church said nothing, opting to simply smoke and drink more.

"How close are you to getting this horsemen shit taken care of?" I pressed. "Won't it set off a chain reaction and bring hell to our doorstep?"

"Well." Church sat forward. "Let's hope we can just pin it on my old man, and I walk away without a scratch. I don't give a shit what any of them do. They can go feral and tear each other to pieces, but I still wouldn't care." He paused. "But if shit goes south and they come for us, I'll kill them all without hesitation, and I'll own the fucking city. I don't have time to look over my shoulder. I prefer to look forward."

I said nothing, knowing Church tended to grow darker the longer he was in the Underground with his father. It was how his life was. He had to adapt or get eaten. Quite literally.

Didn't mean I had to like it.

"Keep yourself in check," Stitches said, clearly on the same page as me. "You tend to fall a little into the black when you're there too long and exposed to all that shit."

Church let out a soft chuckle that sent chills down my spine. I hated him like this.

"I'm the king of the black. I invented it, brother."

"Church, we worry," I said. "Life is hard enough without trying to tug you back from the brink."

"I'm fine." He sat back abruptly. "I'll be fine. I always am."

"Don't forget who you are," I said evenly.

He eyed the camera for a moment. "I'm the King of the Underground."

I sighed, knowing he was in one of his moods. "I'm going to duck out. You and Stitches have a good talk. I'm going to go check on Sirena." I turned and made to leave, needing to get out of there before I lost my shit.

"Asher," Church called out.

I sighed and turned to face the phone.

"I will be home soon. I better not come back to find Sin has tried to make a comeback, or I'll finish what we started in the cemetery with him."

I clenched my jaw and said nothing while Stitches let out a soft curse in Spanish.

Turning, I swept forward, grabbed my jacket on the way out, and stepped into the cold air, praying for some damn peace.

If not for me, then for Sin.

I felt he deserved it.

# SIRENA

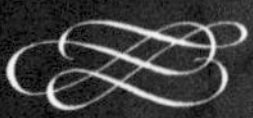

$\mathcal{I}$ stared down at the pink, sparkly polish on my nails. I hadn't painted them in ages it seemed, and it felt nice to do so with Cady.

"So I told him he could go fuck himself if he was going to be that way," Cady said, finishing her story about some guy named Jake on campus who wanted her to put out, but she wouldn't because he insisted on recording them.

"I don't know how you deal with all your guys," she continued. "Do they do stupid shit like that?"

I shook my head for her, making her sigh.

"I'm glad you're lucky in love. I'm waist-deep in the cesspool, it seems."

I patted her hand, letting her know it would be OK. She did seem to have bad luck with guys.

"You know, last year at Megan Keeley's party, I made out with Lucy Travers."

I raised my eyebrows at her admission.

She nodded, smirking at me. "It was fun. Girls are softer, you know? They aren't just looking to screw. At least the ones I've known aren't. Sure, it's a good time and all that, but they actually can hold a conversation, unlike all the guys I've known."

I watched her examine her black nails.

"Mom called. Asked how things were going here. I told her I wish I'd have gone crazy sooner. She didn't like that." She laughed. "But she said Jerry's being a dick and hasn't been home much. He's probably railing his secretary or something." She paused. "Does he have a secretary?"

I shrugged, not knowing or caring what that jerk had, but wishing my mom would leave him. I had no idea what she saw in him.

"And Adam." She sighed.

I stiffened at the mention of his name, my pulse roaring in my ears.

"He had his meds adjusted. He's been so much better since. He's apologized for the shit he said that night." Her voice grew softer. "I truly believe he's sorry. He wasn't himself. He brought me those roses."

I glanced at the red roses on her dresser, my stomach in knots.

"So I know he was a complete dick. I wanted to kill him that night, but he really did apologize and has been so good since. I-I'd like you two to get along. I think he might be the one."

My heart was beating so hard and fast I thought I was going to pass out.

There was a knock on the door, making her look to it.

"Listen, I invited him over tonight because he said he wanted to apologize to you in person."

*No. No. NO.*

I had to get out of there.

She got up, and the moment she did, I pulled my phone out and tried to call Ashes. He didn't answer, making me panic further. I swept down my list and hit Sin's name. It rang twice before he answered.

"Siren?"

"H-help," I choked out, my voice trembling as Cady opened the door. "P-please."

"Where are you?" he demanded.

"C-Cady's."

"I'm on the way. I'll be there in a minute. Hang on, OK?"

I said nothing, breathing heavily into the phone.

There was no way in hell I was going to stay in here. I had no way to protect us. Getting to my feet, I disconnected the call from Sin and put my phone into my pocket. I was going to go out the damn window if I had to. I'd face a broken leg before I faced the monster who hurt me.

I wasn't ready for it. Not yet. I wasn't strong enough.

I was just about to smash open the window and make the dive when Cady opened the door further and let out a sigh.

Bryce stepped into the room, and his hazel eyes zeroed in on me.

Without contemplating my next move, I rushed to him and threw my arms around his neck.

He hugged me back, his lips at my ear as he leaned down for me. "What's wrong?"

"L-l-leave. H-home."

"OK." He didn't question me. He simply tightened his hold on me for a moment before moving away.

"Where are you going?" Cady asked, frowning as we moved past her. "Rina? What's wrong?"

"Uh, we had plans tonight." Bryce put himself between me and her. "Sorry. I canceled on her and then was able to come, so I headed here since I knew this was where she'd be. We'd stay, but I also promised Ashes I'd get her home. So. . . raincheck?"

Cady sighed. "I guess. Rina, are you sure you're OK?"

I said nothing, wrapping my arms tighter around myself.

"Fine. We'll talk tomorrow."

"Come w-with. . .?" I tried to beg her. I didn't want her alone with Adam.

Her phone buzzed, and she waved us off before closing the door.

I stared at the heavy door, my heart in my throat.

"Come on," Bryce said, putting his hand on the small of my back and leading me to the elevator. He pushed the button, and the doors slid open. We stepped inside, and I let out a choked breath.

Bryce fixed his gaze on me. I had no idea why he'd shown up when he did, but he was a godsend. Maybe Ashes really did send for me.

"Sirena, what's going on?"

"A-A—" I couldn't get his name out. "C-Cady. N-not safe."

He frowned at me for a moment before pulling his phone out and sending a text. His phone rang a moment later.

"Hey, yeah, she's worried about you. What's going on?" He was quiet as he listened to Cady on the phone, nodding his head.

"I don't know. I guess that's good. I'll let her know. She'll relax now. Yeah. OK. Bye." Bryce hung up and tucked his phone away.

"She said Adam called and isn't coming tonight, so she was going to hang out with Jasmine O'Laughlin in her dorm instead since she'd asked her to earlier. Whatever is bothering you is OK. Cady's OK."

I nodded, relief rushing through me.

The door dinged open at the bottom level, and we stepped out into the lobby. Bryce quickly took my hand and led me outside into the cold night air.

The tension dissolved the more distance we put between us and the dorm until I could almost function.

"You're not OK," Bryce said, breaking the silence. "Sirena, what's going on?"

I shook, my arms still around myself. I'd forgotten my jacket at Cady's.

Bryce pulled me to a stop, then took his jacket off and wrapped it around me. He was a lot bigger than me, so the coat hung loosely around my body.

"Look at me," he murmured, concern on his pretty face. "Sirena?"

I shook my head. I didn't even know what to say. More than anything, I wanted to save my sister.

Then, I needed to kill Adam.

It was the only way.

The darkness peeked out, reminding me it was possible if I could just let it out and learn to control the dangerous capabilities I possessed.

The darkness and bravery were the same thing in this instance.

The terror in that moment was greater.

I had no idea how Bryce knew I was at Cady's. I wanted to ask, but the words weren't there.

I needed to learn to defend myself. And more than that, to kill without remorse.

"I wish you could tell me what's going on." He sighed before reaching out to adjust the jacket on me. "I don't ever get to see you anymore. It's so hard. I actually have something for you in my dorm. I was going to bring it, but I heard Jasmine O'Laughlin telling Amanda Perry that Cady wouldn't be going to watch movies in her dorm tonight because she was going to hang out with you. In my excitement, I rushed out without it. Do you want to come back to my place?" He shuffled from foot to foot, his face showing me all I needed to see.

Exhaling, I reached for his hand, noting how cold he was, before tugging him toward his building.

✝

"CHOCOLATE WITH CHERRY FROSTING," Bryce proclaimed, handing me a pretty cupcake.

I'd relaxed enough to take it from him with slightly trembling fingers. I loved these cupcakes.

"I also have a lemon one and carrot cake with cream cheese frosting." He showed me the little box of cupcakes he had. "I knew you really liked the chocolate one, though, but you can have these ones too. Take them home with you. I kept a few for myself."

I didn't bite into my cupcake. I simply held it in my hands.

Bryce reached out and carefully took the cupcake from me, then placed it on his bedside table.

"Cady said Adam was on his way over. I don't know if you heard her telling me when she opened the door tonight. She told me to get lost." He took my hand in his and held it. "Do you want to talk about it?"

I rocked back and forth, hating the sound of that monster's name.

"I know this place gets overwhelming, but you're not alone. I don't want you to ever think you are." He paused and cleared his throat. "Mirage came to see me."

I continued to rock, trying to hold myself together.

"He told me what happened, Sirena. I-I know what happened to you that night. I'm so fucking sorry. God, if I could change it. . . I-I went into the woods that night. I tried to get to you in the hopes we could talk. That I could. . . hell, I don't know. Prove my feelings." He let out a breath. "It doesn't matter. You know how I feel, and I'm not here to push that on you. I just want you to know you're safe with me. You were on day one and will always be." He squeezed my hand again.

I placed my hand over his and finally looked into his eyes.

I had feelings for him too, but everything had become so complicated.

"When you're ready to talk, you can talk to me. I'll make sure things are taken care of." His words held an ominous tone to them, but maybe it was just me and all the feelings ricocheting through my body.

"I hate you were hurt," he said fiercely, his hand trembling in mine. "I fucking hate it. You're a bright star in the dark, Sirena. This place is that dark place. Don't lose your shine. Promise me you won't, and I'll make sure the monster is found."

I stared into his hazel eyes, my body relaxing.

"Promise," he murmured. "I can't lose you. I need you. You're all I have here."

He leaned in and rested his forehead against mine.

I closed my eyes, relishing his warmth. His familiar smell. The way the butterflies converged in my stomach. The same ones I'd ignored when we'd met and every day since.

"Do you think in another world you'd have been my girl?" he whispered.

I knew deep in my heart that I wanted to try to be his girl in this life. Bryce made sense. He was sweet. Caring. Kind. He'd take care of me and keep me away from all the ugly.

My watchers would never go for it. It was the same deal I was facing with my feelings for Mirage/Asylum and Sin. I wanted to take them all and love them forever. It was unconventional, but it was what I wanted.

"You don't need to answer," he continued in a soft voice. "It's probably best that I don't know."

I cradled his cheek, wanting to tell him so many things.

"Don't," he said, his voice trembling.

I wanted to do this. I wanted to have a choice. My entire life, I'd never had a choice. This could be one of mine. Maybe I'd feel guilt and regret it, but I was so tired of feeling guilt and regret over wanting things in my life.

Church's words to me flashed through my mind.

He terrified me, but I loved him. He needed to understand I could love them all.

I shifted so our lips were a breath away from each other.

"Sirena," he pleaded softly, closing his eyes. "*Cupcake.*"

There was a loud bang on his door, jerking us apart. The pounding had nothing on my pulse rushing through my body, my ears filled with the noise.

The door banged open, bouncing off the wall, before Sin entered the room, Mirage behind him.

Sin's gaze darted to how close Bryce was to me. He lunged forward, but Mirage was quick to get between them.

Bryce immediately moved to shield me from Sin's fists as he got to his feet.

"What are you doing here?" Bryce demanded.

"Sirena called Sin. She was scared. We went to Cady's, and she said she was with you," Mirage explained. His blue eyes moved from Bryce to me. "Little bunny, are you OK?"

I gave him a slight nod.

"Perfect. Then, no issues here. Come." Mirage held his hand out to me.

I looked from his hand to Bryce, who wore a pained expression on his face.

"There will be plenty of time to be alone with her," Mirage said, his focus on Bryce.

Bryce stepped aside, and I got up.

He was quick to grab my hand and pull me against his body, his lips at my ear.

"I'm going to win you, Sirena. Whatever it takes, I'll be with you too."

I kissed his cheek and stepped away from him as I took Mirage's hand. My heart was in my throat, and there was a weird hope in my heart that his words were true, as scary as it was.

"Bryce. You should be working." Mirage handed me off to Sin, who didn't wait to pull me out of the room and down the hall, leaving Mirage with Bryce.

"I was worried sick," Sin snarled, tugging me along roughly. I stumbled, trying to keep up with him. He led me into the elevator and smashed the lobby button on repeat angrily, swearing while he did it.

"What the fuck, Sirena? You can't call someone asking for help and then disappear!" He was so angry that his cheeks were red. He punched the wall of the elevator, making the car tremble from the impact. I shrank into the corner, away from him.

He continued to rant and rave before grabbing my hand, then dragging me out of the elevator and to the outdoors.

I still didn't have a coat, and the cold bit at me roughly, making me shiver.

Sin was still yelling, tugging me along behind him.

"Fuck, Sirena. Goddamnit!" he yelled. "I thought you were being hurt. I didn't think you were shacked up with fucking Bryce Andrews. What the fuck were you thinking? What were you even doing with him? I rushed over to help you, and you didn't even need any damn help! You were too busy being cozy with that asshole. Fucking damnit. You can't cry wolf and then expect everything to be OK! You can't do stupid shit like this and hope everything works out! You know it doesn't. You know it fucking ends up in you practically dead in the woods!"

Tears rolled down my cheeks as he screamed at me, his breath coming out in white puffs.

"I can't get to you every damn time you call, so the next time you make a fucking call to me begging for help, actually need the help!"

"I-I'm sorry," I choked out, shivering. "What does it matter, Sin? You don't have to come—"

He lunged forward, his face inches from mine. I jerked back, but he wound his arm around me and tugged me closer.

"It matters because you matter. It matters because it's you, Siren. It's *you*," he whispered. "You matter to me."

I swallowed at his words, his warmth soaking into me as he continued to hold me.

His eyes darted to my lips.

"I would fucking die if something happened to you. Do you understand me?" He gave me a slight shake. "I'd go with you. I would. I couldn't handle a world without you in it. It's not a world worth living in. It's fucking not. You don't understand the hold you have on me. The hold you've had on me since the day we met. Every cut, every bruise, on my body, I do in your name. All that pain dims in comparison to the pain I feel at not having you. Each day it grows. I-I can't—"

I closed the space between us and crushed my lips to his.

He didn't move beneath me. No kiss back. Nothing.

Confusion raced through me, and I pulled away.

He stared down at me, his bottom lip trembling before he lost control of himself, grabbed my face with both hands, and crashed his lips against mine in a soul-penetrating kiss. I fell into the kiss, deepening it like I was searching for my next breath.

He pushed us backward, and I hit a tree along the trail, the snow shaking free and gently coming down on us in a white, powdery mist.

Sin knew how to kiss. He poured his soul into it, his tongue thrashing alongside mine like he was trying to burn everything about it into his memory. Like he was never going to get this moment with us again. His tongue ring clanged against my teeth, but I didn't care.

What he took, I freely gave, letting go for a moment to feel him. To know him.

"Tell me to stop, Siren. Tell me," he rasped against my lips. "I'm scared of what I'm capable of if I don't."

"I'm not afraid of you, Sinful," I answered back. "I'm not."

He let out a growl and pressed his lips back to mine, stealing my breath in one moment and delivering me new life in the next, his hands back to cradling my face. Then, tangling in my hair.

He broke away, leaving us both breathless.

He said nothing as he stared down at me, but he didn't have to. Everything was written on his face and etched into his gray eyes.

His words were his truth.

My kiss was mine.

I looked past him and stiffened.

He turned away to see what I was looking at. Immediately, he released me.

"Asher," he rasped. "I-I-"

Ashes didn't say anything. He simply stepped forward and took my hand in his, pulling me away.

Still silent, he placed his jacket around my shoulders as Mirage came out of the building and trotted over to join us.

Mirage's blue eyes took me in before he looked to Sin, then Ashes.

Luckily, he remained quiet.

"Asher, man. I'm sorry. I-I lost control. I wasn't thinking—"

"That's always been the problem, hasn't it, Sinclair?" Ashes asked. "You never think."

Sin looked crushed as he looked from Ashes to me.

"Siren. I'm sorry."

"Come on." Ashes took my hand and led me away, but not before I looked over my shoulder to see Sin standing where we'd left him, Mirage at his side.

My heart broke.

This wasn't Sin messing up. It was me. I'd nearly lost it with Bryce, and I'd finally lost it with Sin. I was the mess. The factor that was screwing everything up.

We walked home in silence, me hating the fear I was in. I didn't want anything to happen to Sin. He didn't deserve that.

To make matters worse, I couldn't get the kiss out of my head.

"Go to bed, Sirena," Ashes said when we stepped inside the house.

Stitches frowned as he rose from the couch.

"What's going on?" he asked.

I couldn't hold it in any longer. A sob escaped me, and I rushed to my room, my heart shattering.

But all I could think about was how I had to fix this. If it was the one thing I could make right, I was going to do it.

For both Bryce and Sin.

And even Mirage and Asylum.

I was in too deep and didn't have a ladder.

All I had were three watchers who loved me dearly and who were going to completely lose it on innocent people, starting with Sin.

The darkness within me stirred, making me sob harder as I curled into my bed.

It was a place of protection. A place of bravery. A place where another me lived, the me who could handle it all.

I wanted to let it out.

Squeezing my eyelids closed, I focused on how to fix things. How to escape the monster I was slowly becoming.

# STITCHES

"What the fuck is happening?" I demanded. "Where was she?"

I'd been pacing the room since Ashes called to let me know she'd left Cady's and gone with Bryce. Ashes instructed me to stay behind in case she came home. It took all I had not to bound out of the house and find Bryce before introducing him to my fists.

Again.

Ashes went to the couch and settled on a cushion. He stared into the crackling flames of the fireplace before pulling out his lighter and flipping it open and closed as was his way.

I scrubbed my hand down my face and sat on the L of the couch as I waited for him to speak. Whatever it was had to be bad because this Ashes was subdued. Worried. Angry.

A full ten minutes of silence passed by, his flipping of the lid on his lighter beginning to slow.

"Asher?" I ventured.

"I went to Bryce's. I was walking the path to his dorm when I heard Sin yelling. I stopped to listen," he said, his voice soft and shaking.

"What was he saying?" I asked, hoping it wasn't stupid shit that would get his ass kicked. This time, it really would end in his death, the stupid bastard.

Ashes shook his head and went silent again.

It took several long beats until he finally spoke.

"He told her his feelings. Then. . . they kissed."

I stared into the fireplace at Ashes's words. Stunned didn't even begin to describe my feelings. While I could easily see Sin was developing something for Sirena, I never thought he'd do anything about it.

But I'd be a fool to not think so because I was there when he'd brought her back to us. I'd heard his words and seen him kiss her then. Granted, she wasn't conscious, but this was huge.

Especially if Church caught wind of it.

He explained in great detail to me when Ashes left earlier what he'd do to Sin if he caught him getting close. Church was stubborn. So was Sin. This was a fucking nightmare.

I got where Church was coming from on it. He knew Sin was unstable sometimes. He failed to realize we all were. I was stuck in the middle with Ashes between the pair of them. I wasn't even sure which side I was on. While I got Church's side, I was seeing Sin's too.

I rubbed my eyes. "What now?"

"I honestly don't know," Ashes murmured. "Church is against Sin coming back. He'll lose his mind over this. Sirena initiated it, so that means something. And god knows what she has going on with Asylum or Bryce."

We were quiet, contemplating everything.

"Church wasn't opposed to Asylum. At least he didn't really seem that way."

"Well, she wasn't out there kissing Asylum, though. So if she wants him too, that'll be a whole other thing. Right now, it's Sin. And probably fucking Bryce because I see the way they look at one another." Ashes finally sank back against the cushions and stopped flipping his lighter open and closed. "Fuck, Malachi. What are we going to do? Church will be back soon."

I nodded. He was right.

"Well, I think we should let them be together as much as they can be before Church gets back," I said.

Ashes looked over at me. "What? How will that help?"

"They might realize it's not worth it. Sin might be too much of a broody pain in the ass for her. You know he's a grouch. Letting her hang out with him like that might be what they need."

"And if it makes it worse? Then what?"

"Then we deal with it. I don't know how, but I think it gives us some options. Like I said. She might hate him after spending too much time with him. If she does, we never speak of it. Let her get it out of her system."

"He was meant to be with her with us," Ashes said, sitting up.

"Yeah. So. . . it's truly the best option."

"You want him to come home?" Ashes studied me.

I sighed. "Yeah. And no. I'm still angry because of all the shit that happened, but I don't hate him. Not like I did a few months ago. I'm willing to do this. For angel. I want her to be happy."

Ashes raked his fingers through his hair before blowing out a breath.

"You're right." He pulled his phone out and stared down at it for a moment. "Church is still in Chicago. Did he say for how long? An estimate?"

"He said at least a week. He'll be calling Wednesday to update."

"OK. So then, let's do this." He pushed the screen and put it on speaker. The phone rang on the other end several times before Sin answered.

"Asher, man, I can explain."

"Do you love her?" Ashes asked. "No bullshit, Sinclair. Just answer the question honestly. Do you love her?"

Sin was quiet on the other end before he finally spoke.

"Yes."

"Then come over. Church is gone yet, and we want to talk. Sound good?"

"Yeah. I'll head over now."

"Sin?"

"Yeah?"

"Only you, OK?"

"Of course. I'll see you soon." The phone clicked off, and Ashes looked at me.

"Well, here we go," I said. "Are we going to tell Sirena?"

Ashes shook his head. "No. He can tell her."

I nodded, realizing I'd have to give them space while Sin was here. All I wanted to do was hold her close and tell her I loved her, but I forced myself to remain on the couch.

Fifteen minutes later, there was a soft knock on the front door.

"Ready?" Ashes asked.

I looked at him. "We're dead if Church finds out."

"The way I see it, we're already dead." He shrugged and got to his feet, and went to the door.

He probably had a point. Ashes always did.

# SIN

"Don't take any shit," Mirage instructed as he walked with me to the watchers' house. I knew I was supposed to go alone, but Mirage insisted on keeping me company while I walked there, promising he'd leave once we arrived.

"I'll take whatever they give me," I said. "I don't want to fight with them anymore."

"This could go really bad, so make sure you're doing what you need to do."

I straightened my jacket. "What do you mean? What have you seen?"

"Everything has been so cloudy lately." He let out a frustrated sigh, his rabbit ears bobbing.

"You have been quiet."

"I'm trying to figure shit out. Bryce loves her too. Can you imagine all of us with her? Wild."

I shook my head. "I very much doubt I'll be able to come home, and I know they won't let Andrews in."

I knew what I'd seen with her and him when we'd burst into his room. She cared about that asshole too. I wasn't a fan, but at this point in my life, if I got to be with her, I wouldn't bat a lash at who else she chose, as long as I was part of the lineup.

Most likely, though, I was walking into a trap where I'd be beaten to death. It didn't bother me. I was tired of the struggle and ready for it to end. Maybe it was a little depression. Who the fuck knew? I just didn't feel happy. The only thing that made me happy was her. Siren.

We reached the watchers' house, and I stared up at it, my stomach in knots.

"It's going to be OK." Mirage smiled, cocking his head to the right. "Oh yes. It'll be fine."

I dragged my focus from the house and looked at him.

"Love hurts, Sin, but I promise it's worth the pain." He looked over at me and smiled before pulling out his carrot and taking a bite.

I smiled at him. "What will you be doing?"

"Wild animals belong to the forest, my friend. I'm on my own journey of redemption." He clapped me on the shoulder and took a final look at the house before he turned and rushed to the woods, letting out a whoop as he dove through the snow and darkness, disappearing from view.

"Weirdo," I muttered before hauling in a deep breath and going to the door.

It was now or never.

✝

AWKWARDLY, I sat on the couch, staring into the fireplace. It hadn't been like this when I lived here. Everything was normal. Comfortable. Now, I felt like an invader in a space I didn't belong.

Ashes flipped his lighter open and closed five times before staring at the flame and doing it all over again. Stitches's legs bounced as he raked his fingers through his dark hair.

I didn't want to be the first one to speak, so I remained quiet, waiting for them to tell me to say my final words.

"Church isn't home yet. He won't be for at least another week," Ashes finally said.

I nodded, wondering when they were going to nail my coffin closed.

"Sin, do you really care about Sirena?" Stitches blurted out.

I snapped my attention to him, my heart in my throat. "I-I do. I fucked up. I know I did. It's something I live with knowing. If I'd have known. . . fuck." I tugged at my hair. "I didn't know I'd feel this way. I didn't know. It's different than it was with Bells. This feels so much. . . more. It feels real. Like maybe I-I finally got it right," I finished in a soft voice.

I blew out a breath and swallowed, my focus on the fire.

"I know I fucked up my vow. I said I wouldn't touch her. That I wouldn't get close. I failed you guys and I keep doing it. If you want me to leave and never show my face again, I will. Church gave me his hunting knife. I-I'll finish the job—" I pulled the knife out and held it against my wrist, feeling completely out of control and lost. Devastated. Heartbroken. I felt like throwing up.

The bite of pain as the blade pierced my skin made me grind my teeth.

"Stop!" Ashes sprang forward with Stitches and grabbed the knife from me. "What the fuck, man?"

"I'm putting an end to it—"

"You're nuttier than squirrel shit," Stitches snarled. "We've been through enough bullshit. Don't add to it. I don't want to watch your ass die. Prick." He gave me a disgusted look before going back to his seat and shaking his head. "I'm the one who tries to kill himself. Don't take my fucking thunder, douche."

Ashes tossed me a washcloth for my bleeding wrist. I pressed the cloth against the small wound and held pressure to it.

"Do you need to get sutured?" he asked.

"No," I mumbled, knowing it wasn't too deep and wouldn't bleed for long. "I'm fine."

Ashes let out a grunt and left the room anyway, only to return with a bandage. He handed it to me, and I put it over the wound, knowing he wouldn't relent until I did.

We were all quiet for a moment after.

Finally, I asked the question that was killing me.

"Where's Sirena?"

Ashes and Stitches shared a look.

"She's upstairs in her room. Attic," Ashes said. "Waiting for you."

"What?" I looked from Ashes to Stitches and back again. "What do you mean?"

"We mean, you have a week to get shit sorted with her. If you want her, now is your chance. We know Church can be stubborn, but so are you. If Sirena decides she wants you back and she wasn't being impulsive, then maybe Church will let it go," Ashes explained.

"And if he doesn't, he'll probably kill you," Stitches added.

I absorbed the information, so many ideas going through my mind.

"It was always supposed to be us, Sin," Ashes said gently. "Stitches and I are good if you're serious about it. But if you hurt her—"

"I would die for her," I said fiercely.

"I know." Ashes gave me a smile. "She's yours tonight. For the week. Go up there and talk to her. Maybe something good can come from this. Just. . . if you decide you aren't feeling it, I want you to be gentle with her."

"If she wants me, then I'm here to stay," I said, meaning it.

"Well." Stitches gestured upstairs. "She's in her room. We made her one in the attic. Don't fuck this up, or we'll fuck you up."

"I won't," I promised, getting to my feet. My heart was going a mile a minute. My hands shook.

"Sin. Relax," Ashes said. "You're going to do great."

I let out a shaky breath. "Yeah. Yeah. I-I'll be fine."

With those words, I went upstairs and stood outside the closed attic door, my heart still racing. I had no idea what I was going to say to her, so I figured I'd wing it. Maybe a miracle would happen.

I opened the door and let it click closed softly behind me before quietly making my way up the stairs. When I got to the top, it was to see her pretty bedroom. The little twinkle lights she had hung up were the only light. In her bed, she lay beneath the blankets, her breathing deep and even.

Carefully, I went over and stared down at her. From the dim lights, I could see tears dried on her cheeks. The thought she'd been up here crying because of me made me sick. Deciding I needed to make a damn move to try to fix this, I let out a breath and gently pulled back her blanket before crawling into bed with her.

Drawing her into my arms, I held her tightly.

She immediately curled into my body, her fingers twisting in my t-shirt.

I knew she was still sleeping. It took her a moment before her lashes fluttered, and she stared up at me.

"Sinful," she whispered.

"Siren," I answered, my throat tight. I pushed her hair away from her eyes and allowed my fingers to trace the tear stains before running my knuckles along her jaw.

Her eyes asked the question her mouth wouldn't.

"The guys told me to come see you," I said. "They know I'm here. They're OK with it. Well, Ashes and Stitches. Church doesn't know, but maybe I can win him over."

She said nothing, and I thumbed her bottom lip, our kiss alive and well inside my head.

"Siren," I whispered. "Can I kiss you?"

She gave me a slight nod of her head, making my heart soar.

I leaned in and carefully brushed my lips against hers, everything within me on fire. Making this work had to happen. I wanted to prove I wasn't a shit bag, but most of all, I wanted to feel again.

These feelings were different than anything I'd ever felt before, though.

These feelings were like Ashes's fires. Stitches's anger. Church's crazy. A part of me I'd never let go of before, but now that I was feeling it, I never wanted it to end.

I cradled her face and deepened the kiss, never wanting to let her go.

I was here and knew leaving would break me. I didn't need a week to prove my feelings or think about them. Test them. I was in.

Her tongue slid along mine, making me groan softly while tugging her closer. There was no way I was letting this go.

This was it.

The nail I'd been looking for to go into my coffin.

All this time, I thought it was just my bullshit that would be the end of me, but I knew it was her. She was everything I'd always wanted.

She was everything I'd fight for, even if it meant I had to face Church head-on.

Nothing would stop me.

Nothing.

# SIRENA

$S$in didn't push for more with me. He simply slowed his kisses to a stop before he held me in his arms, whispering sweet things to me while I rested my head atop his chest, his heart thrumming in my ear.

"I can't believe I'm here," he said softly. "With you in my arms. It doesn't feel real."

I moved my hand lower on his abdomen. He exhaled slowly as I ran my fingers lightly against the bare patch of skin peeking out from beneath his t-shirt.

"I have so much to say but lack the words," he continued. "I-thank you, siren, for the chance after all the shit I did. I don't know how many ways I can say I'm sorry, but if you ask it of me, I'll do it."

I gently pressed my finger to his lips to silence his worries. He planted a kiss atop my head and went quiet.

Knowing the guys had allowed this to happen filled my heart. I'd been so confused, and I'd really thought that after tonight, everything would just crash and burn. We weren't out of the woods yet since we needed to get Church to allow it, but I was hopeful. It was the best I had right now.

Maybe there was some part inside me that was scared to not be protected. Maybe it was why I was falling hard for the men in my life. It could be a hope I'd have them there to keep me safe. The hope for something more.

I closed my eyes, the darkness peeking out to remind me that the only real way to be safe was to take out those who hurt me so they could never do it again.

I smiled at that before drifting off to dreamland.

✝

I AWOKE the following morning to Sin's arms still wrapped tightly around me. Inhaling deeply, I tried to carve the way he smelled deep into my mind. He smelled of spice and a hint of leather, much like Ashes and Stitches did. The difference was there was no tinge of smoke and cherries, like with Ashes, and no bit of sandalwood and fresh linen, like with Stitches. With my eyes closed, I drew in several deep breaths until I was content, envisioning the way he looked. The way he kissed. How his gray eyes reminded me of stormy skies and how his touch was like lightning on my skin.

Carefully, I untangled myself from him and went into the bathroom, where I freshened up before returning. He'd barely moved, so I crawled back into bed and reclaimed my spot.

"Hey," he murmured, draping his arm around my waist and dragging me back against his body. It felt so weird to be this intimate with him, considering everything we'd gone through, but I definitely didn't hate it. Even through my nerves, I knew this was right. Before he'd ever hurt me, I'd wanted him.

Now, here we were, on the cusp of something terrifying. Despite what he'd done, I felt like he'd paid his penance and deserved to come home. I felt like I could trust him. People didn't save your life if they wanted you dead, and I knew he'd rescued me from the woods with Asylum.

I let out a soft sigh, and he raked his fingers through my hair.

"We only get a week, siren," he said in a low voice. "That may be it. Once Church comes home, it's probably game over."

I pulled away and stared into his sad eyes before pressing my finger to his lips as I did the night before. He went silent, so much concern on his handsome face it made my heart stutter.

It didn't take a genius to know his fears. They were mine too. Church might completely lose it on him. On me. We were playing a dangerous game, me probably more than Sin, because deep in my heart, I wanted more. I wanted Bryce. Asylum. All of it. Even my rabbit.

"What are you thinking about?"

I fluttered my lashes for a moment as a means to clear my worries from my mind, knowing it wasn't going to help, but deciding I needed to just focus on one problem at a time. In this moment, getting Sin home with the guys was my top priority. Everything else would eventually fall into place.

At least, that's what I kept telling myself. Dealing with one thing at a time was what I needed to do.

I said nothing, watching his lips turn into a slight frown.

I didn't like to see him frown. I didn't like for any of my guys to frown. We'd all been through hell and back and needed to smile more.

I wasn't sure how to make that happen, though, except to try to reunite everyone.

"Do I need our notebook?" he continued, his thumb making gentle circles on my cheek as he cradled my face.

I liked our notebook. It was like a history book for us.

I gave him a pleading look which made him chuckle softly.

"OK. I'll go get it." He made to pull away, but I was quick to twist my fingers into his t-shirt and hold him in place.

The smallest smile curled his lips upward at my gesture.

"I promise I'll be right back. Wait for me." He placed a gentle kiss on my forehead, and I released him, letting him go. He probably wanted to change his clothes anyway.

I watched him slide his feet into his boots before he left the room, casting a final look of longing at me that made butterflies dance in my stomach. Once the door clicked closed behind him, I got up and quickly showered before putting on a pair of leggings and a long, pink, cozy sweater.

I stared at myself in the mirror for a few moments, trying to decide what to do with my hair. Finally, I decided to leave it hanging in loose waves around me.

Once back in my room, I sat at my easel and began painting in an effort to keep the fear and worry out of my mind.

It didn't take long until I'd created the image of Sin with his blond hair hanging around him in a shaggy mess, his gray eyes sad and downcast.

"Angel?" Stitches called out, his heavy footsteps coming into my room. I'd been so lost in my painting I hadn't heard him on the stairs.

His warm hand rested on my shoulder, and I finally turned to look up at him.

"Hey, baby," he greeted me softly. "Is everything OK?"

I gave him a slight nod, and he knelt in front of me, taking my brush from my hand and placing it on the easel.

"Can we talk?" He took my hand in his, and I let him lead me to my bed. We sat on the edge of it, both of us quiet for a long time, before he spoke.

"I saw Sin leave this morning. Did you two, uh, I mean, did you guys have sex?"

I remained silent for a moment as he stared back at me before I shook my head.

He blew out a breath and offered me an unsteady smile that looked misplaced on his handsome face.

"I want you to be happy. So does Ashes. It's why we decided to do this with Sin. We have about a week before Church gets back. There's something we need to discuss, though."

I reached for his hand and gave it a squeeze, ready for him to lay the news on me. I assumed it was bad news, judging by how quiet he seemed.

"You don't know this, but when Church spends too much time in the Underground, he tends to become. . . unhinged." He cleared his throat, and my stomach tightened with worry at his words.

"We can already see how it's affected him. He sort of just disconnects. My therapist would say it's a coping mechanism and a way to partition that part of his mind off as a means to keep his sanity. But honestly, angel, he loses a piece of his mind whenever he's there. You and Sin trying to work out your differences can be dangerous if Church snaps. Ashes and I love you to hell and back and will do all we can to protect you. But know that Church is Church, and we're all playing a dangerous game."

I sat quietly, absorbing his words. It wasn't a secret how unhinged Church and the guys already were, but the fear washed through me at what it could mean if he really did snap. I didn't want anyone to be hurt because of me. Not Sin, Ashes, Stitches, Asylum, Mirage. . . Bryce.

Damnit.

I hugged Stitches, the worry over how complicated all of this was taking hold. He let out a soft breath and kissed the top of my head, his arms around me.

"I love you, baby," he murmured. "I'd die to keep you safe. I'd *kill* to keep you safe."

I swallowed hard at his proclamation. I'd do the same for him and the guys.

"Just. . . don't sleep with Sin. Don't let anything happen there. It might be the thread you pull to save the entire thing, you know?" he continued softly. "I know Sin can be a smooth talker, but hold out until it's sorted, OK? Wait for Church to be OK with it. For now, get to know one another. You may hate his grouchy ass."

I smiled at his words, knowing exactly how much of a grouch Sin was but also knowing he'd come a long way since the beginning.

"Oh, angel, we're in hell, aren't we?" he asked, gently raking his fingers through my hair. "Sin fucked up and hurt us all, but I miss him and want him to come home. I worry about Dante, though. Just. . . be good, OK?"

I pulled away and peered into his dark eyes. With a small nod of my head, I agreed to his terms, earning a smile from him.

"Let's get you fed." He got to his feet and offered me his hand, and I took it, allowing him to lead me downstairs.

Life was like taking the stairs. One step at a time.

I repeated it in my head, my lips moving with the words.

The little blip of darkness within me sighed, letting me know we could just say to hell with the steps and jump.

I'd call that plan B.

# MIRAGE

I watched Sin rummage around the room, his hair a wet, tangled mess from his shower, his shirt off with his scars and injuries on full display.

"What are you looking for?" I asked, watching him from the place I sat on the edge of the bed. I noted the new wound on his wrist, my own ugly memories swimming through my head. I shoved those aside and focused on the moment at hand.

"My rosary. It was here a minute ago."

"It's in the bathroom."

He looked at me and frowned. "I put it on my nightstand."

"Yes. Then you picked it up and took it with you into the bathroom."

He hesitated for a minute before stalking back to the bathroom. A moment later, he emerged, the rosary clutched in his hand.

"So they're letting you in, huh?" I watched him grab a t-shirt from his dresser and tug it over his head.

"Not really. I get a week to win her over, then I can deal with Dante."

"Who will try to kill you," I said, cocking my head to the right. "But you'll do the right thing and win him over."

He turned to me, worry on his face.

"Is he actually going to try to kill me?"

I shrugged. "It's Dante Church. Of course, he will. I don't need to be psychic to see that. You just need to have a bartering chip. Well, *we* need a bartering chip."

"Do we have one?" He grabbed his jacket and turned back to face me.

"Maybe. I've been looking into this shit with the fucker who touched her in the woods." My chest tightened with the barely controlled rage I had. I inhaled deeply, hoping to quell the storm within me before continuing. All I'd been doing lately was obsessing over the monster in the woods who hurt her. Who robbed her. She'd always been an easy target, and I was fucking tired of her being in pain. These assholes needed to pay.

"I know it's not Linley, but it has to be someone in the same mindset as he is. A demented sex pervert." I closed my eyes briefly, wishing I could get a clearer image of things.

Sin raised a brow at me when I opened my eyes. "Names?"

I sighed and shook my head. "I don't know. My fucking head feels like a dumpster fire lately. I don't know what's going on with it. Is this what it feels like to be. . . normal?"

Sin chuckled. "I'm not sure because I don't think any of us here are normal, but maybe it's a shadow of normal."

"Shadow," I murmured. "Shadow." I picked my carrot up from my bedside table and took a crunchy bite before getting to my feet.

"Where are you going?" Sin called out to me as I went to the door.

"Out," was all I said before heading to where the distant voices led.

I ROUNDED a corner and nearly ran right into Bryce who was walking while staring at the ground.

"Shit." He let out a gasp of surprise when he realized I was there. "Sorry, Mirage."

I smiled at him, taking in the way he maintained his distance, his gaze darting around the empty path. I cocked my head to the right, surveying him.

"You're always so nervous," I commented. "Or are you?"

He scoffed at me and looked toward the science building. "Thanks for saving me in the woods. I don't remember if I ever told you."

"Don't play games with me, Andrews. You know it wasn't me who saved you. Right?"

He turned his attention back to me. "Asylum. Mirage. It's all the same, isn't it?"

I caught the meaning in his words, knowing no one having heard it would have batted a lash. But me? I saw right through it.

"Sure. We'll let everyone run with that idea. It's worked so far."

He grunted. "OK. Great. I'm meeting up with my friends, so I need to get going—"

"Oh?" I crinkled my brows at him beneath my rabbit mask. "Where are you meeting them?"

"My dorm."

I nodded. "Where were you?"

"Getting snacks." He stared back at me without an ounce of emotion on his face. I liked that.

"What did you get?"

"I got some cookies. A few bags of chips. A couple brownies."

"Not into healthy eating, huh?"

His nostrils flared as he stared back at me. "What do you want, Seth?"

I grinned at the use of my name. "Only making conversation. Sin is off romancing my girl, so I'm out here looking for trouble. Guess I found it, huh?"

"I'm not doing anything wrong."

"You just stole from the cafeteria. We both know we aren't allowed into the storage area. It has a damn lock on the door. Big ass combination, if I remember correctly." I narrowed my eyes at him. "Right?"

He looked away from me. "Seriously, I'm going to be late—"

"Well, you guys always seemed pretty OK. I'll come with."

He hesitated for a moment before letting out a sigh.

"Fine. You should know the group is afraid of you."

I waved him off. "They're afraid of Asylum. I'm Mirage. You know that."

He went silent and began walking, me at his side. I let him be in silence, hoping maybe he'd spark up a conversation. I wasn't exactly sure how he'd fit into the watcher dynamic with the guys because everyone had their *thing*. Bryce was just. . . normal.

Well, outwardly, but I knew better than that.

We rounded the path to his dorm before I decided to break the silence.

"Are you going to ever tell her?" I asked while we walked.

I could feel his tension at my question.

"Tell her what?"

"You know what, Bryce. Don't play stupid. We both know your truth. Are you going to tell her?"

"What would it matter?" he asked glumly.

"For starters, she's under the impression you're a sweet, normal boy. We both know that's bullshit."

He stopped and turned to face me. "Listen, Seth. I don't need this shit right now. I'm not in the mood to be taunted and fucked with, OK?"

"You're still pissed me and Sin showed up, huh? Ruined that kiss you wanted so much."

He let out an angry snarl at me and looked away.

"What would you have done had it happened? Huh? What could you do given the circumstances?"

"I don't know."

"And that's your problem. You don't know shit about what you're doing. Get your shit sorted, Andrews. You keep hesitating. Pull the fucking trigger already."

"And end up like Sin? Like I was in the woods, nearly gutted?" He scoffed. "No thanks."

I shook my head at him. "You're not this person. Why are you pretending to be?"

He let out a bitter laugh. "I am who I need to be in order to survive. I think we all are here. You're more than Mirage and don't claim your identity, do you. . . rabbit?"

I stared him down for a moment. He didn't back away. He showed no fear, further confirming what I knew of him.

"She needs to learn to protect herself," he continued in a low voice.

"You're supposed to be helping me find the guy who did this. So far, you have jack shit for me."

He stepped up to me, meeting me nose to nose.

"I don't take commands from you, Mirage. I'm doing this because I give a damn about her. This has nothing to do with you or any other dick on this campus. Get that through your head. *It's her.* Believe me when I tell you I'm logging the fucking man-hours on it." He licked his lips. "I have a lead."

"Names," I snarled, ignoring the other shit he'd said.

He shook his head and backed away from me. "Nah. I need to confirm it before I give names. Don't need you choking him with your carrot like you did to Linley, or beating him like you did to Eric Phelps." He eyed me. "That's right. I know you beat the shit out of him on the lowdown and are the reason he's been put into the med ward."

"Of course you do," I said to him. He was really starting to anger me. "I'm sure you know about Jason Winkle and Austin Daly too."

"Broken arm. Broken nose. Of course, I know."

I gave him a dark smile.

"You're good at what you do, Bryce. It's why you're here, but I expect better. I want a name. I want to kill this guy. Put that incredible mind of yours to work." I was done. I turned to walk away, but he called out to me.

"Hey, Seth."

I paused and looked over my shoulder at him. "Yeah?"

"Asylum said you can't read minds. That you can't get into them. If that's true, how did you know about me?"

I cast him a sinister smile.

"Sometimes we lie. You already knew that, though."

And with those cheerful words, I left him to mull it over.

# CHURCH

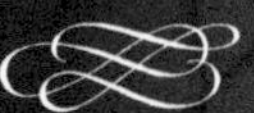

$S$omething was going on back at Chapel Crest, and I needed to get home and squash that shit. Ashes and Stitches were right. The longer I was in the Underground, the more deranged I became. I didn't need them to point it out. I could feel the darkness seeping through my veins with every breath I took in this fucking hell I was stuck in.

I had a little bit of a plan, but it wasn't much. And the last thing I wanted to do was give in and have *a look* at what was happening back home. All I knew was that shit didn't feel right. My assumption was Sin, but it also swung to that fucking Bryce Andrews.

"Lost in thought or just lost?" A familiar voice called out as I walked the halls through the mansion that sat over the Underground palace.

"Asylum," I greeted him, not surprised he was there. I knew he worked for my father. Or at least my father believed he worked for him. I was under the impression he was on our side at the moment, given what I knew and witnessed from him.

We all had a part to play. Asylum played his well.

"Maybe a little bit of both," I muttered, stopping to speak to him.

He smiled at me, and I took note of the blood dots on his face. "Working hard, I see."

"Always." He looked past me, a muscle thrumming along his jaw.

"I was under the impression you were staying behind at Chapel Crest." I narrowed my eyes at him. "To help if help was needed."

"I'm here and there. Don't worry, though. I'm more there than here."

I sighed, hating his riddles.

"I think you love them." He turned his attention back on me. "Here's another one. *In the darkness, he lurks while you do the work. When he finally steps forward, you'll realize the truth. He's as big a part of her as I am her youth.*"

"Andrews." His name was sour on my tongue.

He shrugged. "My advice to you is to let nature take its course. I think you'll eventually change your mind on whoever it is."

"He's never going to join us. He's not strong enough. You know he's not."

"Am I strong enough?" Asylum raised his brows at me.

I studied him for a moment before answering. "You have a better chance than he does."

"Good to know." He grinned at me again. "Listen, Andrews is an issue only if you make him one. Like I said, let nature take its course. And sometimes, that course is a little violent. Wait and see. Now, if you'll excuse me, I have to get back to work. Someone needs an eye exam." He twirled his fork and let out a bark of laughter. "I'd like to come home too, Dante."

He departed, leaving me standing there, wondering what the fuck was truly the matter with him. Maybe he was better at playing the part than I was because he skipped a little before he disappeared around a corner, humming that same damn song Sirena hummed, his fork in his hand.

Knowing I needed to get to the meeting with my father, I pushed everything out of my head and focused on that. If I didn't, I would get overloaded and just lash out.

And that never ended well for anyone.

✝

"DANTE, my boy, you've done well." My father's deep voice interrupted my thoughts. I glared at him and slammed back the drink he'd poured me.

When I didn't say anything, he surveyed me and sat forward, his hands clasped in front of him at his desk.

"You're unhappy."

I scoffed. "How observant, Father."

He let out a soft laugh. "I do not understand why you are the way you are. You have everything, including power and a kingdom. What can I do to make you happy?"

"Let me leave here and return home."

"This is your home."

"This is a pit of despair," I snapped at him. "A place where the weak and unfortunate come to die. As I am neither, I do not see it as my palace."

His lips thinned. "You wish to return to Chapel Crest."

"You know I do."

"Funny, I had a hard time getting you to go. Now look. Clawing to get back there."

I said nothing, watching as he sat back and smoothed his tie. He was wrong about that. I didn't want to go because I was worried about my mother. Leaving her alone to his madness nearly killed me, but she begged me to leave. In retrospect, I knew she did it as a way to give me a chance. I'd gone even though I hadn't wanted to. And she'd suffered as I knew she would. Each day, I hated myself for it.

"I will give you this gift, my son. My pride and joy. I am freeing you as you wish. You may return to Chapel Crest soon. You've learned every aspect of our enemy. I trust in you to deliver the next time I call on you. You will not disappoint me, yes?"

I ground my teeth for a moment as I stared back at him. If I failed,

Sirena would be harmed. The family I'd fought to have would suffer. I had no choice but to obey until the day I had the means to end him and his terror. Of course, it would only give birth to mine.

Funny how things worked like that.

"I will not fail. I always deliver on my promises," I said, my voice a soft, even hum.

A wide grin spread across his face. "You truly are your father's son. I am nothing but impressed with your work. You will be rewarded."

"I only require the safety of my family. For Sirena to be mine," I said. "I ask for nothing else. Sign her soul over to me."

"You shall receive all that and more. Finish this task for me, and I will sign my name on the dotted line for you. Let us have dinner."

"I do not wish to dine here." I tried to keep from grinding my teeth together, my irritation at an all-time high.

He chuckled and got to his feet, completely ignoring my frustration. Or maybe I'd gotten so good at remaining emotionless on the outside he didn't catch it.

"Of course. I have a table at Monico's already booked for us. Come. I'd like you to finish out the week here with me."

"You said I was free to return to Chapel Crest." I rose to my feet, my elation at the possibility of going home deflating quickly.

"Yes, you are free. I would like for you to remain here for a few more days. I do need one more thing from you."

Of course. A fucking catch. There always was.

"And what is that?"

"It's really only a side task. I'd have assigned it elsewhere, but I feel it's a good final job for you for this visit."

"Sounds like fun," I muttered as we walked to the front door. The men opened the door for us, four of them moving in to walk behind. I knew how this worked. He brought two to man the vehicle, armed to the teeth, with the other two following closely in another vehicle. His entourage. It was one of the reasons I couldn't kill his ass. This entire place was crawling with idiots who'd die for him. Idiots who would overcome me since there was a vast number of them prowling the halls. My father's orders were straightforward. If something happened to him, kill whoever did it, even if it were me. It was an issue I was working on. It was why I needed to somehow get him alone or get enough manpower to gut his ass, get out safely, then return to take over.

Of course, there was the issue of loyalty too. Just because the men were loyal to my old man didn't mean they were loyal to me. They feared me, so that was a good start.

"I need you to simply go in and check on him. Make sure he's still working."

We got into the back of the blacked-out SUV, two of the men getting into the front like always. The partition was in place, so I knew they couldn't hear us.

"And if he's not?" I stared out the dark window, watching the scenery move past.

"You're creative. I'm sure you'll know exactly what to do. Ensure he works. I do ask that he keeps his hands and fingers. He does require those to work."

"So I'm free to remove everything else?"

A wicked smile curled his lips upward.

"Bring me the spare parts if they happen to come off. I don't like to waste. You can see to him after dinner."

I said nothing, hating him a little bit more.

*Just a few more days. . .*

Then I'd be home with my girl and brothers. I only hoped I wouldn't be adding Sin to my body count when I returned.

✝

I STOOD outside a wooden door on the ninth level of the dungeon. Around me, the sounds of soft sobs and incoherent babbling sounded out. Typical for this part of the world.

I hated it down here. It was a fucking nightmare sent from the asshole of hell. The quicker I could leave, well, the quicker I wouldn't mentally descend further into my own brand of madness.

With the key card, I buzzed the door open, nodding at the two men guarding the door. Father kept his most prized possessions down here. Many of them I'd never seen before, so only the devil knew what was holed up at this level of hell.

Carefully, I stepped into the dim room. As far as holes in hell went, this one wasn't what I expected. There was a toilet, a sink, a bed, and a computer with five monitors connected to it.

And a man hunched over and staring intently at all the screens of code. He was a tall man. I could tell he'd wasted away after being trapped here many years, but that was typical. He may have been a force to be reckoned with at one point.

"Tell him I'm working," the man called out gruffly with a Russian accent. "I'm only one man."

I walked deeper into the room and stared at the monitors, taking in all the information. I had no idea what any of it meant. Computers weren't really my thing. Ashes spent more time fucking around with them than I did.

"What are you working on?" I finally asked.

"I'm working on breaking into Ivanov's accounts. He has them on lockdown. I've never seen code like this before."

I watched in silence, wondering what my father was up to. Whatever it was could seriously fuck us all if it went south.

"Work harder," I said in a deadly whisper. "Faster. Results are needed now, not tomorrow."

The man stopped typing furiously and didn't move for a moment. Finally, he turned and faced me.

I blinked rapidly at him, something in his face making my guts churn.

He was familiar. Too fucking familiar.

"I am trying. I can only do what I can do. He has me roadblocked at every turn. He's smart. Ivanov's paranoia works in his favor. It always has."

I swallowed. "Indeed."

The man rubbed his eyes and pushed his dark hair away from his face, his blue eyes filled with exhaustion. Black rings from lack of sleep circled his eyes.

"What's your name?" I asked after a moment, my heart thrumming quickly.

He looked up at me from his seat and let out a soft laugh.

"It's funny you should come in here and ask my name. I figured the son of Satan would know it, or does he not give you pertinent information like names when he sends you to do his bidding, Dante?"

I narrowed my eyes at him and pulled my knife out. I gave it a twirl, trying to soothe the monster inside me who wanted answers but feared them.

"Right." He eyed my blade. Judging by the look in his eyes, he'd contemplated attacking. Had he not wasted away down here, we may have been a fair match. He knew better, though. "My name is Anatoly Sokolov."

"Is it?" I demanded in a low rumble.

"It is. Of course, I've gone by many names. I'm sure you've heard of me before. Nathaniel, Frederick, William—"

"Jonathan," I said, a slight wobble to my voice.

He blinked in surprise at me. "Yes. Jonathan."

"Lawrence."

He crinkled his brows as he stared back at me. "Everett told you that one?"

"He told me nothing," I snarled. "You have daughters."

He exhaled, his hands trembling. The careful, strong mask he'd had in place slipped. "Do you. . . know my girls?"

"Yes."

"You-you haven't hurt them, have you? They aren't here, are they?" He went from somewhat cocky to terrified as he rose to his feet. "Please. They are good girls—"

"How would you know?" I asked, anger surging through me. "You haven't seen them in years."

"I-I couldn't."

"Or wouldn't," I snapped at him. "You walked out and left them. Do you even know what happened to them?"

The trembling in his body grew. "What happened to them? Please. .
."

"Cady has gone mad. Tried to kill her stepfather. She trapped him
in his car and set it on fire."

Anatoly's face paled at my words.

"And Sirena." I let out a bitter laugh, taking in the fear in his eyes.
"Someone tried to kill her when she was younger. Left her to rot in a
box in a shed."

He pushed past me and went to his toilet, where he fell to his
knees and heaved his guts into it. I watched, waiting to finish the
story. When he was done, he wiped his mouth and looked at me from
his knees.

"Where is she buried?" he whispered, tears on his cheeks.

"Did I say she was dead?"

He frowned. "She-she lives?"

"Oh yes, she certainly does. In my home."

"What?" He stumbled to his feet, the fear in his eyes morphing into
something that showcased his terror. "You-you have her?"

"I do," I answered as he stood before me.

"Please, I'll do whatever you want. Don't hurt her. She's a good
girl. The sweetest. She's my-my princess. . . She-she dances. Ballet.
Sings. Her voice is like an angel's—"

I let out a laugh at him, angry at him for reasons I wasn't able to
pinpoint. Perhaps it was the fact he'd been under my nose the entire
time and I was angry with myself over it. Or maybe it was because
he'd walked out on her and Cady.

"I remember you," I said, closing the space between us. "That night
with Ivanov. The night my father took you from him. I assumed you
were one of Ivanov's top dogs."

"Tell me about Sirena," he choked out, ignoring my comments.
"Please. Let her go. Set her free. She-she wants to be a singer—"

"She no longer speaks," I snapped at him. "Her ordeal has left her
mute. She wouldn't even respond when I first met her. But after I
claimed her. . ." I smiled at him, drinking in the way he shuddered and
sucked in a sharp breath. "She came around for me."

I twirled my knife again. "She still doesn't speak much, but she's a little crazy these days. I suppose being with me, she'd have to be. I tend to rub off on people."

He lunged forward, his hands hitting my chest hard. I took a step back, my blood on fire with all sorts of wicked thoughts.

Quickly, I caught myself and whipped forward, stopping his next attack and kicking his legs out from beneath him. He went to his knees with a cry, my knife at his throat.

"Why did you fucking leave her?" I demanded as he clung to my arm, my knife biting his flesh.

"I-I had no choice," he rasped. "I could never stay long. It was part of my-my job."

"Who do you really work for?"

"N-Nicolai Reznikov," he choked out.

I released him, letting him fall forward.

"So you were on the inside trying to get Ivanov."

"And De Santis," he said through a cough. "I-I worked both ends."

"For what purpose?"

"Nicolai wanted information. He knew I could get it."

"A mole," I muttered, shaking my head at him. "How are you connected to Reznikov? Blood?"

"No." He righted himself slightly and crawled back into his chair to stare up at me. A thin line of blood glistened on his neck from my blade, giving me a sense of satisfaction that helped quell the fire in my veins.

"Nico and I have been friends since we were children. Our fathers were friends. Best friends. You know how it works in our world."

I did. Children were heirs and ushered in whether they liked it or not.

"I wonder why it is that Nico hasn't looked for you," I said, frowning. Nicolai Reznikov was a monster. He was mostly situated on the west coast but had once had his fingers deep in Chicago. He'd pulled out suddenly, and now his name was simply whispered in terror. De Santis took over most of the city, and Ivanov took what was left. And us. We sat somewhere beneath it all, waiting. Watching. Plotting, apparently.

"Perhaps he has, and you simply do not know about it. Or maybe he's smart to let me go. Waging war on the Underground seems a bad idea, don't you think? Everett's reach is far and wide." He stared glumly at his hands before he let out a soft sniffle.

I sighed. He'd been in this fucking hole for too many years.

"I'd have gone back," he said after a moment while wiping his eyes. He stared at me, so much sorrow on his face it made my skin crawl. I hated seeing sadness in people. It angered me. I had no idea why, so I didn't spend a lot of time exploring the emotion.

"I-I have another child aside from Sirena and Cadence. I'd have gone back for all of them."

I stared him down, knowing damn well Sirena and Cady had no idea they had another sibling.

"Who is the third?" I asked.

He looked away from me. "Why would I tell you? So you can trap her too?"

I let out a soft, dark laugh. "Sirena belongs to me. Trust me, it's better than who she could belong to. I'm a walk in the fucking park compared to my father."

He scowled at me, the fury still alive and well in his eyes as he gazed back at me.

"Do you torture her like your father tortures the people here?"

"No," I answered evenly.

He crinkled his brows while surveying me. "You-you *love* my daughter?"

"I do," I said. "And she loves me."

He shook his head. "Impossible. Sirena is a sweet, innocent girl—"

"Sirena is an adult with a mind of her own. She chose me as much as I chose her. She is mine, and I am hers."

"She would never. What did you do to her?"

"I did nothing she didn't want," I responded fiercely. "Now. Tell me who the other child is."

He glared back at me. "I will tell you nothing."

I sighed. "Listen, Anatoly, I'm not in the fucking mood. Get your shit done here. Fucking off to buy yourself some time won't work. I'll kill you without batting a lash. There are other mediocre hackers out there we can replace you with."

He rose from his seat, his bottom lip trembling. "I want to leave here."

"Then get the fucking job done," I snarled at him.

"Everett will never let me leave. This is where I'll die."

He was right. I was certain that's exactly what would happen to him. I also knew I couldn't be aware of his whereabouts and let that happen to him. It would devastate my specter.

"I'll ensure your freedom if you finish the job," I said, my voice low.

He drew in a sharp breath. "What?"

"For my girl. I'll let you out. She deserves to know why you did what you did. Why you left. And you're going to tell her yourself."

He nodded wordlessly.

"But I want to know the name of your other kid. Sirena and Cady deserve to know they have more family out there. If you die before you're released, then it dies with you. You've already fucked their lives enough."

"And you won't harm her? Or tell your father?"

"I won't give him shit," I hissed out. I put my blade to my palm and made a cut. The blood blossomed out, dribbling down my palm and to my wrist. I placed my hand on his old torn shirt, leaving my mark over his heart. "You have my word and my blood."

He visibly swallowed when I pulled away, contemplating my promise for a moment. "I have another daughter. Her name is. . ." He exhaled and scrubbed his hand along his cracked lips.

"Her name is Bianca. Last name Walker."

I logged her name away. I'd look into her soon enough.

"Get this job done," I said, backing away from him. "I'll see to it you're free. You'll need to be patient and understand it'll take some time on my end, but I will come for you."

He watched me go to the door without a word. It wasn't until I knocked to be let out by the guards and the door creaked open that he finally spoke.

"I really am trying to hurry. I'm not lying. I'm stuck."

"Then get unstuck. Have a good night, Anatoly." I stepped out of the room, the lock clicking into place behind me.

Drawing in a deep breath, I stepped away, knowing I had my fucking work cut out for me. Saving him would be a real bitch.

But I'd do it.

For Sirena, I'd do anything.

# SIN

I sat beside Sirena on her bed, scribbling quickly to her, my heart racing as fast as my hand was. Running back as quick as I could with our notebook in my hand, I'd burst into the house and rushed past Stitches and Ashes, who were playing a hockey game on one of the gaming consoles in the living room. Stitches had sworn as Ashes scored, calling me a cocksucker for apparently startling him and making him lose focus.

I paused over my message and reread it.

**Do you want to build a snowman? I know it's sort of lame, but I've never actually made one before, and I saw the painting you're working on. I like how the snowman's head isn't attached, and he's in the cemetery.**

I sounded fucking stupid, but I'd already written the message. Frantically erasing would just make me look even worse, so I cleared my throat and handed her the notebook.

She took it from me, clearly eager, and wiggled in her seat. The cute move made me smile. Her colorful eyes swept over my message for a moment before she wrote back to me. As patient as I could be, I waited. Finally, she slid the notebook onto my lap.

**I would love to build a snowman with you. I could take your snow-ginity.**

I smirked at her words before looking to her to see her eyes wide and full of innocence. A soft chuckle slipped past my lips, and I shook my head before responding.

**I would love for you to be my first.**

She clapped her hands excitedly before getting off the bed and tugging my hand to follow. Like a kid on Christmas, I did, my heart thrumming excitedly.

"What are you guys doing?" Ashes asked from his spot on the couch. They'd gone from gaming to watching a movie. I took in the way Stitches's leg was jumping and how he rubbed his hands up and down his thighs. He was agitated. It didn't take a genius to know why.

Me. Always me.

In the grand scheme of things, we were all on edge. Time was ticking. Everything had the potential for getting seriously fucked up more than it already was.

"Uh, we're going to build a snowman," I said sheepishly. Sirena grabbed her jacket and tugged it on. Dragging my gaze away from Ashes and Stitches, who shared a look, I grabbed her cute fuzzy hat with the dingle ball on top and pulled it onto her head, earning a sweet smile.

"Maybe go for a walk after. I'll have her back soon—"

"Take your time. A week isn't long." Ashes looked from me to Sirena, a look on his face I couldn't decipher, but the dread weighing down my guts knew. A week until Church returned. I could be dead this time next week.

I had to make this fucking count. A few moments were all I really had at this point.

"Angel, I—" Stitches raked his fingers through his mess of dark hair before he offered her a pained smile. "Remember, OK?"

She went to him and wrapped her arms around his neck. I watched him hug her tightly to his chest and whisper in her ear, to which she pulled away and kissed him gently. She went to Ashes next and offered him a kiss, which he took, deepening it quickly before abruptly breaking it off and clearing his throat.

"Have fun," was all he said when she stepped away from him.

She came to me before taking my hand and pulling me to the door. I cast a look back at the guys to see them watching. Everything about the looks on their faces screamed their concern.

"I'll keep her safe," I said.

"You fucking better," was my answer from Stitches.

I stepped out the door, her mittened hand in mine, and focused on the day ahead of us. I couldn't bear to focus past that. The fear just worked that way for me.

✝

I LET OUT a laugh as Sirena tumbled over the massive snowball in her attempt to make it bigger. The thing had to outweigh her three to one. Her momentum in trying to push it only another inch had her rolling over the top and landing flat on her back on the other side with an audible huff of frustration.

I stopped rolling the middle portion of the snowman's body and went to her.

She stared up at me, her dark hair a wild mess around her, her eyes wide and lips parted. The rosy red of her cheeks and the tip of her nose made me smile.

"Do you want help now?" I asked.

She'd brushed me off before when I offered and handed me a snowball as an indicator to get to work on my own. I'd done it, enjoying how she was taking charge. Now, it appeared she needed me.

With her bottom lip jutted out, she looked from me to her massive snowball before letting out a sigh and nodding.

Grinning, I went to it and gave it a push. I had to hand it to her. That damn thing was heavy. I was surprised she'd done as well as she had.

When I got it to the spot she indicated, she clapped her mittened hands together and grinned at me.

That made twinging my back worth it.

I gave her a wink and went back to rolling my ball. She wandered off and collected twigs for the arms and various other bits in the yard while I heaved the snowball onto the bottom portion. Taking a step back, I surveyed my work.

It was decent. Perfect, actually.

I looked around to see Sirena coming back toward me with her sticks and a few other things in her hands.

"What's this?" I took one of the pinecones from her and eyed it before looking back to her.

She smiled and dropped the pile into the snow before starting another snowball. I watched, taking in how serious she was. Once she had the ball the size she wanted, she placed it beside the bottom portion and came back to me.

I helped her gather the items she'd gotten and held them while she used the pinecones for ears and broke others apart to create eyes and a small mouth.

She pushed a small limb into my hand, and I stuck it into the snowman's torso while she placed the other arm. We took a step back and surveyed our work.

"Not bad," I murmured, drinking it in. "It's a masterpiece." I wound my arm around her waist.

After a moment, she turned to me and went up on her tiptoes. Her lips swept softly against mine, making me let out a contented sigh before she pulled away, her pretty eyes sparkling.

"What do you want to do now?" I asked, brushing a snowflake from her rosy cheek. I looked past her to the sky. It was getting dark, and the temperature was starting to fall even lower. Despite that, she wrapped her mitten around my gloved hand and gave me a gentle tug to follow her. I did without a moment's hesitation.

I'd follow that girl to my very death, that much I was certain.

# ASHES

"Let's go do something," Stitches said, coming into the house and shaking the snowflakes off him.

"What's something?" I averted my attention from the show I was watching on TV and pulled my cherry vape out. I'd been trying to quit, but I knew I'd just smoke more weed if I did that. I supposed, in the long run, weed was better for me. At least, that's what I'd been reading lately.

I'd been trying to distract myself from burning down the house. Or at least a portion of it. Stress typically put me right on the cusp of a forest fire. I was teetering on that delicate line. Knowing Church was most likely going to explode when he got home, I was losing it. Once he found out about Sin and Sirena, we'd have World War III in this bitch. Someone always died when Church lost it. I really didn't want it to be Sin.

Inhaling, I sucked in the sweetness of nicotine before blowing out a cherry-scented ring.

"I don't know. Something. Anything. I need to get out of this fucking house. I hate winter. I hate being stuck here. I hate worrying—"

I got up and went straight for my jacket and boots. The last damn thing I needed to deal with was Stitches falling again. Plus, I needed a distraction too.

"Come on." I looked back at him after pulling my boots on. "Let's go set something on fire and then get some food."

He grunted and followed me out, having already been dressed for the outdoors because he'd been getting high on the patio overlooking Lake Superior.

"Nice," I commented as we stepped onto the walkway.

In our yard was a decapitated snowman with pinecones for ears.

"That's fitting," Stitches muttered. "Maybe Sirena is psychic."

I sighed. "Let's hope not."

"Hey, where's Rina?" Cady called out, trotting up to us, her breath puffing out in white clouds.

"Uh, she's with Sin," I answered. "Why?"

"Damn. I was thinking we could do a scary movie night and some hot chocolate. She makes really good hot chocolate, and I had a craving for some." She frowned and pushed a dark piece of hair away from her face. "Where are you guys going?"

"Out," Stitches mumbled.

"Cool." She fell in step with us.

I glanced at Stitches to see if he'd protest, but he looked deep in thought.

I cleared my throat. "So, what's been up with you lately?"

"Nothing. Just hanging out," she answered.

"Different dude every night?" Stitches came out of his thoughts and looked to her.

She smirked. "Sometimes. I don't fuck all of them."

"At least not at once," he shot back. "You have a sign-up sheet or something?"

She rolled her eyes. "You're being an exceptional cocksucker today, stranglehold. What's going on with you?"

He shook his head and didn't say anything.

"It's Sirena," I said as we trudged to the small shed near our house. I pulled out a key and unlocked the door before stepping inside.

"What about her?" Cady's voice had an edge of concern in it.

"Well, she wants Sinclair now, and Church has threatened to murder him if he touches her. And he's definitely touching her," I said, stepping into the shed. I went to the box on the wall, then pulled out two sets of keys and tossed one to Stitches.

"Wait. And you guys are OK with this? After the shit he did to her?" Cady didn't bother to keep the anger out of her voice.

"She's capable of making her own decisions." I glanced to Stitches, who scrubbed his hand down his face but nodded.

"Yeah, but it's that fucker. He hurt her—"

"He loves her," Stitches said. "We know he does. He's just a fuck-up is all. I think he's over that hurdle, though. Now, he's fallen into the same deep abyss the rest of us have. Only he's still falling."

"What's that mean?" Cady looked from Stitches to me.

"It means when Sin falls, he falls hard. He's. . ." my voice trailed off as I thought about Bells, Sin's ex.

"He's what? A fucking nutbag who should stay away from my sister?"

"No." I shook my head. "Look. He likes her. Hell, he loves her. Church will be back in a week. All hell will break loose. We're all aware of it. Sirena will tell Church she wants Sin. Church will lose his shit. He'll try to kill him. Hopefully, all ends well with Sin managing to get out of it. But understand this. Once Sin makes his mind up about loving someone, he goes all in. And he's in with Sirena. We've seen him."

"If he hurts her," Cady warned.

"He won't," I said firmly. "We trust him."

"Mostly," Stitches muttered as he got on his snowmobile and started the engine.

Cady sighed but didn't pursue the subject. Instead, she climbed onto my ride.

"Uh, I don't think so," I said. "Get off."

"I want to go with you guys. I'm bored. Let me drive that one if I can't drive this one." She pointed to the black snowmobile next to mine.

"Absolutely not. That's Church's. He'd string me up next to Sin," I said.

"Then the other one." She raised her brows at me.

"That's Sin's. No."

"What the hell, Asher? What am I supposed to do then?"

"Stay here?" Stitches called out, offering her a half-assed smirk.

She gave him the finger and turned back to me. "Please? I promise I'll be good. I want to go with you guys."

"You don't even know where we're going or what we're doing," I pointed out.

"Doesn't matter." She crossed her arms over her chest. "I'm coming with you guys."

"For fuck's sake," Stitches called out. "Is this what having an annoying younger sibling is like?"

"Yep." She grinned at him.

I sighed and motioned for her to slide back.

"Can I drive?"

"Claws, you're lucky we're letting you come at all. Just be quiet and move back," I said.

She rolled her eyes at me but obeyed. I got on and fired up the machine before we moved out of the shed and onto some snow.

"Hold on," I called out over my shoulder. "If you fall off, that's on you. We're not coming back to pick you up."

She wound her arms around my midsection and clung to me like a baby opossum.

Stitches rolled his eyes at me as I shook my head.

She let out a squeal as I hit the throttle. We roared out onto the trail, ready to set some shit on fire.

✝

"THAT WAS FUN," Cady said as we walked back into the house several hours later. Night had long fallen, and my nose felt like it was going to fall off my face despite my face mask. I loved snowmobiling, though.

It was my idea for us to get them. If I didn't have my bike, I needed something to cruise on during the winter months.

"You tried to set my fucking coat on fire," Stitches snapped at her.

"But I didn't." She rolled her eyes at him, then flopped down onto our couch and grabbed the remote.

"Motherfucker, I was *in* it!" Stitches yelped, snatching the remote from her. "Asshole."

"You're too sensitive, stranglehold." She grabbed the remote back and turned the TV on. I went into the kitchen, in a feeble attempt to ignore their bickering, and opened the fridge. After grabbing a bottle of water, I returned to the living room to see Stitches threatening Cady with a pillow if she didn't return the remote.

"I'm not watching that B-movie shit," Stitches said. "I'll suffocate your ass if you put it on, Claws."

She raised her brows at him in a challenge. They were driving me nuts.

I reached out and stole the remote from her, making her cry out.

"Asher!"

"Claws." I turned the channel to some feel-good movie about second chances.

"For fuck's sake, Ashes. I'd rather watch that shitty horror movie than this garbage," Stitches groaned. "You know what? Fuck it. Set me on fire. Put me out of my misery."

"Gladly." Cady pulled her lighter from her pocket and flipped the lid, the flame glowing moments later.

Fuck my life.

This was going to be a long night.

I couldn't wait for Sirena to come home. I'd do whatever I could to get a moment alone with her, even if it meant taking time away from Sin.

The alternative was letting Cady set me on fire too. It would be a hell of a lot better than listening to her and Stitches antagonize one another all night.

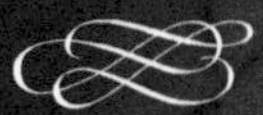

**he snowman turned out good. I really liked the pinecone ears. It was a nice touch.**

I smiled at his words in our notebook as we sat in the cave later that night. I didn't realize he'd had the notebook tucked away in his jacket the entire time, but I was delighted he'd thought to grab it.

We'd wandered through the cemetery before heading to this secret cavern deep in the forest. I liked it here. The heaviness of Chapel Crest seemed far away as I scribbled quickly in the dim light from the heater to him.

**I wasn't going to give him ears, but I was thinking, what kind of snowman doesn't have ears?**

I took in the smile on his face as he read my words. Sinclair Priest was beautiful when he smiled. He was beautiful when he didn't smile, but something about the way his face lit up made me sick with want. Wanting to keep him smiling. Wanting to keep him happy. Wanting so much for him, including his family back.

I was going to make it happen. Somehow.

Church's words slipped into my mind. I swallowed and pushed them away. I didn't want to worry tonight. Or this week. My focus needed to be on Sin right now.

*One thing at a time.*

That little dark cloud inside me peeked around the corner of my mind, reminding me we still needed to make a certain someone pay for what he did to me. Guilt rushed through me at having neglected that.

"Hey. Siren." Sin's warm fingers slid beneath my chin. "Come back, OK? Whatever you're worried about, let it go. Be here with me in this moment."

I stared into his gray eyes and nodded, my throat tight.

It didn't seem to matter how hard I tried. What had happened in those damn woods haunted me like an old ghost. I needed to lay it to rest, but I didn't know how. I couldn't even say his name, let alone do anything about it.

The darkness grew.

God, what I wouldn't give to tear his guts from his body. Wear them like a necklace before I. . .

I blinked, the vision of the hellish destruction in my head clearing.

*Damnit. I was really losing it.*

"What's wrong?" Sin pressed softly. "Talk to me, beautiful."

I blinked at him, my heart pounding. He crinkled his brows as he took in my face like he knew what I was thinking.

"I don't like that you still think about that night." His voice came out in a low, sad, shaky hum, confirming my thoughts. "I-I can't stop blaming myself for it. Fuck. If I could go back in time, siren, I'd change it all—"

I silenced him with a kiss. I hated that he hated himself. He had issues. We all did. It was no reason to continue to punish ourselves over them.

He cradled my face with his hands while deepening the kiss. I parted my lips, allowing him all the control he wanted.

"I want to take the ugly memories away," he whispered against my lips between kisses. "I want to replace them with everything I can give you. My promise is to keep you safe always. My touch. My devotion. My love."

Butterflies fluttered in my chest at his sweet words.

I wanted all of that and more. Without a doubt.

"Fuck, I want to give you a world I never had, baby." He'd managed to shift me back on the couch so he was balancing on his elbows over me, his gray eyes filled with so much adoration that it made my breath catch.

His lips brushed gently against mine before he stared down at me again.

"That night. That I-I did that to you. I wanted to come back, but I was scared. Terrified. So fucking stupid. I knew then that I loved you. I just didn't realize what the feeling was because it was all-consuming. I've never felt anything like it before. I-I believed it was hate." He bit his bottom lip for a moment. "I ran. I wasn't going to come back because I knew what I'd done was going to fuck every-thing up." A pained expression crossed his face which broke my heart.

He made to move off me, but I gripped his shirt and brought him back.

"Stop running, Sinful," I whispered to him.

"Oh, siren." His lips descended on mine again, stealing the breath from my lungs.

It was me who took the lead this time, kissing him hard and deep, desperate to let him know who loved and wanted him. That I forgave him. That I understood.

His hands traversed my body, his dick hard as he pressed between my legs. With my fingers tangled in his messy hair, I tugged him closer and jutted my hips up to grind against him. He let out a soft moan against my lips and rocked forward for me. My pussy vibrated with want as we rubbed against one another.

But just as the heat began to build, Stitches's face entered my mind. His words. My promise.

Damnit to hell.

I broke the kiss off, knowing it was for the best. If I screwed this up, it could cause more issues when Church returned. I didn't want him to return to me fucking someone he was mad at. Risking Sin for an intense orgasm wasn't worth it. When this happened between us, I wanted all the magic, not simply a few minutes of rubbing against each other.

"What's wrong?" Sin's voice came out breathless when I broke the kiss off. "Am I hurting you? I'm sorry." He immediately stopped and moved off me, his fingers in his hair and his eyes downcast. "I-I get excited. I'm so fucking grateful for you, siren. I got carried away. I know you're going through shit, and this might have been too much—"

I sat up and reached for him. He came to me, a sad look on his face that all but broke my heart.

"I'm sorry," he whispered again. "It was too much. I always push for too much."

Desperate, I pulled away from him and grabbed our notebook. As fast as I could, I scribbled a note to him, wishing my words could just come from my mouth instead of only random things at random times.

**It's not you. I want you. I want this. I don't want to hurt Church, though. His feelings on this matter to me too. If I do this with you, it could hurt him. I don't want anyone hurt. I love him like I love you.**

Sin's gray eyes took in my words. I watched as he stared at the paper for a moment before he turned to me, his brows crinkled.

"You love me too, siren?"

I answered by leaning in and brushing my lips against his.

The notebook fell to the ground. He swept me into his arms and clung to me, his face buried in my neck, his arms wound tightly around me.

"I don't know how you could ever love a monster like me, but I am so in love with you too. I am. From the moment I saw you, I knew. I knew you were the one I'd been looking for. I was just so scared." I felt a warm tear drip along my neck before his lips were at my ear, his warm breath tickling my skin. "I fucking love you with every ounce of me there is. I will always love you. You have become my entire world. I only hope I can be a fraction of yours."

He pulled away from me and scribbled those words into the notebook before handing it back to me.

"So you remember," he murmured. "They aren't only words to me. They're promises. I'm yours. In whatever capacity you need or want me, you own me, Sirena. I belong to you now."

I took the pen and wrote the only thing I knew in that moment.

**And I belong to you.**

# MIRAGE

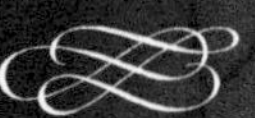

$\mathcal{T}$he worst thing about being wild was the cold. I hated the cold. I stared out at the barren cemetery from the dark line of the woods, watching as Sin walked with Sirena through the darkness to the mausoleum.

"Is it always like this?" I murmured. "Watching. Waiting."

"Always," Bryce answered from my side.

"You really are a shadow," I mused.

"I'm what lurks in plain sight." He let out a sigh and shifted next to me.

"If it helps, I think Sin has finally wiggled his way into her good graces." I watched as Sin pulled her to a stop and kissed her gently beneath the falling snow.

"And you're OK with that?"

I smiled. "She's been through a lot. I owe her. So yes. I'm OK with it. I want whatever she wants. I always have."

"I'm pretty sure she didn't want to be murdered with a shovel."

I ground my teeth at his words. "That wasn't me. That was Asylum."

"Right. Right. Same coin. Different sides. Got it."

I grunted. Honestly, I couldn't wait to just get this shit out in the open.

*Waiting is the hardest part.*

*Don't I know it.*

*Shh. . . the wind is changing.*

*SHUT UP!*

I shook the third voice out of my head and focused my attention back on Sin and Sirena, who had gone to sit on the stone bench near the mausoleum.

"Were you upset it wasn't you trapped in that coffin with her?" Bryce asked.

I was quiet for a moment, contemplating it before I answered.

"At first, I was. I was upset that it happened at all. But you know how Asylum is. He sees things and goes for them."

"And you? You just. . . wait?"

"I'm good at waiting. It's all I know how to do," I said. "Although, I've been getting antsy lately."

"Your inconsistency is killing me," Bryce muttered before pulling his dark hat lower over his head. "So is this cold."

"It's not cold when you're in someone else's arms."

"I'm not fucking hugging you. I barely can stand next to you."

I rolled my eyes at him. "Don't be so dramatic. I'm not telling you I want to roll in the snow with you, Andrews. Besides, I doubt you could handle me. I've heard you're vanilla."

"Fuck off," he grumbled. "And what are you? Chocolate?"

"Me?" I looked over at him. "I'm a spicy little jalapeño, baby."

It was his turn to roll his eyes. "You know, sometimes you and Asylum are hard to tell apart."

I nodded. "Good. That's the point."

"A frustrating one," he muttered.

I ignored him and continued to watch Sin and Sirena. Bryce and I had come out here to walk and talk after I had him go with me to knock Jeff Lowe around a little bit. I'd heard he had some information about who had hurt Sirena. It turned out he was trying to make himself important and had nothing. Well, not nothing. Now he had two black eyes and a broken leg, but hey, some lessons were hard ones to learn. I didn't mind being the teacher.

I smiled at the fact Bryce hadn't tried to stop me. Instead, he'd simply watched silently while the crack of bone echoed through the night. Bryce was as twisted as the rest of us here at Chapel Crest. He just hid it better.

I admired that about him. That and his determination. He was stronger than anyone realized, the watchers included.

"Excuse me," I said, stepping out of the shadows and adjusting my rabbit mask.

"Where are you going?" he demanded in a soft hiss.

"It's a lovely night for a dance," I said, turning to smile at him. "Watch. You'll see."

"Damnit, Mirage. Fucking damnit." Bryce's voice faded away as I moved further from the woods and to the cemetery where Sin and Sirena were still sitting.

"Good evening," I said, stepping up to them. They'd been so lost in one another and their notebook that they were scribbling in they hadn't noticed my approach.

Sirena's eyes widened as she took me in, her lips parting. I loved that look on her.

*Kiss her for me.*

*If I kiss her, it's for me.*

*Prick.*

*Asshole.*

I silenced the voice in my head and looked to Sin.

"Hey. What are you doing out here?" he asked.

"Oh, you know me. Just outside frolicking." I smiled at him.

"Of course you were." Sin took the notebook they'd been writing in and closed it before stuffing it back into his jacket.

"Care to dance?" I held my hand out to Sirena, hoping she'd agree.

"There's no music." Sin shot me a sour look.

"Then sing, puppet," I answered back, not taking my eyes off the beauty in front of me. She cast a look to Sin, who gave her a small nod. It was funny to me she sought his approval. A small flare of anger ignited within me, but I tamped it down, knowing she was that good of a girl and didn't like stepping on any toes.

Her mitten slid against my palm, and I pulled her to her feet and against my body.

"Ready?" I asked, smiling down at her as I placed a hand on her waist and held her other hand in mine.

A tiny smile quirked her lips upward. That was the only green light I needed.

I swept her around the tombstones, the snow kicking out around us, dancing beneath the pale moonlight like we were characters from some gothic Victorian romance.

Just me. Her.

*And me.*

Of course.

Just us.

*Perfect.*

I smiled down at her, relishing in the way her eyes lit up as I lifted her easily over a low grave marker before spinning her around the next.

Before long, her laughter was bubbling out of her and sounding off into the night while Sin stood and watched as a shadow lurked on the edge of the forest, drinking everything in like he always did.

*"Roses and whiskers*

*Don't stop the purrs, mister.*

*This world is too big*

*To go it alone."*

I sang our song as we moved through the cemetery, her smile growing wider with each word falling from my mouth.

*"So follow me through the thicket*

*And just try to fit through the thorns.*

*I'll be right behind you.*

*No need to be alarmed."*

I spun her again before pulling her against my body and staring down into her pretty eyes before softly singing more to her.

*"I'll love you forever*

*And need you for always*
*Remember who we are*
*When we take the monsters down.*
*They'll fall hard*
*But stick next to us*
*For in us, you can trust*
*To get the job done*
*Our pretty little monster.*
*No more tears*
*No more screams*
*We promise to give you the end to some.*
*It's not a battle of fists and hits*
*For you, my monster queen*
*Simply lead the way to the place it all began*
*And we shall leave behind a bloody scene."*


GENTLY, I brushed my lips against hers before pulling away from her. She'd been so lost in the moment that she'd not noticed Sin at our side, but I had. I hoped my words stuck with her. A future that had yet to pass. The help. The training. That was it. Psychological warfare, not violence. Not yet.

"Dance with Sin, pretty girl," I whispered, breaking free from her. "We'll dance again soon. Next time, it'll be in blood."

I placed her hand in Sin's and offered her a smile.

"Until next time, my love."

And then I turned my back and dashed back into the woods.

I always kept my promises.

The answers were coming.

I smiled at that.

# SIN

The week went entirely too fast after I danced again with Sirena in the cemetery after Mirage had left us.

I stayed each night with her after that, her tucked against my body, and my arms wrapped tightly around her like I was afraid she was a dream I'd wake from.

The guys were granting me this grace, but I could see it bothered them that I was hogging her. But I only had a week. Every moment needed to count for us.

I was being a glutton. I knew this. The most the guys got from her was a kiss in the morning and before bed because I always kept her to myself.

"Last night," Ashes said to me while Sirena was in the shower and Stitches was at therapy.

I nodded glumly, knowing the end was near.

"Listen, I know you love her." He opened and closed his lighter five times while he sat on the couch and watched me.

I shifted on the cushion and nodded, my throat tight. The words wouldn't come out without me sounding like a choked-up bitch, so I didn't even try.

"But you know how Dante is. He loses it in the Underground. He's been there for a long fucking time this round. He's already made his feelings known. Just . . . be strong, OK? It'll be shit at first, but we'll get it sorted."

"He's going to kill me." I scrubbed my hand down my face and let out a groan. "Fuck, what am I supposed to do? Say? He's never going to let me come back. I know everyone tells me he'll do what Sirena wants, but Dante also does what he wants. If he's already fucked because of being in the Underground, I don't expect any moments of sentiment from him. I'll take my punishment as he wishes."

"I know, but you shouldn't have to. I get where he's coming from, just like I see where you're coming from. You both love her. He only sees the negative. That's simply how he works. You know that."

"I know I fucked up and want to make it right. That I'm trying to make it right," I said fiercely. "All I know is that I love her with everything I am or could possibly ever be. That I'll stay on my knees forever, begging for forgiveness if that's what it takes. I only want another chance to prove myself." I looked at Ashes to see the expression of sadness on his face. He snapped his lighter closed and looked down at it.

"I know. Just stay strong. We'll figure out how to break the news to him. It may take a few days, so be cool about it."

I nodded morosely, knowing if I jumped the gun, I'd fuck everything up.

The front door banged open, and Stitches came rushing inside, his dark hair covered in snow.

"You need to go. Now," he shouted breathlessly.

I got to my feet, my heart in my throat. Ashes followed, confusion on his face.

"Church. He's back. I saw him in the office only minutes ago. He didn't see me. I knew I had to get here. I forgot to charge my phone, and it died, so I couldn't call. But seriously. Go. He's coming."

"I-I have to tell Sirena goodbye—"

"You can't be here." Ashes's hands landed in the middle of my back. "Get out. We'll tell her."

He pushed me to the door, and Stitches tossed me my jacket.

Desperation raced through me.

"Please," I started, my stomach twisting in worry.

"We'll handle it. I'm sorry." Ashes gave me a look that showcased he really meant it. "Be good, brother. We'll see you soon."

His use of the word brother had me backing away and nodding at him, trying hard to believe it.

"Go," Stitches urged softly. "Don't fuck this up."

I had to leave. There was no other option. With a heavy heart, I turned and went out the door, leaving everything I loved behind but vowing to return soon.

# CHURCH

The last fucking thing I wanted to do was deal with Sully while at Chapel Crest. I'd only watched him fuck a body the day before after I'd gutted it. The places he'd put his dick had sickened me, but my job wasn't to bitch. It was to learn my enemies from their insides out.

And Sully was my enemy.

He thought he was going to be a good servant to me when I came into power.

The only fucking thing he'd be good for is a new rug. I smiled at the idea of skinning him and laying him out to walk on like a bearskin rug.

He'd be the rug in the room where I planned on hanging my father's head from his mounted spot on the wall. Like a fucking animal because that's what he was.

But so was I.

I hoped someday my own kid would do me the honor of putting my sick fucking mind out of its misery.

Of course, I'd not go out before my specter. After that, I'd freely go anywhere anyone wanted. If it was straight to hell, so be it.

But I'd claw my way out to find my girl. A demon on a mission. I knew that much. Heaven didn't have high enough walls to keep me out.

"Dante. You're back. I've only just arrived this morning." Sully greeted me with a half-assed grin.

I said nothing, eyeing him with distaste. His smile faltered a bit.

"We had a good time yesterday—"

I held my hand up to silence him. "We don't talk about shit like that here. Got it? We aren't friends. You're a piece of trash that will eventually get dragged back into hell when the time is right. Until then, you fuck whatever you need to fuck and keep it to your damn self, you sick prick."

He let out a soft laugh. "You can't tell me your dick wasn't hard watching me run my cock through his skull. Maybe I can do that soon to Sirena if you misbehave. Everett said—"

I punched him so hard that he fell over his desk and toppled to the floor. I was on him in an instant, my fist hammering repeatedly into his face. Blood gushed from the cracks I was putting into his skin and pouring out onto his clothes and my hand.

Fuck it.

I was simply going to kill him and send parts of him to my old man. I was done. No one talked about my girl like that. There was no coming back from it.

"Enough!"

I'd been so lost in my rage that I hadn't noticed Vice Headmaster Atkins come in. He tugged me off Sully, who lay on the floor, in and out of consciousness, blubbering incoherently about what he was going to do to me. What he was going to tell my father.

The dead can't scream. I always made sure of that.

"Easy. Dante. Dante. Look at me." Atkins gripped my shoulders and shook me. "Hey. Over here. Dante. DANTE!"

I looked away from the fucked-up face of Sully and back to Atkins.

"There we go."

"Let me finish it," I said in a monotone. "I won't even say you were here."

"But I am here, and I can't let you do that. It's not worth it. You know it's not. Go back to your room, and I'll make sure he doesn't die. Your father would lose it if he died. You know that."

"He'd lose it if either of you died," I said before clenching my jaw hard. "You're both his fucking minions."

"You know that's not true." He gave me an even look. "You know what survival looks like, Dante. Don't pretend like you don't. We're the same. We're both just trying to live."

I let out a snort. He was right. I hated he was.

"Go back to your place. See your friends. It's been too long. I'll handle this."

I glanced to Sully on the floor, blubbering like a lunatic, before turning and leaving the room without a word.

Atkins was a decent guy. Mostly. He was stuck like the rest of us. I knew the feeling all too well. While he didn't make it to the Underground, he did what he had to do here to stay alive. That was just how life worked in our world.

I knew I was covered in that shitbag's blood, but I didn't care. Atkins was right. I'd been away for too long. I needed my family to bring me back down.

As quickly as I could, I made my way to the house, vowing I'd kill Sin if he were inside. When I opened the door, it was to find Ashes and Stitches sitting on the couch with Sirena's feet on Stitches's lap and her head on Ashes's.

"What the fuck happened—" Stitches started while Ashes's eyes widened.

I said nothing and stomped forward before dragging Sirena off them and bringing her into my arms.

She let out a little grunt, still asleep. I took in the dried tears on her face and shot them both a sharp look.

"Why was she crying?" I demanded in a soft, dangerous voice.

"Just. . . a bad day," Ashes said dully. "You know how that goes. We gave her some meds to bring her down so she could sleep it off."

I did know how bad days went.

Without another word, I took her upstairs to my bedroom, determined to make both our bad days into a good one.

When I got inside, I laid her on my bed, noting her deep breathing. She was out. Perfect. I needed this.

I didn't bother to wash the blood off my hands and face. Instead, I carefully undressed her and stared at her beauty, taking in all the dips and curves before stripping my own clothes off.

"So beautiful," I murmured before moving to the bed so I could spread her legs. I parted them easily, taking in the very place I planned on burying myself in only moments.

Fuck, she was perfection.

I'd missed her so damn much while I'd been away. All I'd wanted was to see her. Hold her. Kiss her. Fuck her.

And now I was home, and we were here.

I moved forward and lapped gently at her pretty pink pussy, enjoying how bare she was for me. How she tasted. How her warm body felt beneath mine, perfectly helpless and open to whatever I wanted.

Fuck, it was her I wanted. All of her.

I continued to eat her sweet center, sucking gently against her clit, my dick getting harder by the second as she let out a soft little moan, her breathing heavy.

Carefully, I pushed a digit into her wet channel, noting how gloriously tight she was before adding another. I fucked her with my fingers for a moment, hooking them to hit that spot that could get her off while I continued to flick my tongue against her clit.

She came easily, her orgasm making her unconscious body tremble and her wetness rushing out like a fucking volcano.

I ate it all down, eager for more, but knowing my cock wasn't going to hold out. It ached with want.

I shifted my face away from her pussy and withdrew my fingers before moving forward, my dick in hand. Staring down at her, I took in the relaxed look on her face. Her plump lips. The way her long lashes fanned out against her porcelain cheeks. How her chest rose and fell with each breath she took.

She really was glorious.

Without fanfare, I shoved my way into her hot center, making her body tense at my sudden rough intrusion.

I fucked the same way I shoved into her.

Hard.

She felt like heaven with her pussy sheathed around my cock.

I fucked into her, jostling her while I sucked against her lush tits, leaving my mark along her pale skin.

When I was finished with her tits, I moved to her lips, where I kissed her, never once slowing down on fucking her.

It was when I pulled away to stare down at her that her lashes fluttered.

She was changing. I knew she was. I'd seen it in her eyes before I'd left. She was a sweet little monster deep down inside.

I wanted to tear down the prison she kept herself in and bring her true self into the light.

I'd had plenty of time to think on it. She'd still be my sweet girl, but she'd also be the hellfire the world needed.

That I needed.

I slammed into her hard.

Her eyelids flew open, and she stared up at me, her bottom lip wobbling and tears in her eyes.

"Hello, specter," I husked out, not slowing for a moment. "Your monster is home."

She answered by shifting beneath me in such a way so that she had me on my back. I could have stopped her, but I liked her this way. I liked the monster she was becoming.

She straddled me, my dick buried to the hilt inside her tight heat, and rode me, her tits bouncing in my face.

"Fuck," I groaned out when she pinned my arms over my head and continued her assault.

I rushed to thrust upward to meet her movements, completely lost in her magnificent pussy and everything that was her. My specter.

"Keep riding me like that, and you're going to make me come," I growled, nipping at a breast and making her breathe heavier. "Is that what you want? To make me fill you with my come?"

She answered by moving faster, her hands tightening on my wrists as she fucked me. Her long black hair brushed against my face. My chest. The smell of her perfume flooded my senses.

She was all I knew. All I wanted. A creature as broken as I was who I'd kill for.

I overpowered her and was on her in an instant, hammering away inside her body while she arched her back as her impending orgasm teased her.

Quickly, I tugged her forward so she was on my lap this time. She rode me as much as I rode her back.

And then she came with her head back and her chest heaving, her walls clenching around my dick.

I had no choice but to follow her into oblivion, shooting my load deep inside her with a groan I was sure the guys could hear downstairs.

I loved getting laid.

But I loved getting laid by her the most.

It had been way too fucking long.

We slowed to a stop, and I kissed her gently. Softly.

She pulled away and stared into my eyes for a moment before she ran her fingers lightly along my face, asking the question without words.

"It's Sully's," I answered her silent question. "He pissed me off today. I doubt he'll do it again."

I cradled her face, taking in her reaction.

Slowly, she took my bloodied hand and drew one of my fingers deep into her mouth and sucked.

Fuck. Me.

My perfect girl.

"Oh, specter. I'll willingly give you all the blood of your enemies if you want it." I watched her tongue on my finger. Felt the suction of her mouth as she continued to suck and taste my small gift to her.

"You're really my little monster, aren't you?" I mused when she finally released my finger.

She gave me a tiny smile.

I smiled back.

"Fucking perfect, baby." And it was. I proved it by putting her on her knees and fucking into her body once more, my fingers fisted in her hair as she clung to my headboard.

The perfect welcome home gift.

# SIRENA

*H*aving Sin gone now broke my heart. But having Church back put it back together, even if there were pieces still missing.

The Sinful pieces.

Hell, the Asylum pieces. The Bryce pieces. The Mirage pieces.

I frowned at my thoughts, hating how foul they felt. How wrong they were when I had everything a girl like me could want.

Maybe I was selfish.

Church's lips descended on mine before he stared down at me.

"What's wrong?"

I sat up in his bed and stared down at my hands, desperate to tell him about Sin and everyone else but knowing it would jeopardize a lot of things.

Sometimes I was really brave. Sometimes I was crazy. But mostly, I was a wuss.

I bit my bottom lip as I contemplated how to make my wishes a reality. How I could get Church to see reason for all of it.

But I remembered what he told me when he left and the things he promised if Sin came around.

I felt backed into a corner without a way out. It wasn't just the stuff that happened to me in the woods and my need to scream that monster's name from the rooftops. It was everything. It was building up to a place I wasn't so sure I could tolerate.

I was at the end of my rope with all of it.

Noting I was breathing too hard and fast, I closed my eyes and tried to calm myself. My head hurt. My heart hurt.

Church's warm hand rested on my back for a moment before he shifted on the bed. His fingers brushed beneath my chin and forced my face upward so I was looking into his piercing green eyes, the blood dots from Sully still on his face.

I loved that he'd beaten him. I hated Sully with everything I was. His death couldn't come quickly enough. Knowing he was nursing some painful wounds at the moment made me feel so much better.

"I know it's hell inside your head. Inside your heart. I also live in hell," he said, his voice low. "But there's no reason to live there alone when I'm already there. If you need me, scream my name. You know I'll always answer."

I exhaled and rested my hand against his face, feeling the rough stubble beneath my palm and fingers.

"They're all monsters, Dante," I whispered, knowing the time wasn't right to tell him my secrets.

His green eyes drank me in with each word.

"I want us to be the only monsters left in the end," I finished, my voice barely above a whisper.

"Your wish is my command. Always, Sirena." His lips crashed against mine, sending all logical thoughts from my mind.

I liked that we were monsters together.

We made a dangerous pairing, Dante Church and I.

Someday, we'd show this twisted world what it was like to over-step your boundaries with monsters like us.

CHURCH KEPT me locked in his room with him all evening. Stitches brought us food and left it outside the door for us. It hurt me that Ashes and Stitches were left out in the cold. Lately, all my time had been spent with Sin. Now Church. It wasn't fair to them, and I needed to do something about it.

The next morning when Church tugged me away from the door after fucking me three times in the night, I pushed back and broke free.

He let out a grunt of disapproval, but he didn't try to stop me again. Instead, he followed me downstairs to the kitchen, where Ashes and Stitches were putting some breakfast on the table.

"Hey." Ashes gave me his sweet smile, his gaze darting between me and Church, worry clearly in them.

"Hey." Church released my hand as I went to Ashes and wrapped my arms around him. He relaxed against me and let out a breath.

"Heaven, baby, it's been too long," he whispered into my ear. "I've missed you like crazy."

I squeezed him tighter, letting him know I felt the same way before I released him and went to Stitches.

He gave me a mischievous smile and pulled me close.

"Do you have any idea what it's like to sit down here with Ashes and jerk off on the couch while we can hear Church fucking you all night long? Angel, when I say we felt left out, I mean it."

His words made me smile as he let me go.

"You hear that, Dante?" Stitches called out, his hand still on my waist. "I had to jerk off with Ashes in the living room last night while you fucked her. Bit selfish, don't you think?"

"Absolutely." Church's answer came quickly. "But I never said I wasn't."

Stitches gave him the finger, making Church smile a little before settling in for breakfast. I took Sin's old spot, my heart aching a little more each minute for him, while the guys sat in their seats.

We ate the waffles Ashes made. I poked at my runny eggs, not wanting to hurt anyone's feelings.

"They suck. I know they do," Stitches finally said, giving me a grin. "I made them. Mostly. Halfway. I got distracted. Bored. Said fuck it. They're my fuck-it eggs."

I shook my head at him, biting back my smile.

"Don't eat them. I won't be offended. Asher didn't even bother hiding his hatred for my fuck-it eggs." Stitches pointed to Ashes, who got up and dumped them down the garbage disposal. "He threw them away like nothing. Rude."

"Sorry, man. I like my eggs cooked," Ashes said, moving to clear off the table since we'd finished eating. I watched him, finding myself getting a little warm as his muscles strained against his dark t-shirt.

"Asher enjoys dessert, even after breakfast," Church said.

I snapped my focus to him, my cheeks hot.

"Asher," Church called out.

"Huh?" Ashes turned around, his apron back in place.

"Come fuck Sirena for us."

I quickly drank down my glass of water, knowing my face had to be flaming red. Ashes smiled and strode forward without a word, then lifted me out of my seat before setting me on the tabletop. His lips met mine in a sweet kiss, his hands cradling my face.

Ashes always knew how to make my heart flutter. Always so gentle and sweet. Until he wasn't.

I loved him all the ways he could be.

Even in his frilly yellow and white apron.

Gently, he put his hand to my chest and pushed me onto my back.

"Eyes open," Church commanded as he stared down at me. "Legs spread."

I let my legs fall open. Stitches moved so he was next to Ashes and pulled my panties down my legs for me, praising me for always wearing a dress.

I listened as Ashes undid his belt.

"You're not even going to take off the apron?" Stitches asked, hissing out the question.

"It's a hot look for me," Ashes answered, running his cock along my pussy and teasing me. My breath hitched, and Church tutted at me to be still.

Stitches snorted, and Ashes pushed slowly into my body, making me suck in a sharp hiss of air at how full he made me.

"Oh fuck. I missed this," he husked out, his voice shaking. I noted Church's brows crinkling at Ashes's words before all thoughts left my head and Ashes set to work, thrusting in and out of me like a jackhammer.

"Sorry, baby," he rasped, holding me tightly at the hips. "You feel way too fucking good. God, I love the way your pussy hugs my dick. Fuck." He pulled out and slammed back into me, rocking me on the table.

Church reached out and pushed my dress down and pulled my breasts from my bra, exposing that part of me.

He squeezed and rubbed them, paying special attention to my nipples while Ashes continued working me over.

"Stay still," Church instructed. "Stitches."

Stitches moved onto the table, and I had the sudden thought it wasn't going to hold our weight, but maybe the fall would make the moment more fun.

Church released my breasts, and Stitches straddled my chest, his pants and boxers off, his cock in his hand. He ran the head of his dick along my lips for a moment before pushing inside. I sucked him in best I could, knowing this was just going to be him fucking my mouth. All I needed to do was not bite or gag.

With his fingers twisted in my hair, he fucked my mouth, his cock ramming deep into my throat, making it hard to breathe. Ashes continued his work on my pussy and Church. . . Church watched it all silently with his dick in his hand, stroking himself.

*I wish Sin were here too.*

Stitches shoved into my mouth again, brutally fucking it. I gagged and choked on him, a move that only seemed to spur him on.

"You going to swallow Malachi's come for him, heaven? Huh?" Ashes groaned out, his dick hitting a place deep inside of me that made me want to cry tears of joy.

"I love it when she swallows," Stitches said breathlessly as he continued his onslaught. "Her mouth is fucking perfect. I could fuck her like this all day."

I dug my fingernails into his thighs, making him let out a hiss, his cock buried deep in my throat. It was so hard to breathe, but I loved doing this for him, Ashes, and Church. If they wanted this from me, I'd give it willingly.

"Push her back. I want her head to hang off the table," Church's voice sounded out.

Ashes slammed into me harder, sending me back a few inches so my head hung off the table.

Stitches let out a huff, his dick slipping from my mouth, but my mouth was filled again, this time with Church's dick.

He was ruthless as he fucked my mouth. I tried to keep him at bay by putting my hands against his waist in an awkward position, but he let out a snarl and shoved them down, demanding Stitches get up from where he was straddling my chest to hold me.

"Sorry, angel," Stitches murmured, his voice trembling.

It was an ugly flashback memory for me too.

"Just breathe," he continued. "When you can. Come for Ashes so I can come for you. OK?"

I let out a soft whimper before Church fucked deeper into my throat. I coughed and gagged whenever I could, but that only seemed to drive him into a frenzy because he worked deeper and harder into my mouth, his hands on my breasts, his groans feral and husky.

When he released my breasts, he shifted forward and rubbed my clit while Ashes chipped away at my heat.

"Oh, fuck, she looks good stuffed with our cocks," Ashes said, his hands painfully tight on my hips as he continued to drive into me. "Fuck, I'm going to fill this tight little pussy."

I came hard at his words, knowing I soaked his damn apron because he let out a laugh before pushing so deep I saw stars, his cock twitching as he groaned out his pleasure.

Finally, he slowed and pulled free from me, and Church moved back so I could breathe easier.

But he didn't pull his dick from my mouth. Instead, he instructed Stitches to take Ashes's place.

Stitches did so without a moment of hesitation. He was buried inside me within moments, his hips moving hard and fast, the sound of our slapping skin sounding out.

I gagged on Church's dick again, earning a dark laugh from him. If I thought he'd go easy, I was wrong. He simply continued fucking my mouth like I didn't have a gag reflex and he didn't have a care in the world.

I came again, this time my teeth cutting Church's dick. He let out a snarl and wrapped his hand around my throat and squeezed, his dick so deep I couldn't breathe.

"Careful, specter," he warned, squeezing until sparkles dotted my vision, my orgasm continuing to roll through my body. "Turn me on like that again, and I'll fuck your ass while you try to scream around Ashes's big cock."

I jerked against his body, my nerves going wild as he continued to hold me, balls deep in my mouth and Stitches buried inside me painfully.

"I like the way you fight. Fuck, that's hot." Church released me, and I sucked in as much air as I could when he gave me a moment to breathe, cock-free.

"Fuck. Fuck, fuck, fuck," Stitches shouted, coming hard inside me, his cock pulsing with every spurt. He slowed to a stop, and Ashes high-fived him. Church finally pulled free from my mouth and moved to take Stitches's spot.

I was a mess. I could feel both Ashes and Stitches's release dripping out of me. It didn't stop Church. He burrowed right back into me, his cock taking up residence in what I was sure were my lungs.

I cried out as he worked me over.

"Come on her face," Church rasped. "I want her to be a complete fucking mess for us. We need this, brothers. We deserve it."

If Ashes and Stitches had an issue with his commands, they certainly didn't show it. Instead, they gripped their cocks and pumped them over my face while Church fucked me to the point of my next release.

He cursed as I came all over him. Then he praised me as I shook through one orgasm and into the next as he rolled his hips against the spot that turned me to jello.

"Good fucking girl. There you go, baby. Come for me just like that. Fuck, that's a pretty mess."

I cried, tears rolling from my eyes at how much pleasure I was in. How scared I was for what was to happen, not only with sex but with Sin and the others I wanted.

"Cry for us. More tears," Church groaned. "Fuck."

Ashes reached out and wiped my tears before rubbing them along his cock. Stitches did the same, his moan soft and so full of want that I wept harder, desperate to not disappoint any of them.

My body trembled as the orgasm finally ebbed away. Church took the opportunity to have his and came with a curse of obscenities. Stitches and Ashes followed, their long ropes of white come coating my face, their moans heavy in my ears as they made a complete mess of me.

Church pulled free from my body as I lay beneath the mess.

Then his tongue met my heat, lapping up the mess left behind by him and the guys and driving me back into orbit.

Ashes reached out and began rubbing his come into my skin, Stitches following.

I cried out, my moans so loud I didn't even recognize my voice, as I came a final time. It felt like my soul had left my body before slamming back into me.

Church slapped my pussy, making me jump, before leaving me on the table and coming around to where Ashes and Stitches were standing. He moved between them. I stared up at them, knowing I looked like a complete disaster.

"You look beautiful covered in come, specter. I want you to stay right where you are and think about what a good girl you've been and how good girls don't make monsters upset. Does that sound good?" His words sent a shiver of fear through my body.

"Dante, man," Ashes interjected. "Don't—"

"Or you could just tell me why you haven't been fucking her," Church interrupted.

Stitches and Ashes went silent, and all I could hear was the pounding of my pulse through my ears.

"That's what I thought. Let's let her think about it for a bit."

"At least cover her," Stitches grumbled.

"No, I like her this way. Leave her." Church ran his dick along my lips for a moment before he started pumping it in his hand again. Ashes and Stitches didn't move. They stood right beside him as Church came, his release spurting over my face and adding to the mess.

He leaned down to speak into my ear.

"I want you to really think about this. I know something is up. Tell me what it is before I find out on my own. I know Asher and Malachi. I know how they are when they haven't fucked. What is my pretty little Ghost keeping from me? Hm? You'll get up once I have an answer. Until then, just. . . think." He ran his tongue along my cheek, collecting some of the mess before moving away and leaving the room.

I swallowed hard, trying to not cry and make a bigger mess.

"Sorry, baby. We'll talk to him," Ashes said gently.

"It'll be OK. Give us a few minutes." Stitches added.

I said nothing, my eyes stinging from the unshed tears. Closing my eyes, I drew in a deep breath.

Church was as violent as he was crazy. I knew this. Ashes and Stitches knew this. So I'd do as I was told.

"You know what? Fuck this. Get up—" Ashes reached for me to help me up, but I jerked away from him and gripped his hand. Quickly, I wrote my words onto his palm.

*He knows. I'll figure it out. Leave me.*

"Fuck, baby." Ashes let out a sigh. "Fine. We'll still see what we can do."

"He just needs to smoke a little and come down from being stuck in the Underground," Stitches said, his voice strained. "I'm so sorry, angel. I'll be right here if you want to get up."

I closed my eyes and felt a tear slide out.

I'd made my decision.

I'd wait and hope I came up with a way to tell him without him losing his mind.

More than my life depended on it.

Sirena spent all day on our kitchen table, her tits and pussy exposed and our come drying on her face.

"Enough is enough," I said to Church as we sat down for dinner and ate around her.

Her small body trembled, but she didn't fight it.

"I agree. So someone should tell me what's going on," Church said as he dipped his fork into his mashed potatoes. I watched him eat without any concern on his face. I hated it when he spent time in the Underground. He always came back a complete fucking asshole.

I also knew if Ashes and I fought it, we'd have an even bigger problem. Getting Dante to come down always took time. He stayed near the edge of his sanity for days, sometimes weeks, after returning from the Underground. It had been a long time since we'd had to deal with it. Back then, we had Sin to help. He always had a way to distract him and keep him levelheaded. Now, we didn't have shit but our naked and violated girl on our kitchen table while we ate around her like she was a fucking centerpiece at Christmas dinner.

I'd even tried getting Church to smoke with me. He'd raised his eyebrows, clearly knowing what I was up to, before going back into the house.

"She needs to use the bathroom and eat," Ashes said. "This is bull-shit, Dante. You know it is."

"Yet, you don't deny something happened," Church said easily. "If nothing happened, you'd fight more. I know you better than you know yourselves." He ate again and gave us both a serene look.

Ashes threw his fork, and it bounced off the wall. Sirena jumped when his plate crashed to the floor next. Her breathing picked up.

"Making a mess isn't going to solve anything," Church said easily, gesturing to Sirena. "Ask our tight-lipped girl. It didn't help her so far."

"You're being an asshole," I said. "You know this is bullshit. Just let her up. Maybe we can all talk then. You'll be reasonable."

"Me? Unreasonable?" Church let out a sinister laugh. I noted the goosebumps on Sirena's pale skin and the way she trembled. He was scaring her. This was fucking stupid and ignorant. I could see maybe getting pissed for an hour, but she'd been lying there all fucking day. Nothing we'd tried with him was working. Not talking. Not smoking. Nothing.

Enough was enough.

"Sirena, get up," I commanded. "This shit is over—"

"Don't you dare fucking move," Church snarled, making her quake a little more. "Not until someone tells me what the fuck is going on."

Ashes shot me a look, letting me know we needed to do some-thing. We always let Church lead and have his way. But we had Sirena to protect now. It couldn't be this level of crazy. Not after all the shit she'd been through. Losing her to whatever dark place she drifted to wasn't an option.

"Sirena," I said gently. "Come with me. It'll be OK."

Her chest heaved, and tears rolled from her eyes, but she wouldn't move. I knew she was afraid of Church hurting Sin once he found out. Ashes and I both knew this would end badly. The fact she was willing to take this punishment and remain silent spoke volumes about her heart.

I didn't want to see it shattered.

Fuck, what a goddamn mess.

If only people would listen to me.

Anger rushed through me. I hauled in a deep breath, forcing myself to chill the fuck out before I went completely batshit crazy. I didn't like my girl this way. I didn't like my brother this way.

I'd been so lost in Sirena that I hadn't been paying attention to Ashes and Church yelling at one another. Church shoved his chair back so hard it crashed to the floor, startling Sirena again, before he stormed out of the room, leaving us alone with her.

"I'm telling him," Ashes said.

Sirena gripped his hand and shook her head, tears continuing to roll from her eyes.

I gave her a pained look, wishing she'd just come out with it.

"Message Sin," Ashes muttered. "All hell is going to break loose. He needs to be on alert."

I pulled my phone out and shot a message to him, letting him know Church was losing his fucking mind and to be careful. He didn't respond to me, making me grind my teeth. He was probably off with Asylum, or Mirage, whomever the fuck he was this week, trampling through the fucking dark woods.

Sighing when he didn't answer, I twined my fingers through Sirena's and stood at her side, Ashes on her other side. We stood that way for a long time, both of us clearly trying to work out what we were going to do to fix this. We were both aware everything was fucked, though. If Church decided he was going to punish Sirena more once he found out, we'd have a big problem. I didn't care if I died trying to protect her. I would, and Church could carry that fucking guilt around that he'd murdered me for the rest of his miserable ass life.

Time passed by. It had to be at least an hour before I looked up and saw Church come back into the room, holding a notebook. He sat on the couch without a word.

I looked to Ashes, who wore a frown on his face. Before either of us could say anything, there was a knock on the front door.

"Could you get that?" Church asked in a low voice.

Sighing, I released Sirena's hand and went to the door, really fucking hoping it wasn't Cady because she'd flip her shit if she saw

Sirena this way. But maybe that was a good thing. She'd punch Church in the face so I didn't have to.

I pulled the door open to find Sin standing there.

"What are you doing here?" I snarled at him.

"Church said we needed to talk," he answered.

"I sent you a message and told you to lie low. What the fuck, motherfucker? Are you trying to get yourself killed?"

He gave me a sad smile. "Sometimes death is a nice vacation from a miserable life, Malachi. I've been searching for it for a long time. Maybe tonight it finally finds me."

"Don't do this. Fucking go, Sinclair. Don't. You don't want to see this."

"Malachi, it's cold outside. Let our guest in," Church called out.

I ground my teeth. "Run, Sinclair. The other option is dying. It's not fucking worth your life."

"Yes, she is," he said softly before stepping past me.

Fuck.

Fuck.

Fuck.

# SIN

*I* stepped into the living room to see Ashes standing at the table and Church on the couch.

Neither of those things did I care about.

It was my girl lying half-naked on the table that got me.

"She's pretty, isn't she?" Church stood and moved to his chair before gesturing for me to sit on the couch.

"What the fuck is going on?" I demanded, staring at the beautiful woman on the kitchen table. The woman I longed for. That I loved with everything I was.

"Sinclair. Come. Sit," Church said. "We can talk."

I heard Sirena sniffle, and she shifted like she was going to get up.

Immediately, Church was on his feet and at her side, his lips at her ear, whispering something to her that made her choke out a sob but remain still.

Ashes cursed at him then went and wiped her eyes for her.

I was going to rip Dante's head from his fucking shoulders.

He sat in his seat, but I hadn't moved an inch. Stitches walked past me and took a seat on the center of the couch. A place where he could get between us.

He was always thinking in the language of violence. A lot of things changed in life, but that one was steady as a river.

Ashes flipped his lighter open and closed in the kitchen, his hand wrapped firmly around Sirena's.

"We can get through this a lot quicker if you come sit down." Church held up the notebook. The one with all my conversations with Sirena. I swallowed hard, knowing this was probably the case, when I got the call from him.

I glanced back to her half-naked form on the table and blew out a breath before moving to the couch to sit. I knew going to her could set him off. If there ever was a time to be calm and work shit out, now was it.

"Do you think I'm an idiot, Sinclair? That I don't know what happens in my home?" Church started.

"I don't think you're an idiot, Dante. You know that."

"Really?" He tapped his fingers on the notebook. I tore my eyes away from all the conversations I knew lay beneath the cover and steadied my breathing. I knew I should have told Mirage what was going on, but for once in my life, I wanted this shit over with. If today was the day I was going to die, so be it. I already said she was worth dying for, and I meant it. At least I'd go out knowing I'd finally gotten something right in my life. That I'd truly loved and been loved back. That was all that mattered now. That and her safety. If my death meant Dante continued to keep her tucked away and safe the way he did, so be it.

"Yes," I said.

He let out a soft laugh and grabbed the TV remote. I watched him flip to a different setting and OK it with a password. A moment later, the complete feed of the house came over the screen.

"What the fuck?" Ashes called out thickly.

Stitches scrubbed his hand down his face, his legs bouncing.

Church cycled through every room of the house before turning it off and smiling at me.

"You knew? The whole time?" I asked.

He shrugged. "Yes and no. I never looked. I had this done when

Sirena was sneaking out. If she could get out, I worried someone could get in. I never turned it on and watched it while I was away. However, I did catch a glimpse of you coming into her room. I watched it a little today. Not a lot. I didn't actually need to, though, because I found this in her room. Hidden, of course, but then again." He gestured to the TV. "Not hidden from me."

I swallowed and stared right back at him, not letting any of my emotions show.

"So you and Sirena," he said, eyeing me back.

"Dante, man, just listen," Ashes said, still at Sirena's side.

Church held his hand up to silence him. "You're right. It is time I listen. So, tell me, Sinclair."

"What do you want to know?" I challenged him.

"Everything. All of it. I want to know why you vowed something to me and then broke that vow. Why you're touching what belongs to the watchers. Why you think you can come in and try to undermine me in my own home," his voice rose with each word until he was yelling. "Why the fuck do you think you're good enough for her after the shit you did. She almost *fucking died*, Sinclair. Died. Dead. And Malachi. He was fucked. *Raped.* Each fucking day, our brother was drugged and pounded like a fucking coked-out whore. Then, they had Sirena hurt while they fucking watched it happen. Tell me, what gave you the fucking right to come back into our lives after I said to stay away? Huh? Tell me!" His face was red with his yelling.

My hands trembled as much as my voice did. Him laying my sins out for me that way made me want to put a bullet into my own head. He was right. I knew the point he was trying to make. I was a piece of shit, and nothing would change that. Nothing I did could ever fix what I'd broken.

So I said the only thing I could say.

"You're right," I whispered. "I'm not worth it. I'm selfish. I lied to you about staying away. I tried, but I couldn't. I wanted to come home. I wanted her to be our girl. *My* girl. I-I was stupid. There are no words I could say to ever make up for what I did." I looked to Stitches, who stared back at me, his dark eyes wavering. "I'm so fucking sorry,

Malachi. You didn't deserve that shit. I never would have done what I did had I known. . ." my voice trailed off, and I looked down at my feet as I tried to not cry like a fucking baby. "I'm so sorry. Malachi. Please. I know how badly I fucked everything up. I live with the guilt every day."

"Malachi, tell Sinclair how you really feel," Church said.

Stitches stared back at me for a moment before looking away from me.

"I hate you," he finally said in a soft, trembling voice. "I hate you so fucking much. In my dreams, I see you watching from outside my hospital room. Knowing what you did and never speaking up about it. It fucking haunts me." He wiped quickly at his eyes, my heart a twisted mess.

He grew quiet before his body stilled, and his legs stopped bouncing. Finally, he turned his head in my direction, tears on his cheeks. I stared back at him, wishing it were me who could have been in his place. Wishing I'd never even done any of that shit so no one would suffer the way they had.

I didn't deserve forgiveness. I knew it as I stared into his dark, wavering eyes.

"But I love you as much as I hate you. It's causing me a fair bit of conflict," he finished, wiping at his eyes. "I've also seen how much you care for Sirena. It helps."

I said nothing because my throat was too tight to speak.

Church flipped through the notebook before stopping near the end and reading my words aloud.

"I don't know how you could ever love a monster like me, siren, but I am so in love with you too. I am. From the moment I saw you, I knew. I knew you were the one I'd been looking for. I was just so scared. I fucking love you with every ounce of me there is. I will always love you. You have become my entire world. I only hope I can be a fraction of yours." Church looked at me after finishing, waiting for my answer.

"Those words were for her," I finally said. "So she'd remember."

Church let out a soft snort and looked back to the notebook again without a word. I took that moment to look to Ashes, who stared back at me, worry etched into his face, his hand still clutching Sirena's on the table and his other hand going wild as he opened and closed his lighter.

"Asher." Church looked to Ashes. "What was it Sin told you he'd do? When you two had your little heart-to-heart?"

Ashes tore his gaze away from me and looked to Church.

"He said he loved her and would beg forever on his knees if that's what it took. That he wanted another chance to prove himself."

Church nodded and flipped through the notebook more, clearly reading all our private conversations.

He pulled his knife out of his boot and twirled it between his fingers as he read. Sirena's soft cries echoed around me, twisting my guts like a snake. The thought brought back my memory of William Snakespeare, my retic, and how she was scared of him. How I wanted to teach her not to be. How I wanted to prove to her that not all snakes were bad. Because I was a snake too.

Fuck.

I wiped at my eyes again and looked to her. Her chest heaved. She had to be so cold.

"Asher and Malachi helped me punish her today," Church called out, pulling me from my thoughts. "Of course, they didn't know they were doing it. It took seeing their reactions today for me to realize something was very wrong here. They were feral for her. Like they hadn't fucked her tight pussy in ages. I guess they hadn't." He let out a humorless laugh. "I'm good at reading people. Always have been. Asylum has his parlor tricks, and I have mine. Isn't that fun, Sinclair?"

"A fucking riot," I answered in a monotone, tearing my focus from Sirena and back to him.

"Let's go for a walk. Shall we?" Church rose from his seat, his knife still in his hand. I looked to Stitches, who shook his head *no* at me, and then to Ashes, who pleaded with his eyes for me to just walk away and not onward to my certain death.

"You love the lake, don't you?" Church continued as I got to my feet.

"I do," I answered softly.

"Then I think it's the perfect place, don't you?"

"Yes," I whispered.

"Good. Malachi. Asher. Get her cleaned up. We'll talk when I return." Church stomped past me and grabbed his jacket. I followed and cast a look to my girl lying on that fucking table.

"Dante, don't do this," Ashes said. "Please."

"It's already done," Church answered before pulling the door open and stepping into the night air.

"For what it's worth, thank you for giving me this week with her," I said. "Siren. *Baby.* I fucking love you. M-make sure Bill eats, OK? A-and keep dancing. I want you to dance no matter what happens. I'll see you soon." I stepped out the door to hear her wail my name.

*Sinful.*

I closed my eyes and let out a deep breath. Nothing about what would happen next was good.

"Let's go," Church called out, nodding for me to follow him.

Without protest, I followed him into the dark trees, catching a glimpse of someone darting behind a tree wearing all black.

*Shadow.*

So many secrets were kept in the dark at Chapel Crest.

Mine was out in the open now.

It wouldn't be long until Shadow was brought to light either.

All monsters at Chapel Crest eventually paid for their sins. He'd be no different.

I sent up a silent prayer for him, hoping that if I didn't make it, then maybe he would.

# CHURCH

"*I*t's cold out," I said as we stood staring out at the frozen lake. "Hard to hide bodies this time of year. We'd have to really get out there to do it."

"The lake hasn't frozen in its entirety since '94," Sin answered, his voice showing no emotion.

The only thing I could think about doing in that moment was drowning his ass in the cold waters of Lake Superior and watching him fade away before I gutted him like a fucking animal.

"If you kill me, there will be witnesses. Not watchers." Sin still didn't look at me.

I smiled at his words. "I know. He's been following us since we left the house. He followed me home as well. He's never far away."

He wasn't the white rabbit, Mirage, but he was someone. Someone I'd get to eventually. Fortune smiled upon him for the moment, though, because I had Sin to deal with.

"Shadow," Sin continued. "That's what he's called."

"Good to know." I nodded and twirled my knife again. "Did you mean it? What you told Ashes?"

"I've meant every word I've said since shit happened." He turned to look at me.

"Except that part about staying away from her." I clicked my tongue. "You have your moments of failure, don't you?"

"We all do," he said simply, looking back out to the lake. "This is yours."

I chuckled at his words.

He turned to me again. "You think she'll forgive you, Dante? Killing me won't make her love you any more than what she already does. In the beginning, she was ours—"

I punched him in the face, knocking him a step back. Blood poured from his busted lip and nose.

He didn't attack me back. Instead, he straightened himself and stared me down, letting the blood rush down his face.

"This isn't the beginning anymore, Sinclair. It's the fucking end," I snapped at him. "You had a chance and fucked it up."

He stared at me wordlessly.

"And now, here we are at the fucking lake in the middle of goddamn winter, and you're bleeding all over the damn place."

He grunted at me but didn't snap back. He'd changed. He wasn't the same Sinclair Priest I'd once known. This Sinclair was broken and pieced back together in such a way that left me curious.

"Fine. Let's get this over with." I sighed and rubbed my eyes, my knife in my hand. "Get on your knees."

He stared me down for a moment before dropping to his knees, his focus in front of him at his beloved lake. I often wondered if he viewed it as an escape route. A way to just float away. A place to disappear. I found him here at the lake over the years. It seemed a fitting place as any to end this madness.

I watched him pull a rosary from his pocket and run the beads shakily through his fingers, his lips moving as he prayed.

I twirled my knife again.

That was Sirena's rosary. I'd seen her pray with it before too.

I had a similar one that I often used. Not to ask for forgiveness but to give me the strength to keep going.

I suppose we all prayed differently.

I wondered what Sinclair prayed for.

So I asked.

"What are you praying for?"

He closed his eyes for a moment before opening them and looking at me as I kneeled in front of him. I dragged my knife along his jaw, making him wince as it bit gently against his skin, a thin line of red telling me it was the perfect amount of pressure to ensure he knew I meant business.

"For her," he whispered. "I always pray for her."

I stared into his gray eyes for a moment, the truth clear on his face. He really was praying for her.

"Forever is a long time to be on your knees," I finally said.

His bottom lip wobbled. "It is, but some things are worth begging for."

I nodded at him. "Enjoy eternity, Sinclair."

I rose to my feet and stared down at him.

"Beg me."

"What?" He crinkled his brows at me.

"You said you'd spend your life on your knees, begging for forgiveness. So beg me. And when Stitches comes, beg him. Beg Ashes. Beg Sirena. I want to hear your fucking prayers, Sinclair. I want to see you prove yourself. On your fucking knees, I want to see if your god answers your fucking prayers."

"You used to believe in god too," he said softly.

I let out a soft, mirthless laugh. "Until I realized I could be a god and deal in life and death. You want your second chance?"

A muscle thrummed along his jaw.

"Then beg, Sinclair. Beg us all. And when we finally give in and forgive you completely, you can come home. You can join us again."

He blinked at me for a moment, obviously surprised I wasn't going to cut his throat.

"I want you to prove to me you're worth a second chance." I backed away from him. "Just don't die in the process. It gets cold out here. Maybe I'll see you later."

He said nothing as I walked around him and back to the woods, leaving him on his knees.

If there were a god, maybe he'd finally get off his ass and answer prayers because I knew Sirena would pray for the asshole since he wasn't smart enough to pray for himself.

# SIRENA

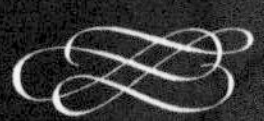

*I* was inconsolable.

I'd tried to escape several times already. Stitches had to hold me down in the tub so Ashes could wash me. It did no good. The moment I was on my feet again, I was tearing to get to the door and out to Sin and Church.

Ashes had me restrained against him on the couch while Stitches kept trying to call someone on his phone.

When the door opened and Church walked in alone, I finally broke.

I screamed his name on repeat, desperate for him to answer me and do all the good things he'd promised me.

"Church! Church! CHURCH!" I was wild with anger and desperation. With pain. With fear. I managed to break free of Ashes, who swore and tried to catch me, but I darted around the couch and threw myself at Church, my fists pounding on him any place I could land a hit.

Church didn't move. He didn't fight me or try to restrain me. He simply took my hits and listened to my screaming his name until I finally collapsed at his feet, my heart completely shattered.

This was all my fault. I'd gotten Sin killed because I was the selfish one.

I sucked in a shuddering breath, not getting nearly enough air. My panic at a world without Sin in it had me completely losing it. I couldn't breathe. I couldn't fucking breathe.

Church bent and scooped me into his arms and held me tightly against his body as I tried to breathe correctly.

"Get her meds," he said gruffly to Ashes, who darted off to do his bidding.

"Dante, man, what did you do?" Stitches asked, his voice wobbling.

"What needed to be done. We'll talk later," Church said. Ashes came back into the room and handed Church the meds. It didn't matter anymore. I hoped he drugged me so much it killed me.

Church carried me upstairs and placed me in his bed before scooting in beside me. A pinprick met my skin, letting me know he was putting me down.

"I hope it kills me," I managed to choke out between my fast breathing.

Church pressed his lips to my forehead. "If I killed you, that would hurt Sin, don't you think?"

My eyelids grew heavy, and I struggled to keep them open.

"He's not dead, specter. Do you truly think I'm that kind of monster?"

My heart raced.

"Sinful?"

"He's alive. For now. He just needs to beg for forgiveness. If he does, he can come home. You can have your watchers. Sound good?"

I didn't know what any of that meant. My mind couldn't comprehend a word of it as the heaviness from the drugs weighed me down.

"He's alive, specter. Pray for him. He only prays for you." He kissed me, and the darkness took over, leaving me silent.

# ASHES

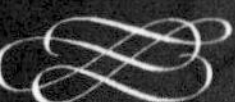

Church came downstairs a half hour after he took Sirena away from us. We'd sat in silence, awaiting his return. The good news was I didn't see any blood on him aside from a little on his knuckles, which meant he'd definitely punched Sin at least once.

We looked to Church as he sat in his chair, his silence making me uneasy.

"Is he dead?" Stitches finally asked.

"No," Church replied, staring back at us. "He's currently at the lake on his knees. Praying for Sirena since that's what he said he was doing."

"Why? What did you do to her?" The thought of trusting him with her never making me falter until that moment.

"Relax." Church waved me off. "She's sleeping. Sin is alive. For now."

"What the fuck does that mean?" Stitches demanded.

I glared at Church, really hoping he wasn't going to piss me off more tonight. I had no idea he'd bugged the damn house. It was an invasion of privacy that we'd get to soon enough once we got the Sin thing sorted.

"Well, he said he'd beg on his knees until he was forgiven. So he's on his knees. In the morning, I expect you to go to him and let him beg you to forgive him."

"It's fucking freezing outside. He'll die," I snapped at him. "What the fuck is your problem, Dante? Huh? You do realize the world doesn't revolve around you and your wants, right?"

He got to his feet when I got to mine.

"Her world revolves around me, and I intend to keep every motherfucker who intends on hurting her out. If he wants in, he can fucking beg."

I shook my head in disgust at him.

"We're going to get him tonight."

"We aren't. He's working on his prayers—"

I got in Church's face, my chest heaving with anger.

"So help me, Dante, I will burn this motherfucking house down with you inside it if I have to. Don't fucking push me on it. Sirena loves him. She wants him. It's *her* fucking choice. *Not* yours. You don't get to decide. *She. Fucking. Chooses!*" I shoved him in the chest before storming past him and grabbing my jacket.

I thought he'd fight me on it. Instead, he pulled his phone out and made a call.

"I need you to watch Sirena while we go out. No. That's fine. Be quick." He hung up, and Stitches got to his feet.

"Asylum is on his way. He's going to watch her while we're gone—" The words weren't out of his mouth before there was a knock on our door.

I pulled it open to find Asylum on our front step, his black beanie pulled low and his cheeks rosy.

Or Mirage, judging by his white rabbit mask.

"What the fuck. You fly here, witchcraft?" Stitches muttered at him.

Mirage smirked at him. "I had a feeling I'd be needed. So here I am."

I sighed and rolled my eyes. Church was cool keeping Asylum/Mirage around, the guy who tried to die with her in a coffin, but had issues with Sin. His logic baffled me.

"I'm a good guy, Asher. You know that." Mirage winked at me. "We want the same things."

"Are you Mirage or Asylum today? I'd like to know so I don't piss you off and have you correcting me every few minutes," I said.

"I'm Mirage," he answered, cocking his head to the right. "Asylum can be a pain, can't he?"

"You're a pain. Keep an eye on Sirena. Church drugged her and knocked her out. Don't fucking touch her," I warned.

"Of course. Fucking the unconscious is Church's thing, not mine. At least not usually. I'll be a good little nutcase and stay downstairs. The cameras are watching." He pointed to various spots in the room. "Am I right, Dante? That's where they are?"

"Some of them," Church commented, grabbing his jacket and shrugging it on.

"Up the stairs. Down the stairs. In the rooms. Even watches while you brush your hair. Or hairs?" Mirage cocked his head to the right again. "Ah, well. Time is wasting. Run to little Sin by the lake before he freezes to death. Sirena, nor Asylum, would not like that."

I crinkled my brows at him.

"You're so fucking weird," I muttered, wondering why he was speaking in the third person. I'd never figure it out, so the point was moot. Instead, I stepped outside, Church and Stitches behind me, and headed off to Sin's favorite spot at the lake.

✝

SIN WAS on his knees facing the lake when we came upon him. He clearly hadn't moved. I admired that, but I knew he had to be freezing.

"Hey," Stitches said, going to step in front of him.

"H-hey," Sin answered, trembling from the cold.

"You should come inside. It's cold out here."

"No." Sin's voice shook as he shivered. "I've not paid my penance. I've not begged. I'm not forgiven. I don't expect to be. Let me die at my spot. Tell Sirena. . . Tell her I'm sorry."

Stitches let out an exasperated sigh.

"Man, come on. Let's go."

"No." Sin shook again but remained on his knees.

"Sinclair," I called out.

"Asher, I'm not leaving. Stop, OK? I accept my fate."

I looked to Church, who frowned in Sin's direction. We all knew Sin struggled with his emotions, and understanding love and all that. This was just one of those instances he struggled to wrap his head around. Everything always had to be so damn complicated with him.

"Sin, please. We can talk at home," I pressed, shivering as the cold wind blew in. If his ass didn't come inside, he'd be dead by morning. There was no way he'd survive these temps in nothing but his jacket. He didn't even have a damn hat or gloves on. He simply stayed on his knees in his jacket and jeans, his fingers running along the rosary he held.

"Take care of my snake," he said, his teeth chattering. "Sirena named him William Snakespeare. He means a lot in more ways than you can imagine. I want her to learn to not-not be afraid anymore. I think Bill will help with that."

"Sin—"

"Asher, please. Just leave me."

I let out a sigh of frustration. I didn't want to knock his ass out and drag him home, but I definitely would if it came down to it.

"Beg me," Stitches broke in.

Sin looked up at him. "What?"

"Beg me to forgive you," Stitches said. "I want to hear you say all the shit in your head to me. Beg me."

Sin was quiet for a moment before he spoke, his voice soft.

"I'm sorry, Malachi. You're one of my best friends in the entire world. You trusted me, and I broke that trust by letting my fear take over. I'm so fucking sorry. I don't have enough breath in my-my lungs to tell you how sorry I am and always will be for what I did and what happened to you and Sirena. I-I don't deserve to live. To be your friend. To be anything more than dust. But I swear to you, if I can come home, I'll prove I'm worth it. That I'm loyal and love you all so damn much. You're my family." Tears rolled down his cheeks before freezing in place. "I want that again. I-I'm begging you to please forgive me. Give me another chance. Let me s-show you how much this means to me. How much you all mean to me. Let me prove what I'm willing to do to-to be a family again. You're all I have in this world. You're all I fucking have. I'm so goddamn sorry. Please, Malachi. Please. Forgive me. I-I'm begging on my knees for you to let me come home. I'll do anything you ask of me. If death is your wish for me, then so be it. Just please. . . know how deeply I ache for my sins. I would take your place in an instant and go through that hell so it didn't happen to you. Fuck, Malachi. I'm sorry. Goddamnit it! I'm sorry." He let out a sob, his head bowed, his body shaking.

I swallowed the lump in my throat at his words, seriously hoping Stitches gave him the green light he desperately needed.

I glanced to Church to see him watching the scene, his face emotionless.

Stitches went to his knees in front of him and cradled his face in his hands.

"You fucked everything up, Sinclair," he said fiercely. "*Everything.* Each night, when I sleep, I relive the nightmare of what happened. Of the forced. . . the way they forced themselves inside my body." Stitches's voice cracked. "But I don't want to lose you either. I'm angry at you for what you did. It may take me a long time to get over it. Not for me, but for what Sirena went through too. Because she suffers even now. She suffers because even going through it, she loved you. Your actions hurt and confused her. She trusted you too."

"I know," Sin choked out. "I know."

"If you ever fucking think of hurting her again, I'll kill you myself." Sin nodded, wordless.

"I forgive you. *Brother.*" Stitches reached out and hugged Sin to him, making Sin weep softly, his body shaking from his tears.

They stayed that way for a long time, holding one another. Finally, Stitches got to his feet and looked to Church.

"I've forgiven him," he said evenly. "My part is done."

Church nodded and looked to me.

I went and stood in front of Sin, who stared up at me, half the tears on his face a frozen mess.

"You hurt all of us. You know you did. I've seen the way you've changed in the last few weeks. You're not the guy I knew. I hate that. I really do. I miss that grumpy fucker." I went to my knees in front of him. "I forgave you long ago. I know what it's like to hurt inside and be confused about it. I get it. I know how much you love Sirena and how much she loves you. I don't want to take that from either of you. I want you to come home to us. OK?"

He nodded, more tears flowing.

I leaned in and kissed his forehead before getting to my feet and giving Church a pointed look.

He said nothing as he stepped around me and faced Sin.

"Beg," he said softly.

"Please, Dante. Please, let me come home to my family. I beg you to give me a second chance. Please. I'm sorry for disappointing you. All of you guys. For all my sins. My mental shit. My-my mistakes. The watchers are my family, and you mean the world to me. I was so afraid of losing you that I didn't stop to think that my actions would be the catalyst for my fears. I-I don't know how to beg harder. What would you have me do?" Sin looked up at him, a plea to his voice. "I'll do it. Anything you want."

Church pulled his knife free from his boot and twirled it along his fingers.

"Make a blood vow to me," Church said.

"Yes," Sin agreed without hesitating.

I looked to Stitches, knowing exactly what a blood vow meant in our world. If you broke it, you died. There were no do-overs. No second, third, or fourth chances. One fuck up, and that was it. Game over.

Church signed his name in blood whenever he did a transaction with his father. Hell, whenever he did any meaningful transaction. It was just who he was.

"Repeat after me," Church instructed. "I, Sinclair Priest, vow to give my life should I ever fuck up. Any misstep that would cause harm to Sirena or my brothers, and I will take a knife to the heart and die on its blade without protest. That I will do what is necessary to protect her from all pain and danger."

Sin repeated his words, his voice quaking more from the cold.

"Hold out your hand," Church said.

Sin did as he was told. I watched while Church cut his hand, the blood blossoming out. A moment later, he drew the knife over Sin's palm.

Church slid his bloody hand against Sin's.

"To the fucking grave, Sinclair. And then back again."

"To the fucking grave, Dante. And then back again," Sin repeated.

"And when we can't breathe anymore?"

"We fucking do it anyway," Sin answered.

"'Til the end, brother."

"'Til the end," Sin's voice shook again, his and Church's blood dripping onto the white snow.

"Welcome home, Sinclair," Church said, pulling Sin to his feet. "Now, let's get you home so I can properly punch you in the face."

I let out a breath of relief before looking to Stitches, who looked how I felt.

"I'm still pissed at you," Church continued.

"I know. And I'll let you hit me again as many times as you want."

"Be careful what you promise me. You know I'm a devil who collects."

"I know," Sin said as I steadied him. He shivered again, but at least the light was back in his eyes.

It was better than the darkness.

Way fucking better.

# SIRENA

The moment I woke, I shoved my blankets off and stumbled to the bathroom. As quick as I could, I did my business before brushing my teeth, my mind racing on how I was going to get out of the house and get to wherever Sin was.

When I was lying on the table in the kitchen, Church had told me if I moved, Sin would surely die and that I needed to let Sin tell the truth. I'd been terrified in those moments, but I had to put my faith in something, praying death wouldn't come to any of my guys over me.

I'd heard them say Sin was at the lake. It was a bit of a walk, and I had to go through the trail in the woods, but I could make it.

Hopefully.

I was terrified of the woods still. It was much easier to get through when someone was with me. Going alone put me on edge, but I'd do whatever I needed to in order to save Sin.

Church gave me enough sleeping meds to put my ass out all night. As groggy as I felt, I was ready for a war if it came down to it.

I didn't bother dressing, opting to remain in the nightgown I was in.

Quickly, I rushed downstairs, rehearsing what I was going to say to Church and how I was willing to stab him to get my point across.

I stopped abruptly as all four guys put breakfast on the table.

"Good morning, heaven," Ashes called out, his face cheerful.

Cautiously, I moved closer and rubbed my eyes. I wasn't sure if I was dreaming.

"Angel." Stitches came to me and kissed me quickly before taking my hand in his and leading me to the table. "We got up a little early to make you breakfast."

He pulled my chair out and sat me down.

Sin looked at me and gave me a smile, his gray eyes filled with exhaustion. But he was alive.

He was alive, and he was here.

"I told you it would be OK," Church said, coming and dropping a kiss on my forehead before going and grabbing a bunch of toast that had popped up and putting it on a plate.

I looked to Sin again.

He reached for my hand as he sat in his spot. They'd put a chair next to his for me.

"Hey," he murmured, bringing my hand to his mouth and brushing his lips against my knuckles. "I'm sorry you were scared."

I said nothing, not believing this was real. Maybe it was a lucid dream.

"It's real," Sin continued softly like he was reading my mind. "I'm here. I'm home."

My heart soared.

I flung my arms around him, making him gasp at my sudden fierceness. It didn't take him long to return my hug, dragging me against his body and rocking me.

"Baby," he whispered over and over. "I'm home. I'm never leaving. You're it, siren. You're it."

Our notebook was slid in front of us by Church. I reached for his hand as I broke away from Sin.

"You can thank me later," Church said, his green eyes moving to stare at Sin. "Keep him in line. If he fucks anything up again, he really will die."

"So dramatic," Stitches said, shaking his head and putting a waffle onto his plate.

Church scowled at Stitches before throwing a piece of toast at him. Stitches whipped his waffle at him, smacking him in the chest, the syrup making the waffle stick in place.

"Motherfucker," Church snarled before launching himself at Stitches as he fell out of his chair in an attempt to get away.

I watched them roll around on the floor together, each trying to shove the waffle down the other's shirt and swearing at one another.

I looked to Ashes, who remained calm and continued to eat.

"Eat, baby," he instructed while Sin poured me a glass of orange juice. "The boys will be boys. It's how they are. Just step over them if they're still going at it when you're done eating. It's what I do."

I blinked at his words and looked back to the pair still wrestling on the floor.

"Ashes is right," Sin said, dropping a piece of toast on top of the pair. Stitches grabbed it and tried to shove it into Church's mouth. "They'll be at it forever. Some things never change."

"Eat," Ashes urged again. "You'll get used to it."

There was a smile on his face as he exchanged a look with Sin.

So I ate while the brothers wrestled one another on the floor while stuffing food down each other's shirts.

✝

"WHAT ARE YOU DOING?" Church asked as he leaned against my doorway later that morning. I glanced over at him before reaching for my shoes to put into my bag. It was Friday. We had classes. I'd missed way too many of them lately and needed to go.

I didn't get my shoes, though. Church took them from me and dropped them behind him before crowding my space and cradling my face with both hands. He tilted my face up to look at him.

"I asked you a question, specter. What are you doing?"

I searched his face, trying my damndest to get the words to come out, but they wouldn't.

"You speak to Ashes by writing on his hand. You touch Stitches. You write notes to Sin. For me, you only stare. What am I doing wrong?" he murmured, his green eyes sweeping over my face.

I exhaled, wanting to tell him he pissed me off last night. That he scared me. That I didn't like it.

"Say it," he whispered. "All that anger I can see on your face. Say it to me. I want to hear it."

I breathed out again, my jaw aching from clenching it. Closing my eyes, I thought about all the anger in my heart. All the despair. The fear. The sadness. The want. The need for revenge. To tell all of them how I felt without little notes and whispers. How I wanted Bryce and Asylum. And Mirage.

"Sirena," Church called out softly.

I focused on the anger. It seemed to be an easier jumping-off point for me.

"You pissed me off," I said, snapping my eyes open and staring up at him.

He nodded. "I know."

"You hurt me. Scared me. I-I thought. . . I thought. . ." The words faltered on my lips before I closed my eyes briefly to gather myself before opening them and looking at him. "Aren't you even a little sorry?"

He was quiet for a moment before he tucked a piece of hair behind my ear.

"I was raised to never apologize for who I am and what I do. I don't know how to really feel those emotions. Sometimes, I think maybe I am sorry, but then I realize that being sorry and having guilt are two different emotions. Sometimes they conflict with one another." He paused and thumbed my bottom lip. "But to answer your question, no. I'm not sorry. I feel nothing akin to either guilt or sorrow in regard to yesterday."

I shook my head at him and turned away, disappointed with his answer.

He grabbed my arm and turned me to face him again.

"Let me finish," he said. "I am not remorseful for my actions. Maybe it's because they were needed. I knew you'd never tell me. Keeping secrets does bother me, Sirena. Especially in my own home. I know who I am. Do you know who you are?"

I frowned at his question and looked down at my feet. The truth was, I had no idea who I was. Inside my head was a mess. One moment, I was strong and brave. The next, I was terrified, and confused and hiding in the darkness.

"That day when you let that little bit of yourself out in our living room," Church continued, tilting my chin up. "I saw you then. I caught a glimpse of the strong girl you keep hidden. I'd love the chance to meet her properly. I think that's the girl who can speak and who doesn't take my shit. She's part of what makes you who you are. I love all the parts of you, but you only give us the little pieces while we scramble to get the whole girl."

I swallowed. "E-even the b-broken pieces?"

"The broken pieces are my favorite part." He brushed his lips against mine. "I'm not redeemable, Sirena. You know I'm not. This is me not only telling you who I am, but I've also shown you my monster. I want to see yours now."

"I'm scared—"

He pressed his finger against my lips. "Fear is also a monster, baby. Don't let it be yours. In this house, there is no fear. You're a watcher's girl now. *Show* the world who the fuck you are if you can't find the words. We're your army in this dark kingdom. Whether you choose to believe it or not, you're the ruler here."

"I-I am?"

He nodded and ran his knuckles along my jaw. "How funny that you can't see that. Whatever my queen wants is what she shall have." He closed the space between us. "Tell me what you want, specter. *My little Ghost.* Tell me their names. *I know there are more than four.*"

My pulse roared in my ears when he pulled away from me, his green eyes sparkling with an emotion I couldn't quite place since I'd rarely seen it on his face.

"You call the shots. Just don't get carried away."

*I call the shots.*

*I choose.*

"But for now, let me handle it until you're ready. Deal?"

I licked my lips before holding my hand out to him. He smirked at me and brought his knife out.

"My sweet, brave girl, willing to make a deal with the devil." He cut his other palm before I turned my palm upward. He made a small slash over it, the sting making me hiss. I pressed my hand to his and twined my fingers with him.

"Maybe I'm a devil too," I whispered.

"I really fucking hope so, baby." His lips met mine in a deep, penetrating kiss before our hands were all over one another, the blood stains marring our skin.

"By the way," he said between frantic kisses. "You're going to come downstairs and fuck Sin in front of me so I can watch."

I groaned against his mouth, making him chuckle.

But when he lifted me, I wrapped my legs around his waist and let him take me downstairs and place me on Sin's lap.

If he wanted a show, I'd give him one. As long as my timid side didn't stop me, I knew I could do it.

That's what queens in hell did. We persevered.

SIN

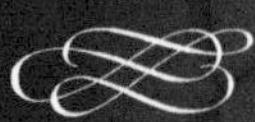

*H*er hand was bleeding, and she had some bloody handprints on her skin. I looked to Church. He raised his brows at me and moved to his chair, matching handprints on his body and his hand bleeding too.

*What the fuck deal did she make with him?*

It worried me to know. I'd left after breakfast with Ashes to rush back to my dorm room to grab William Snakespeare and my belongings. We'd only just gotten back. I thought I was living in a damn dream being home. Things were a little tense with Church, but we'd been at this point before, so it wasn't anything I couldn't get through. This time, I had Sirena as a prize, so the fight was worth it.

I'd kept my distance from her, though. I wanted to ease Church into seeing us together. He was already teetering on the edge of insanity and fury. No sense in pushing him into the deep end.

But damn, him putting her on my lap sent my heart into twists.

He was serious about it.

At first, I considered he was maybe playing a cruel trick on me. Bring me home and make me think shit was finally working out. Have my hopes up high so that when I crashed back to earth after he snatched it away, it would teach me a lesson.

So far, it wasn't like that.

Sirena snuggled against my body, her face buried in my neck. I cast a look to Church to see him watching us from his chair, his body a little stiff, but nothing on his face that said he was going to gut me.

Ashes winked at me and flipped his lighter open and closed while Stitches peered at Bill through his glass tank.

"Is it slimy? It looks slimy," he muttered, giving the glass a small tap.

"He's not slimy," I said. "He's pretty calm, too, actually." I ran my fingers through Sirena's hair and placed a kiss atop her head. "You can take him out if you want."

"Eh, I don't know man. I like rope and all, but this here, friend, is a nope rope. Motherfucker is as long as I am. Dick-wise, of course." He shot me a wink.

I chuckled as Stitches tapped the glass gently again with a tatted hand before shaking his head.

"Nah. He looks like he might be plotting how best to swallow me whole."

"He's not quite big enough to do that yet," I said. "Plus, he already ate."

"Keep him in your room. Just in case." Stitches looked at me, a serious expression on his face.

I smiled at him and nodded. "Sure, man. I'll keep him in my room."

"We could get a cat," Ashes piped up. "Those are nice. I had one when I was a kid."

"No cats," Church called out.

"A dog?" Ashes asked. "Something big. A Doberman."

"That'd be cool," Stitches said, nodding.

"No dogs either," Church continued. "We have enough trouble keeping ourselves alive. No point in adding an animal to the mix."

"Lame," Ashes muttered. "So our house mascot is a snake named Bill?"

"William Snakespeare," I corrected. "Bill for short."

"I think a snake is a great mascot." Church stared right at me. "Don't you think, Sin?"

"I do," I murmured, letting my eyelids shutter closed as Sirena kissed along my neck.

Fuck, it felt good to be loved by her.

To be home.

"Maybe you deserve a welcome home gift," Church continued.

I stared at him through slitted eyes, my heart pumping hard. I knew where he was going with this. I wasn't going to force her, though. She'd stopped me before. Whatever she wanted would be at her speed.

"Specter." Church continued to lock eyes with me.

She pulled away from me, making me ache inside, and got to her feet. With a sweet look on her face, she walked to where she was summoned. Church dragged her onto his lap and whispered in her ear. I watched him caress her as he spoke, his hand running slowly up and down her back.

I ground my teeth at the sight.

Sharing this way was still new to me, and god knew Church and I had our issues with women in our past. I had a feeling he wanted to show me who was really in charge around here, so I watched, desperate to rip her away and hold her close.

Church let out a soft laugh as she buried her face in his neck and twisted her fingers in his shirt.

"She's shy," he called out to me. "Nervous for you to see her. And seemingly a little scared."

"Siren, I won't hurt you," I called out, noting the desperate tone of my voice. *Fuck, pull it together, you damn pussy.*

"See? He wants it too," Church cooed to her as he ran his fingers through her long black hair. "He's seen your pussy before, remember? He's even tasted it."

I swallowed hard at the memory of the time Church brought her here, and we played around with her. I'd been so fucking rock hard that I'd had to jerk off in the bathroom to calm myself later that night.

"We don't have to," I said honestly. "I'm fine if we don't. In fact, I'm better than fine. I'm just grateful to be here."

I didn't mention how nervous I was at my tattered body being put on display. It had been torn to shreds from me punishing myself. Having that reminder out in the open maybe wasn't the best idea, especially if it triggered Sirena. Being self-conscious had never been an issue for me, but now that things had changed, I couldn't help the feelings.

"Let her decide." Stitches took a seat next to Ashes on the couch, leaving me alone along the L part. "I don't want you to force her. We already had a fucked-up time with her when you made her lie on the table with our come drying on her face."

I clenched my hands into fists. I hadn't known that's what she was doing. I believed they'd fucked her and left her there on Church's orders as a way to fuck with me. And sure, it had been a great way to fuck with me, but I hadn't known that shit had happened.

"What's wrong, Sinclair? Don't like the way our house is run?" Church asked, eyeing me.

I scoffed. "You know, there are some things I never liked. I don't like that you came all over her in humiliation and left her out to dry like wet laundry."

"In our defense, we didn't know that's what was going on," Ashes spoke up. "We thought we were simply having fun. She was into it."

I looked down at my hands, not wanting to talk about it. I'd only just gotten home. Pissing everyone off because I didn't agree with any of it didn't seem like the best idea at the moment.

It wasn't until Sirena was kneeling in front of me that I lifted my head.

"What are you doing?" I murmured, drinking her in.

She offered me a gentle smile before reaching out and cradling my face.

I stared into her eyes, completely lost in the colors, wishing I could give her the world. Fuck, what I wouldn't give to be able to.

"What is it?" I asked, my voice barely above a whisper.

She bit her bottom lip, her brows crinkled.

I wished I had our notebook so she could tell me, but it was in my bedroom. Not being able to communicate with her was hard. I wasn't as intuitive as Ashes was, or hell, even Asylum/Mirage.

"I don't know what to do," I continued, reaching for her. I placed my hands on her waist and gave her a squeeze. "I'll do whatever you want."

I studied her face for a moment longer. Knowing the guys were watching me put me on edge too. That whole self-conscious thing came rolling back, this time about how maybe I wasn't talking to her right or touching her properly.

All I knew was that she was my siren, and I was her Sinful. Past that, nothing else mattered.

"I-I want to," she whispered to me.

My heart jumped at her soft words. I knew just how difficult it was for her to speak, so the action itself meant a lot to me.

"Me?" I crinkled my brows as I stared at her.

She nodded, making the breath whoosh out of my lungs. I studied her for a moment before coming to a decision.

Fuck it. I wanted her too.

My lips met hers, and it was like lightning shooting through my body. Her lips parted for me. I was done for.

I kissed her deeply. Tasting her. Touching her. Part of me wanted to take her fast and hard while feeling her writhe beneath me. But another part, a stronger part, wanted to take it slow and savor her in all the ways I'd dreamed of since I'd first seen her.

Carefully, I pushed the strap to her dress down her arm before the other one. In moments, her dress was pooled on the floor around her, her lips still fused to mine.

It had been a minute since I'd taken a girl's clothes off, so I fumbled with her bra, knowing damn well it was Stitches I heard snickering in the background.

Once I had her stripped down to her lacy white panties, I helped her when she faltered with the buttons on my shirt and pants.

The moment my shirt fell open, her hands were on the hard expanse of my torso. Her fingers explored each cut and scar, her kiss slowing until she pulled away to examine me.

I swallowed hard as she pushed my shirt off completely and took me in.

I hadn't been working out nearly as much as I used to, but I was built like a machine, albeit a slightly smaller one. Her fingertips traced over her name on my chest, her eyes drinking each scrawl of jagged letters.

*Siren.*

Her name etched and scarred deep into my body because I belonged to her like a broken toy.

I even said as much.

"I'm your broken toy." I gave her a sad smile.

Her eyes met mine, and she spoke, her voice so soft I could barely hear it.

"And I'm yours."

Fuck me, she was.

I hauled her against me with one hand, all while shoving my pants down with my other one. She was easy enough to maneuver since she was just a bitty thing. In moments, I had her beneath me.

I balanced myself over her on the couch, staring into her eyes, my heart so full I thought it would burst.

I was in love. Completely obsessed with every facet of her being I could wedge myself into. This love was a different love. Anything I'd ever felt for another person before had become completely obliterated. She was it.

I moved away from her, and she reached out for me. Taking her hand, I kissed her knuckles.

"I want to see you," I said, releasing her hand and moving to take her panties off. She hesitated for a moment before allowing me to do so. I let my gaze drift over all her pretty dips and curves, her full breasts, her bare, glistening pussy.

And her scars.

The ones left on her milky skin from a fucking piece of shit who tried to steal her away.

I ground my teeth so hard I thought they'd snap off. When I found this guy, he was dead. I'd kill him or die fucking trying.

"Broken," her voice was still soft, only meant for me. She knew I was memorizing each mark on her body, categorizing every painful way I could think of to hurt the motherfucker who hurt her.

"Not broken, siren. You're perfect," I answered back, trailing my finger along the scar near her pelvis. It was still a little red, but it had healed nicely.

Leaning down, I pressed a kiss to the spot, noting the goosebumps that traveled along her soft skin. I smiled at that, indulging for a moment that I could make her body react that way to one of my kisses.

Slowly, I traveled lower until I was between her legs. I kissed her pussy, earning a soft sigh from her that only ramped me up further. It was when I licked up her heat that she let out a gasp.

Fuck, she tasted good.

I wanted more.

I dove in and ate her, each of her tiny moans and hip thrusts just encouraging me more. My tongue over her clit. Around it. Sucking. Licking. Tasting. Her breathing picked up when I inserted my middle finger deep inside her wet channel. I even groaned at the feeling while I continued to suck along her clit.

In and out, I moved my finger, learning her. Studying her. Logging every bit of information away into my head so I could always please her.

I knew she liked it when I sucked and flicked my tongue against her clit. She liked it when I hooked my finger and rubbed rather than did an in and out. Carefully, I inserted a second digit before I took my other hand and pressed gently against her lower abdomen, quickly learning I could easily get her off.

Her body tightened and arched, her pussy pressed firmly to my mouth, my fingers buried to the knuckles. I rubbed her G-spot until she filled my mouth with her release, her body trembling violently and her fingers tangling in my messy hair as she forced my face deeper into her hot center.

What a glorious fucking mess. She came with the force of a volcano, dampening everything around us.

When she finally came down, I kissed her pussy again before

pulling free. A soft, shaky sigh left her lips as I kissed my way up her body, pausing to lavish her breasts. I sucked and nipped against the flesh, wanting to mark her.

She whimpered against my lips as I worked, leaving behind a kiss which would surely stay red for days, before my lips found hers.

With my body pressed against hers, we kissed softly. Gently. Touching. Exploring. I took her hand and put it between our bodies so she could feel how hard she made me.

I wasn't a small guy, so when she wrapped her fingers around my shaft, I let out a groan that bordered on a feral howl. Her touch just did something to me.

I broke the kiss off and stared down at her as her hand explored me. Her eyes widened for a moment, and she blinked.

A smile touched my lips.

"It's a Prince Albert," I said softly. "The piercing on my dick." I saw the question in her eyes and answered it for her. "It doesn't hurt. It feels really good. I promise it won't hurt you. OK?"

Her eyes wavered for a moment before she let out a soft breath.

She was afraid, even though I said it was OK. Sometimes words weren't enough, however. I'd learned that hard truth recently. Instead, I'd have to prove it to her.

"Do you want me?" I asked thickly. "Inside you?"

She visibly swallowed. I knew that look. She was trying to speak for me.

"You don't need to." I brushed my lips against hers. "If you want it, kiss me, and I'll give it to you for however long you can take it."

Her lips met mine in a fierce kiss, giving me all the answer I needed. With our lips still fused to one another's, I grasped my cock and ran it along her wet pussy before pushing against it.

"I love you," I said between feverish kisses. "Don't ever forget it."

And I pushed forward, finally claiming what had always been mine.

The tightness. The heat. The sound that came from her as I sank deep inside her body was the final nail in my coffin.

I was hers. Forever. There would never be a time when I wouldn't be.

And her?

I'd never let her go. There wouldn't be a place in heaven or hell she could run and hide from me.

When I said I loved someone, it went to the grave and beyond.

She would be my greatest love. My greatest obsession.

I only hoped she was ready for it.

# SIRENA

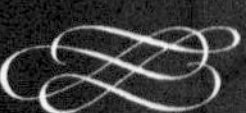

Sin filled me slowly. Sweetly. It was almost too much, but I spread myself wider for him, eager to fit all of him inside me.

And the piercing. While it terrified me, it also intrigued me.

It was when he started moving that I saw the appeal.

With his eyes locked on mine, he made love to me. Deep. Gentle. A little swivel of his hips every now and then to grind himself deep inside my heat. Teasing. Giving. Loving.

I clung to him as he gave me a little piece of himself, his gray eyes all-consuming as he stared down at me. His warm breath blew across my face. My nails made deep indents into his skin. He didn't wince. In fact, he spoke.

"Deeper, siren. I want to feel you claw my soul, baby," he rasped against my lips.

So I dug deeper, earning a groan from him and knowing damn well it had to hurt. I'd seen the scars and marks on his body. My nails were no more painful than what he did to himself, so I gave him what he asked for.

I'd give him whatever he asked for. All of them owned me and could have anything they wanted from me. That's just how far I'd fallen.

Sin picked up his pace, each swivel and grind of his dick inside me making me gasp out in pleasure. The heat grew until my pussy was spasming around him, my release rushing from my body like a tidal wave.

And he rode it, weaving one wave of pleasure into another. With his brows crinkled, he watched me come. Watched me give a silent scream, his name tumbling from my lips like a prayer I couldn't stop repeating. He was learning me. I knew he was because he did it again, his dick hitting that place inside me that sent all logic from my brain and turning me into jello.

The way he could weave one moment of pleasure into the next had me reeling. He was quickly learning all the ways to make me claw at him.

He moved faster, setting a fire inside me, until I was consumed completely, this time his name not so silent.

"S-Sinful. Oh god. Oh my god," I cried out, my nails deep inside his flesh.

He groaned out my name, his cock pumping as he came with me, filling me. His movements grew uneven before he collapsed over me, breathing heavily. He managed to keep most of his weight off me as he buried his face against my neck and clung to me.

"I love you. I love you so fucking much," he husked out against my skin.

I ran my fingers through his messy hair as he held me tighter.

"I'm yours, Sirena. Always and forever." He didn't come up for air. Instead, he held me like I held him, our bodies perfectly molded to each other's.

"I'm yours too, Sinful," I answered back, my voice trembling. "Always and forever."

We'd been so caught up in one another that I'd forgotten the guys had been watching the entire time. I glanced over and caught Ashes's eye.

He gave me a smile, his eyes shining brightly.

Then Stitches. He simply stared back, his lips parted, his hands clasped in front of him as he balanced his elbows on his knees, all his focus on us.

And Church.

He hadn't moved an inch. There was no emotion on his face until our eyes met.

Then he inclined his head at me and gave me a smile.

I relaxed beneath Sin, who was holding me tightly, his breathing growing deeper, his cock still buried inside me.

It was going to be OK. We were finally good.

✝

WE STAYED WRAPPED up in one another the rest of the evening and into the night, making love and sleeping off and on. The guys had left us alone after our first round. I wasn't sure where they went, but they didn't come back until night had long fallen. And even then, they'd gone straight to bed, leaving the smell of smoke behind them. I assumed they were giving us the time together we needed.

Sin made good use of it too. Bringing me from one high to the next, his cock never leaving my body. I lost track of how many times we had sex that night. Sometime during it, he'd lifted me from the couch and brought me to his room, where he continued to work my body over.

By morning, I was so sore I could barely walk.

But I loved it. It reminded me that he was now mine for good.

"I'm sorry," he said as he stood behind me in the bathroom while I brushed my hair with his brush. "You're walking like I've hurt you." He winced, shame washing over his handsome face.

I turned to face him and wrapped my arms around his neck before kissing him. I liked the pain. I liked what we'd done together.

So much so that I backed away and slid onto the counter before I spread my legs for him.

"Baby," he murmured, a tiny smile on his lips. "You're already sore from me. I don't want to make it worse."

I bit my bottom lip and studied him before I put my hands on his shoulders and pushed him downward. His smile grew before he was on his knees, his face buried between my legs.

Each flick of his tongue brought heat. Each suck. Each tender kiss.

He gripped my hips tightly and tugged me forward, then ate me faster.

It didn't take long for my release to rocket through me and flood his mouth. Gushing the way I did was embarrassing because it could get so messy, but these guys seemed to love it, so I let go of the embarrassment a little and enjoyed the ride.

I sagged back against the mirror, completely spent. Sin emerged, his chin and lips glistening from my come, before he dragged me to him and kissed me, the taste of myself teasing my tongue.

"You're the best breakfast I've ever had," he said when he pulled away. "I could eat you every morning for the rest of my life."

I smirked at him, earning a wide grin.

"So be it," he said in a sexy growl.

A pounding on the door had us breaking apart before we could kiss again.

"Sin, man, come on," Stitches shouted through the door. "Listen. I'm an easygoing guy, but you've been hogging her. I want to see her too."

Sin let out a soft laugh and looked into my eyes. "It's hard for me to share."

I smiled at his words.

"We went and burned with Ashes last night. Do you know what I had to do after watching you fuck her on our couch? I had to jerk off in the cold because I couldn't handle it anymore. My come literally froze coming out of my dick. And I'm pretty sure the head of my dick has frostbite. So I'm begging you to not make me suffer and come out so I can see her."

Sin let out a soft laugh, a smile on his face. I'd never seen him look so happy. It made my heart soar.

But Stitches was right. We'd been ignoring the rest of them while we worked through everything. The thought raced through my mind on what would happen if I managed to get others into our group.

It made me feel a little slutty.

But then the darkness peeked out and smirked.

Sue me. I wanted all of them. Maybe I was crazy and belonged at Chapel Crest. I knew this choice was mine. Church had told me it was. But everything was a test with him, and it was one I didn't want to fail. He asked for me to go slow, and so I would. For now. Because, really, I had a lot to figure out.

Sin kissed me again before going to the door and pulling it open. Stitches stumbled in and set his dark gaze on me sitting on the bathroom sink with my legs still spread.

"Perfect. Leftovers," he proclaimed before taking the spot Sin had been in and burying his face between my legs.

I let out a breath, a soft moan following it as I tangled my fingers in Stitches's hair, allowing him to feast on me.

Sin's lips met mine before his hand pushed my top down to cradle my breast, his thumb and forefinger teasing my hard nipple.

When I came in Stitches's mouth, my mind was made up.

I definitely wanted more.

It spoke volumes about my level of crazy.

My darkness agreed.

# BRYCE

*I* watched from my spot in the darkness as Mirage beat the living piss out of Tony Mullins in the center of the clearing.

Tony Mullins.

Sex fiend. Delinquent. 1.2 GPA. Bipolar. Oppositional Defiant Disorder. Single mother. Two siblings, both of whom he abused. Janna, twelve, and Avery, fifteen. Avery he'd put into the hospital. Miscarriage of the baby he forced inside her. He'd beaten her when she'd fought back during his sixth attack on her. He didn't need Chapel Crest. He needed a hole in the ground.

Mirage's fist met his face on repeat.

This was more about submission than anything. Tony really was defiant.

"Fuck you," Tony spat at him. "I ain't telling you shit."

Mirage punched him in the face again before letting him drop completely to the ground in a bloody heap. I watched him pull his carrot from his back pocket and take a bite, his face calmer than I'd expect from someone who was near murdering.

The snow was painted red with Tony's blood, but Tony kept laughing like a maniac.

I sighed from my spot and looked around, making sure we were still alone. That was my job. Be a shadow. Watch. Observe. Report. I was good at what I did. But this was what survival looked like at Chapel Crest.

This time, I wasn't working with fucking Everett Church. I was working with one of his worst nightmares.

Mirage.

My carrot-wielding, wild rabbit friend.

Well, I figured I could call him a friend. We'd been hanging out a lot more now that Sin was trying to win Sirena over. Mirage had told me this morning that when he got home, all of Sin's stuff was gone. I already knew Church was home. I'd known before his feet touched the soil here that he was returning. A perk to being a shadow. Mirage assured me Sin had been successful, as he had returned as a watcher and was now part of the group.

It fucked me over because how would there ever be room for me? My idea of loving someone didn't include sharing her, but I had fallen hard for the silent beauty. I wanted it, and I wanted her to want me. And if I wanted her, she came with them, so I'd have to get used to sharing. It was really that simple.

Disheartening but simple.

A guy like me probably didn't have a snowball's chance in hell with a girl like Sirena, especially when she already had four guys plus Mirage. Asylum. Or whatever the hell was going on with all that. They'd get in before I would.

Sighing, I focused on the scene in front of me, memorizing everything as was my fashion.

"I'm in a foul mood today," Mirage said. "And I don't actually like being violent. It would be a good thing for the both of us if you just tell me what you know about who hurt Sirena Lawrence out here."

"I'll tell you that I know you're a piece of shit," Tony said through a deranged laugh. "That you work for Church's old man. That you're a bigger monster than any of those watcher pricks are. That the black rabbit fucked her sister and realized he wanted the next step up, and it was her. The mute bitch."

Mirage's fist met Tony's face with a loud crack. He released him and stumbled back, his body clearly vibrating with rage.

Tony let out a wheeze of laughter before sitting back up in the snow and wiping at his busted face.

"She's hot. The mute. *Sirena.*" He said her name with a growl. "Big tits. Tiny waist. Beautiful. Those eyes. Mmm. I'd have fucked her too. Who knows. Maybe I will. Maybe I'll get her to scream like the black rabbit did. Bury my dick deep inside her pussy. Fuck her hard. Put another pretty memory inside her head—"

I was nearly coming out of my spot to tear his dick from his body as a means to feed it to him. Hearing anyone talk about Sirena like that put me into a headspace that was not good.

He didn't get to finish his words, though, and I didn't get to be the one to silence him.

Mirage stuffed his carrot into Tony's mouth, making him gag. His arms flailed about as he tried to push Mirage away, but Mirage wasn't a small guy. He forced the carrot deeper into Tony's throat before he was on a knee, making it count.

"You don't talk about my Rinny that way," Mirage snarled. "You never fucking talk about her like that."

Tony's arms fell to his side, but Mirage continued to push the carrot into his mouth until it completely disappeared.

Then he let him fall to the ground.

I watched him stare down at him for a moment before I approached and stood over them, surveying Tony's dead body.

"He fucking ruined my breakfast," Mirage muttered. "That was my last carrot."

"I have cupcakes in my room."

Mirage grunted. "Do you have a shovel in there?"

I let out a laugh. "You know shovels are more of an Asylum thing."

He looked up at me, a sour look on his face. "You're a dick." He got to his feet and glanced at me again. "And for the record, Asylum likes forks. The shovel was a one-time thing."

"Can't dig a grave with a fork," I said.

"Can't dig a grave period in this cold." Mirage adjusted his blood-splattered rabbit mask and let out a sigh. "But I know some friends who are hungry. Take his feet."

It was my turn to sigh as I grabbed Tony's feet, and Mirage grabbed his arms.

"When did I become an accessory to murder?" I trudged through the snow, helping to carry Tony's body.

"What was the date?" Mirage asked with a laugh. "When your world changed?"

"August 5th," I said easily. "The day I met Sirena."

"Then that's your answer, but you already knew that."

He was right. I did.

I knew everything.

It was just what made me so damn special here at Chapel Crest.

# STITCHES

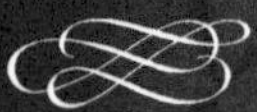

*I* woke up in a cold sweat, three days after eating Sirena out, my chest heaving. My throat was raw from screaming, and I'd clawed at myself during the nightmare.

Sitting up, I rubbed my eyes, my heart pounding hard.

I had nightmares almost every night. Usually, they'd fade away, but this one simply kept going.

My door cracked open, and Sin poked his head in, his torso bare.

"Malachi?"

"Yeah?" I grunted, reaching for my meds on my nightstand. Truly, fuck this shit.

"You OK? I heard you. . ." Sin's voice trailed off.

"Yeah, man. I'm fine. Just a bad dream." I popped a pill into my mouth and swallowed it dry.

Sin stepped into my room and closed the door. The moon was bright, so it lit the place up in an eerie sort of way. Seemed fitting, considering my nightmares.

He walked forward and sat on the edge of my bed.

"What can I do to help?" he asked.

I grunted and lay back against my pillows.

"Ain't nothing you can do. It's over. This is the aftermath." I lightly touched the scar on my face from where I'd carved off a tat in my delirium.

"There has to be something," Sin whispered. "It's my fault—"

"Look. It's *my* fault, not yours. I'm the one with control issues who lost his shit. That was me, Sinclair. Not you. I knew what I was doing. Don't keep blaming yourself for my issues. They're mine, OK? Stop trying to steal them." I gave him a small smile, hoping to discourage him from chasing this shit. I hated that it happened and wanted to be free from it. That freedom came whenever I opened my eyes and left the nightmares behind.

"If I wouldn't have—"

"Listen to me, Sinclair. We could argue about this all night, OK? I could blame my mother for spreading her legs and letting me be created. It's her fault I'm here at all. So don't do this shit. I'm dealing with it."

"Are you?" He peered at me, a frown on his face.

"I am. I'm not strong like Sirena is," I mused. "I tend to dwell. I admire her for her strength."

"She is strong," he agreed. "But she hurts too. She wakes from bad dreams."

"I know," I answered simply. "I've held her through them, and she's held me through mine. I guess we're bonded in the same darkness. She. . . *gets* me. Shared trauma." I shrugged and looked away, my throat tight with the thought of her going through being hurt the way she was by the monster in the woods. I remembered my fear. Knowing hers made it that much worse.

Fuck, I wanted to hang whoever hurt her with my rope from the highest tree in the forest. I prayed I got the chance. Maybe we'd play piñata with him. Beat him as he hung, until his guts sprang free and slopped to the snow below.

"*Yo prevaleceré*," I said. "I will prevail. It is the only option."

"And you will. I know you." Sin laid back beside me in bed.

I smiled at that.

"Did you get a tattoo?" I asked, having noticed dark marks on his back before he got into bed.

"Yeah. I, uh, saw Cass Whitman a few days ago. Had him tat Sirena's claw marks onto my back. They were still swollen, so he had no issue making them permanent."

"Nice," I said. "Wish I'd have done that. Guess there's still time to get her to claw my back, huh?"

He let out a little laugh, settling in further beside me.

"How's Sirena?" I finally asked.

"Church came into my room and took her to his," he answered, staring up at my ceiling. "I expect he's apologizing in his own way."

"Most likely."

"I have been hogging her lately, haven't I?"

"Yep." I popped the p on the word. "But I get it. When I finally gave in, I did the same. I probably drove Church and Ashes nuts with it. So it's cool. You deserve to have time with her too."

He was quiet for a moment.

"I'm scared," he finally said.

I looked over at him to see the worry on his face.

"Of what?"

He shook his head. "She's so fragile. So delicate."

"Let me stop you right there. Sirena is fragile like a grenade, not a flower. You have to have noticed she's changing." I'd noticed the change in her after the forest incident. It was like a fire had been lit inside her, and she was trying to work out how best to let it out without it consuming everything. It reminded me of Ashes, the supreme control he managed over his life, and the struggles he endured to maintain his sanity.

"I have."

"She's becoming a lot more than she was when she got here. Hell, she even communicates these days. I think she's only going to get better. I pray she does."

"I pray for her too." He held his hand up to show me a rosary. "She gave me these. I use them, well, all the time."

I smiled at that. She'd softened the old asshole up a hell of a lot in the past few weeks.

"I also pray that we find the son of a bitch who did that to her," he whispered fiercely. "Mirage has been looking. I was helping, but we kept coming up to dead ends. I don't know how else to get her to tell us."

"Maybe she wants to just forget about it." I knew the feeling, but I also knew this shit couldn't go unpunished.

"Maybe, but I-I can't allow that. He needs to pay. I want to make him pay, Malachi. More than I wanted to make Bells pay for killing my kid." His voice had lowered and taken on a dangerous tone I hadn't heard since Bells's demise. "And you know what I did about that."

I did know. He'd choked her to death, and Ashes had burned her body before Sin took her remains and hid them. And me. I'd been there. To be fair, I hated that bitch too, so I was fine with her death. I may have even done it myself to put Sin out of his misery.

"Then what should we do? Ashes and I have tried to find the person too. Nothing. Whoever did it was a loner. He didn't share it, or he has a very niche group, and they're all tight-lipped."

"I don't know of anyone." Sin sighed. "Fuck. It's driving me crazy."

I agreed, feeling the same. I wanted the prick dead too.

"For now, let's only focus on her. We can work shit out and talk to Asylum and see what he has to say."

"Mirage," he corrected me. "At least I think he's Mirage right now."

"Fine. Mirage. Speaking of that basket case, what's up with him?" I asked.

"What do you mean?"

"You know what I mean. Is it multi-personalities or something? Schizophrenia? What's his deal?"

Sin let out a soft laugh. "It's. . . complicated. I'm not even sure I understand it. I'm assured there's a purpose, so I'm trusting the process."

"Be nice to know what the fuck the process is," I grumbled. "I worry he's going to lose it and hurt her. I've seen the way she looks at him, and I know how unpredictable he can be." Whenever we were on campus, her eyes would seek him out. It used to bother me before we were all stuck in the facility together. Again, with the shared trauma.

Then there was that fucking Bryce Andrews. Mr. Cupcake Man. Fucking douche. She always looked for him too. It ate me up he had her before us. I was working on it, though. I'd been trying to put my jealousy aside because I knew he was important to her. It was a battle I'd been fighting a lot lately when I thought about that guy. Maybe it was because I felt like there was something more with him, and he was just here playing a part. Being on edge was becoming an everyday thing for me, it seemed. Maybe I was the one with the paranoia.

"She looks at him that way because she loves him too," he said, his voice thick.

I let out a sigh. "I know she does. And she should. He did a lot for her in the facility. I simply wish he would be more open with us. He's just so. . . weird."

"He is weird. Imagine living with him," Sin mused.

I snorted at that. "Was it weirder than only interacting randomly with him?"

Sin looked over at me as I rolled on my side to face him.

"He's odd. He has a routine he sticks to. He reminds me of Church a lot. Stickler for shit. He has a better way of getting his way. Church commands it. Asylum wills it, if that makes sense."

"Like he has some kind of mind control."

"I wonder sometimes if he does."

"But Asylum. Mirage. Can you tell when he switches?" I studied Sin to see his gray eyes rake over my face.

"Aside from the mask and carrot? There's a lot more to him than his illness. In fact, his *personalities* aren't really his issue."

"It's the voices, isn't it?" I pressed.

He winced and looked back to the ceiling. "I think the voices are definitely a problem for him. Them. Whatever you want to call it. The struggle is there. But who would he be without them? I think it'll lead us somewhere good. I always followed Church, but honestly, I think we should let Asylum help out more."

I nodded, knowing Asylum knew his shit. I'd never known him to steer us wrong. In the beginning, I hated him. Deep down, I think I always knew he was cut out to be a watcher. The issue would have been he was working for Everett doing god knew what. Now, he's come out with it and even saved Sirena in the facility. People who weren't on your side didn't do that shit. At least, I hoped they didn't.

We were quiet for a moment before Sin spoke again.

"I miss him," he murmured.

I frowned. "Who? Asylum?"

"Yeah. I like Mirage a hell of a lot, but he's more unpredictable than Asylum is. He's scarier, truth be told. You guys haven't seen or heard him. He's gentle, sure, but fuck, when he's pissed. . ." his voice trailed off.

"Is she. . . would she be safe around him. . . when he's like that?" I asked, the worry alive and well within me.

"There are two things I know for certain in life. One is that I would die for Sirena without hesitation. The second thing I know is Mirage would predict that moment and push me aside so he could hold the title. Does that answer your question?"

It did.

It helped relax me.

We were quiet again as we lay in my bed.

"Sin?"

"Yeah?"

I looked over at him. "I'm glad you're home. Seriously. I've missed you."

He stared back at me, a sad smile on his face. "I've missed you too."

"Want to stay with me tonight? It'll be like that time we had that sleepover at your place, and we drew all those dicks on Ashes's face."

Sin let out a snort of laughter. It was good to hear. It felt like forever since I'd heard it.

"He was so pissed he set my bed on fire. My mom was so mad," Sin chortled.

I grinned at the memory. Ashes had calmly left the room as we sniggered. Returning moments later with a can of gasoline he'd gotten from the garage, he proceeded to pile Sin's clothes on his bed before he dumped the gas onto it. Then, he dropped a match into the mess. It had gone up like the Fourth of July. Even the fire department had shown up. Sin was out of clothes and had to borrow some from me since Ashes had torched his.

Ashes wasn't allowed to sleep over at Sin's house again after that.

It had been a long time since then. It was a fun memory. Even Ashes had laughed it off after it happened. It took about a week since the dicks needed to fade off his face, but he was a good sport.

"So, will you stay? No dicks?" I asked.

Sin stopped laughing and nodded. "Yeah, man. I'll stay. I'll fight the demons with you." He gave my hand a squeeze.

"No dicks," I added.

His lips quirked up. "No dicks."

I exhaled, a memory coming back to me of the aftermath of when Sin was shot by his father. How he'd wake in the night screaming. Thrashing. Crying for his dad to stop and his mom to save him. I'd stay at his house and curl up beside him, holding his hand and promising him everything would be OK.

"Do you remember—" I whispered as he held my hand tightly.

"I never forgot," was all he said before we both went quiet.

I closed my eyes, knowing I wasn't fighting a half-assed battle anymore.

It helped me to sleep peacefully, Sin's hand in mine.

# CHURCH

*L*ife had returned to normal. Mostly. We had that rabbit shit looming over our heads. Knowing the prick who hurt Sirena was out there drove me to the edge of my sanity. I still needed to have a word with Asylum/Mirage over him meeting up with her and not coming out with it. That shit pissed me off. I was attempting to take things slow. She was happy, so I was. Again, mostly.

I'd been back a week. Classes were fine. We were fine for the most part. Having Sin home should have felt good, but it didn't. I figured that had more to do with me trying to trust him again than anything else.

But I'd read their notes to one another. I'd seen the way he fucked her in front of us. I'd never seen him that way before, and I'd seen him with a lot of women, including Bells, whom he had been head over heels for.

This love was different for him. It had changed him. Even I could see that, and I didn't typically spend a lot of time giving a shit about people's feelings.

Something felt off. I tossed it aside, assuming it was simply the fact that the rabbit was still running wild and probably watching us, knowing he'd been balls deep inside our girl just weeks before. Probably smirking and feeling like a god.

I wound my arm tighter around Sirena's waist as we finished classes for the day. I'd had her in my bed last night, and Sin had her in his the night before. Ashes the night before that. And then Stitches crawled in with them, leaving me and Sin to sit in the living room. We'd silently agreed to play a video game and hadn't physically killed one another, although the fighting game we played would suggest it wouldn't be long.

I called that progress.

"Hey, Sunday." Cady bounded up to us and draped her arm over Sirena's shoulder, Bryce right beside her.

"I hope you're not talking to me," I grunted.

She rolled her eyes. "Of course I am, Churchy boy. Sunday. Church. Get it?"

"It's not funny if you have to explain it," Bryce muttered.

We stopped at Sirena's locker. I watched her meet Bryce's eye, her cheeks blooming pink. The smallest smile touched his lips before he cleared his throat and looked away. If I didn't know better, I'd think he was going to reach for her hand.

I had to cool myself off. Struggling over the entire Sin thing had me worn out. I knew what I'd told Sirena about her choosing but for fuck's sake. Anyone but this shithead. Bryce Andrews wouldn't be able to keep up with us. Ever. He was our polar opposite. The only thing he probably ever killed was a pint of vanilla ice cream.

"Andrews," I snapped at him. "Why are you here?"

"I came to see Sirena," he answered without missing a beat. "We barely see one another anymore. I think that sucks. I'd like it remedied."

I looked him up and down, taking in how he had his uniform perfectly pressed and his tie tied. Mine was barely held together because fuck this place and everyone who ran it.

"You would?" I snickered at the audacity. "Not happening, cupcake."

His cheeks darkened. "Maybe I wasn't clear, Dante. I'm not taking no for an answer."

I blinked in surprise at him before snapping out of it and taking a dangerous step forward.

Sirena was quick to intervene and get between us.

"I assure you no is my answer, and your response is to walk away before I rip your dick off and stuff it into your mouth like it's your new pacifier."

"Good grief. Chill." Cady grabbed my hand and gave me a tug back. "They're friends. And who cares if it turns out to be more? You're not the boss of her."

Cady was pissing me off.

"She's mine." I ripped my arm away from Cady. "I own her."

"She's not a pair of pants you can stick your dick in," Cady surged back. "Seriously, Rina, what do you see in him?"

Sirena was growing more upset as the seconds ticked by.

"What's going on?"

I looked to the newcomer.

"Asylum," I muttered back in greeting.

"Mirage," he corrected. "Is everything OK?"

"No, it's not," I snapped at him. "We've discussed this before. You know it's not."

"We have?" Mirage frowned "When? And what isn't OK?"

I let out an exasperated breath, forgoing what Asylum had told me about letting nature run its course. "*Fucking lunatic.* When I saw you in the Underground. I told you I wasn't OK with Andrews trying to hone in on Sirena."

Mirage nodded. "Right, well, that wasn't me. That was Asylum. Sometimes I don't get those messages. My apologies." He tapped the side of his head.

Motherfucking mental case. I thought my shit was bad, but it was hard to keep up with Asylum and his many fucking personalities. That made him unreliable.

"I'm not unreliable," he said to me, his voice soft. "I'd appreciate it if you didn't have that opinion of me."

I breathed out hard. This was pissing me off.

"Andrews, fuck off," I said, turning my focus back on him. Sirena placed her hand on my chest and shook her head at me.

"I'll go with them," Cady said.

"So will I," Mirage added. "Besides, don't you have therapy in a few minutes? I happen to have it on good authority that Stitches took a piss on Sister Janice's desk during his Bible study class. So. . . he's going to be late getting here because he was assigned lines or a week in the hole. Obviously, he took the lines."

And Ashes and Sin were already at their group therapy. Fucking damnit.

I knew I was beat here. It helped that Cady and Asylum—er, Mirage—were going to be with them. Even though he confused and pissed me off more than anything, I did trust him.

"Fine." I relented, hating that I had to. I never relented. Fuck.

I placed my hands on Sirena's waist before kissing her. She immediately gave me her submission, which encouraged me to prove who she belonged to in front of Andrews. When I broke the kiss off, she was breathing hard, her lips swollen from my kiss.

"Be good," I warned her. "Remember what we talked about."

She said nothing, but she didn't need to. She was a good girl when she had to be. And in this instance, she needed to be because I wasn't ready to share again.

# SIRENA

"I'm sorry," Bryce said the moment Church left us. Cady had winked at me and scooted off, leaving me with only Bryce and Mirage. I knew she was trying to give me the time I needed with them. I loved her for that.

"It's fine. He'll be OK." Mirage waved Bryce's words off as they flanked me. I had no idea where we were going, but I'd grabbed my jacket, and Mirage had taken my backpack from me.

"I need you to stay warm." Mirage stopped me when we reached the doors and pulled my hat over my head.

I gave him a tiny smile that made his blue eyes light up. I took note of the carrot hanging out of his back pocket and shook my head at his antics. He truly was trying to be his own person. I had to admire that about him. It had to be rough always living in Asylum's shadow since, let's face it, his shadow seemed to swallow everything around it.

Mirage smirked at me, making me wonder if he knew what I was thinking. When he didn't elaborate, I looked back to Bryce.

"We can just go to your place if you want," he said. "I didn't really have a plan other than seeing you."

I was good with that plan. More than good with it. I gave his hand a gentle squeeze to show him, earning a relieved look.

"So I heard Sin is back with the watchers," Bryce said as we walked. One of his curls fell out from beneath his hat and bounced against his forehead. He cast me a quick glance. "And he's with you now too."

I locked eyes with him for a moment before focusing on the path in front of us. The hurt in his voice was apparent, but I was still working on one thing at a time.

"That part is solved," Mirage said. "Sin is home."

I peeked over at him, still intrigued by how he simply knew things.

"Maybe it's beginning to be that time where you focus on the next one," he continued.

I kept walking in silence until we stopped at one of the vending machines for Bryce. Staring at my feet, I got lost in my thoughts on what Mirage said about focusing on the next one.

The next guy.

"It's not me," Mirage murmured as Bryce shook the machine for eating his dollar and cursed.

I followed Mirage's eyes and knew he was talking about Bryce being next.

My feet became my focus again as I realized I didn't even know how to traverse that part. I'd never even kissed Bryce, but he'd quickly become someone I cared deeply for and wanted to explore the possibilities with. He already said he wanted to. The problem was doing it without upsetting the guys.

Maybe I needed more time to acclimate to all of that so we were comfortable before I plowed on. . . or got plowed further.

My cheeks heated at what was going through my mind.

"I just want some damn crackers," Bryce muttered, shaking the machine again. "Everything in this place sucks. The damn machine in the cafeteria ate my other dollar. I'm out of money, man."

"I got it." Mirage stepped away from me and went to the vending machine.

"You have a dollar?" Bryce sounded hopeful.

Mirage scoffed, and then the noise of a crash sounded out and made me jump. He'd knocked over the vending machine and was kicking it. The front cracked a bit, and he shoved his boot through with the next kick, completely obliterating the entire front.

"There. Get as many as you want," Mirage said as a few students scattered away from us.

"You're insane." Bryce shot him a look, but he still bent down before grabbing a bunch of snacks from the wreckage and stuffing them into his bag. "That's because I know they overcharge my parents for what I get out of this place."

"The anger management classes could use some work," Mirage agreed, grabbing snacks with Bryce. "They're certainly not helping me. I think they just piss me off more."

A hand came to rest on my back. I thought maybe it was one of my guys, so I turned to face them.

Instead, I came face-to-face with my nightmare.

Adam Larson.

My breath caught as I stared up at him.

"Hey, Sirena," he greeted me, a sly smile on his face. "It's been a while, hasn't it?"

He'd moved his hand to my waist.

I was frozen. Completely frozen.

"You're still so pretty," he whispered in my ear. "That pussy still tight for me, baby? I think I'll be finding out soon enough."

"What the fuck are you doing?" Mirage was between us in an instant, shoving Adam away from me. "You looking to die, fuckmeat?"

Adam let out a laugh. "Sorry, man. I was seeing if she knew where I could find Cadence. My bad for forgetting she doesn't speak. Silent little church mouse."

Mirage's fist flew out lightning fast just as Bryce grabbed me and pulled me behind him to shield me. I didn't need to see to know Mirage had connected with Adam's face. The loud crack and grunt let me know he'd been successful. And if that hadn't been my first clue, the blood dripping into the snow was the second.

"Get fucking lost," Mirage snarled at him. "And don't ever fucking touch her again. I've killed pricks for less."

"Whatever." Adam stumbled to his feet, holding his bleeding face. "I'll see you around, Sirena."

And with that, he tucked tail and retreated. The moment he was out of my sight, I, too, turned and ran in the opposite direction, desperate to be as far from him as I could be, his words on repeat in my head.

Again. Again. Please, god. Not again. Don't hurt me. Please. Please. PLEASE.

"Sirena! Hey!" Bryce shouted.

I couldn't stop. I needed to put as much distance between me and Adam as I could. I'd been fine on campus because he hadn't been around, but now he was definitely making an appearance and torturing me. Testing me. Teasing me.

I ran faster, knowing I'd lost Bryce and Mirage somewhere behind me as I wove my way through alleys and trees.

I looked over my shoulder, taking note I wasn't being chased. I collided with a hard body, the impact sending me stumbling back. Before I could hit the ground, strong hands caught me at the waist and dragged me into the dark recess between the theater building and the gym.

"It's me. It's me," Mirage's voice came out as I squirmed in his hold, terrified out of my mind. "Rinny. It's me."

I collapsed against him and cried into his chest.

He wound his arms around me. I had no clue how he'd gotten ahead of me, but he had.

"Shh. It's OK. It's OK. I'm here. It's just me and you." He rocked me in his arms, murmuring over and over that I was OK.

"Breathe. Please breathe. That's it. You're fine. Everything is fine now. Just us."

As much as I wanted to be fine, I couldn't. My brain wasn't working.

"You can do this, Sirena. You're stronger than you think. Let it out. Fuck, let that strength out. It's not darkness. Not the way you think. It's what I have. What *we* have. Come on, baby. *Come on.*"

I shook my head.

I couldn't.

*"You fucking can,"* he growled at me. "Damnit, I need you to, Rinny. Everything depends on it. You've overcome so much. Take control. *Please.* I need you to do this. *We* need you to do this."

I tuned his voice out, losing myself inside my head. My safe place. The place where I wouldn't experience pain. The place where it was dark.

Mirage's voice sounded so far away. Eventually, it gave way to silence, leaving me in a place where no one could hurt me.

Except myself.

Because even though I was safe from everyone else, I wasn't safe from me.

And that may have been even more terrifying.

# SIN

"I need you." Mirage's voice came over the phone, Bryce's voice in the background. I was clearly on speaker because I could hear him speaking.

"What's wrong?" I got up and left my group session without a backward glance. I knew everyone had their own thing going on this evening. Church had talked about skipping, so I had no clue what was happening.

"It's Sirena. She's having some trouble. I need help getting into the damn house."

"What are you talking about?" I broke into a run and headed in the direction of the house. "Fuck. I can take her back to my dorm, but I think I just need to get her warmed up."

"Bryce, try the back door. Sometimes Stitches forgets to lock it after he smokes," I said, running as fast as I could get my feet to carry me. "Is she OK?"

"She's. . . out. I don't know. Fuck."

I swallowed hard. "I'll be there in a minute. Keep her safe."

I cut the call off and phoned Church as I continued my run. I suddenly wished I had done more cardio because the cold air was killing my lungs.

"Sin," Church's gruff voice came over the line. "What's wrong?"

"S-Sirena," I gasped out, seeing our house in the distance and making out Mirage's figure on the front step holding a limp Sirena in his arms.

"What happened?" His voice came out tense, and I could hear him curse at someone before a flurry of movement because he was obviously running now too.

"Don't know. Mirage called. He's at the house with her. I'm almost there."

"Get to her. I'll be there in a minute." Church hung up, and I raced up the steps to get to the door as Bryce came around the side of the house, looking worried and frustrated.

I unlocked the door and ushered them inside.

Mirage took Sirena to the couch and laid her on it.

My chest constricted as I took her in. Her eyes were open, but she'd checked out.

"Fuck, what happened?" I whispered as Mirage shifted her to remove her coat.

"I don't know. Adam Larson pissed her off when we were at the vending machine. He was being his typical dipshit self and saying stupid shit," Mirage said, pushing her hair gently away from her face.

I noticed his busted knuckles and the drying blood and realized Adam Larson probably had a broken nose.

"What did he say?" I demanded.

"Just being a dick," Mirage muttered, checking out on me and focusing completely on Sirena. "Rinny? Hey. Come on. We can't do this. Come back, OK?"

He began humming that song I'd heard so often, his hand clinging to hers.

I backed away before going to the hall closet and getting a heavy blanket for her since I knew she had to be cold. All I could think about was losing her and questioning why.

Why did this shit need to keep happening? It wasn't fucking fair. I couldn't lose her. Damnit, I couldn't. My heart couldn't handle it. I knew I needed to pull myself together, so I drew in a few calming breaths.

I came back in to find Mirage still humming and Bryce sitting on the edge of the couch, worry written all over his face.

It took me a moment to realize what I was witnessing.

Two more guys who loved her dearly. It was what love in action looked like.

There was no time to dwell on it, though, so I covered her when Bryce moved aside for me.

Admitting it killed me inside, that she'd gone blank again like she had before.

Church burst into the house with Ashes and Stitches on his heels. Bryce was shoved aside as they all gathered around her.

Bryce tensed but lurked on the edge of the group, his focus on everything going on. Instead of dwelling on that, I kept my attention on what was really important, and that was our girl.

"She's... fuck," Stitches rasped. "No, man. Not again."

"It's fine," Ashes said, his voice shaking. "We've done this before. She came back before. She's only... taking a break. She's been under a lot of stress."

"Right," I murmured. "Stress."

"What happened? Tell me everything," Church demanded. It was Bryce who spoke because Mirage was too busy humming to her.

He quickly recounted the tale.

"Then Mirage found her and called me to come help. Now we're here," Bryce finished. "I really think she needs to be seen at the facility—"

Church rounded on him in an instant. "Fuck the facility."

"What about O'Brien? The doc?" I asked, looking to Church.

He was quiet for a moment before he nodded and pulled his phone out. I knew O'Brien was one of the few good ones left here. If Church trusted him, then I trusted him. It helped that I'd seen him in action with her. He appeared to give a damn and hadn't put out there anything which had gone down with her before after all that other shit happened.

Church turned away from us and spoke quickly but softly into the phone.

"Siren?" I called out, taking her other hand. *Damn, she was ice cold.* "Hey, it's me. It's Sinful. I know you're in there. Come on. We need you to come back. We can talk. I-I have our notebook."

I watched as she didn't respond to me. With each passing second, I could feel parts of my heart begin to crack.

*Please, don't break it, baby. Please. I'm begging you.*

"He's not here," Church proclaimed, hanging up. "He said he won't be back until tomorrow. He had a family emergency and is traveling back as we speak. He said to keep her comfortable, and if anything changes, we need to call the wards." The way he said that made me think he wasn't going to follow through.

Knowing what I knew about this place, I was with him on it.

"He's going to call me when he's back in the morning. He wants us to bring her then if she hasn't improved," Church continued, his voice thick and wavering. I glanced at him to see the muscle thrumming along his jaw. He was going to lose it.

Three... two... one...

"I want Adam Larson," he snarled, backing away. "I want that motherfucker on his knees, begging for his life."

"I'll go with you," Stitches said, backing away, a fierce look on his face.

I was torn between ripping Adam to shreds and staying with Sirena. Sirena won easily, though, so I stayed and looked to Church.

"Make it hurt," I said in a rough voice.

"You can count on it," he answered before walking out the door, Stitches on his heels.

Ashes leaned over her and placed a kiss on her forehead before he backed away.

"I'm going to go with them. That pair isn't a good combo. Take care of her," he murmured before departing, his lighter in his hand.

Bryce took a seat at Sirena's feet and said nothing. All he did was continue to watch her. If I had to guess, I'd say his mind was going a mile a minute. He looked like someone who was thinking. And worrying. That part was apparent as his hands trembled.

And Mirage. He kept humming to her and holding her hand.

I sat on the edge of the couch beside her, just watching. Whispering to her. Praying, the rosary she'd given me in my hand, the beads making a soft tinkling noise as I moved through my prayers.

Eventually, Mirage fell asleep and lay on the floor beside her. Bryce did the same, none of us having spoken to one another the entire time. I looked at the clock finally and saw nearly three hours had passed.

Carefully, I reached out and gently shifted Sirena so she was on my lap. Her eyes were still open, and she had no reaction at all to my touch. Her skin was colder than usual, so I covered us with the blanket once more and cradled her in my arms, whispering my entire fucking being to her.

"Please don't go away again, siren. I need you to stay. This life is nothing without you. I don't want it if you're not here with me. Please. You still haven't gotten to hold Bill. Or dance more. Or even tell the others you love them too," I finished softly. "We need you here. You don't even know how much you've saved us by coming into our lives. Don't go. OK? Stay, siren. Please."

I closed my eyes and continued to hold her tightly until sleep took over.

Maybe when we'd wake, she'd be back.

It was the last thing I prayed for right after Adam Larson's death.

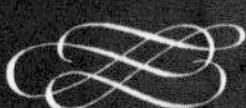

*N*othing.

Adam Larson was gone. His friends claimed they hadn't seen him in hours. Even after Stitches broke Sam Duncan's arm and blackened both eyes, they maintained their story. If he were smart, he'd stay gone because I knew his time on this planet was limited. My anger grew by the second, while Church and Stitches wouldn't be able to be pulled back from the ledge.

I was the only one with a bit of control left.

Thank fuck because I was teetering on the edge of burning down the building where Adam's dorm room was.

Maybe my therapy was working.

When we reached our home, it was well past dark. Bryce had fallen asleep at Sirena's feet, and Mirage was on the floor by the couch, a carrot on the floor beside him. And Sin.

He held her in his arms.

He'd have a hell of a crick in his body tomorrow.

I couldn't help but admire him, though. He'd come so far.

"It's nice," Stitches murmured. "He loves her so much."

"He does," I agreed, taking in the pair.

Church said nothing and walked over to them. Carefully, he

untangled Sin's arms from around her and lifted her from him before taking her upstairs to his bedroom.

I sighed and looked to Stitches.

"You know how he is," he mumbled, rubbing his eyes.

I did know how he was. He was most likely upstairs undressing her as we stood there in the living room. In moments, he'd sink inside her body in a feeble attempt to bring her back before his anger would take over again.

He'd done it before, and Dante Church was a creature of habit.

I went into the kitchen and took care to be quiet as I boiled a pot of water for some quick spaghetti. Even if my heart wasn't into eating, I knew we needed to because we'd need our strength.

I was just taking the food off the stove when Church made a reappearance, his lips turned down into a deep frown. Stitches shot me a knowing look and put plates on the table.

I stopped to watch Church tuck Sin's blanket back up around him before putting one over Mirage.

He hesitated for a moment before grumbling and putting one on Bryce too.

I let the tiny smile out before turning back to the food.

"Should we wake them?" Stitches asked.

"No. Let them sleep. Some of us should get some rest," Church answered, sitting in his place as I set the pot of noodles and sauce on the table.

"How is she?" I ventured, taking my seat. Stitches did the same and doled some spaghetti onto his plate halfheartedly.

"Same. Just. . . not there."

"Did you. . ." I whispered.

Church looked at me, his green eyes wavering. "It didn't work."

I nodded and didn't say anything, hating he did shit like that but knowing it was simply who he was. It helped to know she wouldn't tell him no either, had she been conscious for it. In fact, I knew I'd have even joined in.

I supposed that said a lot about me as a person too.

"What's the plan?" Stitches asked.

"She sees O'Brien tomorrow if nothing has changed. If she needs to be monitored at the facility, one of us will always be with her. Like last time." Church rubbed his eyes.

It was as good a plan as any at this point.

"What about Larson?" I looked to Church, who hadn't touched his dinner yet.

"He dies," he said simply. "I don't even fucking care anymore. Students go missing from here all the time. He'll simply be another one."

"Tony Mullins is missing," I said.

"He's dead." Mirage came into the room and rubbed the sleep from his eyes. "I killed him when he pissed me off."

I raised my eyebrows at his proclamation and watched as he took Sirena's chair at the table and scooped spaghetti onto one of the plates Stitches had put on the table.

Church narrowed his eyes at him.

"Asylum," he started.

"Mirage," Mirage corrected.

"Excuse me for not keeping up to speed on what fucking personality you're sporting," Church snapped back.

"These noodles are crunchy," Mirage muttered, seemingly not caring what Church had said. "My compliments to the chef."

"Sorry," I muttered. "Guess my heart wasn't into it this time."

Mirage scooped more into his mouth and nodded. "I get like that too when I kill someone." He looked at me, his blue eyes wide. "Sometimes I go on autopilot, you know? Just to get it over with."

"How often are you killing people?" Stitches asked, looking confused.

"Too often," he answered back. "I'm not really the violent sort."

"Uh." I let out a nervous laugh. "Seems like maybe you are if you're knocking off people on campus."

"People? I hardly call some of them people." He ate more before letting out a sigh and cocking his head to the right, and mumbling. "No, I'm trying. What the fuck? It's fucking cloudy. You know it's fucking cloudy. OK, Mister-Fucking-Bionic-Vision. I know. I will.

Not fucking happening. No. *I said no.* Fuck off." He went silent and ate again while I exchanged looks with Stitches and Church.

"Are you OK?" I asked gently, looking over to him. I knew stress could make some conditions worse. I wasn't sure how it worked with Seth's schizophrenia and other issues, but I assumed maybe it wasn't helping him. The last thing we needed was for him to lose it.

He slammed his fork down, his hands shaking.

"I said no," he snarled. "Let me do this. I can handle it. *I can handle it.* Stop. Stop. FUCKING STOP!"

His breathing came out harshly as he sat in his seat. I exchanged another look with Stitches and Church before Church spoke.

"Asy-I mean, Mirage," he started. "What's going on?"

Mirage closed his eyes for a moment and drew in a few deep breaths before opening them and staring at Church.

"Sometimes it gets loud inside my head," he said, a look of vulnerability sweeping over his face. "Things have been cloudy for me lately. Nothing makes sense. I get. . . frustrated. I'm sorry if I've made things uncomfortable. It's not my intention."

"You're fine," I said, giving him a forced smile. "As long as you don't kill any of us."

He scoffed. "I don't like to kill people. I mean. . ." His Adam's apple bobbed. "I'm complicated."

"I think we all are," Stitches piped up. "Do you want to smoke? We can mellow out."

Mirage contemplated his question for a moment before nodding. "Yeah. Sure."

Stitches got up and left the room to get the drugs, leaving the three of us behind.

"So where is Tony's body?" Church asked.

"Oh. Yeah. That." Mirage started to eat again. He swallowed before answering. "We cut him up and fed him to the wolves."

I grimaced at his words, my stomach twisting. It shouldn't have bothered me, but the image of him hacking up a body and feeding it to the wolves like a treat made me a little ill.

"Were you ill when you helped dispose of Bells?" Mirage leveled his gaze on me and cocked his head to the right.

I let out a huff of laughter. "No, I suppose I wasn't."

"Then this would have been no different. The wolves are my friends. They chase me." He pointed to his white rabbit mask. "We like to play these games. I always reward them."

I shivered at his words, not even wanting to know how many people he'd fed to the wolves.

"Not as many as I'd like," he answered my thoughts.

"I hate that you do that," I muttered to him.

He shrugged. "Me too, Asher. Me too."

Stitches came back in and lit the joint before taking a big inhale of it and passing it to Mirage, who finished his spaghetti. I watched him take a hit before blowing it out. He handed it off to me.

Sighing, I took it, wishing I wasn't out of my vape because counting smoke rings right then seemed like maybe a nice stress reliever. I inhaled before passing it off to Church.

"So count your blessings instead," Mirage said softly to me. "They matter more than smoke rings. Now eat. We need to be strong. This next part may hurt."

Chills raced over my skin at his words, but I didn't press him for more answers. I wasn't quite sure I could handle them right then, anyway.

# CHURCH

$S$he wasn't better.

She was still just a shell, lying in my bed with her eyes wide.

Her pretty, lifeless eyes.

I'd fucked into her body when I'd brought her upstairs, weeping over her with each thrust. Begging her to return to me. To us. I needed her like I needed my next breath.

"OK," I said into the phone later that morning as I spoke to O'Brien. "I'll be there soon. Sully is off campus?"

"Yes. He left this morning. Atkins is still here."

"He's not an issue," I said, staring at Sirena, who lay like a perfect doll in my bed. I hadn't slept last night. Mirage had gone back to sleep on the L of the couch while Sin and Bryce curled up on the other side. Ashes and Stitches had sat in my room with me. We'd watched Sirena all night and talked about nothing and everything.

Now, it was time to get her some help since my brand of help wasn't cutting it.

Gently, we washed and dressed her before Ashes went downstairs and started my Bronco.

"Dante?" Stitches asked after whispering something into her ear I couldn't hear.

"Yeah?"

"Will you promise she'll be OK?" The note of fear in his voice made me look at him.

"She's going to be fine. She has been before. When things are too much, she checks out. She always comes back," I said thickly. "She always comes back to us."

He nodded and didn't say anything. Instead, he followed me downstairs as I lifted her into my arms.

Sin came out of his bedroom wearing different clothes, his hair a mess, and his eyes rimmed in dark circles from having a shitty night of sleep.

"Hey." He crossed the room quickly and stopped in front of me, his face pinched with worry.

"She's the same," I answered. "I'm taking her to O'Brien. We'll take turns watching over her like before. I'm taking the first watch."

"OK." He nodded tightly before brushing his lips across hers. "I love you, siren. I'll be there soon."

"I'll call if anything changes," I said as Stitches opened the door. The plan was for him to go with me across campus to the facility and drop her and me off before returning home with my Bronco. If anything changed, I'd call the guys to come help me. It was unlikely I'd need help, but we had to stay open to that possibility.

We rode in silence, Stitches driving and me holding Sirena on my lap. When we got inside, the wards were already waiting with a stretcher at the door. They took her to her room, Stitches following us.

"So, no improvement?" O'Brien asked as he stared down at her in the bed. A nurse bustled around setting up an IV. I watched as she inserted the catheter and hooked Sirena up to the bag of fluids.

"No," I answered.

"She did blink this morning for me," Stitches said. "I-I asked her if she knew where she was. She blinked once for yes."

I hated that he was so damn hopeful because if she didn't come back, he'd be fucking crushed, and we might lose him too. Knowing that made everything that much worse. In fact, I was sick to my stomach over this shit. While I wanted to kill Adam since I thought he was a prick to begin with, I knew my specter needed me right now. Adam's time would come soon enough.

"Well, let's keep her here and see what happens. I'll give her some meds. Make sure she's got some fluids, and we'll watch. Dante, watch some TV. Hang out. I'll make sure there's food for you. You have a private room here with everything you'll need. I'll be in and out. Press the button if you need me or anything. Got it?" O'Brien looked me over.

"Yes," I said. "And remember, this doesn't get out to Sully or my father."

"I'll do what I can. I only have my trusted ones working with me today. I can't guarantee anything, though. You know that. This place has people we think are allies when they aren't." He looked disgusted as he said the words.

"I'm aware." My answer came out dry and just as disgusted.

"Malachi, stay out of trouble," O'Brien warned before leaving us.

"I'll be fine," Stitches said, looking at me quickly. "I won't fuck up."

"I know you won't. Too much is riding on all of this. We'll get it sorted. I promise." I hugged him to me before releasing him. "Go home. Try to rest. Eat. Shower. Keep Sin in line. Make sure Ashes doesn't burn the damn house down. He was really twitchy last night."

"I know." He let out an exasperated breath. "I'll make sure Cady doesn't know either. She's like gasoline on an already blazing fire."

"Truth," I mumbled, putting my focus back on Sirena.

"I love you," Stitches said to her before kissing her once more. "And I love you, man. Call me. Text me. Please."

"You know I will," I said, watching as he went to the door.

He cast one final, heartbreaking look at Sirena before leaving us in silence.

I took her hand in mine and gave it a squeeze before pressing my lips to her knuckles.

"What movie do you want to watch?" I asked, sliding into bed beside her, the remote in hand. "What was it you liked? Lord of the Rings?"

I found it on a streaming channel and hit play before kissing her temple and settling in completely, my eyes heavy. I prayed she'd be back to normal when I woke up.

Fuck, god, please.

# SIN

It had been nearly four days since Sirena's episode, and Church wouldn't leave her side. He was supposed to be taking turns with us, but he'd refused to leave whenever we'd go to relieve his watch.

I knew he needed to get out of there, or he'd end up going nuts and being committed himself.

At least he'd been letting all of us visit, including Mirage and even Bryce, although he did kick him out after ten minutes.

Bryce took it in stride and just kept going, though. I admired that about him. I didn't know a lot about his life, but I assumed it had been shit. He seemed fairly normal to me, so his being at Chapel Crest always stumped me.

It didn't matter though. He was slowly growing on me.

Then there was the issue of Cady. She was a damn dog with a bone when it came to Sirena. We kept heading her off whenever she'd come over looking for her. It was always excuse after excuse. She couldn't be disturbed because one of the guys had her. She was napping. She was out with Stitches. Ashes wanted to show her something with fire. On and on, the excuses went until I was certain she was going to camp out in front of the house.

"She's a pain in the ass," Stitches grumbled as she left our house later that morning.

"She is," I agreed. "But she's Sirena's sister. They're close."

"Yeah, yeah. You think I could hit her with a snowball from the front step?"

"I think she'd tear your head off then torment me into giving her information on Sirena."

"So, no?"

I chuckled sadly, hating I was laughing at all, everything considered.

I gathered my bag after putting on my jacket and boots.

"Where are you going?" Stitches asked, frowning at me.

"It's my turn to swap with Church."

"Fuck, man. He's not going to swap. He practically shoved Ashes out of the room yesterday."

"Then I'll stay and be a pain in his ass. I'm going. I don't even care. I want my turn," I said firmly. I went to the door and paused. "Can you give Bill a rabbit? He needs to eat today."

Stitches wrinkled his nose. "Man, come on. You want me to kill a rabbit?"

"You're Dante Church's brother, and you're telling me you can't kill a rabbit?" I shook my head at him. "It's not you who kills it anyway. Put it in his habitat and let him have some fun."

"That's fucked up," he muttered. "Maybe I'll call Mirage over to do it."

"Whatever you need to do. Thanks."

He cursed softly as I closed the door behind me.

For a guy who had killed people before, he sure was a softie when it came to furry creatures. Maybe he really should get a cat like Ashes suggested.

✝

"I'M FINE. You don't need to switch with me," Church said as I sat down in the chair beside Sirena's bed.

"Listen. I know shit's been bad between us lately, but it's going to get worse if you don't fucking leave," I said, locking my glare on him. "The rest of us have a place here too."

Instead of fighting me on it, he got up and kissed Sirena on the forehead before kissing her lips. He looked at me, his eyes filled with exhaustion.

"Fine. You're right. I do need a decent night of sleep. If anything happens—"

"I will kill anyone who walks through that door and even looks at her wrong," I said firmly. "She's safe with me. I promise. I meant what I said. I'd die for her."

He studied me for a moment before giving me a nod and leaving the room.

As surprising as it was, it was also a huge relief. I didn't want to fight with him anymore. We used to be close, but now it seemed like it was forever ago. Having those moments come back to us meant a lot to me. I only needed to figure out how to get us there again. I prayed it happened sooner rather than later because I missed him like crazy.

✝

NIGHT HAD FALLEN. They'd come in and replaced Sirena's bag of IV fluids and gave her a new blanket, which had obviously been kept in a warmer. She hadn't moved an inch all day except when the nurses came in to change her clothes and gave her a sponge bath. I'd stared out the window during it as a way to give them some privacy.

Now, she slept and had been for the better half of an hour.

The TV droned on in the background. It was some romance movie. It struck me as odd that Church had been watching this shit. I supposed maybe he figured she'd like this stuff.

And hell, maybe she did. All I knew was that I was desperate to find that out and more about her.

No one had seen Adam on campus, so we couldn't even take our frustrations out on him. Everything was at a standstill. No Sirena. No Adam. No fucking answers.

"I miss you," I murmured to her as I held her hand. "What can I do to bring you back? I can't stand that you're here, but you're not. It's killing me. Please. I don't know what to do, siren. Fuck, baby. I just need a sign to know you're in there and simply working on things so you're stronger. You're already so strong, though. And you have me now. And you could have Mirage. Asylum. Even Bryce if you wanted him. I'm sure of it. We need you to come back. We're so lost without you." I crawled into bed beside her and straddled her small body. Carefully, I took her face in my hands and cradled it while leaning down, my lips a fraction from hers.

"You are my Sleeping Beauty. Let me be the prince who wakes you. Please," I whispered. "I'm begging you, siren. Come home. I need you so fucking much."

My tears fell on her face as I brushed my lips against hers. I lingered for a moment before pulling away, my heart heavy because she continued to sleep.

Maybe I wasn't her Prince Charming.

My heart sank at that thought while she continued to slumber.

So much for fucking fairy tales.

It didn't matter though. Maybe I'd have to rewrite the story. Tell it a different way.

Maybe in this story, it was the villain who woke the princess.

"Please let me be the villain," I whispered before kissing her again.

# SIRENA

*Please let me be the villain.*

Somewhere far away, I heard Sin's voice. My heart jumped at the sound of it. It felt like forever since I'd heard anyone. Or registered any presence aside from the darkness.

I'd been wallowing in it for ages.

I wanted to go home.

I dreamed of the guys. Mirage. Bryce. Asylum. Church. Stitches. Ashes. Sinful. All of them were begging me to come back. Making promises to protect me. To keep me safe. To love me. To do anything I asked of them.

But I didn't want that.

I wanted to protect myself. I wanted to be the one who could handle my business. The fear that dwelled inside me needed to go away. There was only one way to make that happen.

Stop wallowing in the darkness I hid in and become it.

The darkness was what my guys were. It made them stronger. I hid behind my trauma. Embracing it could change everything.

*Please let me be the villain.*

Maybe I wanted to be a villain too.

487

All I needed to do was wake up. Take what was mine. Claim it. Own it. I could be brave. . . right?

*Please, god, I want to be brave.*

He begged me softly. His voice grew clearer. Dampness. He cried quietly, not wanting anyone to know he was doing it.

Sinful.

My Sinful.

*Please. I want to be brave. Help me. Please, god, help me!*

*Open. Open your eyes and just face it. OPEN YOUR EYES.*

I snapped my eyelids open and stared blearily around the room for a moment before I took in Sin curled against my body, his face buried in my neck, his body shaking as he cried.

Every muscle screamed at me from not moving, but I managed to lift my hand and rake my fingers clumsily through his messy hair.

He pulled his head up and stared down at me, his gray eyes bloodshot from crying.

"Siren?"

I let my eyelids drift closed for a moment before I opened them and cradled his cheek, his rough stubble beneath my fingers.

"Sinful," I whispered his name, my voice raspy.

"Oh, fuck. Sirena." He dragged me to sit up before wrapping his arms around me and squeezing me until I almost couldn't breathe. His lips peppered kisses all over my face before he finally released me.

"You're back. You're here." He stared at me in wonder, like he couldn't believe I was a real person.

I didn't feel like a real person. In fact, my body felt foreign to me.

But I was here. Awake. Alive. Back.

"Y-you need to eat. You haven't eaten in days." His voice shook. I watched him grab the call button and hit it several times until a nurse bustled in.

"She's awake. Get O'Brien. Get her food. Now," Sin snapped. The nurse looked terrified but rushed away to do as he commanded.

I liked that he made people move like that.

In fact, it made me more than happy.

Sin laid me gently back against the mattress and stared down at me. "I have our notebook."

I gave him a tired smile, desperate to just say my feelings and forgo the notebook. "I f-feel weird."

"I know, baby." Relief swept over his face at my words.

It didn't feel right to speak.

"You haven't eaten in days. You need food. You'll feel better once you have some."

Moments later, the doctor came in and went over me from top to bottom. I didn't answer his questions. He was a nice man, but my voice wasn't for him.

He seemed satisfied with me, though, and told Sin he still wanted me to stay the night. Sin agreed, and I didn't fight it. I wanted the weirdness I felt to go away.

Or maybe I needed to adapt to it.

The lights hurt my eyes.

"Your food is here." Sin moved so the nurse could put the food on the tray. Sin adjusted my bed a little so I was sitting up better.

The nurse didn't stick around. She booked it out before Sin could give her a second dirty look.

I really did like him domineering and in power mode.

"Eat," he said softly, lifting my spoon for me.

I parted my lips and ate everything he fed me, right down to the weird cold peas.

"How are you feeling? Better?"

I said nothing, watching him worry over me.

He didn't need to worry for me. None of them did. I was tired of people always being scared I was going to break because of how weak I was.

"I need to call the guys." He pulled his phone out. "We've been so worried, baby. So fucking worried. We thought we'd lost you." His voice trailed off.

Anger surged through me.

They didn't deserve this. None of them deserved to constantly be going through this with me.

I needed to be brave.

The words kept repeating in my head.

I needed to be a villain too. Princesses ended up captured. But villains. . . they were in control.

And that's what I wanted.

Control.

I held his hand for a moment before he kissed me again. When he pulled away, he put the phone to his ear and spoke.

"She's back."

No.

She wasn't.

*I* was.

The brave Sirena. The one who lurked in the darkness. The one who wanted to merge that darkness with her guys and make a stronger world for all of them.

A ghost of a girl who wanted more.

And one who would get it.

# STITCHES

I watched Sirena smile as she sat on the couch next to Ashes three days after she returned home. She'd been more quiet and withdrawn. It didn't seem possible, considering she didn't speak much to begin with, but this was different. It was almost like she was always lost in thought.

But she was here, and that was all that mattered.

To say we were thrilled was an understatement. O'Brien told us he believed she had some PTSD, and certain episodes triggered it to the extreme. As a coping mechanism, she'd retreat inside her mind.

As long as she came back to us, I'd learn to handle it if that's what was going to happen. O'Brien suggested that with the right medication and therapy, she may be able to find coping mechanisms to overcome it.

She'd sat and listened to him talk about it without anything akin to caring on her face. In fact, she just seemed. . . lost.

Mirage had been in and out all week checking on her. Each time he'd arrive, her face would light up. Yesterday, I'd watched her run her thumb lightly over the scars on his wrist when she didn't think we were looking. I knew Ashes had seen it, too, because he'd frowned at the movement but had looked away without a word. I was grateful

Church hadn't seen it. He may have mentioned the possibility, but that didn't mean shit when it came down to it.

And Sin.

I knew his ass had seen the affection she'd shown Mirage.

I didn't have any issues at this point with Mirage. Asylum. Whoever the fuck he was. It was that shared trauma bond. I was all for anyone who was willing to save our girl. The only thing I found myself concerned with was Church. If this were going to happen, it needed to happen slowly so he could acclimate, and it certainly couldn't be hidden.

But was it hidden if I knew about it?

I let my legs bounce as I mulled everything over.

I'd been so lost in thought I hadn't noticed her move to sit beside me. Her warm hand rested on my thigh, slowing my bouncing to a stop.

"Angel." I smiled at her, immediately relaxing.

She stared back at me, concern in her pretty eyes.

"I'm OK. Just thinking."

She hooked her pinky with mine, and I was done for. I sank back against the cushions, my heart full.

Her lips brushed against mine, my pinky still hooked with hers. She always knew all the ways to touch me in order to bring me back to life.

Fuck, I loved her.

She moved on her own accord and straddled my lap in one of the pretty dresses Church had bought her. Of course, I wasted no time gripping her pert little ass, giving her a squeeze as I did so, her lips still on mine.

It wasn't often I let her lead, but I wanted her to do whatever she wanted so much that I relented, despite my surging desire to throw her onto the cushions and rail her into next week.

Her kiss deepened, her tongue doing a delicious swan dive into my mouth. When she ground against my aching dick, I let out a groan she eagerly swallowed down.

I'd completely forgotten the guys were in the room with us. It didn't matter, though, because it wasn't like we'd never fucked together before.

She didn't waste any time getting my clothes off. I let her too. Fuck, like I was going to even attempt to stop her. She could do whatever she wanted to me. I was hers.

Having her back once more was a dream come true.

She trailed her lips along my jaw and down my neck while continuing to rub against me.

"You're going to make me come if you keep doing that, angel," I husked out. Having her warm, cotton-clad pussy rubbing against me had me nearly going insane. I gripped her ass tighter and helped her slide against me.

She let out a soft moan against my skin, nearly sending me into orbit.

*Don't come. Don't come. Don't come.*

I'd never blown my load early before, and I didn't want to start now.

But fuck, it felt good to have her against me like this. So hot. So needy.

"Need some help?" Ashes asked, sliding in next to me, his voice gravelly.

"Fuck, yes," I managed to groan out.

Her lips left me as she leaned over and began kissing Ashes, her hot pussy still rubbing against my dick.

It wasn't helping.

I needed to be inside her.

I fumbled to get to her panties, but I managed to shove them aside before lifting her by her ass and bringing her down on my cock.

With a groan, I sank deep inside her, her moaning against Ashes's lips as I burrowed deep.

*Fuck, her pussy felt good.* So warm and tight.

My favorite place.

I pulled out and thrust back inside her. A soft sigh of pleasure feathered out across Ashes's lips. With his cock out and in his hand, he pumped it slowly before she took over for him.

It was Church who joined a moment later and shifted her so her head was back, and he was giving her an upside-down kiss. Sin watched us from his spot on the couch, not moving a muscle, his snake, Bill, draped over his shoulders.

Church pushed the top of her dress down, exposing her full breasts. I fucked into her pussy as he massaged her pert tits. She continued to jerk Ashes off, her body jostling gently while I fucked her.

The fact that she was becoming so coordinated in paying us all attention made me even harder. She truly was perfect.

"Sinclair, get over here," I managed to call out.

He hesitated for a moment before he approached, that damn snake still on him.

"Fuck, really?" I choked out, eyeing the snake while fucking Sirena. She'd now turned her head, and Church had his cock in her mouth while she continued to jerk Ashes.

"I'd like to try something," Sin said.

"I'm pretty open to trying a lot of things, Sinclair, but fucking a snake isn't one of them," I grunted, slamming upward into Sirena's pussy. It jostled her, and she clearly bit a little on Church's dick because he let out a hiss before tangling his fingers in her hair and pushing deeper into her mouth.

"No one is going to fuck Bill," Sin said. "The fuck?"

"Just putting it out there," I groaned as he took a seat next to me, his pants coming off in the process.

Sirena's mouth popped off Church's dick, her face twisted in what I knew was her oncoming release.

Her hand slowed on Ashes. Within seconds, her head was thrown back, and she was dampening everything around us as she came on my cock. Her release gushed like a river, making me howl in pleasure as I followed, adding to her mess.

Breathless and with her chest heaving, she fluttered her lashes before sliding off me and going to Sin.

He was quick to pull her down onto his waiting cock, fucking into the mess I'd already made in her pussy.

His groan let me know he had no issue with it.

"Mm, siren," he rasped before sucking one of her hardened nipples into his mouth, his dick buried balls deep inside her.

She ground against him, and we watched.

It was when Bill moved forward and flicked his tongue against her cheek that I stiffened and cast a quick look to both Church and Ashes. Church kept his eyes narrowed, and Ashes leaned forward, his hand slowing on his dick.

Her eyes widened, but Sin gripped her by the neck and brought her lips to his.

"He won't hurt you," he said before slamming upward into her, his lips on hers.

Bill slithered over to her as Sin fucked her pussy. We watched Bill wrap himself around her shoulders while Sin continued to bury himself over and over inside her.

It was all too hot and a little terrifying, especially when she took the lead and rocked on his dick, pinning his arms above his head.

And he took it, that damn snake coiled around the pair. It was like watching two demons in hell fuck.

"S-Sinful," she cried out his name as she came.

He let out a feral groan, his body tensing as he followed her.

She collapsed against his body, Bill resting his head on her shoulder and flicking his tongue out at me.

"That was both hot and a little frightening," I said, edging away from the snake. If Sin was looking for a way to keep her to himself, Bill was a damn good barrier, especially when it concerned me.

Church smirked at me after taking a seat next to Sin on his other side. Church tugged her off Sin's cock and pulled her down on his own, Bill coming along for the ride.

"You want in?" Sin asked, stroking his cock, his piercing glinting beneath the lights from the living room.

I wrinkled my nose and looked to Ashes, who shrugged.

"I, uh, think I'll have to build up to that," I said, still wondering if the snake was as slimy as my brain said it was.

Ashes let out a laugh and clapped me on the shoulder before

getting up. "I'll try anything once," was all he said before he went to Church and Sirena and pushed his cock inside her mouth while Church continued to plow into her pussy, Bill looking like he was on an amusement ride as he rested his body around the pair.

I shook my head, a smile on my face.

I hoped Bill wouldn't be a permanent fixture in our carnal activities.

Because honestly, I may be a little afraid of snakes.

But it wasn't enough to keep my cock in my pants.

Fuck it.

I reached out and touched Bill's scales and shuddered.

Yeah, I'd have to work up to the snake thing.

I didn't mind watching, though.

Maybe that just made me a crazy weirdo too.

I was OK with that.

# SIRENA

*I* felt better. My head was getting clearer. I'd been working on embracing my inner strength the past two weeks since coming home.

I thought I was doing a good job of it, especially since I'd fucked the guys with a snake wrapped around me. The entire ordeal made me feel like a goddess. I'd loved it so much that Sin and I had done it several times together alone in his room. Feeling Bill slither around us, binding us closer together, just did something to me.

Mirage and Bryce had been gone the last few days. Mirage had been coming to see me almost daily but had told me the last time he was here that he'd be going away for a few days with Bryce and would be back. He didn't elaborate on it. He'd simply squeezed my hand, adjusted his rabbit mask, and left. He was never without his mask. It was constantly fixed in place, his bright blue eyes peering out from beneath it, his jaw and lips exposed. I couldn't count the number of times I dreamed of kissing him.

He'd given me a knowing smile but hadn't ever pushed for it.

Maybe that meant I was supposed to make the move.

I glanced at Church as we sat together on the couch.

"Baby," he murmured, kissing my palm before going back to reading the book he had.

I smiled at the action. I'd never felt so much love before. These guys kept amazing me. They continued to put up with all my crap, even the episodes where I slipped away on them, without complaint. I owed them for their devotion. I hoped someday I could really show them what they meant to me.

Stitches and Ashes had left earlier that morning to do something for classes, and Sin was at therapy. Church was set to leave for his therapy soon.

Sighing, he looked at his watch before closing his book.

"I have to go," he said, kissing me. "I don't want to leave you here alone. Come with me—"

I silenced him with a kiss and shook my head.

I knew the plan. Stitches and Ashes would be back before Church. I'd be able to safely wait for them in the house after Church left. It was only a few hours, and that didn't bother me in the slightest. I never got a lot of time to have the house to myself. The idea of it excited me.

He scowled and looked away from me. "I worry, Sirena."

I placed my hand over his and gave it a squeeze.

He looked back at me. "I can't even look at the cameras. Ashes made me disconnect them because it violated our privacy."

I raised my brows at him, knowing damn well the ones outside were working.

He smirked at me, clearly knowing what I was thinking.

"Fine. You win this round. I know you want to try out those new paints we got you."

I threw my arms around his neck and hugged him tightly.

He seemed surprised by the action but collected himself quickly before returning my hug and holding me tightly.

"I love you, specter. More than you'll ever understand." He kissed my temple, his hold growing tighter. "Mine," he whispered.

I closed my eyes and breathed in the way he smelled. The woods. The wild. The cold.

"Mine," I whispered back to him.

✝

I BRUSHED the black paint along the canvas, staring into the image I'd created of me peering out from the darkness.

That familiar feeling within me stirred, reminding me it was still ready for me to grasp.

I focused on the painting, wondering what it would feel like to become the girl in the portrait. To embrace that darkness. The bravery. To be uncrushable.

Lightly, I traced my fingers over the drying paint, the feelings stirring within me.

*It's yours. Take it. Be brave. Be the darkness. . . Join the guys and revel in it. . . Untouchable. Be untouchable. It's all psychological.*

My phone buzzed with a video call, and I snapped out of the alluring thoughts before snatching it up, wondering if it was Sin because he was supposed to be back a half hour ago.

Sin's name appeared on the screen. I accepted the call, my heart thrashing violently when Adam's face came onto the screen.

"Hey, church mouse," he greeted me with a grin as my blood ran cold.

*How does he have Sin's phone?*

"I bet you're wondering how I'm calling you from your boyfriend's phone, huh? Well, let me answer that question for you." He panned the camera around to show the coffin I'd been in with Asylum not all that long ago.

"He's inside. But wait. I need to show you this. You're going to love it." The camera shook as he went to the coffin and showed me what was inside.

Sin's naked body was pressed against Cady's. He'd somehow knocked them out and had them tied to one another, completely naked. Blood dripped from a cut on Sin's head, and Cady's face was bruised.

"Guess what they did for me when I threatened to get you next?"

He turned the camera back on himself. "It's not hard to guess. They're still naked."

Nausea rolled through my guts at his words and what they meant.

"Tell you what. I was going to just kill them and leave them here. Honestly, they'd not feel a thing because I really knocked them out. I figured I was having so much fun, so why not invite you to play?" He grinned like a lunatic at me. "So here are the rules. You come to me, right here in the cemetery. I'll let them go if you come with me. They get to live. You get to save them. Your dear, sweet sister who was already willing to die for you, and Sin, who begged me to leave you alone. You should have seen their faces when I told them to fuck for me in order to save you. I think there's something there. Maybe they can bond now." He let out a cackle. "You should have seen him when he came inside her. The way he kissed her. Fucked her. How she took his big cock and moaned beneath him."

My hands shook as he continued to vividly describe the nightmare he'd created.

"Listen," he suddenly grew serious. "I know Sin hurt you before. Put you into this box and left you with that nutjob, Asylum. I'm paying him back, baby. He deserves this. And your sister. She knew I scared you, and yet she didn't care. She kept fucking me. Telling me you'd be fine when you clearly weren't. I mean, you did recently have another mental break and all. Come to me. Let this be their punishment for their crimes against you. Trust me, their sex was on fire too, so I know they both enjoyed it. You can make this your last big gesture. Free them. Let them live in the guilt. Come on, what do you have to lose? I mean, aside from maybe your life?"

I swallowed hard, my breathing uneven.

"Right. The rules. Come to me. Tell no one. If anyone finds out, I'll kill both of them and make you help me. Oh! Doesn't that sound fun?" A maniacal glint glimmered in his eye. "I can hold your hand while we push the blade through their necks." He let out a gleeful laugh. "You have ten minutes to get here, or I'll start stabbing." He held out the knife Church had given Sin and let out another cackle. "Tick-tock, little mouse."

The call disconnected, and I stared at it for a moment, the darkness pressing against me from all sides.

I had to be brave. I had to do this.

*God, please! Help me!*

*Please save Cady and Sin.*

I repeated the words over and over inside my head as I tried to steady my breathing. I had to do this. It had to be me. No one else or I'd be risking their lives.

I pulled myself together before going downstairs and running out the front door without my jacket, my heavy boots on. Luckily, it wasn't nearly as cold today as it had been lately. It had to mean spring was coming soon.

At least, that's what I told myself as I darted into the woods, my heart in my throat.

# SIRENA

"**W**elcome," Adam greeted me as I stepped into the mausoleum, my lungs burning from running so fast. "Oh, you wore a dress for me. I love it. You look beautiful."

He reached for my hand, but I snatched it away from him, the nausea twisting like a snake through my guts.

"Right. You want to see them first." He rolled his eyes at me and nodded for me to follow him. I did so, stopping to look down at Sin and Cady inside the coffin, their naked bodies pressed firmly against one another.

"It looks unnatural, doesn't it?" Adam mused.

I watched in horror as he lifted Sin's hand and shoved it between their bodies, making it clear he was placing it between Cady's legs.

"He fingered her for a moment before they fucked," Adam said, grinning at me. "I assumed it was prep work, but whatever. Fucking on command clearly isn't Sinclair's thing. He needed a little motivation, so fingering her pussy and kissing her seemed to help."

I swallowed down the bile threatening to claw its way up my throat.

"Listen. You did a really good job. I'm proud of you. So, I'll give you a reward." I watched as he shook Sin violently. "Hey. Hey, shitbag. Sinclair. Fuckface. Wake up! Wake up, you stupid cocksucker." He smacked him a few times and shook him roughly before Sin's eyelashes fluttered, and he opened his eyes.

It took him a moment to come to, but when he did, he was clearly in a headspace where he understood what was happening.

"Look who came to watch you and Cady," Adam proclaimed.

Sin's gray eyes met mine, so much sorrow in them it made the nausea twist faster.

"L-leave her a-alone, Adam," he choked out.

"I will. I'm going to," he promised, looking serene. "I just need you to get out of the coffin and say goodbye. Wake Cady so we can move this show forward."

Sin tore his gaze away from me and nudged Cady, his hand still stuck between her legs. It was hard for me to watch, but I knew he had no choice in it. Her lashes fluttered a moment later, her eyes meeting his.

"H-hey. I need you to wake up. S-Sirena is here."

She squirmed against him, tears dribbling from her eyes as she struggled to break free.

"Easy. Easy," Adam said, reaching out and fisting my hair tightly. I let out a whimper as he kicked my feet out from beneath me. I fell to my knees hard, the pain of hitting the concrete making tears erupt from my eyes.

Adam shoved me, sending me falling to my side, my elbow cracking the concrete. The pain seared through me, and I tried like hell to not let him see it.

With Sin's knife, he cut them free and tugged each one out. Cady scrambled to me, her skin like ice.

"Rina. Rina," she wept.

Sin's fists flew, but Adam slammed his fist back into his face over and over while Sin struggled inside the coffin. With Adam winning, Sin's arms went limp, and Adam tugged him out and tossed his naked body onto the cold floor.

Cady crawled to me, but before she could get to me, Adam had her, his fingers tangled in her hair. He shoved her down beside Sin, who let out a groan and sat up. He made to swipe for Adam again, but Adam tutted at him.

"You try anything like that again, and I'll cut the tits off your girl," Adam said firmly, coming over to me. He fisted my hair and brought me to my knees. With ease, he dragged me over to sag in front of Sin and Cady.

"Sirena has agreed to come with me in exchange for your freedom. Honestly, Sinclair, I fucking hate you. I think you're a worthless piece of shit who needs to die after what you did to her. The watchers think they're really something. Newsflash! They ain't fucking shit when I'm in charge." He let out a booming laugh. "Church thinks he's just so perfect. Daddy's number one boy. He's fucking worthless compared to me! I'm better! *I'm fucking better!* Everett loves *me*. Not him. I'm the one he should be leaving shit to! I matter. I fucking matter!" Spit flew from his mouth as he shouted. "I'm going to prove I can take what I want better than that fuckshit Dante can. I'm meant to lead the watchers and rule the Underground." Adam gripped my hair tighter. "She's a hell of a prize. Everett is going to fucking love me forever for grabbing her for him. Fucking Dante. What an idiot." He laughed again.

"Don't fucking do this," Sin warned, his voice husky, the blood pouring down his body from his busted face. "Don't. She's good. She's pure. Let her go. Take me instead. If you need to hurt someone, hurt me. Not her."

Adam chuckled. "Taking her is hurting you, Sinclair, or haven't you been listening? It's hurting all your fucking watchers. So exclusive. No one ever had a chance to join. It's bullshit!" He screamed the words, spit flying from his mouth. "Just because I'm a little crazy doesn't mean I didn't deserve a chance. I deserved a fucking chance! I'm one of you too!"

I let out a shriek as the knife he was holding came slashing down, the blade catching me across the chest. The burning ache ebbed through me.

It wasn't a deep cut and barely got me, but a dribble of blood trickled out, and that was all it took for Sin to lose it.

He lunged forward, knocking Adam back. I went flying halfway across the room, landing hard and banging my head off the edge of the pedestal the coffin was on. My vision swam as Sin and Adam beat on one another. Frantic, I plunged my hand into my pocket, but my phone wasn't there.

*Damnit. Damnit. Damnit!*

Cady tried to help, but Adam clocked her so hard she hit the ground, not moving. As fast as I could, I crawled to her, my ears ringing, and wrapped my body tightly around hers.

*I have you. I have you. I won't let him hurt you.*

*Be brave. I have to be brave. Please. . .*

I was torn away from Cady, Adam's fingers back in my hair. Sin's chest heaved as he got to his knees. His eyes were so swollen there was no way he could properly see out of them.

"I'm done with this shit. You couldn't let it go, could you?" Adam snarled. I let out a cry as he bent down and crushed his lips to mine, the taste of his blood tainting my mouth.

"Don't. Don't," Sin warned, his voice a choked garble. I knew he was close to losing consciousness. He'd been beaten half to death. "Please don't hurt her. Adam. Please."

"Is that how you begged your father?" Adam asked.

Sin let out a soft sob.

"He still shot you anyway, huh?"

Sin's shoulders shook. "D-don't do this. You don't have to do this."

"You're wrong. I do. Unlike your old man, I'll actually finish the job. I'll make mine finally proud of me." He released me and rushed forward. A scream tore from my lips as he plunged the knife deep into Sin's body. The gray of Sin's eyes met mine briefly before he fell over, clutching the knife, his blood dripping out.

I couldn't stop screaming. Adam tried to reach for me again, but I kicked him as hard as I could in his knee, sending him cursing to the ground. Scrambling over to Sin, I cradled his face in my hands, my tears dripping onto his battered face.

"No. No," I repeated. "Sinful. Please. No."

His lips trembled as he gazed up at me through his swollen eyelids. "I-I love you," he whispered. His bloody fingertips brushed lightly against my face as I sobbed over him. "Be brave, baby. I-I know you can be. So strong. So-so beautiful." He gave me a sad, watery smile. "Just run, Sirena. Please. *Run. D-Dance for me.*" His hand fell away from my face, and his eyes closed. His breathing was shallow. I knew. . . I knew this could very well be the end for him.

I couldn't accept that.

I cried loudly, his name on repeat, as I clung to him.

Mirage's words echoed through my head as the darkness surged forward.

*It's not a battle of fists and hits*
*For you, my monster queen*
*Simply lead the way to the place it all began*
*And we shall leave behind a bloody scene."*

Adam ripped me away, cursing my name as he dragged me through the mausoleum. Sin faded away from my view, only the cold to greet me as I was taken through the woods back to the spot where he'd hurt me the first time.

To the very spot where everything changed.

I smiled as he threw me into the clearing, knowing exactly how this next part was going to go. When his fist connected with my face and I hit the ground, I let out a soft laugh, knowing my monster was coming.

Adam shoved me onto my back and held me down, his bloody face looming over mine.

"You like this, you little bitch? Huh? Why are you smiling? It's just us now."

I let out another huff of laughter, knowing things were going to end badly.

As I lay beneath him, staring up at the dusky sky in the cold snow, I prayed for my strength. I prayed for my Sinful. I prayed for my darkness. I prayed for anyone who crossed me. It's what we learned to do at Chapel Crest. Pray for the sins of others. Pray for ourselves. Pray for strength. For guidance.

But for me, I let my last prayer be for Adam's death.

And sometimes, as I was quickly learning, prayers were answered.

# MIRAGE

She was gone. Taken. I knew she was.

Church came home to find the house empty. He reviewed his outdoor cameras. We watched the screen as she raced outside in nothing but her thin pink dress, her boots on her feet.

We'd been searching for the better half of an hour for her. Instead of breaking up, we did it as a team.

It was why we were racing through the cemetery towards the mausoleum, the only place we hadn't been yet on campus.

The door was open.

Fuck.

Night had fallen, but it was too hard to see inside the place.

Bryce's phone rang. He pulled it out as we surged forward.

"Cady? OK, yeah. We're here." He hung up as we continued our run. We were halfway across the snowy, dark cemetery.

"What's going on?" Church demanded.

"They're in the mausoleum. They're hurt," Bryce panted, trying to keep up. We really needed to work on his cardio, but I wasn't about to focus on that right then.

*She's not there. She's not fucking there.*

*Then where is she?*

*I-I don't know. Fuck. I can't see anything. She's. . . not there.*

Church was the first to enter the mausoleum, Ashes and Stitches close behind him. I came in next, with Bryce at the rear.

My insides wanted to become my outsides as I stared at the mess. Cady and Sin, naked. Cady sobbed over his body.

Church fell to his knees at Sin's side, and Ashes took his jacket off and wrapped it around Cady, his hands shaking.

"A-Adam," she choked out. "It's him."

"I knew it," Bryce murmured, moving back to the doorway.

"No. No. NO!" Stitches shouted, falling next to Church.

"Sin. Please, man," Church choked out. "Hey."

Nothing. Silence greeted us.

"C-call the wards. We need help." Church looked wildly at me. "Call the fucking wards! Find Adam."

Bryce pulled his phone out and made the call while I continued to stare down at the scene. The knife protruded from below Sin's right lung. His breathing was barely visible and was uneven. If I had to guess, the blade was firmly embedded in his lung.

An arc of pain cut through my head, sending me to my knees.

Sirena's face popped into my head.

*Help. Please. Seth. Help me.*

I couldn't see where she was, only that she was hurting. Her pain ripped through my body, letting me know she wasn't on a pleasure cruise. Then, more. Darkness. So much of it.

Finally.

I staggered to my feet.

"What is it?" Stitches demanded, holding Sin's hand, his jacket now over Sin's body to keep him warm.

"I-I need to find Rinny. I need Rinny. S-stay with him. I'll get her." I stumbled out of the mausoleum and into the night air, my body feeling like a fire had been lit inside it.

"Did you see where she was?" Bryce demanded, coming out from behind me.

I shook my head, my hands on my knees.

He was quiet for a moment before he finally spoke.

"I think I know where they are."

I straightened, giving him the benefit of the doubt. He was a shadow, after all, and had been proving his worth.

"Let's go," I said, breaking into a run next to him, my soul on fire.

✝

It was just like Bryce thought. The clearing.

Night had fallen, but I could easily make out Adam on top of Sirena in the same spot as he'd hurt her before.

White hot rage soared through my body. It was doubled when I felt Asylum rear his head within me.

We burst into the clearing, my fist making contact with the side of Adam's head in a sickening crack. He fell off her and fumbled to put his dick away as Bryce rushed to pull her to safety.

"Hey, welcome to the party," he spat at me. "So you know, we're down a member. I killed Sinclair not long ago."

"We're about to be down two then because you're next," I snarled back.

He let out a laugh. "I was just about to fuck your girl. Again. That's gotta suck to know I've had my dick in her more than you have."

I tore into him, beating him until he was on his knees, his face bloody and his chest heaving with each breath he tried to rake in through his broken ribs. I circled him, noting Sirena was moving against Bryce, and he was trying to hold her back.

"Let her go," I whispered, feeling her monster stir around us. "It's time."

Bryce released her, and she came over to stand beside me. Her small body trembled, and she had a cut across her chest and a bruise forming along her cheek.

"Hello, little monster," I whispered, adjusting my rabbit mask.

"Seth," she answered back, her voice shaking slightly.

"We always knew it would come to this," I said, staring down at

Adam who swayed on his knees, clearly a little knocked out of his head from my hits. "Asylum is coming."

"Good." Her words came out softly. "I want him to be here for this next part."

I felt her doubts floating around us.

"You're brave, Sirena. You always have been. It's time to take control of everything," I said, taking her hand in mine and lifting it to my lips where I kissed her knuckles. "We're right here with you."

She stared up at me for a moment before I released her hand and pushed my knife into it.

"Enjoy," I offered, backing away from her, ready to watch the birth of a real fucking monster into our dark world.

A smile curled her lips upward, her colorful eyes darkening with the rage she'd hidden away for so long.

And then she descended on Adam like a storm, the knife glinting beneath the moonlight.

Adam's shrieks echoed through the night as Bryce stood beside me.

"Is Asylum really coming?" Bryce asked while we watched the carnage.

"He's already here," I said through a smile.

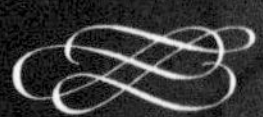

The blade tore through Adam's flesh like he was butter. I relished each of his screams, the darkness which had been lurking on the edge of my soul finally breaking free and blanketing my entirety.

With each stab, each slash, a new part of me was born.

His blood poured from his body longer than his screams did, which was a pity because I'd finally started having fun.

He gripped my wrists with bloody hands, his eyes wild as he stared up at me, his body covered in his blood.

"I-I loved you," he choked out. "I'm not-not myself sometimes. . ."

"Me either," I answered, pushing my blade deep into his throat. His eyes widened, and he garbled for a moment, the blood pooling in his mouth before he went silent.

I stared down at the mess I'd made. He was almost in pieces.

"What are we going to do with the body?" Bryce asked softly, his voice pulling me from my thoughts.

"I have some hungry friends deep in the woods," Mirage answered.

I rose to my feet and turned to see Mirage and Bryce staring back

"He's been taken to the wards. There's nothing we can do but wait," Mirage said gently like he knew what I was thinking.

I nodded, knowing he was right. We still had work to do out here anyway. Sin would want me to finish what I'd started.

I stepped forward and stood in front of Bryce.

He stared back at me with hazel eyes, his curls falling across his forehead.

Leaning in, I pressed my lips against his soft ones. He fell into my kiss immediately, deepening it before relenting to allow me control. Our tongues tangled for a moment before I broke away from him, leaving a bloody handprint on his face.

"Soon," I said, stepping back. "Shadow."

He nodded at me, his Adam's apple bobbing.

Next, I went to Mirage, who gave me a smile.

"You're a mess," he said.

"So are you," I countered, taking in the blood splattered on his white rabbit mask. I reached forward and traced my fingers along the edge of the mask. Carefully, I pulled the mask off to see his true face.

So familiar.

"There you are," I whispered, trailing my fingertips along his cheekbones. He closed his eyes as I touched him.

"Come, my love. We have work to do," he said, taking the mask from me and pulling it back over his face.

I took the hand he offered and let him lead me into temptation, Bryce right next to us.

I'D NEVER CUT up a body before, but it wasn't nearly as hard as I thought it was going to be. Adam came apart easily enough. Mirage guided me while Bryce kept watch. Bryce was good at watching. He was always watching. I loved that about him. I hoped it came into play later on because I wanted him to watch me do all sorts of dirty, terrible things.

For the parts I struggled with, Mirage came along and showed me how best to disconnect bone. The cracks sounded well into the night until our work was done. Beneath the moonlight, I stood between my white rabbit and a shadow, watching as the wolves devoured Adam.

When it was over, and I felt sickly satisfied, a new sort of rush coursed through me. Mirage took my hand in his and tugged me through the woods. We didn't stop until we reached the cemetery.

"He didn't hurt me," I said as Mirage pulled me into his arms and stared down at me. "I wouldn't let him."

"My pirate princess," he murmured.

I smiled at that.

I felt Bryce watching us from the edge of the tree line as Mirage moved with me, dancing through the tombstones beneath the moonlight.

"Dance, Rinny. Sin would want you to dance. Do it for him. Do it for you."

My heart swelled. Sin told me to dance. When my dance was over, I'd go to him and tell him all about it. We'd scribble in our notebook for hours before he pushed me onto the mattress and made love to me.

It was the hope I kept in my heart as I prayed for him to be waiting for me when this was over. To not leave me.

"For Sinful," I whispered before allowing Mirage to sweep me through the tombstones.

I let out a wild laugh, feeling free for the first time in my life. I sang our song with him as we moved and twirled along the stones, my body light, the darkness free.

"I love you, Rinny," Mirage whispered as he tugged me against his body and swayed, peering down at me through his white rabbit mask.

"I love you too," I answered back before he gave me a twirl away from him. I kept spinning, laughs bubbling out of me as I danced through the tombstones, the world spinning above me.

Strong arms captured me, and I stared up into familiar eyes, the mask gone.

"Asylum," I whispered. "You're back."

"Never actually left, firefly," he answered. "May I have this dance?"

I smiled up at him, knowing I was still covered in Adam's blood.

"You're dressed perfectly." He dipped me low, his lips a breath from my own. *"No guilt, no shame. The siren dances for Sin. The Ghost rises. Her army of darkness will win,"* he said before sweeping me into his arms, our song continuing.

Cryptic words as usual, but I liked the way they sounded.

I knew I had to take moments like these. I deserved them. When the sun rose, I'd be at Sin's side again. But for tonight I'd dance for him. I'd dance for me.

For us.

And tomorrow, I'd pray for this dark world.

Because good girls made really perfect fucking monsters.

*To be Continued in Shadow: The Boys of Chapel Crest*
*Pre-Order Now.*
**Thank you for reading Sinful: The Boys of Chapel Crest. Please consider leaving your review.**
**Want more from the watchers? Check out the Chaos Universe, a dark RH crossover world where their stories continue. You can find the Chaos Universe books on Kindle.**

# ABOUT THE AUTHOR

Affectionately dubbed Queen of Cliffies, Suspense, Heartbreak, and Torture by her readers, USA Today and International Bestselling author K.G. Reuss is known mostly for making readers ugly cry with her writing. A cemetery creeper and ghost enthusiast, K.G. spends most of her time toeing the line between imagination and forced adulthood.

After a stint in college in Iowa, K.G. moved back to her home in Michigan to work in emergency medicine. She's currently raising three small ghouls and is married to a vampire overlord.

K.G. is the author of the Black Falls High series, Kings of Bolten, the Boys of Chapel Crest, The Everlasting Chronicles, Emissary of the Devil, The Chronicles of Winterset, and many more with a ridiculous amount of other series set to be released.

Can't get enough? Visit her website at www.kgreuss.com or join her reader group at www.facebook.com/groups/streetteamkgreuss

Find her on TikTok at https://www.tiktok.com/@kgreuss

# ALSO BY K.G. REUSS

May We Rise: A Mayfair University Novel

As We Fight: A Mayfair University Novel

On The Edge: A Mayfair University Novel

Into The Fire: A Mayfair University Novel

When We Fall: A Mayfair University Novel

Double Dare You

Double Dare Me

Church: The Boys of Chapel Crest

Bells: The Boys of Chapel Crest

Ashes: The Boys of Chapel Crest

Stitches: The Boys of Chapel Crest

Sinful: The Boys of Chapel Crest

Shadow: The Boys of Chapel Crest

Asylum: The Boys of Chapel Crest

Emissary of the Devil: Testimony of the Damned

Emissary of the Devil: Testimony of the Blessed

The Everlasting Chronicles: Dead Silence

The Everlasting Chronicles: Shadow Song

The Everlasting Chronicles: Grave Secrets

The Everlasting Chronicles: Soul Bound

The Chronicles of Winterset: Oracle

The Chronicles of Winterset: Tempest

Black Falls High: In Ruins

Black Falls High: In Silence

Black Falls High: In Pieces, A Novella

Black Falls High: In Chaos

Hard Pass

Kings of Bolten: Dirty Little Secrets

Kings of Bolten: Pretty Little Sins

Kings of Bolten: Deadly Little Promises

Kings of Bolten: Perfect Little Revenge

Kings of Bolten: Savage Little Queen

Barely Breathing

The Middle Road

Seven Minutes in Heaven

www.ingramcontent.com/pod-product-compliance
Lightning Source LLC
Chambersburg PA
CBHW040328020826
48978CB00013BC/949